Let the light shine through

A. MARIE

Editing: Rebecca, Fairest Reviews Editing Service
Proofreading: Judy Zweifel, Judy's Proofreading
Cover Design: Murphy Rae
Cover Photography: Regina Wamba
Formatting: Champagne Book Design

Playlist

Music plays a big role in my writing.
You can find the link for the full Spotify playlist and
more on my website amarieauthor.com

SUPERG!RL—Stefania

bad guy—Billie Eilish

So Am I—Ava Max

Basic—NiGHTS

Sweet but Psycho—Ava Max

Princesses Don't Cry—Aviva

Sociopath—StayLoose, Bryce Fox

Boy Toy—Marisa Maino

Wasted—Jesse McCartney

So Bad—Brandon Colbein

How to Be a Heartbreaker—MARINA

You Don't Own Me—SAYGRACE, G-Eazy

Nights With You—MØ

Cool for the Summer—Demi Lovato

Headcase—Kailee Morgue, Hayley Kiyoko

Crave—Ruth B.

I Didn't Just Kiss Her—Jen Foster

Explosion—Zolita

Church—Aly & AJ

Monster—Gabbie Hanna

Terrified—Terror Jr

Fine—Spencer Sutherland

Deathbeds—Bring Me The Horizon

Let Me—ZAYN

Hydra—Julia Wolf

Let Go—Lynnea M

No Right To Love You(Acoustic)—Rhys Lewis

Sucker(Acoustic)—Ben Woodward

Someone You Loved—Lewis Capaldi

Empty—Olivia O'Brien

DaNcing in a RoOm—EZI

The Boy Who Cried Love—Anastasia Elliot

Fuck Feelings—Olivia O'Brien

1 Shot 2 Shots—Che'Nelle

My Name Is Human—Highly Suspect

Horizon—Luna Blake

Funeral For A Lover—JJ Wilde

Get Better—Leslie Mosier

Young Fighter—Nate Fenwick, Evie Clair

Afterlife—XYLØ

The Night We Met—Lord Huron

For the ones we still need.

This book is a 95k-word mature new adult romance standalone.
It contains foul language, consensual sexual situations, mild
violence, and drug and alcohol use intended for audiences 18+.

Depression along with subjects dealing with cancer
and death are present.

Prologue

Black surrounds me as far as the eye can see, mocking me, and a bead of sweat breaks from my hairline, running down my temple. One at a time, I roll my sleeves up to my elbows, stalling.

This—public speaking—has never been my strong suit.

Fucking sucks. Especially for this. *For him.*

"Hi," I say finally, scanning the crowd of unfamiliar faces. "I'm, uh, Roswell Andrews-Smith."

Nothing. Not an ounce of recognition.

That's small-town upstate for you. Nobody gives a shit who or what you are here. They're too caught up in their own lives to worry about anybody else's.

Not like the scene I'm used to.

Or was, I guess. *Was.*

"Or you might know me as Roz."

Crickets.

Cool.

Because if nobody recognizes me in this place, then chances are nobody else in town will recognize me either. I've been gone a long time.

Not long enough.

Aside from visiting my parents every now and then, I had no plans on coming back here permanently. Not now and sure as fuck not like this.

"Big Red and I, uh. I mean Salvy." *Fuck!* "Salvy and I were teammates, but more importantly, we were friends." Best friends—brothers practically—but who cares? He's gone.

Dead.

Forever.

Just like our friendship.

What does it matter that he lived doing what he loved? He also died doing what he loved, so…was it worth it? Really? Doesn't seem like it from where I'm standing—at his *goddamn funeral*, getting ready to relay some great memory to a church full of strangers, like it'll somehow give meaning to a person whose death was completely meaningless.

And our friendship? No one here will understand what Salvy truly meant to me. Not even from a sappy story straight from the horse's mouth.

If I ever get around to telling one…

Gripping the edge of the wooden podium, I glance around again. It's the energy. Mine. Theirs. It's all…off.

I'm off. Off the mountains I crave more than air. Off my fucking game in everything else I try to do. Just off, period.

In the front row, my parents take turns consoling Salvy's mom, Diane. It was only as a favor to my mom back in sixth grade that I asked Salvy to come up to our cabin with us for a weekend of skiing and snowboarding. I used to think it was because she knew I struggled to make friends on my own, but now that I'm older, I wonder. I wonder if it was just her way of keeping her heart from hardening over during the frigid New York winters. She can be…complicated. Judgmental. Harsh at times. But she'll never turn down an opportunity to look like the ultimate hostess. Thank God too because that little redheaded fucker, Salvy, became my best friend after that trip up north together and we've been inseparable ever since.

Were. We *were* inseparable.

I hang my head, rolling it side to side as I focus on the brilliant red tie I wore in his honor.

Why him? Why now?

We were the best snowboarders on that mountain that day and

yet…it wasn't enough. Salvy's now a statistic, a fucking number, for the very sport that bonded us nearly ten years ago. His mom will never see her son again. I'll never see my partner in every stunt we've ever pulled—on and off the slopes—again. All for what? Because we liked the snow more than the heat? Because our blood ran icier than others'? There's not a boarder alive that could argue that fact.

Salvy and I got identical contracts from our sponsor for a reason. We were the team to beat and everyone knew it. We requested, chased, begged for any boarding time we could get because it was what we wanted. What we loved.

But what if we hadn't? What if we would've spent more time off the slopes than we did on? Would Salvy have missed the avalanche that ultimately took him out?

On a sigh, I lift my head, instantly noticing a new face. One that wasn't here before. One that's different from every other face locked on mine. Different because not only is she wearing a white shirt in a sea of black dresses and suits, but she's also smiling. At me.

Hands in her pockets, she leans against the back wall, bending a knee to prop one of her Vans under her ass. She's still dressed in black, too, but in what looks like a men's suit. It's open in the front, revealing her two-sizes-too-big white V-neck that practically hangs from her thin frame as she lowers her head conspiratorially. Long dark curls come to a stop well below her chest and that out-of-place smile of hers is still stretching her full pink mouth.

Our eyes connect and her lips widen, showing a full row of teeth whiter than her shirt.

Who smiles at a funeral? And why?

I swallow and I swear her gaze drops to my throat before returning to mine. It's so bleak in here, I can barely see—usually it's all twinkling white hills and frisky gray skies—but amongst the mass of dark clothing, and even darker expressions, this girl's like a beacon of light.

Nothing feels bright anymore. It's all just…dull. Silent. Not the kind of silence you seek out, but the kind that finds you, then swallows you whole. My life is now muted.

Except her smile. There's nothing quiet about her smile. I can't take my eyes off it, wishing I could hear it myself. Feel it. Taste it.

She pulls a hand from her pocket, motioning with her heavily ringed finger for me to speed it up, almost like she's got somewhere to be.

I hold back a scoff. In the end, we're all going to the same place. Somewhere Salvy arrived way before he was supposed to. Definitely before I was ready for him to. He was always like that though. *Eager motherfucker.*

The thought tugs at my lips, and I straighten with the reminder fresh in my mind.

After a cough, I start again, "In all the years I'd known Salvy, he was always the first one down every line we carved. Not because he was the fastest, or craziest, but because that's just who he was." Sounds of agreement echo around the packed room. "Yeah, I guess he figured the sooner he got to the bottom, the sooner he could start back from the top all over again. I never told Salvy this, but that was one of my favorite things about him—without fail, his goofy-ass smile would be waiting at the top of whatever new mountain we were trying to conquer."

I tell them about our time in Saas-Fee, Switzerland, leading up to the avalanche, all the while my thumb rubs a divot on the aged podium, over and over again, the spirals mimicking the swirling inside my chest from remembering those final days. I haven't talked about our last trip together yet. I've always been on the quieter side, much to the frustration of my sponsors, parents, and practically any girl I've ever hooked up with, but ever since Salvy died, I don't feel like talking at all. To anybody. About anything.

Maybe I did choose the silence. It's safer. You can't hear anything you don't want to.

"It wasn't supposed to end like that," I choke out. "But if Salvy really did rush to the final finish line, I hope to God when it's my turn to join him, that his smiling face is there to greet me one last time."

The center aisle distorts in front of me as my vision blurs and my ears fill with deafening white noise. I manage to give the girl in the back one last look before stepping off the altar. She watches me the entire time, smile still in place. I can't decide if I should return the smile or flip her the bird. What's her deal?

I find my seat beside Salvy's mom, my dad clapping me on the back a little too hard to be supportive.

"Buck up, boy. Time to get back out there already." Both my parents have been saying it since I touched back down in the States. They think I should shake off my best friend's death. They think I should get back to work, grinding my ass off.

For what though? To meet the same end Salvy did?

I don't want to do anything that has to do with my old life.

The priest drones on while I fight the urge to yank my tie off. *Fuck.* This is the most clothes I've worn since…ever. Bet Salvy's getting a real kick out of watching me squirm in this clown suit. *Only for you, Big Red. Only for you.*

Throughout the readings—there's so fucking many—I catch myself trying to spot the mystery guest out of the corner of my eye, but every time I send a side-eye down our row, I can only make out the first few pews, nowhere near the back.

After my fifth failed attempt, I give in and tug at my collar roughly. I need air. But not this air. Where everybody else's lungs beg for oxygen, mine scream for the mountains.

That's what nobody seems to understand but pretends to nonetheless. The need, the constant pull from wherever I am to the white powder I've always thought was more addictive than any other—snow. Even here, even now, the itch to strap up and ride the fuck out until nothing exists except the sound of my board slicing through my own lines…it's strong. So fucking strong.

The urge is still there, but the follow-through is not, and the longer I go without snowboarding, the easier it'll be to ignore that impulsive feeling entirely.

With a closing prayer, the funeral concludes with a not-so-subtle invitation to take things elsewhere. My mom insisted—of course—to hold the reception at our house, so after I receive a kiss on the cheek from her, Dad leads her away to the waiting town car. The caterers have been there all day preparing, but my mom will want to go over every little detail before the first guest arrives.

I'll take Salvy's mom over after she has the chance to make the rounds.

Speaking of…

Scanning the small courtyard, I snag on one person in particular.

Bingo.

I make sure Diane is all right, then pass through the wrought-iron gate, stopping under an impressive maple tree to peer down at her—the girl from the back. She's sitting on a skateboard with her arms resting haphazardly on bent knees as she stares up at the sky.

The arches of my feet tic. Even though I haven't skateboarded since I was a kid, a deck's a deck and this one calls to me just the same.

I silence that, too.

"It's a bluebird," I say, and she lifts her pointer finger, telling me, "Actually, it's a Crow."

She raises a second finger. "Two." Her eyes finally meet mine. "Do you know what that means?"

I glance up, noticing two Crows soaring high above our heads.

"A change is coming."

More change?

"Good or bad?" I ask, watching them.

"Good."

A good change…what would that even look like right now?

My eyes fall to find hers again, and I tell her, "I was talking about the weather. Bluebird…it means it's a clear day. Perfect weather for boarding."

"Snowboarder." She nods her head. "Right."

"Not anymore."

Her head stops all movement as she stares at me openly.

Despite the calendar saying it's now officially spring, winter's still in full swing here in New York—thankfully—and the frigid bite to this March day is a welcome relief from the sweatbox the ancient nave inside was. Immune to Jack Frost's cruelty myself, sweat continues to form on my back, but this girl's sitting only inches above the still frozen earth, probably freezing her ass off.

My jacket's already sliding off my shoulders and down my arms. It's gentlemanly. At least they make it seem like it is in the movies. It might actually be offensive now that I think about it, but I don't care. I need air and she needs…

What *does* she need? Why is she here?

I drape the jacket over her shoulders, causing her to finally blink, and just like that, her smile reappears, not as big this time though.

"Have we met?"

Her eyes—round, brown, and insanely hypnotizing—drop to the crunchy grass under her shoes, giving me a perfect view of her untamed locks. Soft, shiny curls fall around her shoulders as she leans forward to flick a blade of stiff grass off her Vans. As she's reaching down, the skin at her cleavage, exposed by her deep V-neck, is nothing short of translucent, and I'm pretty sure I can see each and every beat of her heart.

Tha-thump. Tha-thump. So calm. So sure.

I wish I could feel that again.

"No," she says nonchalantly.

Okay. "Did you know Salvy then?" I'm really hoping she says yes because if she doesn't, her smiles…they might mean something I won't like.

There's never a shortage of opportunists when your name makes headlines.

It might've been naïve thinking my return to my hometown would go completely unnoticed but it's never been an issue in the past. Usually, I'm able to slip in and slip out with no one the wiser, but now I'm back, living here full-time, and that might be a bit harder to pull off.

I'm so busy running my eyes over her…everything, I almost miss her say quietly, "I don't think so."

She stands suddenly, slipping her arms through my jacket's sleeves, which sets off a chorus of jingles. The girl's got at least one ring on each finger, maybe even each knuckle.

"Sounds like he was a good time though."

I step back, giving her—or me—some space, and nod. "He was."

A gust of chilled wind whips past, ruffling her brunette hair, and instead of pushing the unruly strands from her face, she leans into the breeze, letting them tease her pale skin. The move strikes me as familiar. Like something I'd do. Like something I do.

Something I *did*.

"Well, I'm Roz," I say, sticking my hand out even though I still don't really understand why she's here. She doesn't seem to recognize me and she didn't know Salvy. Maybe she's a friend of the family?

But no, that doesn't check out either, considering she hasn't so much as waved in Diane's direction. So far, she's only been focused on me. *Is* she here for me?

She hums, giving me a once-over while purposely ignoring my outstretched hand.

"You were lucky."

My eyebrows clash together. That's all I've been hearing lately. *"You're lucky it wasn't you."* Really? Because I don't feel very fucking lucky.

I snatch my hand back and she smirks, bending to pick up her skateboard.

"You had a great friend you loved and trusted…not everybody gets that. And I'm sure he loved you, too. You have a kind heart."

Her words are…unexpected. She thinks I'm lucky, not because I didn't die, but because I had someone in my life that meant a hell of a lot more than words condensed into a seven-minute eulogy could ever express.

Fighting past a lump in my throat, I ask, "How do you know that?"

"You've had one eye on her the entire time." She gestures behind me, but I don't have to look to know who she's talking about. Diane's been my main concern since I returned, especially today. I didn't think it was something a total stranger would notice though. Is she a stranger?

"Her? You don't know her name?"

"Diane," she says matter-of-factly, and I breathe a little easier. So she does know the family.

But then she points at the church's stained glass front, telling me, "At least that's what they said in there."

So…

"Why exactly *are* you here? It's kind of fucked to crash a funeral, no?"

Her thin shoulders shrug my jacket up to her ears. "This place does a nice job."

A blizzard couldn't cover the surprise on my face.

For funerals?

"Do you go to a lot of these?"

"Sometimes."

She turns for the street, and without hesitation, I follow after her. This I gotta hear.

Over her shoulder, she says, "I'm just saying, I wouldn't mind if my funeral was held here."

Again, that's not what I was expecting to hear.

"Are you planning on dying then?"

She stops to look at me finally, saying, "Not today."

The board drops to the asphalt, breaking the silence—*the* silence? *my* silence?—and I blink, long and hard, considering her words.

When I open my eyes again, she's already got a foot on the board. She's leaving. Now. Without me even knowing her name.

"I couldn't help but notice you inside." *To put it mildly.* "You were the only one smiling." That same smile grows, waiting for me to continue. "Is there a reason?"

"I just thought you'd be a good one."

Good one?

"Roz, honey, are you ready to go?"

Waiting for me next to the short wrought-iron fence, Diane's anxiously clutching her small purse that I know is only full of tissues—both clean and used.

"Yeah, just give me a minute," I tell her gently, then quickly spin around to ask, "Good for what?"

My question goes unanswered, however, as I find the spot in front of me now empty. I rub at the back of my neck, watching the girl still wearing my jacket skate down the street, untamed hair blowing out behind her like a superhero's cape.

Is that who she is then? A skateboarding crusader that goes around rescuing choked-up speeches at funerals?

Seems unlikely, but crazier things have happened.

"I was wondering if I'd see that again," Salvy's mom tells me on the way to my truck.

"What's that?"

"Your smile."

Catching my reflection in the window, I see she's right. The person that pulled me from the void, even if it was only momentarily, left me without a backward glance or a way to ever see her again. Am I even gonna get my jacket back?

Fuck. Me.

I hope you're laughing your ass off up there, I send to Salvy mentally before sobering at the thought. The last time I was this riveted by something was in Switzerland, when Salvy and I went up on a little heli trip. We became obsessed, so much so we flew back up there the next day. And look how that turned out.

Everyone talks about addiction being dangerous, but nobody ever warns you about avalanches being one of the deadliest consequences of all.

Chapter 1

ROZ

"Is that the last of it?" my roommate, Fletcher, asks from the kitchen as I head back out the front door, so I throw up my pointer finger above my head in answer.

Not long after the funeral, I ran into one of my old buddies who went to middle school with Salvy and me. After catching up, he invited me to move in with him and his roommates. I didn't know where I would ultimately live once I moved back here, but after staying with my parents for a couple months, I knew it wouldn't be there. It's one thing when I'm jetting around the globe to different events with only short stints back at home, but it's another to be there every damn day with the constant pressure to return to something I already swore off.

Anyway, I needed out, and Fletcher needed someone else to help with rent, so I took him up on his offer. According to my phone's lock screen, it's already June, but I couldn't pinpoint what day or week, even if there was a gun to my head. It all blends together into one giant endless stretch of time. The hands on the clock move but nothing changes. At least not to me.

I don't think it's technically summer yet, but I guess it's warm enough to pass because we're opening the pool today. The party we're hosting might be the real reason, but I stopped paying attention to the excuses my roommate makes for throwing parties. I just show up—physically.

Mentally...I don't know where the fuck I am anymore. Grabbing another case of spiked apple cider apparently.

I reach for the last box in the back of my lifted Chevy, freezing when I hear a whirring—one that sounds a hell of a lot like…

The whirring grows louder, like it's getting closer, but there's nothing on the only sidewalk I allow myself to actually scope out. Unfortunately, during Fletcher's pitch to get me to move here, he left out the fact that the house sits directly across from an all-girls high school, so I make it a point to never let my eyes wander over to that side of the road. He got a great deal on the historic Victorian after a fraternity beat the ever-living shit out of it and has been trying to fix the place up bit by bit to increase property value, but since high school girls are too young for everyone that lives under this roof, I've been keeping my eyes—and every other part of my body—firmly on this side of the road.

Now though, there's something—no, *someone*—that has my full attention as I chance a peek across the street.

Russet-brown hair tied into a gigantic sloppy bun sits atop a face I've been thinking about since March. A face sporting the smile that drew me in from the beginning.

The same girl from Salvy's funeral is riding her skateboard past the finial fencing to the hundred-year-old Jacobethan Revival-style school.

It's not that she's in front of the school that bothers me—any-one can breeze past it—it's the uniform she's wearing. The white long-sleeve dress shirt half sticking out the bottom of a black sweater vest, the tie hanging loosely from her neck, the plaid knee-length skirt, and the brown heavy-duty boots—it all really, really bothers me. And nothing bothers me anymore.

Does she *go* there?

She swings a look over her shoulder to check for cars, then she's jumping the curb flawlessly and crossing the road. Straight to my side. Straight to me.

Before I can react, her round eyes rise, connecting with mine, and it's like I'm right back to that first day meeting her. Everything stops, freezing the world until it's just us. Her and me. Me and her. *Her.*

She jerks her chin in acknowledgement, then ollies on to the curb before continuing on her way, trying to leave me for the second time. *Um, what?*

I dart forward, croaking out, "Hey!" and scowl at my own voice. Is that what I sound like?

She twists her head to the side, letting her smile do the speaking, and I halt. Why am I getting the sudden urge to join her? It's taking every bit of my control to stay where I am and not jump on that board and ride wherever she's willing to take me right now, and fuck, I thought it was getting better—the urge. I thought it was getting weaker.

Fortunately, she actually stops this time, snatching her board by the front as she doubles back to the driveway. To me.

She's really here?

"I didn't know you lived on Greek Sac."

What now?

At my confused expression, she explains, "Greek Sac…it's like Greek Row but on a cul-de-sac."

"This…isn't a cul-de-sac."

"Yeah, I know. Whoever came up with it is an idiot but every campus in the country has a Greek Row and you gotta stand out somehow, right?"

This isn't a campus either, sits on the tip of my tongue, but I don't bother voicing it. She obviously knows this place better than I do.

She nods to the house at my back, asking, "Are you a new recruit?"

Yeah, right. College life didn't interest me in the slightest, and now that I know what it's like living with three other guys that can't find the time to clean the piss stains covering every surface of every toilet but somehow do have time to host a party every weekend, I can confidently say it still doesn't.

I have to swallow several times, loosening up my dry fucking throat. "It's, uh, it's not a frat house anymore." *Barely.* "A buddy of mine bought it and I'm just crashing with him for…a while." *Is this temporary? I haven't really put that much thought into it.*

She nods along, surveying the expansive yard. Fletcher kept the run-down volleyball net up along with the plywood beer pong table. For whatever reason, those things aren't frowned upon here. Neither is having dozens of other fraternity and sorority houses line the same street as an all-girls high school.

"What about you? Are you a high schooler?"

I've never wanted to be more wrong in all my life than I do right now. *Please, please say no.*

"Sort of."

What does that mean?

"Do you go there?" I try to point, but my hands jostle the box in my hold, the glass bottles inside clanking together awkwardly.

"Do you need some help with that?"

My chest puffs behind the box, and I give her a headshake.

"I missed a year, so I'm making up the classes I'm allowed in."

One of my eyebrows arches.

"They're obsessive about their rules." She tips a shoulder, then starts walking around the side of the house, looking back, expecting me to follow.

I do, if only to see where she thinks she's going.

"Our views differ on certain subjects."

In a matter of two well-calculated strides, I catch up to her, walking alongside her, listening, watching. She's the most interesting thing I've come across since…I first saw her.

"But I have enough credits to graduate next week, so it's all good."

That sounds vague. And complicated.

I want to ask her why she took a year off. I want to ask her what her views are and how they differ from her school's. I want to ask her what her name is. Anything to keep her talking. But the words get stuck somewhere between my brain and my tongue and all I can do is stare at the side of her face, memorizing her profile.

We enter the backyard and she breaks away from me, rushing

over to open the built-in cooler the previous occupants made for the same reason we're using it. It's made to look like a part of the complicated grilling station though—probably in case the cops ever showed up—so only people that have been here before know about it.

Not bothering with offering her help this time, she immediately flips up the top of the box in my arms and starts unloading the bottles into the cooler herself.

I consider putting the box on the ground to help her, like a decent human being would, but once I catch her scent, I stay rooted. Vanilla and…rosemary? Is that right? Rosemary? A fucking herb? Whatever it is, it's sexy. I'm also detecting a salty tang—probably from skating—that makes it that much more mouthwatering. Makes *her* that much more mouthwatering.

Jesus Christ. Now I'm keeping the box in front of my body for a completely different reason.

I force another swallow to ask, "So, you've been here before then?"

All the bottles of cider now transferred, she closes the lid to the cooler, then uses her arms to lift herself on top of it, taking a seat that's more at my eye level.

Before she can answer, Fletcher bounds down the patio steps, shouting, "G!"

My face stiffens. My back stiffens. My everything stiffens. They *know* each other?

And who the hell is "G"?

The girl doesn't move, save for spreading her legs wider to accept Fletcher's weird, not exactly friendly but possibly more than friendly, hug. *What the fuck?*

While I'm busy debating if I should detach his head from his body, my roommate steps back and faux punches "G"'s arm.

Yeah, I'm gonna have to rip it off. Clean. Off.

Thankfully, the girl doesn't fake anything when she punches Fletcher's arm in retaliation and my roommate all but folds over in pain. She does have enough rings to rival any set of brass knuckles I've seen.

Fletcher gets ahold of himself enough to ask her, "Where have you been? Haven't seen you in a while."

She pulls on the loose tie at her chest and bends a knee to place her foot on the cooler, completely unconcerned about exposing… whatever she's got going on down there—panties? No panties? Did she forget she's wearing a fucking skirt?

My gaze shoots to Fletcher's and the second his drops even a millimeter, I toss the empty box, nailing him in the side of his thick skull.

"What the shit?" he complains, rubbing his temple, and I spin on my heel, facing him, locked and fucking loaded.

Fortunately, a chuckle so warm and rich rings out, stopping me in my tracks. The girl's now sprawled out on her back—knee still bent, damn it—laughing. As much as I try not to, I let my eyes drop, and I can tell from here she's wearing some sort of boy shorts under her skirt. They're actually not bad. They cover everything just fine with extra material to conceal even the bottoms of her ass cheeks, but it's the thought of those ass cheeks that has me licking my lips, then side-eyeing Fletcher. He's still fucking with the box I threw at him, which saves me from having to put him in a headlock. For now anyway.

"What's so funny?" I ask, pulling Fletcher's attention away from the box as he snarks off with, "Look who's talking all of a sudden."

No longer laughing, "G" sits up, studying me. She doesn't say anything and neither do I. If Fletcher's still here, he doesn't either. Is he still here? I honestly wouldn't know. Once again, it's just her and me. Me and her.

The corner of her lips pulls to the side.

Her.

"Um, okayyy…" Fletcher says. "Seriously, Gia, where've you been?" *Gia?* "Tell me you're coming to our party tonight. I promise my boy won't throw anything else." Out of the corner of my eye, I see Fletcher send me a pointed look that I ignore. If I find him scoping out Gia's panties again, I'll fucking throw all right. He should plan accordingly.

Only when Gia drops her leg back down do I break from her stare to return Fletcher's scowl with my own.

"Fletch, Fletch, Fletch, when will you learn?" Gia hops down from the cooler, tugging her shirt sleeves farther down her wrists. "I *am* the party." With that, she turns to leave, calling out over her shoulder, "Later."

And as much as it hurts to watch her go, I can't think of anything else I'd rather look at in this moment.

As soon as she's out of sight, I round on Fletcher, demanding any and all information about Gia, starting with how he knows her followed closely by her age. Actually no, age trumps all.

Chapter 2

GIA

I return Mr. Robinson's wave. He only waves at me when he's happy, and he seems to only be happy when I skate on the opposite side of the street from his flower shop, which is why I just weaved my way through traffic like a noob when I got lost in my head—again—and almost rode across his beloved sidewalk.

I make a mental note to swing by later with chalk to leave my second-favorite widower a nice note to find in the morning. It's been a while since I did that. Hopefully it doesn't rain before he has a chance to see it. June can be stubbornly chilly, annoyingly soggy, or blissfully warm—sometimes all in the same day. *Ah New York, you moody bitch you.*

I attempt to scissor back and forth over the crumbly concrete before giving up and hopping off my board entirely. With my fave spine tucked under my arm, I head inside the bakery I've been meaning to stop by. It's completely peanut-free, which is fucking awesome, not because I have a peanut allergy, but because other people do, and it's about time we acknowledge that shit. I've even been trying to switch out some of my dad's vendors to help make our pizzeria more allergen-friendly too, but it's slow. And difficult. Dad's stuck in his ways.

A girl about my age, maybe younger, greets me as soon as I enter and I take her in before returning her friendly smile. She's wearing a baggie sweatshirt she keeps pulling on that has me wondering what she's so self-conscious about along with a slouch beanie hipsters wear to look cool. She seems like she genuinely prefers it though, which instantly warms me to her. Also, she's got a shy kindness about her my dad probably wishes I presented to our customers.

That thought has me almost laughing out loud as I say, "Hey," then glance at her name tag, "Kylin."

"It's Kyle actually."

Dope name.

"I like your sweater, Kyle." It says *I'm not a morning person*, which with her working in a bakery, she no doubt has to work early mornings on the reg, especially if she's still in school, so…poor Kyle. "What's the best thing on the menu?"

Recovering from her whole face blush—shy *and* innocent—she recommends a fantastically high double chocolate cake with salted caramel filling. I order three slices, shovel one into my mouth, then leave her a hefty tip that makes her blush all over again.

Kyle's adorable.

I'll definitely be back.

On the way out, I spot a girl from my Lit and Comp class stopped at a red light, so after watching—hilariously—as her eyes grow wide when I ask if I can catch a ride, I hop in her passenger seat. I left my truck at home this morning, wanting to skate to school instead, but I'm not up for trying to ride all the way to my dad's pizzeria juggling two slices of cake. Our academy didn't teach us that particular life skill. *Shame.*

Luckily, it's a short drive—I can only handle so much digital hardcore music before I lose my shit—but I leave her one of the slices as compensation anyway.

One foot through the door and my dad's voice booms across the small dining room as he stands behind the counter, cheesing at me. It's fairly early, so there aren't many diners yet, but still, he acts like he didn't just see me this morning. He begins singing opera in an exaggerated voice, using the handle of a pizza peel as his microphone, and I let out a groan, pretending I don't absolutely love this kind of thing. He knows I'm full of shit though and sings even louder just for my benefit. Pure perfection, this guy.

I let him carry on for a while longer, soaking in his show like it might be his last—you never know—then when I can't take it any-more, I snatch up a nearby metal spatula and croon out my own part of this unrehearsed duet. Winding between the tables, I work to keep pace with my pops, stumbling over the foreign words but not car-ing one bit. Opera isn't about perfection, it's about emotion. Exactly what life should be.

"Dad, enough already," I mock scold after our song comes to a close. "You're gonna scare away our best customers," I say, pointing at the one table that's currently occupied. I have no clue if they've eaten here before, but they seem like good people and by that I mean they stayed for our whole performance and didn't throw food at us.

"Gia, come give me some sugar."

I hand him the last slice of cake, pleased with myself for being so literal, then I kiss both of his cheeks, just as happy to be figurative, too.

We work side by side for the rest of the evening until my boy, Rowdy, shows up asking what our plans for the night are. He sug-gests a luau over on Greek Sac but I'm not feeling it. Coconut bras and sarongs? Not for me.

Mentioning Greek Sac reminds me of the guy from earlier—*Roz*. His roommate, Fletcher, mentioned them having a party tonight, too. At least if people are swimming there, I can play that shit off, a lot easier than I could at a luau.

Two pizza rolls and an order of fried ravioli later, I've persuaded Rowdy to not only spread the new plan to everyone else but to be my ride for the night as well. I even promise to play wing-woman for him until he finds someone else to keep him busy. He's so easy to like, but he has this habit of getting super shy whenever he meets new people, so I usually have to wear my hype-woman hat just to get the conversation flowing. We're like Lance-tailed Manakin birds, working in a pair to only get one of us laid, except without the ridic-ulous dancing display.

Whatever. It's all good. He's a great guy, my best friend, and has a hell of a quad collection. If he was as confident hitting on women as he was racing four-wheelers, shit, we'd all be in trouble.

Rowdy waits until the dinner rush is over, then we're off to my house so I can change. And although the idea of Roz going apeshit over my underwear again does sound amusing, I need to change my whole outfit because this schoolgirl uniform covered in clam sauce ain't gonna cut it. If it was *my* clam sauce, then maybe.

Despite my best efforts, I crack up at my own joke, filling the foyer with peals of laughter when we walk in the front door. Rowdy gives me a weird look but doesn't ask, going in search of the remote for the TV instead.

"Where did you stash those cookies?" he calls out when I'm half-way up the stairs, and my eyes roll all on their own. Didn't he just eat? Like a lot?

Ignoring him, I grip the baluster, spinning to the right toward my room and saying, "Hi, Mom," as I pass before pulling up short. I back up a step and twist my head. Both hands on the frame, I adjust the portrait a hair to the left, then stand back to admire it. "Better," I whisper.

My mom left this earth three years ago, but there isn't a day that goes by that I don't talk to her. Sometimes to this picture hanging on the wall, sometimes in the dreams she visits me in, sometimes in my heart where I know she'll forever be.

She was one of those people, the kind that everybody liked. She could light up a room with her smile alone. That's what made my dad fall for her…him and everyone else. The warmth of her affection was unparalleled. She warmed everybody with her love, and the day she died, we were all left shivering.

Finally alone in my room, I strip my school clothes off, hoping the clam smell goes with them since I don't have time to shower. The rest of our boys don't want to walk in until we're all there because Fletcher can be a dick sometimes about the numbers being even, and having that many guys show up at once would totally screw with his chances of scoring with the opposite sex.

Sure, Fletch.

I'm so glad I never hooked up with Fletcher, he's too narrow-minded and just basic overall. Plus, Armida told me he squeals like a pig when he comes.

The Double-crested Cormorant springs to mind and I bite back a smile. The day my mom and I saw one of those at a nearby lake was a good one for sure, but I don't want to ruin the memory by associating it with Fletcher's mating rituals, so over at my retro-looking Bluetooth record player, I flip my Billie Eilish vinyl album before loading it on to the turntable and hitting play on "bad guy." With the volume maxed, I go in search of something clean to wear.

I end up choosing a baseball jersey but ignore the buttons down the front to show off my thick sports bra underneath. My stomach will be exposed but that I can handle. I finish it off with a pair of leggings that have the knees slashed and my white Vans—the ones I wore when I met Roz actually.

That guy. There's something about him. That light brown hair with an ever-so-slight curl to it. Those light brown eyes that match not only the hair on his head but the constant five o'clock shadow he rocks like a boss. Gawd, my fingers ache to scratch that jaw of his. I wonder if the stubble is soft like downy or rough like sandpaper. I'd be willing to let my thighs find that out the hard way. What can I say, I'm an equal opportunist like that.

And that voice. Even with it sounding a little off today, that voice could still trigger earthquakes with how deep and gravelly it is. I swear *I* shook the first time I heard him speak.

Then, of course, there's the grief hanging off his every breath. Abandonment of any kind is the hardest pill to swallow. Even the most hydrated peeps struggle to ingest being left behind by someone they love. Keeping it down is a different story entirely.

Kind of like my French teacher. Last fall, her husband of seventeen years divorced her, after carrying on a six-month affair with a much younger woman. *Naturally.* Clichés suck but cheating husbands suck even more, which is why once the frost set in, I dipped unused tampons in water, then stuck them to the exterior of the guy's car to freeze overnight. I got detention for missing opening announcements the next day but watching him drive to work with what looked like flying sperm all over his ride was worth it.

Pranks aside, my teacher hasn't smiled since. She doesn't even realize it wasn't her fault, that his desertion has nothing to do with her at all. She sits in class, teaching one of the most romantic languages day after day, yet scorns the very notion. Romance isn't dead; loyalty is. Her ex was a tool of the dullest degree and she deserved better. She *deserves* better. Someone who actually appreciates affectionate gestures—like over-the-top corny flower arrangements—and the feelings that inspire them.

Flower arrangements…

After freeing my hair from its bun, I hustle downstairs to dig through the bin under the giant chalkboard we used to write all of Mom's medications on. It got to be a lot, and we needed a way to keep track of everything. Near the end though, the medicine was only doing more harm than good, so she started leaving little notes on the board instead. Her loopy cursive from her last message is still written on it. *Adventure.* She didn't need to put anything more. Adventure's what it's all about. Not money, not cars, not what people think of you, not what next year holds. Life's about the here and now and what you're willing to do with that opportunity to make the best of it while you can. She was the perfect example of that. My mom fucking *lived.*

We didn't know this last scribble would, in fact, be her last, but it ended up being her best quote and I'm glad it never got erased. It's not the best handwriting, since her body was shutting down all function, but she wanted to make sure we'd remember. That *I'd* remember. I sprayed the entire thing with hairspray after she died to preserve it, so I always can.

I pocket a handful of chalk, asking Rowdy if he's ready as I pass behind the couch he's lounging on, and steal the bag of chocolate chip cookies right out of his hands to eat one.

Rowdy and I became friends in fifth grade when I still went to a co-ed school. He's the one that got me into four-wheelers, which may very well be what saved me from losing my mind from the continuous estrogen drip straight to my veins for the last nine years of all-girls schooling. Aside from skateboarding, we're practically the same person—minus his punk fauxhawk I like to ruffle any chance I get. Oh, and that extra appendage he's got swinging between his legs.

"I was eating those!"

I turn around, walking backward to the door, and mumble around a bite of cookie, "Munchies. We need these for later." And by "we," he knows I mean "me." "Now let's go. I need to make a stop on the way over to Greek Sac." I pause at the threshold to grab my keys, my favorite feather pinky ring, and some cash from the entryway table. "By the way, are my bracelets still in your console?"

Rowdy groans, dropping his head back. "G, why you gotta leave your shit everywhere? I'll never get a girlfriend with your jewelry all over my car." I open my mouth to argue when he starts ticking off his fingers. "And workshop. And room. And I swear I found one of your earrings in my laundry room the other day."

"That's crazy."

"That's what I'm saying."

"No," I start, moving out to the front porch, "not that. I mean you stepping foot in a laundry room. Why the hell would you do that?" I smirk over my shoulder, bounding down the steps.

Rowdy doesn't wash his own clothes. I know because I've seen his grandma, who lives with him and his parents, wash, fold, and iron his shit. Creased lines down the front of his work slacks and everything. Like damn, dude, a rogue earring is the least of your worries. Learn how to clean your own undies, then we can discuss adding a girlfriend to the mix.

"Watch yourself, D'Amico," he warns, closing the front door and tugging on the handle to make sure it's locked.

I flip him off over my head, purposely letting my various rings clink together.

"Where are we off to anyway?" he asks on his way down my front steps.

"You up for a little vandalism?" I raise my eyebrows, licking the corner of my lips, awaiting his answer.

His huff of irritation counts as a yes, right?

Right.

Vandalism is a strong term, one I prefer to exclude from my

everyday vocabulary—except when it's for the greater good. *Ahem, frozen tampon car.*

"To the fleuriste, please," I tell my best friend once we're seated inside his orange and black Ford.

"What the fuck is that?"

"French."

"You know I took Mandarin for foreign language."

"Flower shop. To the flower shop."

"I thought you liked the guy that owns that place," he says slowly.

"I do. I just think someone else might like him, too."

Instead of raising his key to the ignition, Rowdy lifts his eyes to the roof.

"Come on, Rowdy." I open his console, finding my bracelets right where I left them. "Let's go spread some amore."

"Now *that's* Italian." He laughs as he starts the F-150.

"Love doesn't have a language."

"Okay, Cupid."

"But if it did…" I can't keep the smile off my face.

He pulls away from the house, groaning, "Don't say it."

"U and I would be next to each other in the alphabet," I say, poking the dimple in his right cheek.

Rowdy tries to shake my hand off, but I catch him smiling.

Chapter 3

ROZ

"**S**o, now you're back here? For good? *Hard.*"

I stare blankly at the guy, T.J., for what feels like the twentieth time in the last hour. It's been one hour too long in his presence, but he's the only person that doesn't seem to mind carrying an entire conversation practically by himself. So far I've gotten by with only a couple obligatory nods or headshakes, but I'm starting to regret even those. He's just so fucking annoying. He sprinkles the word "hard" over pretty much everything throughout his less-than-interesting commentary.

"Your birthday's coming up? That's hard. You won't celebrate it this year? Hard. You should come to my birthday. It's gonna be harddd."

People that do that kind of thing either don't know what else to say or they like the sound of their own voice. T.J.'s gotta be both.

And I'm not going to his birthday party. What are we? Six?

"Bruh, if I was traveling all over the world to exotic locations," I think the word he's going for here is remote, "I'd never come back to this place."

I didn't tell him I used to snowboard professionally. I know I didn't because I haven't said a single word to him since he approached me, which tells me he did some kind of homework on me, and for the first time all night, I actually *want* to open my mouth to say something, anything. I just need to get the fuck away from T.J. already.

Before I can though, he says, "Aw shit, she came through after all. Party's over boys, hide yo' girls. Gia's here to snatch 'em up for herself."

The mention of Gia has my neck damn near snapping to catch

sight of her as she slowly strolls through the yard with a joint perched between her half-parted lips and a stream of smoke lazily curling upward. On both sides of her are rows of people, mostly dudes, and with another masculine outfit on, Gia blends in, almost like she's one of them. Almost.

"Gia's, uh." I cough, expecting cobwebs to come up. "What do you mean Gia's here to take the girls?"

"Fucking look at her." T.J. snorts while I try not to do the same. Look at her? I can't fucking stop looking at Gia. "She's on a pussy-*only* diet." He slaps my chest and the sting on my skin speaks of the extra force he put into it as he says, "Trust me, bruh, bitch ain't worth the trouble."

So her appearance symbolizes her sexual orientation? That's the stupidest shit I've ever heard of. A person's style, a person's personality, is not a person's sexual preference.

And, apparently, she's a bitch, too?

Regretting ever letting T.J. talk to me, I put some distance between us so no one can mistake me for one of his friends. I try not to associate with dumbfucks if I can help it. Their stupidity is like noxious gas, just one small whiff of it can cost you brain cells.

One of the guys Gia arrived with leans down near her ear, whispering something. She takes the joint from her parted mouth, passing it to some other chump beside her, then together, the two of them beeline toward a group of girls. Gia's friend waits a few feet away while she starts talking up the girl with neon-green hair and a one-piece lodged up her ass. Seriously, that can't be healthy.

Did I misread everything? *Not that there was a lot to go off of.* Gia dresses in a masculine way, yeah, but in a way that's still feminine somehow. I can see that tonight with her wide-open shirt and sports bra showing a soft tummy with a hint of toned abs. Never mind the leggings that mold to her like a second skin. The girl she's talking to with the swimsuit showcasing two flawless globes for ass cheeks holds less appeal than Gia does even being the most over-dressed person here.

It's true I didn't get a feel for who Gia was into, but I sure as fuck hoped. I hoped…for what exactly? That she'd like *me*?

I don't even like me right now.

"Hey, cowboy."

The object of my thoughts is suddenly staring up at me with that signature smirk of hers. The lights around the yard make all fifty of her bracelets shimmer, causing me to imagine any other jewelry she might have on but isn't showing.

Fuck. What am I doing?

I swallow thickly. "Cowboy?"

Gia points at my torso with hands that are covered in purple, orange, and blue…chalk?

"Shirtless, abs of steel. Cowboy."

Ever since I was a toddler, I've run hot. There was even a running joke in the media about how I managed to win so many competitions. They liked to say it was because the snow melted away from my heightened body heat. Hell, I would've competed shirtless if it wasn't against regulations.

"You ride, don't you?"

"Not anymore…" She looks at me expectantly. "But that was a snowboard."

She waves me off, saying, "It's all the same."

Is it though?

Another one of her buddies comes over to pass off a lit joint before leaving us alone again. With her busy studying the glowing red tip, I ask, "What's with the chalk?"

"I didn't have any arrows."

I frown in response and she says, "Cupid's arrows," like that explains everything.

After a moment of silence that I normally feel comfortable in, but now feel panicked by, I blurt out, "So," grasping at another topic, "T.J. was just telling me something interesting about you."

I wince like my balls just got flicked. Why did I say that? It's *her* sexual preference. She doesn't owe me an explanation.

A dry laugh escapes her throat as she peeks up at me, saying, "I bet B.J. did."

B.J.? "Do I even want to know what that means?"

She rolls her eyes, finally taking a hit and wincing herself. "Touchy, touchy. Maybe you need this more than I do."

I accept the expertly rolled joint from her to take a much smaller drag than she did. I don't care. I don't have anything to prove to anyone anymore.

"Better?" she asks, and I shake my head, making her laugh. Growing serious, she takes the joint back, staring me down. "How long did you go?"

"Go?"

"Without talking."

My jaw locks in place.

"Before this afternoon, when I stopped by, how long had it been since you talked to someone else?"

I don't answer her. I wouldn't even know how. It's not like I was counting the weeks. Wait, was it actually weeks?

"And tonight? Have you talked to anyone here?"

I open my mouth, but she's quick to add, "Other than me?"

"Yeah. Your boy, *B.J.*" Twelve words I'll never get back, too.

But maybe it was worth it to get the scoop on Gia.

Meh. I'd rather get info directly from the source. T.J. can go dig himself a hole.

"It's not what you think," she says on an inhale, holding in a mouthful of smoke before blowing it out in one big cloud.

"It stands for Blue Jay. He's a Blue Jay."

I nod my head like I know what she means by that, but then, no. I don't fucking know.

"What?"

"Blue Jays are beautiful…on the outside. They're related to Crows, so they're actually scavengers and they can be pretty ruthless." She intentionally points a finger at T.J., not caring when he frowns, noticing. "Just like him. Pretty to look at but fucking rotten on the inside."

I don't think he's pretty, but I could believe the rotten part. Easily.

"Do you compare everyone to birds, or just him?" I ask, remembering the way she was watching the Crows at Salvy's funeral.

She shrugs, her lips pulling to the side.

"All right, what about your friend?"

"Which one?"

I scout around for her right-hand man, finding him off to the side, whispering into the ear of the green-haired girl with the wedgie.

Glancing between him and Gia, I frown. I thought…

"He's a Cockatoo."

I guess I can see it. His hairstyle does resemble some form of a mohawk.

"And them?" I point to some girls that keep shooting Gia judgy looks.

Her brown eyes barely land on the trio in question before saying, "Blackbirds."

I motion for her to elaborate, and she sighs. "None of them are strong enough to stand on their own, so they stick together to better their odds."

"At what?"

"At making it through life unscathed? I don't know. You'd have to ask them."

"I'm asking you." I know there's more she's not telling me.

"A question for a question?"

We hold each other's eyes until I jerk my chin in agreement. I don't really want to know about the girls. I want Gia to keep talking. I could listen to her all night, even about birds. Or people.

"Okay, check it." She rolls her shoulders back, straightening her spine like she's getting ready for a presentation, and I smirk. "There's no clear leader, right? They may have their own thoughts and ideas, but they feel more secure acting on them in a flock rather than risking branching out separately. Each part is actually intelligent when you get them alone," she rolls her eyes in the girls' direction quickly, "but nobody acts individually without the others following along in solidarity."

I watch the girls with new eyes. I would've never thought of them—or anybody—like that, but Gia's right. You can see it in the way their eyes skirt to each other for constant reassurance.

"Blackbirds. They fill the sky with murmurations, but they're not exactly beautiful. Sometimes they can even be haunting."

"How do you know all that about them?"

"They went to my school."

She blows a kiss at the whispering trio, making them finally turn away…as one.

Through my growing smile, I ask, "What about me?" but she tsks, saying, "You owe me an answer first."

With a lift of one of my eyebrows for her to continue, she asks, "Why aren't you talking?"

"I am."

"Before today."

"It wasn't a choice. I just didn't have anything to say."

"There's always a choice," Gia says softly, studying me, and I shift my weight from one foot to the other, sticking my hands in my pockets.

Louder, she tells me, "I like your voice."

"Yeah?"

"Yeah. You should use it more. You never know who's listening."

"Nobody's listening."

"I am."

Okay…

My shoulders bunched up near my ears, I say, "So… What bird am I?"

Unceremoniously as all hell, she pops a shoulder, saying, "Not sure yet," before strutting away without another word.

What? She has every other person here pegged, down to the tiniest idiosyncrasies, but she doesn't know which bird I might be? She either doesn't want to tell me or she just doesn't want to be bothered with new classifications.

But if that were true, why'd she say "yet"?

Hours. It's been hours of this shit. I tried doing the math—what the fuck else was I supposed to do?—and I don't think it's an exaggeration to say that before today, before Gia appeared, I did go weeks without talking to a single fucking person. But I didn't care about those weeks. I didn't even notice. Now though, in the *hours* of silence since Gia waltzed away from my ass, now I care. Now I'm noticing.

Everywhere Gia goes, I can't help but watch her. I promised myself I'd give her space—for my sake more than hers. If she isn't interested, then why torture myself? But not talking to her is even more painful.

I finally said *something* to *someone*, but now I'm back to this purgatory where I watch the world move on but am no longer an active participant in.

For the briefest of moments, I was a part of it though, at least it felt like it. Gia made me feel like it.

Her voice suddenly rising has me treading closer, closer than I've dared all night. T.J. being in the same circle gathered around Gia may or may not be the final tug on my restraint at staying away, and I climb the stairs to the patio, giving myself a better vantage point.

"A woman sleeps with different people so she can feel wanted. A guy fucks everything in sight to prove his worth. She gets labeled a slut while he looks like the man. How is that fair?"

My eyebrows shoot to my hairline. She's got a point. Half the gathering crowd agrees while the other half shouts their own objections, which sound like mouth farts and reek like ignorance. It's actually pretty embarrassing.

With my beer bottle hovering up near my mouth, I take a quick smell to rid myself of the bitter odor all while keeping an eye on Gia. The guys in her corner seem to have her back, but a couple of them jostle her in the excitement and I don't like it. I don't like it one bit.

"So where does that leave your reputation, G?" T.J. asks Gia, his stare piercing hers while all the other eyes in her corner drop to the ground with the subtlety of an atomic bomb.

What's going on?

Gia shakes her head. "Men always care more about women's reputations, meanwhile you should be worried with your own."

T.J.'s eyes narrow, but Gia doesn't back down an inch. In fact, she hops down from the same spot on the cooler she was perched this afternoon to step closer to him.

Cocka-dude surges forward, leaving his current squeeze to stand beside his friend, and my own feet make the final move to push through the tight circle. Now if someone jumps, I can jump, too.

"Girls talk. A lot." Even over the music, I can hear T.J. swallow. Gia backs up with her arms spread wide, eyes still on her opponent. "I know about every guy's sexual competence at this party." She pauses to bite her lips together like she's trying not to laugh before adding, "Or lack thereof—and not from personal experience."

Her gaze darts to mine briefly before landing on my roommate to say, "Right, Fletch?"

I swear my feet try to move me again, this time in Fletcher's direction, but I lock all my muscles up to keep from doing anything hasty. Fletcher did sing like a popstar on autotune after Gia left earlier, swearing on every member in his family tree that he and Gia were *just* friends. But he also left out the small fact that Gia doesn't even like guys, so…

A girl that looks vaguely familiar, like she's slept over before—and not with me—doubles over laughing, which triggers Fletcher in some way because he immediately shoots daggers at her as his face turns beet red.

Hmm.

T.J. speaks up again, saying, "Bruh, maybe we should put your shit on blast. You know, since you want things to be *fair*." He sticks his hands up innocently, shrugging.

Oh yeah, he also calls everybody "bruh," even females.

"Be my guest." Gia props her ass against the cooler, finally letting that smile loose. Maintaining eye contact with an arch in her brow, she tells him, "But if we're really making things fair, Titus Jennings, does that mean everyone gets to hear about *your* shit, too?"

Why'd she say it like that? Like in this instance, she actually does know from experience?

T.J.'s face darkens and I slip the neck of my beer bottle down between my pointer and middle fingers, ready if he makes a move for Gia, but luckily, he storms off in the opposite direction.

I'm lost like a polar bear in the goddamn desert right now, but I wait until the commotion dies down before going for another beer—where Gia's still posted.

My eyes meet hers as my hand lands on the lid. Without breaking the connection, she shifts to let me open it, and after picking one out, I slam it back into place, then match her stance, leaning against the cooler beside her.

"So, you and T.J.?" I let that hang in the air, hoping she'll fill in the blanks, but she doesn't, forcing me to try to piece this shit together on my own. "Because he said—"

"That I'm a lesbian? He's been spreading that lie for years."

My gaze snaps to hers, but she looks away, blowing out a breath to tell me, "I've been with both."

"Are you bisexual then?"

"Mmm, I don't know." She squints, considering it. "Maybe. I don't really do the label thing, but I'm about the person more than their gender, so… I'd probably say pansexual."

"What are your pronouns?"

Her eyes swing back to mine so hard I almost tip over, but I don't blink as I meet her stare head-on.

Slowly the suspicion melts away and she grins, saying, "She/her," then more seriously, "Thanks for asking. Most people make their own assumptions about me."

I sit for a minute, waiting to see if she'll say more, but she never does.

"Why does T.J. bother telling people that?" He went out of his way to make me think Gia wasn't into guys at all. Why?

Gia blinks up at the blackening sky, explaining, "I let him go down on me once," but some unidentified noise escapes my throat, making her stop to glance at me before continuing, "and he was so bad, I mean *so bad*, that I told him he could stop. Actually, I'm pretty sure I told him to leave." She laughs. "Anyway, I don't think his fragile male ego ever recovered because he's been telling people I'm only attracted to women ever since."

"Jesus Christ." I scrub a hand across my chest. "Now I'm picturing his face between your legs."

She's the one to make a strange noise now, saying, "Don't. He didn't spend much time down there."

"You don't care?"

"Well, yeah, I kicked him out of my house."

"No, that he lies about you."

"Oh. Nah, not particularly. If anything, the fact that he tries to pass that off as damaging information speaks to his character. I just told you I've been with women and I don't know you, so obviously, even if I was a lesbian, I'd have no problem admitting it openly. B.J. saying I am doesn't hurt me in the slightest, but I mean, he can't even eat pussy properly, so his credibility is shit as far as I'm concerned."

I guess? To be honest, I never even considered it an option. If you like pussy, you should eat pussy, and you should try to eat it well. Personally, I fucking *love* pussy.

"Well, I don't think I'd be so understanding."

She shrugs, pushing to fully stand. "Maybe you're insecure."

Excuse me, what?

As she goes to leave, I dart my hand out to catch her bracelet-lined wrist. It's the first time I've touched another person's skin for…who fucking knows. Her skin is warm, not as warm as mine, but I was expecting her to be cold for some reason.

"How do you figure?" I rasp out when she doesn't pull away.

Gia maneuvers her arm so that my hand slides down into hers and delicate fingers caked in colorful powder tangle with mine until we're holdings hands. *We're holding hands.*

"I know who and what I am. I also know what I'm capable of."

She blinks suddenly like she's waking up, then yanks her hand from my grasp.

What was that?

"And I don't really worry too much about what other people think about me. But we all saw how freaked T.J. was when I threatened to expose his 'skills,' right?" Gia plants herself directly in front of me, so we're toe to toe and lowers her voice to say, "So maybe yours are lacking, too," before stepping away.

No. Not yet.

With one quick tug on her waist, I bring her right back, putting our faces only inches apart.

Those chalky fingertips of hers dance across my throbbing chest, making me *feel* again. I fucking feel.

I almost lose my train of thought completely as my eyes close, but the way I figure it, she doesn't have anywhere else she needs to be right now.

Here. With me. *Perfect.*

I open my eyes to see her pupils dilate.

Almost perfect.

"If you want to put my skills to the test, all you gotta do is use *your* voice." Because I like hers, too. A lot.

She pops an eyebrow. "Who says I even like you?"

I pop one as well. "Who says you don't?"

Sparring with Gia is getting my blood pumping—everywhere—and along with my confidence, I also feel some of my former self return, not all of him but enough to make me feel alive again, more alive than I've felt in months.

Her gaze disconnects from mine to scan the rest of the party, reminding me we're not actually alone.

Something flashes across her face before she brings her eyes back, saying, "Wanna have some fun?"

My grip on her tightens automatically. I wasn't kidding when I told her all she had to do was ask. She could ask me anything right now and I'd go along with it, if only to spend a little bit more time in her presence. I'm not ready for this to end. She's escaped me twice now and I'll be damned if I let her do it a third time.

"What'd you have in mind?"

Slipping from my hold, Gia winds through the throng of tightly packed dancers, forcing me to roll onto my toes when I lose sight of her, and just when I'm about to go after her, she appears on the other side, closest to the pool—closest to T.J.

I'm confused. How the fuck is anything to do with him considered fun?

Another girl she must've pulled from the mass starts dancing on Gia, then I'm walking before consciously making the decision. Unfortunately, I'm not the only one focused on her every move. T.J. and his followers drool like a bunch of pubescent boys watching two girls dance together only a few feet away.

I have absolutely no idea what the fuck Gia's doing or how exactly I fit into all this, so I stay put, waiting for a signal from her... assuming she's gonna give one.

Faces are flushed—T.J. and his objectifying friends. Hands roam over tits—thankfully only the two girls. And asses are bent and rubbed to the point that I can't even tell who's who anymore, just that it's still Gia and her friend. Unless a third girl snuck in...

Nope, there's only two.

I think.

T.J. breaks from his crew, rubbing his hands together while eyeing Gia with a sick gleam.

Gia's gaze flies to mine as I make my way over, but I give her a subtle nod, reassuring her. He's not touching her.

Before Titus Jennings can even get within reach of either girl, I yank his ass back, shoving him toward his slobbery friends. His shoe catches on the pavement, causing him to face-plant, and I crack a smile a mile wide, asking him, "Was that worth it, *bitch?*"

As the song changes to "Basic" by N!GHTS, two sets of feminine hands snake around to my chest and my smile falls along with my gaze. *What's this?*

Using Gia's bird associations, the dancing pair resemble a couple of Vultures circling their next meal and, goddamn, devour me now. Never have I been this fucking ready.

The duo takes turns teasing along my back, chest, and abs as they sway to the music, drawing it out. I do my best to focus on every featherlight touch, but it's getting harder and harder to concentrate with each pass of their fingertips over my skin, giving me goose bumps. I never get goose bumps because I never get cold. But this, this isn't cold at all. It's straight fire.

One on each of my sides, they latch on to a hand, then arch backward, nearly touching the ground with the tips of their hair. I let them hang for a beat, then with equal tugs, I bring them crashing back into my torso simultaneously. I wrap an arm around each of them, noting how good it feels to be stretching my muscles again.

Gia blinks up at me through heavy lashes before twisting to park her ass against my dick while her friend uses the distraction to skate out of my reach. Boomeranging right back to us though, Gia becomes the filling in a sexy-as-fuck sandwich, but the other girl isn't satisfied with only being a sidepiece. I see it in her eyes as she leans into Gia's space, aiming for her lips, but in a split-second decision, I cup Gia's cheek myself and pull her face to mine, sealing my lips over hers. I eat up her moans, releasing one of my own when I feel her friend's hands twist into my hair, holding me to Gia, then my lips become her playmates while I give her free rein to do whatever the fuck she wants. Nips, bites, groans—they're all here. Gia's rough and has no qualms showing me what she likes.

Well before I'm ready for it to end, the hands on my scalp disappear and Gia pulls away. With the spot in front of us now empty, I glance around, finding her friend back in the crowd, already dancing with somebody else.

Gia faces T.J., grinning confidently at him, and everything finally falls into place. The dancing, the wind-up, the kiss. It was all for show. To teach T.J. a lesson. That Gia can, and will, get anyone she wants, which unfortunately for him, isn't T.J.

The rub though? I'm not fucking playing.

So, spinning Gia around, I snatch her lips up all over again, this time showing her what *I* like.

I hear T.J. mutter something under his breath as he passes by us but I couldn't care less. I'm not stopping for him. I'm not stopping for anything.

My tongue dives deep, swirling and licking followed by more licking and swirling.

This kiss is different than the first. There's no audience to cater to. No point to prove. There's no other reason besides us both wanting to kiss each other. And fuck, do I want to. Judging by the way Gia's nails are digging into the back of my skull, I'd say she does to.

Fuck, I can't get enough of her flavor.

Gia laughs and I taste that, too.

I break away to graze down her neck, needing to taste even more, when something…fishy maybe…has me involuntarily rearing back for some fresh air.

Noticing we're near the pool's edge, I pretend to take stock of our surroundings, but the pucker in Gia's eyebrows tells me I didn't school my features in time.

Not a moment later, I feel a hand slip from my front pocket, the space lighter than usual.

"What—"

The ice-cold water cuts off my words as my back hits the glassy surface. With my feet under me the next second, I'm able to stand in the pool, growling as water runs down my face. *What the fuck was that?* My eyes instantly search Gia out but she's still in the same spot as before. She simply stares down her nose at me, not even remotely sorry for pushing my ass in here. I may not have a shirt on, but I'm wearing my regular shorts with all my shit in the—

Wait.

I reach in my front pockets, palming my wallet still tucked safely inside.

Gia steps closer to the ledge, my phone clutched in her hand. At the same time my stomach bottoms out, she has the nerve to calmly smirk down at me.

My back filled with tension, I lurch forward, freezing when she twists to toss the device, along with something else, onto the grass. Eyes on mine, she…steps off. She fucking steps off into the water, joining me in the pool. Fully clothed.

Stunned, I can only flinch from the splash, but seeing her fully submerged, I snap out of it to help her to standing.

Every piece of Gia's outfit, including her shoes, is soaked through and weighing her down, yet she's grinning from ear to ear as she throws her arms around my neck, acting like we're going for a regular ol' swim.

She's not a thief. She's just crazy.

A smile slowly overtakes my face.

I'm starting to think crazy might look good on me.

Chapter 4

ROZ

We stay in the pool while the party carries on without us. We stay in the pool even when people begin to leave. We stay in the pool until Gia's lips turn blue and I offer to warm them up.

We get out when she agrees to let me.

On our way to the front yard, we find her sidekick with the same green-haired girl from before pressed against the side of his tricked-out F-150. Neither of his hands are visible but both of his elbows are moving…rapidly.

Gia jogs over to them before I can stop her.

"You jumped on his back," I say once she's back by my side.

"Mmhmm."

"And kissed him."

"On his cheek, yeah."

"While he was dry-humping someone."

Pushing through the front door ahead of me, she jerks a thumb behind her, saying, "There was nothing dry about what they were doing."

To keep her from tracking water anywhere else—our clothes are dripping all over the threshold—I grip her middle with both hands, resting my chin on her shoulder.

"Maybe you were getting an eyeful?"

Her breath feathers over my face when she twists her head to the side, asking, "Of Rowdy? Or the girl?"

My eyes hold hers but drop when she follows up with, "I'm madly in love with Rowdy."

How does that work? She's in love with him but doesn't mind him finger-fucking another girl right in front of her.

"But not in a sexual way."

"Then…in a romantic way?" I ask, trying to keep up. Madly in love is serious. I've never been madly in love with anyone. Or anything.

That's not true.

I used to be madly in love with snowboarding. It was…everything. My life's mission.

And now I don't have one at all.

Gia snorts, shaking her head. "Definitely not. Rowdy's my closest friend and I fucking adore him but we've never been like *that*." She says "that" like she's talking about the monster under the bed—if you don't draw attention to it, you're safe.

"Besides, I already told you it doesn't matter what's between someone's legs." I feel her hand glide up my thigh, and on a curse, I press myself into her ass, letting her feel what's between mine. "I only care what's under their ribs."

She shivers, or I shiver, or we shiver, I don't know. I just know something intangible passes between us, and while neither of us openly acknowledges it, we both feel it.

But Gia's eyes widen a fraction and she pulls away, ending the moment by asking for the bathroom. She doesn't wait for an answer either, just finds the correct door all on her own.

The door closes, then the bathtub faucet turns on, making me frown.

Okay. Maybe she's rinsing off?

Climbing the stairs leading to my room, I change from my wet shorts and boxer briefs into a pair of gray joggers sans underwear. I sleep naked, so this is already too much clothing but…propriety and all that.

I grab a plain white tee and a pair of athletic shorts—also sans underwear—for her before heading back down.

After an embarrassing amount of time lingering outside the

bathroom, I finally knock and my plan to leave the outfit by the door flies out the window with most, if not all, of my rational thought when she says, "Come in."

On an exhale, I push open the door, imagining Gia in some sexy pose, waiting to pounce. What I don't expect to find is a mountain of bubbles covering her body as she chills in the filled tub, her head tilted back with her arms resting on the lip while holding a bottle of wine.

Umm.

How'd she get wine in here? Better yet, who the fuck bought it?

Draped across the shower rod, her wet clothes continuously drip down on to the bubbles below, popping them by the dozens.

She cracks an eye and says, "Hi."

"Hi." I cover a cough by pointing to the quickly disappearing bubbles. "Where did you find those?"

She glances at the counter and I busy myself by picking up the bottle, studying it very intently to keep my eyes from wandering. There's no expiration date, but there is a heavy ring of crusty build-up around the cap. I make the mistake of smelling it, my nose stinging from the overwhelming sea breeze freesia scent.

Gia's laughter fills the cramped bathroom. "Hey, it's better than clams."

My eyes go wide as the bottle slips from my hold, falling to the floor with a loud *crack*. Well, that's the end of that. Thank God.

"Don't act like you didn't smell it."

I mean, I did, but why was it there?

"Clams?"

"My dad owns a pizza shop," she says, setting the wine bottle on the edge to slide her body farther down in the tub. "I put in a shift before coming here."

That scenario sounds infinitely better than anything I'd come up with on my own so far.

Fully submerged, save for her head, she asks, "For me?" and I realize I'm clutching the clothes I brought down for her in my other hand.

I give her a slow nod, working to keep my eyes on hers. Nothing of hers is showing, but still, they're distracting—the bubbles. Because I know what they're hiding.

I don't *know*…but I'd like to.

"Unless you had other plans?" *Like, I don't know, staying naked.*

"*That's* not happening." She says it the exact same way she did about love—the romantic kind—but then her hands clap together loudly, sending clusters of bubbles airborne, and she watches them float above her head for a minute.

I follow her gaze, losing myself in the clouds, too.

"Roz." Gia's voice snaps me out of the bubble-filled fantasy. "Towel?"

With rigid fingers, I grab a towel from under the sink, stealing a peek at the top of Gia's shoulder as I hand it to her. There's a small circular scar that looks like a tiny burn, and even though she's careful to keep most of herself covered by the water, I still catch the mark. *How'd she get it?* Even in the pool, she chose to keep her baseball jersey on. She could've easily taken it off and swam in her sports bra, but she refused every time anyone suggested it. I didn't think anything of it at the time. But now…now I'm wondering.

I'm quick to recover, meeting her eyes again to ask, "Need anything else?"

"Anything?"

"Anything."

"Here." I place the box of cannoli in her open palms, then drop down next to her on the couch. She's drowning in my shirt and shorts but pulls them off as if they're her own. Hell, she probably has the same outfit at home.

When she doesn't respond, I look over, finding her frowning at the package.

"You don't like them?"

"Shit, you don't like cannoli?" Fletcher asks. "Isn't your dad famous for his cannoli?"

"That sounded dirty," Johnny, another guy that lives here, says without looking away from the TV screen.

Apparently, my roommates don't have anything better to do, because while I walked to the neighborhood store to buy something sweet for Gia, they decided to take up the usually deserted living room to play video games. They brought their own gaming systems out and everything.

"He's won some competitions," Gia tells Fletcher, but to me, she says, "Sorry."

I shrug, telling her, "That's all they had."

Our other roommate, Nathan, takes them off her, immediately stuffing one in his mouth before mumbling, "Al's, right?"

Gia nods, falling into an easy conversation about her dad's restaurant—a pizzeria with award-winning cannoli.

I didn't realize my roommates knew Gia. Or knew of her. Aside from a brief introduction when I first moved in, I've never spoken to Nathan about anything. Same with Johnny. This is actually the first time I've even been in the living room for longer than a few seconds.

If I would've…I don't know…*tried* with my roommates—at all—I could've run into Gia sooner. Maybe. She's been going to the school just across the street the entire time I've lived here and I didn't notice. I haven't noticed much lately. I haven't *done* much lately.

I haven't done anything.

After an hour of stats, kill shots, and trash talk, I take a break to grab one of the cannoli for myself. Nathan side-eyes me like he can't bear the thought of losing one, but I bought the fucking things, so I take it anyway, sticking the powdery shell in my mouth. With half the cream-filled tube between my lips still, a sneeze to my right pulls my attention from my roommate in time to catch Gia hitching a leg over both of mine to straddle my lap.

My hands fly to her thighs in an instant, gripping them tightly. *Hell yes.*

Our eyes watching the other's, Gia leans forward, slowly taking the exposed half into her mouth, brushing my lips in the process. With a crunch that could raise the dead, she bites down, and I follow suit. Some of the sweet filling gets stuck between us, but using only my tongue and lips, I do my best to clean the mess before she even gets the chance.

A throat clears beside us, giving Gia a grin I can't wait to watch spread into a smile. Or a moan.

"Time for bed, cowboy," she whispers, and not needing to be told twice, I lift her as I stand, helping to wrap her legs around my body, then climb my stairs with Gia secure in my arms.

With her help, the door's open and quickly shut behind us. My feet are already aimed for my bed, but Gia breathing the word, "Whoa," trips me up, causing me to stop and follow her gaze.

Posters—my posters, specifically—line my wall.

She wiggles out of my hold, shuffling over to get a closer look. I trail behind her as she goes but keep my eyes on the back of her head, wondering what she's thinking. Wondering what she sees.

Some have other pro-snowboarders in them; others feature Salvy. Most have me somewhere in the photo, whether I'm mid-air or posing, but they're all the same—my career, my whole life.

"These are you?" she asks, her face a foot away from a magazine feature I did last year, and even though she's not looking at me, I shrug. It's me, or what used to be me, but it doesn't feel like that anymore. I feel disconnected from my old life now. These posters, my face may be on them, but I no longer identify as the person they're portraying.

Or maybe I do, but wish I didn't.

"You're pretty good, huh?"

Were? Or are?

She turns her gaze on me and I shrug again.

"You love it?"

There's no mistaking what tense she's using this time. Do I love it...*still?*

Another shrug.

"But you quit."

This one isn't a question at all, but I answer anyway, giving her a single nod.

She spins suddenly, walking over to the side of my bed before sitting on the edge of the mattress. Throwing herself backward, she stretches her arms above her head, onto the other side. To the ceiling, she asks, "Why do you keep them up?"

"I don't know," I mutter, folding my arms over my chest.

"Are they happy memories at least?"

I study my former life like Gia did, running my gaze over each and every one. My entire existence summed up in less than three minutes with a grand total of thirty-something posters. Some of them I don't even remember. I was there for all of them, but I wasn't always *there*. Time passed quicker then but still just as blurry as it does now. Just like these days, I didn't *try* to appreciate it. I didn't appreciate anything and now it's gone. All of it. Everything.

An embarrassment I've never experienced before washes over me and I adjust my footing, the swishing sound filling the room.

"You rock when you're nervous."

Gia's staring directly at me, so dropping my arms to my sides, I blurt, "What?" adding more irritation to my tone than necessary.

"Maybe it's not just nerves," Gia muses to herself before telling me, "When you're standing still, your body kinda rocks, sways from side to side, and sometimes you even pitch forward and then backward on to the balls of your feet, like you're dodging something." *I didn't know that.* "And whenever you look at my skateboard, your fingers flex."

I drop my gaze. That part I did know, but I didn't think it was noticeable to anybody else.

I guess I'm not the only one that's been paying close attention.

"Anytime someone mentions snowboarding or the snow or even just winter, pain flashes across your face so raw, it's hard to look at without feeling gripped by it as well." My eyes connect with hers. "It's like you left your heart on the slopes, but the rest of your body hasn't figured it out yet."

After a moment of silence I welcome with open arms, she adds, "Maybe it's just waiting for you to change your mind."

"I can't," leaves my lips like a confession. It is a confession. I can't risk it. I can't go back out there just to end up where Salvy is—dead with only long-forgotten, dust-collecting posters to remember me by. I want more, I just don't know what more is. What more there could be. All I've ever known is snowboarding.

"Tell me about him." Gia's voice calls to mine, coaxing it out of its hiding place—out of the comfort zone I've given it these past few months—and after several swallows, I join her on the bed, lying the opposite way, then I do something I haven't done since Salvy's funeral—I talk about him. Openly. Without censoring what we did, how we lived, or who we were.

"Big Red?"

"He had red hair." The reddest. It wasn't just me that called him that either, that was his nickname in our sport. What made him easy to spot even with a helmet or hat on. You could see his flaming red hair anywhere on the mountain.

Until you couldn't.

Until *I* couldn't.

We're both quiet for a minute, then I see her finger in the air, circling the same way she did the day at the funeral. I oblige, and she continues listening intently, her occasional questions spurring me on until I'm telling her about more than just Salvy; I'm opening up about myself, too.

"I didn't take you for a cuddler," she interrupts to say.

I lift my head to see her better. "Oh yeah? Why's that?"

"That perma-scowl of yours scares people away. Then that deep voice terrifies the ones brave enough to stick around."

I notice my face is screwed into a scowl, so I try to relax the muscles. She's right though. Some blogger wrote an entire piece about it once—that I look like I don't know how to have fun. And the voice… what can I say? It's been that way since I finished puberty.

"So, which one does that make you?"

The mattress shakes from her shrug. "Whichever one saves me from being cuddled."

I'm on her almost instantly, making her laugh a low, throaty sound from being caught unprepared.

"I think you'd like my cuddling," I accuse, staring down into her half-mast eyes.

Her lips fall open from her laugh, revealing the tip of her tongue—the tongue she uses like a well-aimed whip instead of a careless caress—and even though I've been dying to kiss her again, I hold back. I hold back with everything I got…until she arches an eyebrow in question, then I press my lips to hers in answer.

I don't rush, more than happy to take my time exploring, but Gia growls out her impatience at my pace, fisting my shorts and tugging. Something tells me if I rush this, I'll regret it, and if I were on my feet right now, I know I'd be rocking side to side like a fucking pendulum.

Peppering kisses down her throat, I pull back. Wild, air-dried curls fan out from her head like an homage to Medusa, except instead of turning my entire body to stone, only my lower half is affected by going rock hard at the sight.

I skim my hand along the band of her sculpted stomach exposed by the bunched t-shirt, making her breathing—and mine—quicken.

Sliding down, I get an inch above her belly button before she stops me, rasping out, "Do you have a condom? Rowdy stole mine and my cookies."

Cookies…

Cookie jar.

I drop my forehead, sighing. *Shit.*

"I'll be right back."

Replacing the baggy fabric, I jog back downstairs, eyeing the empty living room on my way to the kitchen. Luckily, I manage to find the cookie jar without needing a light and lift the lid to reveal a fully stocked supply of condoms. As far as I know, it's never actually had cookies inside, hence my spontaneous midnight quest for something sweet.

Gia asked for a treat while naked in a bath. It was either walk to the store, any store, or learn to bake on the spot. I chose the quicker option.

I take one condom out before thinking better of it and reaching back in for two more.

Back up the stairwell in record time, I step through the door while holding my breath, then immediately release it—quietly.

At this point, I shouldn't be shocked by anything Gia does, yet finding her fast asleep where I left her somehow surprises me.

Reluctant to rearrange her and risk waking her up, I decide to adapt to the unconventional position by lying next to her with our heads at the foot of the bed. I keep my hands to myself for all of four seconds before scooping her head gently and placing it on my shoulder with my arm wrapped snugly around her back.

Gia nestles in deeper, fully tucked into my side, and I kiss the top of her head to keep the smile on my face from spreading any bigger.

I knew she'd like my cuddling.

Chapter 5

GIA

My arm brushes my mother's nearly unrecognizable shrinking frame, leaving me to wonder how much longer until she disappears altogether. How does someone just stop existing? I'd wished I'd never have to find out, but here I am, watching the excruciating process in person.

An ominous shadow falls over the backyard.

"Ooh, look. A Falcon."

With a thin, shaky finger, she points out the brown bird of prey circling above the dozens of birdfeeders decorating our backyard. My mom's hospital-style bed is stationed directly in front of the bank of casement windows in our living room, giving her an unobstructed view of the feeders my dad built for her, along with the birds hitting them up for food.

"Should I go scare him off?" I ask, and a huff of air leaves her mouth, causing my head to rotate to hers. Seeing she's not in pain—well, more pain—I relax a little.

"Not yet."

We watch him soar for a while longer before she says, "Your father's a Peregrine Falcon, did you know that?"

I shake my head. "How so?"

"Well, the incredible speed for one thing."

I laugh, nodding. My dad's always rushing from one task to the next, rarely slowing down to enjoy things—the exact opposite of my mom.

"But also, the wisdom, vision, and protection they signify."

My nod slows as my nose begins to burn. That sounds like Dad. His intelligence and foresight are why our family-run pizza shop is what it is today, but as our family deteriorates, I worry Al's Pizzeria will, too. Because if it does, then there goes our only source of income.

I don't know how he's able to go into work right now. I haven't left the house in weeks because I'm terrified. I'm terrified I'll lose her if I do. I'm terrified to sleep for the same reason. That's why if I do get any sleep, I get it down here, next to my mom, just in case.

But my dad, he has to sleep because he has to work, otherwise my mom wouldn't have a shot at survival at all. The cancer didn't respond to the first round of treatments. Or the second. We still had to pay for them though. We still have to pay for them. Probably will for years to come. Never mind the fact that we're beyond actual treatments now. Now we're just…waiting. For a miracle.

Or for an ending—to the suffering, not the bills. Those don't go away just because the person they're for does.

"There's Leila," my mom says about a tiny Hummingbird hovering near one of the feeders full of specially made nectar before it darts away.

She does this thing where she compares people to birds. In fourth grade, just after her own mom had passed away, she attended a class field trip to a local nature preserve. She said she was holding a cap of sugar water the center provided to all the students when a Ruby-throated Hummingbird came right up to steal a drink. It made her think of her best friend, Leila, who loved sugary drinks and would steal sips off my mom's any chance she got. Laughing for the first time since her mother's death, she told Leila about the comparison, which she swears was the moment that changed the trajectory of her life by kick-starting her passion for birds and everything they symbolize. The Hummingbird didn't just remind my mom of her best friend, it taught her about the beauty in the world. The laughter, the fun, the things life's all about.

I've even started making them too sometimes—the comparisons—but the girls at my school don't always appreciate the way I view things, people, life, so I save all my observations for Rowdy instead. Before—before my mom was bedridden without much hope—when I'd still get out and go four-wheeling with my best friend, I'd stop to snap a picture of any birds we might encounter in the woods, and even though he's the fastest rider I know, Rowdy would always slow down and wait for me, knowing who they were for. My mom and I'd go through the pictures afterward and I'd tell her all about their behavior, since the hospital she spent most of her days at didn't have many birds for her to watch. People, but not birds. Sadness, not joy.

Death, not life.

I'd bring it to her though—all of it...birds, joy, life.

Now I can't even chance that. I've already missed most of my sophomore year to stay at home with her. We can't afford that kind of help. If we could, my dad would be here right now, taking a day off to be with his dying wife. But that's just it, he can't.

Eventually, I'll have to return to school, but I don't really want to go back to the all-girls academy. I want diversity. I want acceptance. I want to go where people don't whisper behind my back because I walk and talk differently than them. Some girls like it, how I am, and I've even liked a few of them back, but never in the way they want. They want like a boyfriend, or whatever, but I'm not a boy. They assume because I dress like a guy that I don't still feel like a girl, but I do. I'm just...me. It's hard to explain, but I don't fit into a box and sometimes that's exactly what the archaic school feels like—one big box full of required knee-length skirts.

But knowing our family's current situation, my academy actually offered to let me finish the rest of my high school career there on scholarship, as long as I help out other young women in our community, which is pretty hard to argue with.

I just want to make my mom proud and she's the reason I went there to begin with, so I'll do it, but I'll do it for her. Whether she's here to see it or not is irrelevant.

"I wish I was a Hummingbird," I say under my breath.

My mom's forehead wrinkles, revealing a light sheen of sweat. "Why?"

I sit up, telling her, "So I could go backward, too."

Hummingbirds are the only birds that can not only fly backward, but do it with great speed and accuracy. If I could, I'd go back in a heartbeat. I'd go back and cherish every moment I could with my mom because I already miss her and she's not even gone yet.

"Oh, but sweetheart, there's nothing back there for you."

Eyes on her rapidly reddening cheeks, I say, "You are," then reach up to feel her forehead. The skin under my palm burns and I yank my hand back, searching for the thermometer. She cannot have a fever right now. She can't have one ever. If she does, her body isn't strong enough to fight off whatever infection might be causing it. Her body isn't strong enough to do anything anymore.

No thermometer in sight, I run my hands over the rest of her body, my stomach a giant aching knot.

Something touches my back, but when I peek over my shoulder, I don't find anything. Frowning, I wipe a hand across my face, pulling it away from my own hot skin.

What the hell?

Now that I think about it, my entire body feels flushed. No, not flushed. Like it's on fucking fire.

Why am I hot though?

I'm yanking on the clothes stuck to my overheated skin as a ray of light cuts across the room suddenly, making me blink.

"The Cardinal's here, isn't he?" Cardinal? He?

My mom's eyes close softly, her breathing slowing.

Tearing my gaze from her, I scan the yard quickly, not seeing the bright red bird anywhere.

What is she—

"Gia…don't scare this one away. Okay?"

But the only Cardinal I know is—

My eyes pop open, only to close again thanks to the harsh streak of sunlight reaching through the blinds straight to my brain.

That can't be right. The sun usually shines on the foot of my bed first thing in the morning. Unless I slept in.

I spring to sitting, reaching for my phone on the nightstand. Only grasping air, I look over to find nothing. Not my nightstand. Not even the…wall?

What. The. Hell?

My eyes settle on the window directly in front of me. I'm not late. I'm at the wrong end of the bed—Roz's bed. I fell asleep somewhere else. Shiiitt.

I drop backward on an exhale, landing on something much firmer than a pillow, and Roz—in all his naked-torso glory—stretches an arm over my chest, pressing the damp shirt to my skin.

The night rushes back to me in pieces, but from the parts I can recall, it's safe to say we didn't have sex.

But so…why the sweat? And who the hell initiated the cuddle-fest happening right now because I don't cuddle?

I need to find my phone and check on my dad.

First, I have to get out of this…embrace. Before I combust. *Good gawd, it's hot in here.*

Carefully rolling out from under Roz's arm, I'm just off the bed when I remember my current clothing situation. A tee and shorts won't cut it. Not today.

The alarm clock in the corner of the room mocks me and my idea to run home. I could…if I started now. And actually ran. *Great.*

The deepest, sexiest, most panty-melting—*if panties are your thing*—voice asks, "Where do you think you're going?" but I'm already glancing around the room because I actually don't wear panties.

"I, uh, I have something," I tell Roz, moving for his closet.

"Can it wait?"

Roz lifts his head from the mattress to track me but ends up wincing, rubbing his neck.

I check the time again and shake my head.

Lucky for me my neck feels fine. Roz's chest made for a beautiful pillow—both practical and decorative.

I grab a pair of pants stiff enough to pass as riding pants, then disappear out his door. Downstairs, I discover my sports bra dry—thankfully—and…folded? The rest of my outfit from last night still hangs on the shower rod above the bathtub, wet as a spring morning, but my bra rests on the counter folded—wait for it—into quarters. The only thing I can't seem to find are my boxer briefs with a smiley face on the crotch. *Someone's hard up around here.*

I snatch up the bra, changing into it, Roz's pants, and the shoes I had the genius idea to place over a vent last night before heading back upstairs too fast to worry about anything else.

Roz has his head in his hands, sitting at the end of his bed when I walk in and he immediately glances up, eyeing me.

"Can I borrow a hoodie?"

He nods cautiously, pointing to a tall dresser, and without thought, I turn around, putting my back on full display. Two mistakes in one morning. Damn.

A sharp inhale the only sound in the room, I grimace but hold steady, refusing to react. It's happened before and it usually isn't that big of a deal. They ask, I redirect the conversation. Plenty of fun all around. I just didn't expect it to happen so soon. Roz is cute. I wanted to play with him at least a little longer.

"Gia?"

I remove a midnight blue sweatshirt from one of his drawers, ignoring him and his loud-ass stare. For such a quiet guy, Roz's attention is deafening. You know when Roz is focused on you. You can *feel* it.

"Gia."

Gentle hands fall on my hips, keeping me in place, but when I go to lift the sweatshirt over my head, he catches it, throwing the item across the room in a not-so-gentle way.

Fucking great. I guess we are doing this.

Soft fingertips ghost across my back, raising the tiny hairs there, and I shut my eyes, mentally cursing myself for acting so thoughtlessly. I'm always careful.

But Roz…he's different. Roz is sweet. And respectful. The only other time I've ever been asked about my pronouns was when I got sent to the head of school for sitting like I had a ten-inch dick under my skirt—my words, not theirs. Although the way they asked what I identify as, I'm sure they were thinking it.

Also, Roz smells good. Amazing actually, like the smell of fresh snowfall on a lazy winter weekend.

But being respectful and smelling good don't matter in the grand scheme of things.

"What are these? What happened?"

I scoff, opening my eyes. "Life." Life and…nope. Not happening. I've already ruined enough of today.

He spins me around and the concern on his face threatens to destroy me. His golden eyes scour mine, so I hide them, concentrating on the scruff on his jaw. I got to feel firsthand just how soft the thick stubble is, but after today, I doubt I'll ever get to again.

I cup his jaw with both hands, pressing my lips to his harder than I should. *Three mistakes.*

"I have to leave," I breathe against Roz's mouth, then in the next instant, I've got his sweatshirt up and over my head, swiping my phone on my way out. Yeah, I'm totally stealing his clothes again, but somebody jacked my underwear. When in Rome…

I'm halfway down the driveway, dialing Rowdy when I hear my name.

Roz—still shirtless, still drool-worthy—catches up to me before I can get my phone to my ear, asking, "Where are you headed?"

Frustration laces his tone, making his voice even deeper, and I have to fight a shiver. He wants to know more than where I'm going. He wants answers. Answers he won't know what to do with. Answers that'll make this so much more difficult than I need it to be. What either of us needs it to be. He's such a mess and he knows it.

But what he doesn't know is how much bigger a mess getting attached to me would be.

Rowdy's voice echoes through the earpiece, so I put him on speaker, keeping my gaze downcast.

Seeing that Roz didn't even bother with shoes to run out here has me shaking my head as I ask Rowdy, "Hey, can you take—"

Roz's finger hits the end button, disconnecting the call.

"I'll take you."

The persistence is unexpected but not unwelcome—surprisingly. I suppress the smile sneaking out, telling him, "Fine."

Four.

Twenty minutes later, wide eyes shoot my way.

"I thought I was taking you home or something. Not that I'm complaining," Roz admits, "but, where exactly are we going?"

He's wearing a pair of faded black jeans along with a black and red flannel he rolled up to his elbows, reminding me of the first time we met.

I point to the open gate. "Through there and to the left."

If it wasn't for his tie, that pop of red against his all-black suit, catching my eye, I never would've stepped the rest of the way inside the church that day. I don't always crash strangers' funerals, but when I do, I try to stick to the outskirts, so I can still watch those affected but from afar. After my mom passed away, I became fascinated with the way people handled the death of a loved one. Would their sadness muddy the rest of their lives? Or would they roll with the proverbial punches with renewed optimism? Some people smile timidly, some people weep openly. Some people don't even know what to think, let alone how to act. How are you supposed to *feel* when you lose one of the most important people in your life?

In my opinion, as long as you're feeling, you're good.

I wasn't planning on staying to listen to Roz, but once I heard that gravelly rasp of his stumble over his own name like he couldn't even stand the sound of it, I was hooked. I wasn't sure how he was dealing with the loss of his friend exactly, just that he was doing it alone—by choice. Roz was torturing himself up there on that podium, and in that moment, I couldn't stomach leaving him to struggle. After a little prompting though, he opened up like a Parakeet showing off its new vocabulary. Just like last night. He shared a lot with me, more than I thought he would, and it was tempting to come to his rescue again. I had to remind myself I'm not his savior.

I *have* to remind myself I'm not his savior.

Roz parks where I tell him to but hops out, going to stand at the front of his sparkling black Silverado as he looks around at our surroundings.

What does he think he's doing?

"Are you racing?" he asks when I finally make my way out to him and I give him a mocking frown.

"A bunch of little girls, Roz? That's not really my style. I race men bigger than you." I poke a finger to his chest, walking backward and saying, "Thanks for the ride," before spinning to receive hugs from a dozen or so pint-sized girlies in riding gear a hell of a lot thicker than what I got going on this morning.

"Good morning to you, too," I laugh as they crowd around me, jumping right into telling me all about any new tricks they've learned on their four-wheelers. My academy wanted me to help young women in the community, and after seeing a lot of girls with the desire to learn about four-wheelers, but not the ability or space, I volunteered to teach them. The owner of this track knew my mom from high school and I'm pretty sure had a crush on her, so he lets me do whatever I want. I store a couple quads I've long outgrown on site, but the rest the girls bring back and forth themselves, meaning their parents transport them since they're all pre-tween-to-tween range.

Once I graduate, I won't technically have to keep doing this, but I don't know if I'll be able to make myself stop.

"Gia?" An eight-year-old named Iris tugs on my sleeve while I grip the bars of her nasty Tao Cheetah, checking the brakes. This one isn't mine, but her dad has no idea how to maintain the expensive machine, so I always do an inspection on it before letting Iris loose on the track. "Who's he?"

He?

I glance over to see who she's talking about and what do I find? Roz.

He stayed.

Standing awkwardly near the area where the parents usually sit to watch, Roz is getting appreciative looks from the moms, meanwhile the dads are all up in his business. *Is he…?* Yup, he's signing autographs on random shit. With a scowl etched on his face that makes him look like he's about to be sick.

"I'll…be right back," I tell Iris, and jogging over to Roz, I take hold of his arm, apologizing to the man trying to get some snow-boarding tips as I pull him away.

"Thanks," he murmurs once we're out of earshot.

"Don't thank me yet, cowboy. I'm putting you to work."

I give Roz a quick introduction to the motor-pixies, then show him how to check if the chains are tight and the tires are filled. The trails around here are hell on ATVs, so we actually have our work cut out for us.

Maybe it's a good thing he stuck around.

Streams of excited whispers fill the early morning air with one name mentioned repeatedly—Roz. He's got one of the younger ones glued to his side, captivated by everything he does, while the oldest ones stay back a few feet, shooting for annoyed indifference, even as they sneak glances at him every chance they get.

I understand though. Roz is hard not to look at. Especially when he bends down to have a conversation with the newbie who just so happens to be missing all four of her front teeth, giving her a challenging lisp that keeps her from talking—even to me—in order to save herself the embarrassment of spitting all over the place. Or when he picks up two giggling girlies at a time after they question his strength.

The man is so standoffish, it's almost laughable to watch him now, entertaining my little four-wheeling troop. Scratch that, it *is* laughable. Laughable but endearing, too.

He's going to make a hell of a dad someday.

Just as fast as the thought appears, I shove it into the same cave I keep other useless topics I shouldn't waste time thinking about.

I busy my hands, and mind, for the next hour, working until my fingers are covered in grease and my cheeks hurt from smiling so big.

Once all the quads pass inspection, Iris pipes up again, asking, "Is he your boyfriend?"

Beside me, Roz clears his throat, but this time, I know it's not from underuse.

"Why? You wanna steal him from me?" I ask her, and the collective snicker that follows gives me my answer.

"Tell you what…first one across the finish line gets him for the day."

All of them, even the older girls, scramble to mount their four-wheelers as I free another smile of my own, knowing the feeling all too well. *I'll be riding soon enough.*

"For the day, okay?" I remind the animated bunch, then brave a sideways glance.

Roz is wearing the same expression he had the moment I first laid eyes on him—pure panic. But in a charming, not even remotely fair, kind of way.

"Ready for a girlfriend, cowboy?" I tease as I shoulder past, aiming for the starting line.

He catches up to me but doesn't bother with a response. Not that I need one. I'd bet my rebuilt Raptor he's never had a serious girlfriend before. His admissions last night basically confirmed it.

Lucky for him though, that's not about to change on my watch.

Fully aware of the stare coming from my left, I raise my arms, counting the revving racers down before shouting, "Go!"

I pivot to watch the line take off, but when I sneak another peek at Roz, he's not looking at the track at all. He's still watching me.

"So? Was that some kind of community service sentence or something?" Roz asks, twisting the pink and purple bracelet on his wrist as he drives one-handed.

Seconds after the race started, two girls simultaneously drove off-track, forcing me and Roz to fly into action, getting them back into the game before they could lose too much time. Then…it happened again. And again. And again. We were so busy returning stray riders to the track, we almost missed a towheaded cutie with baby fat still coating her cheeks take first.

We were exhausted, caked in mud, and out of breath, but couldn't keep the smiles off our faces as we met back up at the finish line.

Minnie, our first-place winner, immediately caught Roz by the hand to slide one of her handmade bracelets onto his wrist. Him staring down at the tiny hand positioning the braided pink and purple yarn was the first time I'd seen Roz lose that little bit of chipped ice on his shoulder completely. He came close last night when I shoved him in the pool, but not entirely. He *wanted* to let go then. This time he just fucking did. And it was beautiful. I had to pretend to dust my pants so quick one tear ended up escaping before I could blink it back.

"Kinda."

"What does that mean?"

"It started out as a way to fulfill a volunteer requirement but… it's not really like that anymore."

He nods, gazing out the windshield, then quietly, he says, "You love it."

"It's the closest I'll probably ever get to having kids," I whisper back, regretting the words and my decision to bring Roz along.

But he needed this, didn't he? It was good for him.

His head turns my way. "Why's that?"

"You know how it goes…being tied down." I make a face, so I don't have to lie.

"Right…" He trails off, his eyes back on the road but skimming quickly left to right. "They tie you down…to what?"

"Them."

"As opposed to…"

"Earth."

"And that's a bad thing?"

I shrug. "Could be."

"Why? Where are you going?"

Roz holds my gaze for a beat longer than a person who's driving should.

"Home."

"What?" he huffs out, his eyebrows pulling together.

"That's my driveway," I say, pointing at the turnoff to my house as we blow past it.

"Shit." Slamming on his brakes, he says, "Sorry," then flips a bitch in the middle of the deserted road. Thankfully my dad and I live in a heavily wooded area, so there's hardly ever any traffic out here. It makes skating on it easy, just sketchy since there's no sidewalk to retreat to if a car does come along.

Rowdy's already here, waiting next to my 1975 Ford F-250 with our quads piggybacking in the back—his YFZ's front tires are kissing the seat of my Raptor, which is standing up with its two front wheels resting on the cab of my truck.

Dashes of electricity zip over my skin from the sight.

Today we're staying local since I have to work and Rowdy has a Pokémon card tournament later. He's been going to them for years. Not even joking. It's his "thing." Watching birds is mine, smashing Poké peeps is his. I've tagged along a few times, and since I don't actually play, it's like watching paint dry, but with super dope people, making it a good time still. They legit bring themed favors for everybody, even their opponents.

Rowdy meets my eye through the windshield, giving me a look but…it's not like that with Roz. Like always, there's no temptation beyond the physical kind. Rowdy's probably just trying to rile me up, so I can ride my hardest out there today. *As if I'd give anything less than one hundred.*

Something nags at me. Something I woke up with and haven't been able to shake since.

What *is* it like with Roz? What am I doing?

A chunk of mud falls from my shoe onto Roz's rubber floor mat with an audible *squish.*

Tearing his eyes from my Poké-obsessed friend, Roz waves me off, saying, "I'm used to it. I was a snowboarder, remember?"

As soon as he says it though, his entire attitude changes. Morphs from happy, grounded Roz, holding hands with a mini admirer that won his pretend affection fair and square in a muddy race, to an adrift grump punishing himself over an unfortunate accident that killed his best friend.

Roz. Roz. Roz.

When he finds himself, he's going to be a force—again.

After meeting Roz, I searched him up. Of course, I did. Guy's a fucking beast on the side of a mountain, and a couple hours into my research, some might otherwise call stalking, I found myself wishing I could see him in his element. In person.

But the way his fingers are tightening around the steering wheel tell me the chances of that ever happening are as slim as me finding last night's underwear.

Fletcher. Fucking Magpie.

Roz would never. He cuddles. He's a cuddler. Cuddlers don't steal used underwear.

Instead of worrying about where I'm going, Roz needs to figure out where he's headed because he definitely doesn't belong here. His brand-new, shiny truck behind my vintage rust-bucket pickup says as much, the contrast as glaring as the sun pushing through the clouds outside.

Talk about wasting time.

Back to my own cave I go...

I reach up for my hood but stop, remembering I'm in a sweatshirt. Roz's sweatshirt.

Oh well. I'm not a cuddler. I have no problem nicking outfits.

With a jerk of my chin, Rowdy approaches the passenger door, but the moment his hand touches the handle, Roz hits the lock button. I know I shouldn't, but I laugh anyway. I wasn't kidding when I said my best friend's a Cockatoo. He's playful, affectionate, and loyal, but when it comes to those he loves, he's also protective with a fierceness nobody sees coming until it's too late. In this case, his bite is so much worse than his bark, and his bark can be pretty bad when he's pissed.

I hold up my pointer to Rowdy, telling Roz, "Thanks for your help today. Pretty sure the girls like you more than they like me now." Screw that, I know they do. I'll probably catch hell from them the next time I show up and he's not with me but...life's unfair.

Roz drops his stare to his wrist before redirecting it to the passenger window.

"So, that's it, huh? On to the next?"

Eyeballing him, then the full bed of my truck, I answer, "Always," and in this moment, we're not exactly speaking the same language, but we seem to understand each other nonetheless. A battle of wills can only end with someone breaking first, but like he said last night, I can't.

Releasing his breath, he unlocks the doors, mumbling something about later. Nothing is promised in this life, and later is no exception, so I keep quiet as I grip the handle.

Before I can overthink it, I plant a kiss on the inside glass of the passenger window, leaving a print of my lips behind. It's the only "later" I can manage.

Rowdy hands me his all-black trucker hat as soon as my feet touch the ground and I fit it to my head, parting ways with him at my tailgate, each of us going for our respective doors.

I hear Roz lower his window and ask, "When can I get my clothes back? *All* of them?"

Rowdy ducks inside the cab of my Ford with a knowing laugh and a muttered, "Good luck with that."

"I'll trade you," I tell Roz, "when you find my underwear."

"Underwear… What?"

"Lifted straight from your bathroom. I was gonna have Rowdy make MISSING signs and everything."

Rowdy says, "I'm not doing that shit," ruining my joke.

I shake my head at him, scolding, "So rude," before closing the door on Roz complaining about not having my number. "I would do it for you."

"No, you wouldn't. You've stolen *my* underwear."

"Yeah, to wear. Not to…whatever Fletcher's planning on doing with mine."

We pause, listening to Roz peel out of the driveway. Gravel sprays everywhere, even dinging off the back of my tailgate and I close my eyes, pretending it doesn't bother me—not the damage to my ride, but the thought of never seeing Roz again.

Once it's quiet again, I open them.

Rowdy only lifts his eyebrows, asking, "Fletcher stole them?" like all this is normal.

I guess he has a point. One time a girl keyed the side of my truck…with me still in it. She wanted the usual—public displays of affection, dates at the local hotspots, the whole nine—and I didn't. It wasn't her specifically, just like it's not Roz specifically. I don't want that stuff with anybody.

Do I? I did kinda do the PDA thing with Roz, didn't I?

No, that was a sloppy hook-up for entertainment purposes. And I was high. It doesn't count. It barely counts.

I was completely sober today though, and I still wanted to kiss him. I could've. I would've… Does that count?

Whatever. This isn't the first time I've pissed someone off with a swift kick to their ego and it won't be the last.

Ask T.J. Rejection rolls off my tongue more fluently than Italian and the seventeen phrases I remember from French do. It has to because the alternative…

Shaking the thought away, I turn over my ignition, answering Rowdy's question. "Fletcher stole them." I don't know for sure that it was Fletcher, but it was totally him.

Either way, I'm sure Roz is about to find out.

I wonder if sex is the only time Fletcher squeals like a pig.

Chapter 6

ROZ

The stain on the ceiling above my bed changes from a sunny-side-up egg to Saturn, depending on which eye I'm closing while looking at it.

Egg.

Saturn.

Egg.

Saturn.

Even though the growing stain obviously means there's a leak of some kind, I'm grateful for it. The rest of my room is bare now that I ripped all the posters down, so it's literally the only thing to look at. Yesterday it was just a nipple, but today it's a planet. Or food.

My stomach growls, reminding me it exists, so I place a hand on it, petting it like an old dog. When my stomach dips, feeling completely foreign, I sit up, looking down at myself. *When was the last time I ate?*

I've been up here in my room for…

I did leave this morning, I know that.

But that was to go to the bathroom, not the kitchen.

Last night? No.

Yesterday? *Did I eat yesterday?* I don't think so.

I actually can't remember the last time I ate anything. Or showered.

I flop back on my bed.

Fuck. I should get up. I should eat. I should human.

But…

I don't fucking want to.

Do I even need to? My stomach will shut up eventually, and there's nobody around to smell me. I haven't heard from any of my roommates since the day I punched Fletcher in the nose, and it's not like anyone else is coming around. Hell, my corpse could be rotting up here and no one would know.

Am I rotting?

I take a whiff.

"Jesus Christ," I mumble, bolting upright again. I just might fucking be.

With a towel and a change of clothes, I head downstairs to grab a shower, only to end up staring at the stream of water with the same concentration I used on the stain.

Maybe I could jump in the pool.

And sink to the bottom. At least then I wouldn't reek up the house.

Shower it is.

I switch the water to scalding though, just to see if I can actually feel it.

I turn up the volume, using the button on the steering wheel. My mom's voice comes through the door speakers, louder but not any clearer. I hate talking on the phone, especially while driving. Any idiot walking outside could make out more of the choppy conversation than even I can. She's going on and on about having me over for dinner one of these nights and I'm trying to figure out where to schedule such an event—before or after doing absolutely fuck all?

After getting out of the shower, I decided to take it one step further into the land of the living by checking my phone. The battery died several days ago but charging it would've required me to get out of bed and well…I let it die. *I let it die.*

I actually felt bad seeing how many missed texts I had from my parents but my appetite reemerged with a fucking vengeance, so I made myself leave the house to find something to eat. It was either that or crawl back in bed with a packet of ketchup.

But now that I have something a bit more substantial in my stomach, I'm cruising the pathetic main street of this tiny town—or hamlet, as it's called here in New York—while my hand grips the top of the steering wheel, my focus on the faded pink and purple threads decorating my wrist more than the conversation with my mom. I've been wearing the bracelet ever since the day I got it. The day that could've been perfect had Gia actually stuck around and not run off with another man. A man that practically stole her out of my truck to mark her with his own clothing. I can't even lie. That shit stung. Bad.

I know it's the corniest shit in the world, but I cannot make myself take the fucking bracelet off. It reminds me of her. Not just her but also the version of myself I haven't glimpsed since before Salvy's death. He's gone. *I'm* gone. But that day I didn't feel like it.

Not like now.

"Maybe you can bring that roommate of yours," my mom says. "Fletcher always has the most fascinating architecture insights. He's a wonderful conversationalist, Roswell. You could learn a few things from him."

It's true, Fletcher's a wealth of useless information about building facts, past and present, which is why he bought the fixer-upper frat house in the first place, but I haven't talked to him since we got into it. Fletcher didn't even have the balls to admit he stole Gia's underwear. I found them myself after tearing through the whole house searching for them. I would've mistaken them for Fletcher's because they were actually men's underwear, but he had them hidden in his nightstand between the pages of a porn mag featuring women posing in different sport settings. And which sport was Gia's underwear bookmarking? Skateboarding, of course.

Once I had them in my possession, I was planning to clean them along with the rest of Gia's outfit, so I could return it all to her house, but after washing everything, I realized that was all I had to look forward to.

That was *all* I had to look forward to.

That's. Fucking. It.

I come to a stop at a red light, telling my mom, "I talk fine." When I feel like it.

Or when Gia's around, I think with a ghost of a smile. Jesus, she was an experience. I let her in more than any other person, besides Salvy, and I still know next to nothing about her—like what all those scars marring her back are. Much like the small one I saw on her shoulder, they resembled cigarette burns. But everywhere. And different sizes. It was fucked. Whatever, or whoever, made those marks had to have caused Gia a lot of pain.

And, I'm not okay with that. I'm not okay with the idea of it possibly still happening, or the idea of me not being able to stop it—her hurting. I've spent more time with a bowl of soup than I have with Gia, and I somehow still care more about her well-being than…well, fuck, most people.

But she doesn't seem to feel the same way. At all. Gia ditched me for someone else, something else, some*where* else. And just like when Salvy died, I was left wondering what the hell I was supposed to do next. Where I even fit anymore?

The light turns green and I pass a bakery one of my roommates—I think Johnny—mentioned something to Gia about the night she stayed over. Apparently, she knew it too because she recommended…some kind of cake, I can't remember, but now that I know where it is, maybe I can check it out sometime. It'll give me an excuse to get out of the goddamn house and something to actually talk to my roommates about. It's not much, but it's more than what I've been doing, which is jack shit.

"It's just that when you're in the public eye, you need to know how to handle certain topics, certain *questions,*" my mom stresses.

What questions? I've already told the media everything I'm willing to share, and I'm no longer in the public eye, so what does it matter how I answer things?

"Mom, that's not my life anymore," I say, trying not to lose my patience. She knows damn well where I stand on this. Both my parents do. We went over it almost every fucking day when I lived with them.

"Like life, snowboarding isn't dependent on who's alongside you, Roswell. It's a solitary endeavor."

"What are you talking about?"

"Snowboarding may have brought you two together, but you shouldn't give up the reason Salvy and you were so close to begin with. Doesn't that undermine the whole purpose?"

"There's no purpose to any of this. None," I grit.

Sweat pools between my hand and the steering wheel, making my grip slippery, and I have to flex my fingers, shaking them out.

Why is she even pushing this again? She of all people knows I don't need the money. I didn't have to move in with three other guys; I chose to. The earnings I made from competing were always split up and invested—wisely—so that it would last even longer because I never wanted to depend on my family's fortune. Living off snowboarding forever was the ultimate goal, but not realistic in any way. The average age for snowboarders to retire is around twenty-two, which I just turned…last week? Has it been a week already?

Anyway, I shot for a long career but planned for a short one. Not this short, but still, I'm doing fucking fine for money, so there's no valid reason for me to return to snowboarding as far as I'm concerned.

Other than needing the snow like fish need water.

But no.

I don't. Not anymore.

I need something else. Something to keep me occupied, so I'm not imagining shapes out of water stains on the ceiling for multiple days in a row. Fun. I need fun that isn't tied to my dead best friend. I need distractions. Lots of them. I need…her.

Wait. Is that her?

Spotting an obvious female form in obvious male clothing has me doing a double take.

Maybe.

Maybe's good enough for me.

"I gotta go," I rush out to my mom, promising to call her again soon. I can't do a dinner with my parents yet; I need to work up to that, but I think I can manage a call.

With a hard swerve that may or may not be illegal, I pull over to the side of a small park, parking half on the sidewalk, half on the tiny shoulder. It's not exactly what I'd call a park, more like a long stretch of grass between two busy roads, and instead of a parking lot, it has a plaque. A plaque I ignore as I approach the only picnic table here. It's directly under a tree, and the woman—that might not even be Gia now that I think about it—stretched out on top of the metal has her arms resting above her head like she's working on her tan, except she's fully dressed. Overdressed to be exact. It's nearing ninety degrees out and she's in baggy jeans and a long-sleeve shirt…but in the shade?

Yeah, this has Gia written all over it.

I lick my lips, propping my shoulder against the tree to cross one foot over the other while taking her in.

Damn, it's been a while.

I knew she was supposed to graduate sometime this month, so in a moment of weakness, before Stain-gate set in, I drove by her dad's pizza shop. The reader board out front confirmed Gia had graduated, and I considered going inside. To congratulate her. To see her.

I chickened out though. Instead, I went home and tore every piece of the old me off my wall. The me that I could look in the mirror on any given day and recognize instantly. The me that knew what he wanted and went the fuck after it. The me that was fearless.

But standing over Gia now, unannounced, and watching her body contract with unhurried breaths doesn't make me feel brave. It makes me feel like a fucking creep actually.

What the fuck was I thinking?

"Got my underwear?" she asks out of nowhere, making my eyes

snap to where Gia's gray shirt's riding up, revealing a thick waist-band of what look like boxer briefs just above her jeans.

Fuck me, she's wearing men's underwear again. I thought the pair in Fletcher's nightstand might've been a fluke, like maybe it was laundry day for her, but I'm glad they're not. They're hot on her. So fucking hot.

My question now is, did she take them from somebody like she stole my clothes? Because I actually like the idea that they might be hers. Like really like it. But the other option? That they could belong to some other dude? Not so much.

Not at all.

"Got *my* clothes?" I challenge back, not caring what answer she gives as long as she gives one.

Gia tips her aviator glasses down her nose, pinning me with those dark brown eyes of hers. "Not on me."

Fuuuck.

I give her a smirk, telling her, "I could change that." I could change that so fucking fast.

She pushes her glasses back into place to face the sky again.

"Come back to my house and I'll get you your clothes," I say.

"But I don't have anything to trade."

Even better.

"I'm not too worried about it. I'll get 'em from you some other time."

She waves a hand through the air. "Nah, you can keep them. I like your shit better anyway."

"This doesn't seem very fair. Your underwear isn't even my size."

"I wouldn't mind seeing you try."

"To fit into them?" My voice cracks, embarrassing the shit out of me. Gia got me to do one crazy thing, not even by choice either, but there's no chance of me squeezing my junk into a pair of too-small boxer briefs.

I adjust my shorts just thinking about it. I like my fit snug but not *that* snug.

Gia must see—*is she watching me?*—because she laughs and

the sound goes straight to my veins like a dose of heroin. Not that I know what heroin feels like, but it's gotta be fucking potent for so many to fall victim to it. And Gia's laugh is that powerful. That addictive.

"You do know you're in the shade, right? Most people work on their tans in the sun."

Gia rolls her head to the side, saying, "You don't know? The sun can kill you."

Her eyes, hidden behind glasses, track mine as I venture closer, putting me less than a foot away from her.

A diesel truck passes by, covering my noisy-ass swallow.

An outstretched hand and I'd be touching her. The urge to do just that runs up my arm, across my shoulder, settling at the base of my neck. I roll my shoulders, trying to alleviate the tension, but it's no use. Gia's within reach, and Jesus, do I want to reach.

I swear she knows what I'm thinking because she starts rocking her bent leg, almost like a tease. A dare. Back and forth, back and forth, until finally her jeans brush the backs of my fingers.

My hand clenches into a fist. A fist I contemplate biting my teeth into, just to keep from grabbing her because if I did, I don't think I'd be able to let go. Not this time.

"Congratulations, by the way. On graduating."

That sounded less pathetic in my head.

"Mmm," she says as a thanks, I guess, before saying, "You look like shit, cowboy."

"That makes one of us then."

"Does it?"

"Yeah, it does. You look good, Gia."

I've traveled around the globe and, hands down, Gia's one of the most attractive women I've ever caught sight of, even without a single stich of makeup. Gia's naturally gorgeous, so she doesn't need it, but if I didn't know any better, I'd think she was trying to mask her physical appearance by wearing oversized men's clothing all the time.

But that's just Gia, she does whatever she wants. She dresses her own way and goes her own way. A way I wish she'd trust me with.

"Why do you call me cowboy again?"

Her reasoning before was muddled at best. I've always been shirtless, but I've never been referred to as a fucking cowboy. Ever.

She rights her face again, saying, "You look like a good ride."

"You mean rider?" That's at least along the lines of the first answer she gave.

"Nope."

Okay then.

"At least you got that part right," I mutter, and she asks, "Did I?"

I stuff my hands in my pockets, nodding even though she can't see it. *Can she?*

"Did someone tell you that specifically or are you just assuming?"

Well, come to think of it…

Damn, did she really just call me out like that?

"I'll let you in on a little secret, Roz, women are vocal. Very vocal. If we like something, we say something."

"I've never had any complaints." Which has to count for something, right? "And they always get theirs before I get mine," I add on. That much I am sure of.

Clicking her tongue, she says, "I could fake an orgasm so good right now, you'd have to stick your hand down my pants to know the truth."

Wha—

No, there are no words. None. The image that statement produces…that's where my energy goes. And stays.

Until…

"Mmmm."

A single moan escapes Gia's throat, and one moment I'm standing in scraggly grass, fighting to keep myself in check, the next…the next I'm on the table, hovering over her, wondering how I can drink the sound straight from her mouth. Never have I been so parched and I just came out of a self-inflicted fast.

She barks out a laugh from the sudden change but screw laughs, and everything I said about liking them, I'll take every last one of her moans—now.

On strong arms, I remain suspended above her by mere inches, fully aware we're in a public space but not giving a shit at the same time. She called my bluff; I folded. And here we are.

Gia says, "Hi," before starting up the swish, swish, swish of her leg again, hitting the outside of my hip this time. Another tease. Another dare.

I drop a knee just under the apex of her thighs, blocking out the pain caused by the mesh-pattern tabletop. Her breath stutters, so I raise my knee, up into those baggy pants of hers, to press it against her pussy.

"Hi."

Gia reaches up to run a finger along the skin below my beanie, rubbing between my eyebrows, and my eyes close from the contact as I commit the gesture to memory. I've dreamed of her touch for weeks, but it's nothing—*nothing*—compared to the real thing.

I open my eyes to find hers no longer hidden under glasses. I don't even know where the glasses went. Or care.

"How'd you find me?"

"I don't know," I tell her. "You just kind of appeared." Just like the other times.

She raises her eyebrows but doesn't push the issue—thankfully. I don't know how to describe it and I don't really want to try. She's not there, then she is.

Then she's not again.

She's like the moon. Or the sun.

"You don't know? The sun can kill you."

If Gia is the sun, there are worse ways to go. *Like starving yourself to death inside your bedroom.*

Flyaways dance in front of her face and this close I can see there's some kind of white cream, probably lotion, gathered along her hairline.

A smile spreading at her lips pulls my attention from it, but just as I begin to lower myself, she shoves me clear off—we're talking over the side of the table—and I bust my ass on the built-in bench.

"What the fuck was that?" I'm getting sick of her pushing me, damn it.

She just sits up without so much as an apology and hops off the table, grabbing her skateboard I hadn't even noticed before. "Let's go," is all she says as she strolls across the pitiful park.

So, this is still happening then? Whatever *this* is.

Gia places her deck in the back of my truck, then turns around, motioning her finger at me to hurry it up—again.

With a shake of my head, I hit unlock on my key fob, letting her in first while I massage my tailbone on the walk over to join her.

"Where to?" I ask in my Chevy and the smile I get in return tells me everything I need to know.

This should be good.

Chapter 7

"**A** skate park?"

"Don't say it like that."

I tear my gaze from the janky-ass skate park to glance at Gia. "Like what?"

"Like you don't want to be here."

I don't.

I mean, how is this any more private than where we just were? This place is crawling with people. Skaters, BMX-type bikers, people on actual roller skates, and kids. Lots of kids. Everywhere.

Oh…

"Are you volunteering here?"

Gia laughs dryly, climbing out. "That depends."

"On?"

"Your skills."

Skills? These skills? *My* skills? I'm not even a skater. She is.

Outside, I find Gia raised on to her tiptoes as she tries to retrieve her skateboard from my truck's bed and have to stop to enjoy how good she looks. My truck's lifted too, so she's fucking stretched.

Fuck me.

But a quick glimpse around confirms I'm not the only one appreciating the view, and my jaw tightens past painful while I grab her by the hips to pull her backward. Using my body as a shield from outside eyes, I set her back flat on her feet, sandwiching her between me and my truck. I box her in with my free arm to grab her skateboard myself, pressing into her until my cock's flush with her backside, then

I bury my nose in her hair, inhaling as deeply as I can. All I smell is vanilla and rosemary this time, no repulsive deterrents whatsoever. *Fuck you, clams and sea breeze freesia.*

And this moan, the one she releases from our bodies' brief but intentional contact, puts that ridiculous attempt at a moan she forced back at the park to shame. To. Shame.

"Mmhmm," I murmur against her ear. "I bet I can tell if you're faking or not."

A humorless laugh rumbles in her throat while I lean down to feel the vibration against my lips through the veil of her hair.

She breathes out, "Roz," and I stop myself from grinding my dick into her ass. Barely. The urge is strong though.

Husky as all fuck, I rasp out, "Yeah?"

Spinning around, Gia catches me off guard by gripping my jaw between her fingers, then biting my top lip and sucking it into her mouth. When I chase the move, trying to deepen the kiss, she releases my face entirely and pulls back.

"Baby, I'd eat the fuck out of you if you let me," I all but growl, pushing into her.

"I know."

"So let me."

"Roz, I wasn't going to fuck you on an uncomfortable picnic table and I'm not going to fuck you at a crowded skate park, so get your shit under control," her gaze falls to my dick, "and let's skate."

My head rears back from the shift in attitude. I wasn't trying to fuck her right here. *Not really.*

I want to though. More than I want to skate. Skateboarding is associated with snowboarding because a lot of other professionals dabble in both to satisfy the need for carving year-round, but I'm not one of them. I haven't been on a skateboard since I was nine or ten.

A little kid flies by on a scooter. *Is that a scooter?* Jesus, they got it all here.

Anyway, I'm done with riding—everything—and I tell Gia that.

"Play my game and I'll play yours."

"What game is that?"

She ducks under my arm and I turn to follow her, glad my cock didn't get to full hard-on status yet. I'm definitely a grower.

"Without stopping to think about it, tell me what you want?"

"You."

Gia's eyes widen.

"I didn't, you know, mean it like that. That's—"

"And what exactly do you want with me?"

"Uh…" My eyes dart around the semi-fenced-in cement jungle. "Answers. You avoid every question I ask."

"What do you mean? I told you about B.J."

Some guy rolling by grabs his crotch, shouting, "I'll take a BJ!"

Gia catches me as I step forward on autopilot and yells back at him, "You're not my type, Duncan!"

Through narrowed eyes, I continue to watch Duncan skate away, but ask Gia, "Do you even have a type?"

She attempts to take her board from my grasp, but my clenched fingers don't relax enough to actually let go until I finally break my stare from across the skate park. It's deposited by my feet, ringing out like a judge's gavel in a courtroom followed by my sentencing.

"For every drop-in you complete, I'll answer a question, starting with my type."

I groan, adjusting my beanie. "I didn't agree to this."

"Your pit stains say otherwise."

Seeing she's right—my armpits are fucking soaked—I whip my shirt off, tossing it at her.

"And that's not my first question."

She catches my shirt, laughing, and sticks it in her back pocket so the material drapes down. Hands on her boxer-brief-covered hips, she asks, "Then what is?"

The noise of the busy skate park comes into focus. The metallic clang of boards grinding against rails, the whir of worn wheels rolling across the pavement, cheers echoing from someone landing a new trick correctly. It's all so different.

It's all too much.

A grungy-as-fuck guy with face tattoos rips by us, bumping

knuckles with Gia before dropping into the bowl we're standing at the top of, and I get caught up watching the way his body moves, anticipating the curves and dips, the way his face zones everything else out until it's just him and the ride—the thrill.

That. That's the fucking same. The same rush I've gone after for what seems like my entire life.

Why did she have to bring me here? Aside from the actual mountains, this is the last place I want to be. I've been avoiding anything to do with snowboarding since Salvy's accident, and this entire scene might as well be my old sport's younger, uglier stepbrother.

The kid on the scooter wipes out landing a jump and not one person so much as bats an eye.

Definitely grittier, too.

As weird as it sounds though, there's something comforting about it all. Being among outcasts looking for an escape from society's norms pressed upon all of us. I got it my whole career. My image meant more than my skills sometimes and I hated that. I snowboarded because I wanted to, not because some people liked how I looked doing it.

I guess it doesn't matter now. Along with my best friend, I lost my desire to chase that feeling. The one I've only been able to achieve slashing through the backcountry or dropping on firm descents. The one that makes me feel inconceivably alive while simultaneously outrunning death.

I look over to find Gia's eyes on mine.

Until she appeared.

Gia makes me feel alive again. Gia makes me feel, period. Every day's been more of the same. The monotony of normal life holds less appeal than I thought it would. Except for when Gia shows up. Whenever she's near, I never know what'll happen next, just like on the side of a mountain. Out there I was known for slicing nimble and playful lines, but this girl makes my old ways look straight amateurish with her all-out spontaneity.

An image of her shredding some fresh white powder herself forms and I can't shake it out before it takes hold, needling its way into my psyche. I want to see it. Firsthand. With me by her side.

Fuck. What am I doing?

Clever fingertips writhe up my abs, over my chest, stopping at my collarbone. The fact that we're standing next to the equivalent of another pool, albeit an empty one, does not escape my notice and I let Gia know it, latching on to her waist and telling her, "You better not push me."

"Then who will?"

I search her eyes, trying to figure out exactly what she means.

"So, what's your question?"

"Will you go out on a date with me?"

I hadn't planned on starting out the gate with that one, but her fingers massaging my skin is messing with…everything.

"What do you call this?"

Some dumbass skating past lets out a catcall astronauts in orbit could hear.

"Overcrowded foreplay?"

"Kinky." She wiggles her eyebrows, nodding her head to the side and dropping her hands as she steps back. "Now, show me what you got, cowboy."

I stare down at her skateboard, flexing my stiff fingers. "I want to up the stakes."

"Go on."

"A kiss for every trick I nail, too."

"Done."

I have no idea if I'll be able to land one trick, let alone multiple, but I gotta try. If I'm going to do this, something so close to what I swore off, I'm damn well going to make it worth my while—hopefully.

Since I always ride goofy-footed, I place my left foot on the tail, right at the lip of the bowl, letting the majority of the board hang over the edge, then wait, allowing the atmosphere to envelop me. The noise is fucking overwhelming compared to the silence I just left a few hours ago.

Luckily, Gia gives me enough time to acclimate before offering some pointers, but when she finishes, she thumps my back, making some smartass remark about me being a cowboy that I decide to let slide.

"You know…I didn't specify where I wanted to kiss you."

Looking me dead in the eye, she says, "And I didn't ask you to," before pushing my ass over the ledge—again.

Jesus Christ, this girl's gonna kill me.

As it turns out, skateboarding is like riding a bike—as long as you don't overthink it, your body remembers the movements as soon as you're back in the saddle. It's also almost identical to snowboarding, if you remove the snow, ice, trees, and sporadic deadly avies, but increase the noise. Holy shit is it loud here. The conversations, the music, the wipeouts, there's nonstop noise. That's one thing about snowboarding I always loved, how the snow would cut out everything except the telltale signs of nature to remind you whose territory you're really on.

So far I've gotten Gia to divulge *bits* of her childhood along with some details of her dating life. I'm using that term loosely here because Gia seems to date about as much as I do, which means she doesn't. Ever. She didn't have a problem listing out some of her one-night stands though, causing me to nosedive and fall straight to the ground. Yeah, that sucked. I got a body count too, but I'm not fucking sharing it. Goddamn.

At least I didn't have to waste a question asking Gia her type because judging by the names she gave, she doesn't have one. I haven't touched on anything that'd explain the scars on her back either even though it's been on the tip of my tongue. The setting feels all wrong. I'm also not sure what to make of her referring to her mom in the past tense, but not her dad. Every time she lights up like a Christmas tree while sharing a memory from her childhood, I want to ask, but again, now doesn't seem like the appropriate time to dig too deep. I've just been keeping a mental running list of things to ask at a later date instead. When we're alone.

Gia's also swimming in a debt of kisses owed—to me. Some of the tricks in skateboarding are similar enough to snowboarding that I've been able to stick a few without wiping out. And on the ones I don't land, Gia's helped me through them. She's a great teacher. I can see how the girls at the ORV park are so talented at such young ages. She's got this way of making you feel like the most successful person from learning just one new thing. It makes you want to try again and again and again.

Don't get me wrong, the prize of kisses we agreed to doesn't hurt, but I'd do it anyway, just to have her look at me the way she's been looking at me and talk to me the way she's been talking. I'd do *anything* to stay in this moment with Gia, where the only thing I feel is alive.

"Trippy back tail, bro," some guy standing beside Gia tells me when I skate over to where she's been sitting on the ground. Yes, she's sitting calmly in the middle—literally—of the skate park, completely unafraid of the chaos surrounding her. Every few minutes, someone carves inches away from her, but she insists on watching from down here. With arms draped over her bent knees, she looks just like she did the first time she stopped by my house, except this time, I don't have to worry about her ass showing.

"It was all right," I tell him, downplaying it, but Gia's quick to argue, saying, "It was fucking butter," peering up at me through her lashes.

I used to compete slopestyle, so tricks aren't hard for me to master. A quick back tail is nothing compared to the shit I've done.

The guy nods his head, agreeing, "Smooth criminal," then takes off across the pavement, leaving us alone. *As alone as we're gonna get here.*

The sun went down hours ago, leaving behind the more serious skaters along with their crews and…girlfriends maybe. I don't know. All I see is Gia.

"What now?" I ask her, but pulling out a joint from her pocket as she straightens a leg, Gia just shrugs.

I put my hand over hers and shake my head. I don't know what's after this, but I know what I want to happen, and I need her fully aware if she plans on settling the serious debt she's accumulated tonight. Hell, she'll want to be present for the ways I plan on kissing her.

Her eyes flit between mine until suddenly, she stands, taking the board with her, and says, "My turn."

All I can do is watch as she tears up the entire fucking park. Others tune in too, scoping out what this beautiful woman is capable of but, unlike when we arrived, I don't interfere—yet. I'm just too fucking mesmerized to do anything else. No surface goes unclaimed as her own personal playground when Gia skates and the picture I had in my head earlier, the one of her snowboarding next to me, is quickly replaced with a much more realistic version, one where I work to keep up with her. I already knew she was crazy, but it's so much more than that. Gia's fucking fearless. Nothing scares her, nothing I've seen anyway.

She stops next to someone's wireless speaker, cranking the volume. The owner, I'm assuming, jerks a lazy nod, his eyes bloodshot even from here. SAYGRACE's newer remix of "You Don't Own Me," featuring G-Eazy, floats across the cement seconds before Gia blows me a kiss, then sucks in a hit from the joint the guy passes her.

My lips twitch with a grin. *Point taken.*

Gia coasts around a curve and right behind her an older guy swerves dangerously close, mimicking her move. This is the third time he's done something similar, but I can't tell if Gia even realizes he's there because she's not acting like it. Either that or she just doesn't give a shit.

But I do.

My attention is cut between Gia and the asshole tailing her, and with my fists already pumping at my sides, I push off the stair rail. The longer I watch him go out of his way to ride her ass, the hotter my chest and the backs of my arms get until not even the night breeze can cool my overheated skin. Nobody else seems to notice what a dickwad this guy's being but me. *Is this a regular thing?* There's been plenty of accidents since we got here. Hell, people on skateboards running into other people on skateboards should be a trick all its own from what I've seen, but something about this feels different, almost malicious, like the guy's got a problem with Gia specifically and is fucking with her on purpose because of it.

I stride closer, careful to keep an eye on him, but, too busy tracking his whereabouts, I fail to notice Gia rolling back down a mini ramp…right into the fucker. I was studying him, but he was studying her.

Gia's side takes the full impact as she collides with his already prepared shoulder aimed directly at her, then my breath catches in my throat when her body bounces—*fucking bounces*—off the concrete when she falls to the ground like a limp doll.

Luckily, the rest of my body doesn't need more than a heart pounding with fired-up blood to run across the park and knock the guy responsible out cold. The satisfaction of seeing his ass bounce off the ground as well never even comes because I'm at Gia's side the next instant, drifting my hands over her thin frame.

"Are you okay?" Such a stupid question, I know, but it's all I can choke out with my lungs not functioning properly.

Shallow moans are my only answer before I'm pulling at her clothes. With her still on her side, I go to lift her shirt for a better look at her back but freeze when her arm tightens, blocking access.

My eyes shoot to her face. What the fuck? I need to see if she's hurt.

Footsteps pound across the pavement until a circle is formed around us, everyone worried about Gia rather than the asshole still passed out next to us.

Gia's eyes are still closed, but she gives a subtle shake of her head, and I grit my teeth. *Fine. Fuck.* The back stays hidden.

Gently, I roll her onto her back—praying she's not ignoring an actual injury for the sake of keeping her scars out of sight—then get to work checking over the rest of her. I keep my touch light but steady as I make my way over her wilted body, looking for any hint of damage. For every wound I find on her, I'll happily replicate on the person that caused it.

My eyes snag on a spot of blood blooming at the bottom of her shirt and a shiver runs up the length of my spine, spreading out to the rest of my body. As the first time I've ever felt truly cold, my internal organs feel like they're about to buckle from the unusual sensation and I'm immediately brought back to that last day with Salvy. He was there, right fucking there, and then he wasn't.

Just like Gia?

No.

My head bows toward the stain, wanting to drive it away with sheer willpower alone. I couldn't do anything for Salvy and the fear of not being able to do anything for Gia feels just as suffocating—if not more.

Hovered over Gia's abdomen, the broken skin on one of my knuckles produces a couple more drops of blood, my shaking hands causing them to fall onto the fabric below. As I watch the small pool of blood—my blood—grow bigger, I finally allow some of my normal warmth to seep back in while straightening my spine again.

Gia's eyes are already open and fixed on mine.

"What hurts?"

So soft I barely catch it, she whimpers, "My heart," but then shakes her head to close her eyes, severing the connection.

"What happened to your heart?"

A smirk pulling at her lips, she mouths the word, "You."

"Yo, G, you okay? You took a gnarly spill."

I shoot the kid a look that says *no fucking shit* before helping Gia up to sitting.

While cradling an arm close to her chest, Gia tells everybody gathered, "I'm all right."

I'm tempted to scoop her up in my arms right here, but doubt she'd let me. Plus, the motherfucker beside us is sitting up too now, glaring at both me and Gia, so I have that to deal with as well. I get the hatred thrown my way, I leveled the guy, but what the fuck is his problem with Gia? He ran into her.

"Hey, fuck you, Mitch," she says as she gets to her feet, and my gaze passes between the two. *She knows him?*

"Fuck you, G. You don't even belong here. This park's for dicks, not chicks with strap-ons, so do us all a favor and kick fucking rocks already." Mitch spits out a mixture of blood and saliva, and I pull Gia out of its path on instinct.

Is he fucking kidding me?

Once again, Gia's being judged and labeled based off her appearance alone. No wonder she doesn't like labels, everybody's already put their own on her without even bothering to get to know her.

And that's bullshit that she can't skate here. It's not that Gia's good at skateboarding for a woman, she's fucking good, period.

I competed against women that had been snowboarding since they were two years old. And I don't mean for fun either. We're talking their families moved across the country just so they could train full-time—while they were probably still in diapers. Those girls were geared up, same as the men, flying down slopes like they were born for it—shit, maybe they were—and discounting them because of their gender was a mistake I never even considered making.

Mitch is just another dumbfuck spewing the same toxic waste the world is already full of. Before today, it'd been days, if not longer, since I'd moved more than just my eyelids, but now I feel like the rest of my body is finally awake again, ready to fucking go. A few rounds with Mitch would be nothing.

"Strap-on? Dude, my balls are bigger than yours. Your vert ramp showed me that." Gia grabs her crotch to emphasize her point, earning a nice little "ooh" from the crowd until her hand slides into mine, then I swear a silence falls over the entire skate park. Even when she brings my right hand up to her mouth, kissing the busted knuckles, nobody makes so much as a sound. It's the first time all night I've been able to block everyone else out, pretending it's just us—her and me.

Murmurs pick up though as Gia drops our hands, leaving behind a streak of brilliant red blood on her lips. She smiles, and despite the heavy coating of what-the-fuck settling around us, I smile back. And because I must be crazy too, I kiss her, full on the lips, not even bothered by the taste of my own blood. Actually, it's kinda hot.

She breaks the kiss to spit back at Mitch, the red-tinged wad landing an inch away from his old-school Vans, and tells him, "Your insecurity really did a number on your reality to make you think you're better than you actually are. Ask anyone here, you're a shit skater and an even shittier person. My skills outmatch yours in every. Single. Aspect." She grabs her crotch again, getting the same reaction from everybody as before. "So the next time I ride here, because I *will* be back, make sure to stay the fuck out of my way." With her thumb, she pushes the remaining smear of blood into her mouth, even licking the tip with her tongue, and *that* is hot as fuck. No kinda about it.

Mitch's bruising face screws up in disgust, but Gia's tugging me away before I can add my own two cents. As much as I'd love to teach him a lesson, I feel like Gia already did.

After retrieving her board, we head for my truck and a few hands pat Gia on the back, which I see her wince through even though she tries like hell to hide it.

Using both hands, I carefully help her into the passenger seat, then buckle her in before going over to the driver's side.

With my beefy engine masking all the outside noise, I ask, "What was all that about?" not wanting to sound ungrateful but also needing to know. "The kiss? The blood?"

Her soft laugh falls over me like a trance. "Sometimes you gotta out-crazy the crazy."

I let out a low chuckle myself.

"At least now, maybe he'll think twice before fucking with me again," she says more seriously, and I hope to God she's right. I don't know what I'd do if he did. I don't even know if I'd be around to find out.

Gia rolls her head to look over at me. "So?"

"So?"

"Still want that date, cowboy?"

If only she knew.

Chapter 8

GIA

For some reason, I'm not entirely sure of, I tell Roz to go to my dad's pizzeria. Since it's a weekday, my dad should be home and in bed already, leaving the place to us. I've been here after hours, of course, but usually to clean, or prep for a big event, or take inventory, but never for a…date. Is that what we're calling this?

What a weird-ass day.

First, I woke up thinking about Roz. After weeks of trying to forget about the guy, he was literally all I could think about. I found myself wondering what he was doing, if he'd washed my lip print off his truck yet, why he hadn't returned my underwear already. He didn't have my number, but he had my address. He could've brought my clothes by any time in the last three weeks. At least I thought he would.

I *hoped* he would.

Ending up in the park near his house after a long ride around town wasn't intentional per se, but I wasn't exactly avoiding it either.

Then, he showed up. Just materialized in front of my face as if my overactive thoughts alone summoned him. And I knew instantly why he hadn't dropped off my clothes. Roz had been torturing himself—again. I don't know what he's been up to for the last few weeks, but I know what he hasn't been up to and that's being a part of the beautiful, complicated world we're lucky enough to temporarily inhabit.

I could've told him to fuck off. I probably should've. It's weird how much I think about him. Worry about him. *Dream* about him.

But I didn't. And now look at us. Me, with a possible broken rib, and Roz, thinking we're out to a romantic date.

I just wanted to push him a little. I wanted to see if he had it in him still—the drive, the will, the life. He does. He so fucking does. Roz is choosing to waste it though.

I deactivate the alarm once we're through the front door of Al's, then give Roz the abridged version of the tour since I'm keeping most of the lights off anyway.

Guys dig candlelight, right?

A snort escapes me before I can stop it. Good gawd, what is happening? I never try this much.

In the walk-in cooler, I dump a handful of ice into a bag before swiping a prepared calzone on my way out. No idea what's in it, but I'm starving. That skunk earlier was the worst of the worst and gave me the munchies without any high whatsoever.

The pan is pried from my grasp as soon as I enter the kitchen and Roz motions to the chair in the corner, telling me to sit down.

Doing as I'm told—seriously, what the hell's happening?—I take a seat, watching Roz fumble with preheating the industrial-size oven. I don't have the heart to tell him it's the wrong temperature but how bad are burnt edges, really? As long as the cheese inside is melted all the way through, I'm good.

While the oven heats, he sets the pan aside to squat in front of me. His eyes go straight to my shirt and I know what he's going to say before he even opens his mouth, so without wasting either of our time, I grip the hem, ready to remove it myself.

Roz shoots a hand out to stop me though, saying, "I'll do it."

Carefully, so fucking careful, he lifts the material up and over my head. The room is dimly lit without the usual brights on, but I know he can see everything. I keep my gaze on the floor, wishing he'd get it out of the way and just ask. It's not like he hasn't already.

All he says is, "Show me where it hurts."

Gluing my eyes to his, I point to the general area, then he starts feeling around my rib cage, trying to pinpoint what might be the cause. My rising hiss is cut short by the oven's *ding*, letting us know it's at temp.

Roz puts the calzone into the oven before returning to the spot in front of my chair and, using whatever medical degree he must think he earned somewhere along the line of being a professional snowboarder, he continues poking until we find the most tender spot. To reach the injured rib just under my sports bra, he slides his fingers under the band, applying more pressure. I gasp out a string of curses but Roz doesn't ease up one bit. Just as I contemplate shoving him and his imaginary doctorate off, his touch finally softens to gentle skin-deep circles, allowing me to release a choppy breath.

"Nothing's broken. It's just bruised."

"Yeah, now it is," I scoff.

In a slow descent, he leans forward to replace his fingers with his lips, then the word "sorry" is murmured against my skin, making my eyes close.

A whisper of my own comes out. "Six."

"Six what?"

"You only get six more kisses."

I take the following silence as Roz thinking of an argument and open my eyes to watch it play out. According to our little bet, he earned a total of eight kisses—anywhere he wants. Before this one, it was that kiss after Mitch checked my ass like a fucking lacrosse defender. The blood was a bit dramatic, even for me, but whatever. Roz rolled with it easily enough, which was more shocking than the fact that Mitch actually got one over on me. I'd heard his ass shadowing me, just like every other time I've skated there, but I didn't expect him to take things to a physical level like he did. *Such a dick move.*

Featherlight kisses trace a path up my neck as I fight a smug smile. I stand corrected, he didn't have an argument after all. He was just plotting.

That was almost too easy.

When his lips find mine, instead of another kiss, he breathes, "Five."

"That was at least fourteen kisses right there."

Clear golden eyes stare back at me as he repeats, "Five," against my lips.

"I don't—" I don't get to finish because Roz's lips crash against mine, cutting off my argument. In the next breath, I'm lifted off the chair and held to his front while my legs fold around his hips.

Spinning us around, he sits back down with me straddling his lap. Not once does he break the kiss and not once do I think about the count. That's the thing about Roz, he's tricky as hell. He weaves his way in without me even realizing it, then boom, we're both shirtless and making out before the main course is even served.

At least this kind of date is more my speed. Maybe by dessert I'll be over all of…this.

My hands tangle in his semi-wavy hair, using the leverage to move his head for a better angle. I brush my tongue past his lips and am rewarded with a groan so deep I feel it in my toes. His top lip is bitten between my teeth, then sucked on as his hands grip my ass tighter. My baggy jeans aren't working in either of our favors as we press together, trying to get as close to the other as possible, and I'm about to stand up and lose them when a shot of pain radiates through my chest.

"Fuck," I grit as I tear my mouth away, placing my forehead on his.

"I'm sorry."

The way he says it, it's clear this is one of those all-encompassing apologies.

"Don't be sorry. You didn't do anything."

Roz shakes his head and I pull back to stare at him.

"That's just it, I didn't *do* anything. I knew that guy was up to something and I didn't fucking stop him."

On an eye roll, I stand from his lap to gather plates and napkins.

"I didn't need you to do anything."

I can and did handle myself. Mitch is not the first guy to talk shit to me about my lifestyle and he won't be the last. Some men cannot fathom why I'd want to be *like* them but not *be* them. I dress like I have a dick, but I don't want one, and to someone who's already convinced their gender is superior, that's incomprehensible. Mitch's dick is probably shorter than his balls when he's soft, yet he still believes it rules the world, and anyone without the same anatomy should bow the fuck down. He's pathetic.

Roz tracks me across the small space, his breath pouring out of him as he crowds my back.

I'm still in my sports bra and jeans, which is basically what he's in—minus the bra, of course—and I know I'll have to erase the security footage before we leave. I don't need Dad asking questions about Roz, questions that'll make me think about him even more.

Maybe Roz and I can be friends. Friends that kiss a few times before deciding friendship is where it's at.

"When I was seventeen, Salvy invited this guy he'd met the day before to go snowboarding with us. As soon as we got off the lift, he started taking digs at me, like he knew me, you know? We'd just met him and I still wasn't that big yet, so I shook it off. Some guys just like to talk more shit than others. About halfway through the day though, he dared me to do a Misty Flip. I fucking took it, thinking it'd shut him up, but he wanted me to do it off his inverted snowboard while it was still strapped to his feet. So instead of a jump, he'd essentially be on his back and boost me into the air himself, using his board. It all happened so fast that nobody got a good look at what happened. Nobody…but me. At the last second, right before I slid off his board, I looked down and saw his face. It was full of spite and anger, which isn't that uncommon in competition, but that wasn't what we'd been doing that day. We were just fucking around, not competing. That's what Salvy and I took it as, but this guy, he took it somewhere completely different."

A shiver that has nothing to do with being shirtless racks my body.

"The front of his board went lax while he kicked the back end with everything he had and that force mixed with that day's howling-ass tailwind, I biffed it going so fast, the landing compressed one of my vertebrae, resulting in a compound fracture between my ribs."

"Shit."

"Yeah. It took me out for months. I had to get surgery and do physical therapy, everything. To this day, it was the worst injury of my entire career."

"Was he one of your competitors?"

"We found out after the fact." He nods, his nose nudging my hair. "I saw that same look on Mitch's face, and I wish I would've done something about it sooner. I could've protected you."

"I don't need you to protect me from anything."

I close my eyes, holding my breath. This is why we can't be friends. Roz is deep. His devotion for the people in his life is deep, and the deeper the devotion, the deeper the wounds.

He turns me around to face him, then bends to my eye level. "I'd rather break my back a hundred more times than watch you take another hit like tonight's."

"I know."

"No." He shakes his head, straightening. "You don't."

That sounds serious. Way too serious.

"I'm not the girl you take home to your mom. I'm not the person you get attached to. You're used to conquering the impossible, so I get it. I understand the challenge you see with me, but I'm no challenge, Roz. I'm the one-night stand you forget to brag to your friends about because by the time morning comes, I'm already long gone." Usually. Tricky Roz got me to stay the night but that was a one-off. I can't let it happen again.

I won't.

"The only memory I leave behind is the kind fever dreams are made of," I whisper, and speaking low himself, Roz says, "I'm not looking for attachments." *But he might.* "I've never introduced a girl to my mom." *He deserves the option though.* "I don't kiss and tell." *That's what they all say at first.* "And fevers don't faze me."

I eye him a moment longer.

"So, you're cool with this not going anywhere past a one-time thing? A hook-up?"

Those golden eyes turn murky, but then he nods slowly, saying, "Yeah."

Dropping my gaze to the floor, I shove the plates and napkins into his chest, telling him to take everything to a table. "I'll bring out the food when it's ready."

Roz's muscular back disappears through the swinging door, making my ribs hurt worse than they did after the run-in with Mitch.

I grab the forgotten bag of ice, shifting it from hand to hand while staring at the melting cubes inside.

Cool. He says he's cool, but…for how long? Because everything has a shelf life. Everything and everyone.

"Fuck, I forgot what being full was like," Roz says, pushing away his crumb-filled plate.

Most professional athletes have to cut calories, so they can maintain a certain weight. Snowboarders aren't one of them. The serious ones probably eat closer to a triathlete's diet, not just because of the physical demand, but also the harsh conditions they have to power through. You tread up a steep incline—on snow, in snow, *through* snow—while wearing multiple layers of clothing, I don't care who you are, you're burning calories faster than an incinerator.

Roz has lost weight since he quit snowboarding. He's lost even more weight since the party at his house. It was obvious as soon as I laid eyes on him. I'd like to know why. Why is he losing weight when he's no longer hoofing it up summits?

I pinch off the last bite of crust, popping it into my mouth. Roz shifts in his chair and I can tell without looking that his feet are pitching back and forth under the table.

"That, uh, that was the best thing I've eaten, probably ever."

"Ever? You've eaten all over."

"I was hungry."

"Mmm."

When he found me at the park earlier, Roz's voice was better off than the last time I saw him, but not by much. He does have a deep voice, but it's soothing, seductive. Not scratchy. It only gets scratchy when he's gone a long time without using it. If he wasn't talking to anybody and he wasn't eating enough to get full, what's he been doing?

"Aren't you used to it by now though? From working here?"

I shake my head. "Used to it but not sick of it. I love eating here." Aside from cannoli, my dad's cooking never gets old to me, but he legit makes the best calzone, even if it hasn't won him any awards yet. Whenever he uses ricotta for savory dishes, he adds chopped jalapenos to kick up the otherwise bland ingredient. It might be a bit controversial, but it also gets rave reviews, so whatever.

"It probably helps that you're high."

"I'm not high," I scoff. "That shit wasn't even medical grade."

Shit. That last part wasn't really supposed to come out. Everyone knows I have a high tolerance from smoking the good stuff, and I'm sure most people know why, but it's not really talked about. At least not to my face. On the rare occasion I am offered someone else's less desirable stash, I smoke as little as I can or avoid it entirely. Life's too short for bad weed. Seriously.

I glance up to see Roz's eyebrows raised.

"I need dessert."

The eyebrows go even higher. "What? Now?"

"Yeah, now." I gesture to the empty plates. "I need to balance out all this salt." Always. I've always had this thing about balancing out the sweet and savory when I eat. I can't end on a salty note, or a sweet one. There has to be an equal amount of both for my taste buds to be completely satisfied. It's a habit. Or character flaw. Whatever. The two are usually interchangeable.

"It's gotta be…what? After two o'clock already? Where are we going to find dessert now?"

"It is?" I guess we both lost track of time because I had no idea it was already the next day.

"Don't worry about it." I wave him off. "There's probably something in the kitchen."

Before I can move, Roz stands, saying, "Stay here. I'll see what I can do."

Now my eyebrows are the ones hitting the ceiling. I mean, okay. Dr. Roz is suddenly Chef Roz. I'm into it.

Hook-up. He's a hook-up.

Roz reappears a few minutes later, wearing a shit-eating grin and holding a small bowl of something I can't see.

Setting it in front of me, he says, "I brought two," then brandishes two spoons from behind his back with magician-like flair. *And the talents continue.*

I scan the bowl. "This is whipped cream."

"It was all I could find," he explains, sitting across from me.

"You had the chance to strip naked and cover your dick in whipped cream before coming back out here and you didn't take it?"

His face registers so many different reactions I almost feel bad. Almost.

Regret finally flickers, and I laugh. Yes, he did, in fact, miss a once-in-a-lifetime opportunity, one I would've enjoyed the hell out of.

I scoop some cream on my pointer finger, then hold it out for him, waiting. Our eyes on each other's, his tongue sneaks out to take a small taste. I swear the lick goes straight to my pussy, and when Roz's mouth closes over my finger, all the way to the base, devouring the cream completely, I have to clench my thighs together.

With a jerk of my chin, I invite him over so I can have a taste, too—he's not the only one with an appetite—but sadly, he releases my finger to shake his head, telling me, "I only have four kisses left."

"So use 'em." I shrug. Like duh, dude, that's what I'm getting at.

I lick up the finger he just sucked, giving him another nod, but again, he refuses. *What the hell?*

Instead, he eyes the bowl, saying, "I thought you said you wanted this."

So we're playing that game.

Propping my ass on the table, I swing my legs around, over to his side, keeping them spread wide.

"Maybe I want something else now."

"You owe me four more kisses, anytime, anywhere." He tilts his head to the side, glancing up at me with half-lidded eyes. "But I'm not cashing in on them right now."

Damn. He's trickier than I thought.

Looking down my nose at him, I say, "So you can't fuck without kissing, is that it?"

The second the words are past my lips, Roz is out of his chair, standing in front of me. With one yank, my ass is at the edge of the table, then his hand wraps around the back of my neck, keeping me in place as he slams his mouth down on mine. And oh gawd, is it a good kiss. I will say, even though I liked the taste of Roz's blood on my tongue, the sweet cream makes for a much tastier addition.

I have to tilt my head back to accommodate the height differ-ence, but any pressure in my neck is immediately rubbed away by Roz's hand, kneading it like he's the one that grew up in a pizzeria.

Roz's kisses are something to behold and I kind of wish he had more to spare. A strong hand at the top of my spine like a puppet master controlling his marionette, a tongue as talented as its owner, and thunderous groans that make me quake all combine to make for the perfect storm rolling through my body.

"That finger I just sucked on?" he asks on a breath as he pulls back just enough for his eyes to bore into mine. "Did that count as kissing you?"

"Um, no?" What are we talking about? And why?

"So if I sucked on your fingers before making you use them to ready your pussy for me, would that count as kissing you?"

I go to shrug, then think better of it. I have to choose my answer wisely here, so I can reap any and all benefits offered. Fortunately, he doesn't bother waiting for my reply.

"Or what if I prepped you myself? What if I used my tongue to lick up your sweet pussy, huh?" He jerks our bodies together, his hard length crashing against my center and sparking like a flash of lightning.

His hold on my hair tightens and my eyes close on a delicious hiss.

"Is that kissing?"

Not precisely, but his descriptions are creating a lot of gray area that I don't care to examine right now. Can't we worry about semantics later? I just want this ache to be soothed and Roz sounds like he knows exactly how to do it.

I open my eyes and mouth to tell Roz that but seeing his eyes dilated to the point of no return has me staying quiet. The gold is nothing but a thin ring around black pupils.

Gawd, I want him.

"When I finally do bury my cock deep inside your pussy and my teeth sink into your shoulder to keep you from fucking moving so I don't explode…is that considered kissing you, baby?"

I'm already shaking my head. Nope. Definitely not kissing. A bite during sex is like adding pepper to bacon, an absolute necessity if you want to make it even close to good.

Then suddenly, I'm angling my face to said shoulder, trying to stop the sneeze ripping from my sinuses.

Roz drops his lust-soaked tone to ask, "Are you okay?"

"I'm fine. Must be something in the air…" I trail off, not wanting to outright lie.

My hands fly to the waistband of his shorts, but his free hand clutches mine, keeping me from removing his last bit of clothing.

Cock.

Block.

Literally.

"Where the fuck have you been hiding this dirty mouth of yours?" I ask.

With both my hands caught in one of his, he slides the other hand around to my throat, grasping possessively while flashing me a smile so sinful I should already be in flames. His thumb rubs back and forth, letting me know he's not an actual threat and ignorance never looked so good, so tempting.

"Waiting."

Waiting…

Waiting for what? Waiting for life to return to normal? That's not how life works. Life is here and now, but it's constantly changing—that *is* the norm. It's up to us to change with it because if we don't, it will pass us by.

"Where have *you* been hiding, Roz?"

Roz's grip on my throat disappears as he steps back, returning to whatever mental hell he keeps banishing himself to ever since his best friend died.

"I…don't know."

A few minutes pass and I hop off the table, stopping to dip my finger back into the whipped cream before bringing it up to my mouth and sucking it clean myself.

"Let's get out of here."

"What about the mess?"

"The mess…" *Which one?* The mess I'm making by drawing this out? Or the mess we just made?

I eye Roz's busted knuckles.

"Do you know how to scramble video feed?"

"Um."

"I'll show you." Luckily, my academy did teach me that particular skill, just not directly.

Chapter 9

ROZ

Gia's all over the place. I can't keep up if I tried. No, fuck that, I can't keep up even *when* I'm trying. One minute she acts like I have some kind of effect on her heart, the next she's making me swear not to develop feelings for her.

And now, instead of dealing with any of it, she wants to up and leave.

She has this incredibly frustrating knack for disappearing right when things are getting good. What the fuck is that about? I told her I wouldn't get attached but that doesn't mean I'm ready to say good-bye just yet. We can hook up, and we will, I just don't want to rush it because then it'll be over and she'll be leaving all over again.

She doesn't want labels? Easy. I've never really liked them my-self either.

She wants great sex? Check my resume. It's kind of my specialty. Or, at least I thought it was until Gia started planting seeds of doubt in my head.

I can't actually care about her aside from fucking her senseless? Well, fuck. Houston, we have a problem—a big one.

Maybe, *maybe*, that was a possibility before I saw Gia lying in a helpless heap at the skate park because now, I'm not so confident. A lot changed in that moment. I changed in that moment. We changed in that moment, whether she'll admit it or not.

"What happened to your heart?"

"You."

What does that even mean? I'd give anything to know.

I'm just coming out of her dad's office when she's finishing up with the dishes. I offered to clean them but she insisted. I don't know shit about video reconfiguration, but Gia explained it enough that I was able to erase the footage of us in the kitchen. I don't really understand why I had to since Gia's nineteen years old and the most we did was make a quick stop at second base. Her dad must be strict or something.

With Gia's back to me, more of her skin is on display than usual. She hasn't bothered with putting her shirt back on—thankfully—and without her bulk of bracelets on either, I swear I can make out more of those burn-type scars on her wrists. With most of the lights off, it's hard to tell, but I'm pretty sure they're the same as the ones on her back. What are they? Who put them there?

The thought of someone, anyone, inflicting any kind of pain on Gia has my fists tightening by my sides.

The moment Gia realizes I'm standing here, her backbone stiffens, making her shoulder blades stick out like an angel's wings.

I go over and pick up her long-sleeve shirt we abandoned hours ago. *Hours.* Shit. It's almost morning and we haven't even slept yet. Not that I'm thinking of going to sleep. I just left my bed. And after not leaving it for several days in a row, I have no desire to get back in it. Not alone anyway.

Gia places the last spoon on the rack, then I help her put her shirt back on along with the bracelets she set aside. She'll tell me about her scars someday, hopefully before I use up my last kiss.

Fully dressed again, she smirks up at me, asking, "Do you have a flashlight?"

Here we go…

"How much farther?"

Using my Chevy, Gia drove us to an empty parking lot with one broken light post but thousands of weeds growing through cracks lining the old asphalt and now we're hiking alongside a decent-sized creek, or kill. New York calls them kills because that's not morbid at all.

Gia's leading the way with a flashlight I found in my glove compartment and I'm trying not to fall too far behind. This girl moves when she's on a mission.

"It's up here." Quieter, she says, "Somewhere."

"Do you even know where we're going?"

"Of course."

A few more steps and I hear her murmur, "Sort of."

Why would I have expected anything else? Gia wants to hike in the dark to an undisclosed location that she may or may not be able to find.

Sure, let's do it. I'll bring the flashlight.

Oh, wait…

"Fuck me," I mutter, letting out a laugh.

"I tried. Remember?"

"Is that when you passed out?" I toss out, bypassing a thick evergreen branch.

"Um, yeah, obviously," she throws right back before saying, "Seduction tires me out."

I laugh again, stretching my shirt away from my stomach for some airflow. Despite the cold bite of early morning air, the dew is penetrating everything, making my clothes feel soaked all the way through. Normally I'd just take the shirt off altogether, but ticks are such a problem around here, I figure the added protection outweighs the irritation.

"No, that was my first time doing that."

"What? Seducing someone?" I look up in time to see Gia stumble and my hand shoots out automatically, catching the back of her shirt before she can right herself. Her rib must be hurting her, yet here she is, tromping through the fucking woods, leading me on some kind of adventure.

I shake my head, picking up the pace.

"Sleeping at someone else's house."

My eyes drop to the ground. She was very clear about not sticking around 'til morning.

"Staying over at anyone's house actually," she muses. "I don't do that. Ever."

I lift my eyes to the back of her head.

"Not even at your boy Rowdy's?"

Her head shakes.

That answer, combined with her confession just before it, makes something primal in me stand taller. My steps fall easier, my stride a little more confident.

Does it even matter where she's taking me anymore? No, not really. I'd blindly follow Gia anywhere as long as the promise of *something* more hangs in the air and what she just said sits heavy around us. I can practically see her admission join our little troupe. I smile at it, I fist-bump it, shit, I put my arm around it, welcoming the enlightening news into the fold. She doesn't do sleepovers, not even with her best friend, but she fell asleep at my place, with me—with ease.

Time passes in a more comfortable silence as we make our way through the woods, stopping every so often for Gia to take pictures of birds with her phone. The first time she did it, she turned to me with a blush and said, "Old habits." Personally, I don't mind. She could be taking pictures of every dust particle floating about and I wouldn't say a word. Everything she does fascinates me. I just wish she'd tell me about it. Tell me about her. I want more than just the table scraps she gave me…yesterday? Damn, this might be my longest date yet.

All of a sudden, she spins around, shining the flashlight under her chin ominously. A smile tugs at my lips before I can school my features. She doesn't even need it anymore—the sun's just starting to come up, so there's enough light for us to see—she's only using it for effect at this point, but I'll play along.

"Roswell Fancy, Jr., are you ready?"

I hold up a finger. "That's not my name. It's Roswell Andrews-Smith."

She drops the flashlight to her side, rolling her eyes. "Same thing."

"No Junior either. I'm the first."

"Ugh, don't tell me you're going to be one of *those*," she groans. "The kind of person that names your child after yourself."

I start to correct her that I have no such plans but something strange crosses her face, something I can't quite put my finger on, before she turns away so quickly, making me question whether it was even there to begin with.

"We're here."

Behind Gia, there's a small set of natural waterfalls that I honestly didn't think the creek could handle.

"So, we found it then?"

"Not yet."

What? More hiking?

She steps up to me, blocking the view with an even better one, and everything else starts to fade away as her brown eyes take hold of mine. My fingers, hanging limply at my sides, venture out, seeking hers. She brings her hands forward too, touching my fingers with only the backs of hers.

"Close your eyes," she whispers, breaking the spell.

I shake my head, not ready to let this moment go, but she nods, smiling.

"You won't push me, will you?"

"Just trust me, Roswell Andrews-Smith."

Even though my own eyelids threaten to revolt, I close them, telling her, "That's Mr. Fancy to you."

A small laugh reaches my ears just before the sound of rushing water comes into focus. Birds chirp overhead, leaves flutter to the ever-growing ground, twigs snap in the distance. Everything's intensified with one of my senses cut off, even the buzz passing between our fingers.

Our only connection breaks and I swear I'm about to open my eyes, then Gia's at my back, pressing her front flat against me. The new, larger buzz intensifies until that's all I can concentrate on and every bit of her body touching mine becomes visible as I memorize her curves with my mind alone. The more I visualize Gia's milky white skin, the more I wonder why the fuck I didn't touch it all when I had the chance. I told Gia I'm saving my last three kisses, but I didn't say anything about keeping my hands to myself.

Gia's breath swirls across my cheek as she says, "Open."

Working past a squint, I'm met with the first sunrise I've seen in a long time. At the crest of the falls sits the tips of the sun's rays gracing us with a warm, colorful morning greeting. My breaths slow to match Gia's while shades of pink, purple, and orange fill the sky above us. Her inhales become mine until we're breathing in sync, my back not to her but for her.

Gia's been avoiding me in a frustrating dance of give-and-take, but she chose to bring me here…for some reason. That has to mean something. It *does* mean something. Watching the sun come up with the woman that brought light back into my life will be imprinted onto my mind for the rest of my days. No fever dream I've ever had could even come close to this.

My cheeks are just starting to heat when Gia speaks, her voice soft and nearly unrecognizable. "Thank you."

"For what?" I spread my hands out in front of us. "This was all you."

"For trusting me."

Her chin falls away from my shoulder.

Toying with her sleeve, Gia avoids my gaze as she asks, "Can you take me home?"

"Sure…" Hope bangs around in my chest, begging to be let out, but before I can ask if she means my home or hers, she looks up and says, "I need to be there when my dad wakes up."

Is that why she doesn't sleep anywhere else? Because of her dad?

"Um, yeah. No problem. You okay to walk back to the truck?"

I reach my hand out for hers, and even though she says, "Yes," she takes it, and we step over a raised tree root together.

"So…"

"So?"

"How long are you planning on drawing this out for?"

"What do you mean?" She's the one that brought me here.

"You're down to three, cowboy."

Aw, she's on to me.

"Just two now."

"Real—"

I tug Gia to me and press my lips to hers, except this time, I'm the one pulling away when she tries to deepen it. Her eyebrows draw together over her still closed eyes.

"Thank you."

She finally looks up at me, grinning, and asks, "For what?"

"Listening."

Chapter 10

ROZ

Gia wouldn't let me walk her to the front door, but she did leave another kiss on my truck's passenger side window, so… there's that. I never got around to washing the first one off, so now there are two of Gia's lip marks to tease the fuck out of me each and every time I drive somewhere.

I'm reversing out of her driveway when I notice her phone still on the passenger seat and I weigh my options for all of three seconds before shifting into Drive to pull forward again. Luckily, it's the same model as mine, so with one swipe, I turn on her Bluetooth, then AirDrop her my number. *There.* Now she can get ahold of me… if she wants to.

At the front door, it gets a little more complicated. I obviously can't call her, but I also don't want to leave her phone on the doorstep. I don't want to risk waking her dad up either. He seems like an asshole.

Hoping she's still nearby, I knock, wincing at the loud interruption to the peaceful morning. Almost instantly the door flies open, but not with Gia on the other side.

Gia's dad—I'm guessing—greets me with a confused sort of frown. He's wearing a polo shirt with the collar popped and a kitchen towel thrown across his shoulder.

Now I'm the one confused. I thought he'd be sleeping.

"Oh, uh—" I stammer, trying to think of a lie for why I'm here. If only I could recite a Bible verse under the guise of pushing some religion, but fuck, I can't even remember a full one to spout.

Why do I have to lie? We're both consenting adults.

"Gia forgot this." I jiggle the phone between us but keep my eyes on his. If he flinches…I don't know. What could I even do? I'm not fucking running, that I do know, but can I actually beat up Gia's dad?

Why am I considering beating him up at all? Do I need to beat him up?

"Why the hell are you knocking then?"

"It's—"

His face relaxes into the same secretive smile his daughter wears, then he turns around, saying, "Just come in," before disappearing down the hallway. From somewhere farther inside, he says, "It's for you."

Gia's head pops into the hall. "Don't just stand there. Come in already."

Um, what? So, her dad's not upset I'm here? And they're both okay with dudes just walking in their front door?

Gia takes her phone from my hand before settling herself on one of the stools at the kitchen peninsula, and without lifting her eyes from it, she pats the stool next to her.

Only when I'm seated does she finally look at me, shaking her head and tsking, "Tricky."

My eyebrows jump and she gestures to my number still displayed on her screen.

"Maybe if you would've let me walk you to the door, I could've given it to you normally," I say through unmoving lips.

"What's that? What happened?" Gia's dad asks.

Gia keeps her eyes on mine but speaks to him, saying, "Roz is mad I didn't invite him in."

The back of my neck heats. *Jesus Christ.*

When I glance up, her dad's looking at me expectantly.

"I hope I didn't wake you, sir." My truck is throaty as hell. I made sure of it. One after-market upgrade later and my Chevy chuffs like a lion prowling the savanna.

"Sir," Gia mocks.

"I only wanted to ensure Gia made it home safely, but since she thought you were sleeping, I stayed in the driveway until she got inside okay."

Gia goes quiet next to me, but I don't dare break eye contact with her dad. With them in the same room together, I notice the resemblance easy enough, but if I didn't know this was her dad, I'm not sure I would have. Where Gia's skin is fair, his has more of a warm tone to it, like he just came inside from an afternoon of gardening in the sun. Their hair is the same color, but while his is straight, his daughter's is wavy like the sea. He's also shorter than Gia, but their eyes have the same sense of humor lining them, especially when he tries and fails to hold back laughter of his own.

"I haven't slept past five a.m. since I graduated college and took up the restaurant life." The father-daughter duo share a laugh. At my expense.

Haha.

"And please, call me Al."

Under the overhang of the granite countertop, I wipe the sweat from my palm on to my shorts, then extend it to Al for a handshake, introducing myself. We look each other in the eye and all I see is humor. No worry or suspicion or anger—nothing cruel at all—just a welcoming energy.

Noticing the cuts on my knuckles, he gives his daughter a frown, scolding, "Gia."

"What? It wasn't me," she chuckles.

"Uh-huh," Al says, looking pointedly down at her shirt that's still stained with my blood, before telling me, "My daughter has a certain…influence."

My gaze seeks hers out.

"Yeah, she does," I say.

Unless I'm reading this all wrong, her dad isn't strict like I assumed.

"Are you hungry, Roz?" Al asks with a low chuckle, turning back to his skillet of fried potatoes.

"I could eat."

Gia snickers, but I try to keep a straight face, remembering my earlier words about eating—her, specifically.

Someone else comes through the front door—sans

knocking—and not a moment later, Rowdy appears, greeting, "Good morning." Surprise colors his face, but he tries to hide it by giving me a jerky head nod. I wait until he straightens from kissing Gia's cheek to return it, then watch as he goes around the counter to wrap Al in a hug.

The whole scene is very…cozy. It's cozy as hell actually. Cozier than anything I grew up with. My parents' house, when I bothered going back to it, never felt cozy.

Cold. That's the word that comes to mind when I imagine my childhood home. Once I started traveling full-time, I didn't even look forward to coming back to it. I've never been homesick a day in my life.

There's not an ounce of cold in Gia's though. I'm still seated inside it and I'm already craving this feeling. How is that? How can you yearn for something you've never even known?

"You guys heading out or just getting in?" Rowdy asks, taking the stool on my other side.

"Getting in," I say, pulling my beanie off to drop in my lap.

Rowdy nods, rubbing his eyes. His mohawk's ruffled like he just rolled out of bed, and he's wearing what must be his old high school sweats. It's funny because it's the same school I would've gone to had I actually attended in-person school. By the time I was fourteen, I was already doing online classes and had a tutor while I traveled. Salvy's mom wasn't in the same position as my parents, so he ended up attending high school here during the week and saved boarding for the weekends. Racking up wins earned me my own money, so I started flying him out to wherever I was, and as soon as he graduated, it was on—we tore up every competition we could find together.

During all my time away from this town, I forgot how small it actually is. Rowdy's gotta be around Gia's age, and I'm only a couple years older than she is, so it's possible Rowdy and Salvy went to school together. They could've known each other, easy. Gia could've known Salvy even. My roommates knew who Gia was; Salvy might've, too.

If I hadn't gone pro so early, maybe *I* would've met Gia sooner.

A melancholic haze clouds my eyes as I half-listen to the voices around me talk about the strange orders the pizzeria gets.

New Yorkers through and through, my parents have always rejected the idea of leaving their hometown permanently, a choice I'm actually grateful for now because despite never being homesick, this was the only place I considered retreating to when I retired myself.

A glass vase with a large chunk off the lip penetrates my haze. It's next to the stove, which seems like a strange place for a vase, especially an empty one. At the skate park, Gia told me a story about her parents' first date. Apparently Al is a real romantic and showed up at Gia's mom's door with an actual glass vase overflowing with orange-red poppies, a flower popular in Italy but not really given as gifts here. He saw the poppies growing randomly on the side of the road, reminding him of a family trip to Val d'Orcia in Tuscany, so he pulled over to pick some for his date. He wanted to buy a container big enough to fit the wildflowers but went a little too big because when Gia's mom went to take the vase from him, her arms gave out from the weight, causing the top to bang into the doorjamb and chip the lip.

I replayed the story several times in my head because while I've never thought to bring any girl flowers, I know if I did, they wouldn't be from the side of the road. Or in a gigantic vase. But seeing the vase still sitting in the middle of their kitchen all these years later has me rethinking that.

It's not about what goes right, it's about what feels right.

Maybe I could've met Gia sooner…or maybe I'm meeting her exactly when I'm supposed to.

My focus stuck on the vase, everybody else laughs over someone ordering onion rings with raspberry sauce.

"We're not waking your mom, are we?"

I glance at Gia, but her eyes are fixed on her dad. Al stares into the frying pan and Rowdy drills a hole into the side of my face.

Gia finally brings her gaze to mine and I'm already shaking my head, whispering, "Sorry."

Al confirms my suspicion, saying, "Gia's mother passed away three years ago."

Meeting Al's eyes, I say, "I'm sorry," then turn back to Gia, repeating, "I'm sorry."

Fuck, am I sorry.

Surprisingly though, Gia's smiling again. "She would've been up before any of us."

Something settles over her own gaze as she slips into a memory.

Al nods, saying fondly, "Up with the birds."

Rowdy scoffs. "You mean up *for* the birds?"

All three of them share a laugh that I don't understand.

"Vita was a bird-watcher," Al explains.

"She was a bird-*enthusiast*," Gia corrects. "It was more than just watching."

Rowdy leans over, talking out of the side of his mouth. "Vita was obsessed."

"Vita loved birds." Al nods, pointing behind me. Through the living room at our backs, a huge cluster of windows serves as the focal point, and on the other side of the glass, dozens of birdfeeders fill the expansive backyard.

"Wow."

Rowdy rumbles beside me.

"How did she die?" Quickly facing Al again, I add, "If you don't mind me asking."

Smiles, eyes, and maybe even a pin somewhere in the distance drop. *Seriously, what's wrong with me?* I feel like not talking for so long made me lose the ability to converse appropriately. I'm missing cues I swear I would've picked up on before.

Nobody rushes to answer while my gaze touches on every person in the room.

Finally, Al says quietly, "Cancer."

I don't know how, or why, but all the air in the kitchen seems to whoosh out at once.

What am I missing?

"I'm really sorry for your loss," I say to nobody and everybody. I don't know Rowdy more than seeing him from afar a couple times, but it's clear he knew Vita and feels the loss as well. Right? Isn't that why he's all buttoned up now, refusing to look up from his fingers drumming the countertop?

Something feels off, but I can't figure out what it is.

"She was the best person to be around."

"You were lucky," I repeat the words she once told me, meaning them more than Gia could ever understand. More than even I understand. Even in death, Vita's liveliness comes through—loud and clear. "Now I understand what you meant at Salvy's funeral." I've only been here for maybe an hour and I can already tell the energy coursing through the veins in Gia's home is what people long for. What people spend their whole lives searching for. What most assume will just appear one day. Except…it won't. It's not some attainable *thing.* It's the people and their passion for life that make a place special. That makes a house feel like a home.

"Oh, God. You're still doing that?" Rowdy speaks up, gaining Al's attention as well.

With all the men looking at her, Gia shrugs. "We all wear grief differently. Sometimes it's muted," her gaze flicks to mine and I swallow, "other times it's not. Funerals are the one place where you see both displayed simultaneously. There's no wrong way to grieve, but there isn't a right way either, and there's something tragically beautiful about that."

So she was crashing Salvy's funeral. I don't know how to feel about that knowledge. I thought as much but didn't know for sure. I'm offended, on Diane's behalf, but also…grateful? If she hadn't, where would I be right now? Is that selfish?

I haven't wanted anything for myself, haven't gone after anything for myself, since I stepped away from my old life, and now that I have my sights set on something I do want, I can't just give it up because we met under questionable circumstances.

Gia's eyes drop before she adds, "But I don't do it anymore."

When? When did she stop? After meeting me? Why?

Does she feel the same way I do? Somehow I find that impossible. But maybe not. While her mouth tells me she doesn't do attachments, we continue to find each other, like there's an invisible tether connecting us.

Leaning back, I stretch my arm out behind Gia, resting it along the top of her stool's backrest, my fingers grazing her shoulder blade.

Something brought her to Salvy's funeral that day. Something brought her to me. Whether due to some divine intervention or not, it doesn't really matter because I'm not letting Gia cut that tether. Not yet.

Al finishes with the feast, placing it on the counter in front of us family-style. Perfectly crisp home fries, seasoned sausage patties, and fluffy ricotta pancakes with sliced strawberries. Oh, and real maple syrup. Even I know not to fuck with that fake stuff around here.

Gia glances up, meeting her father's intense gaze. Coming around the peninsula, Al breaks the connection to give the back of his daughter's head a kiss. Despite Rowdy already reaching for the pancakes, he stops to watch the tender moment, too. When Al pulls back, a lone tear rolls down his cheek before he wipes it away, then he says something to Gia in Italian that she nods to.

"Roz, it was nice meeting you." We shake hands again. "Next time just let yourself in, yeah?" My head bobs on its own accord. *Will there really be a next time?*

With a fatherly pat on the back to Rowdy, Al excuses himself for work, leaving the three of us to the food.

"He's not going to eat?"

Gia smiles thinly. "He eats while he cooks." Then with more enthusiasm, she lifts a fork to stab a sausage patty, and says, "Dig in, boys."

After that, the three of us fall into lighter conversation and I purposely avoid bringing up anything awkward again. In the moments where I remain silent, I watch Gia and Rowdy together. They're close. Really close. But not in the way I might've thought at first. They're like brother and sister in the same way Salvy and I were like brothers.

As soon as we finish, Gia bolts from the room, mumbling about needing to soak her shirt.

"She does that a lot, huh?"

Knowing Rowdy understands what I mean, I keep watch in case Gia returns.

"She has this way of always leaving people wanting more," he agrees.

I twist back around. That's exactly how I'd describe it. Of course, Gia has me wanting more before she even leaves though. But I keep that fun fact to myself.

Rowdy and I eye the pile of dirty dishes, then each other.

"I'll wash if you dry," he says and I smother a laugh. *Why not?*

Rowdy points to a lower cupboard, telling me where the now-clean platter belongs, and while I'm bent over putting it away, I hear Gia whistle as she enters the kitchen.

"You guys didn't have to do all this."

The telltale sound of a towel snapping against flesh echoes through the house before Gia groans and Rowdy says, "You didn't give us much of a choice when you left us with the mess."

Gia's rubbing her thigh when I turn around, but luckily, she's too busy frowning at Rowdy to notice my jaw drop. Her thighs…they're bare. She's only wearing her boxer briefs now, so essentially under-wear. Just underwear. And a long-sleeve tee, but still…just underwear. I figured she'd come out in my shorts just to rub it in my face that she's still got them, but this, this is *so* much better.

And worse.

This date's coming to an end and she decides now's the time to show more of that body. *"She has this way of always leaving people wanting more."* Yes. The fuck. She. Does.

"And when's the last time you cleaned *anything* at your own house?" she throws at Rowdy, circling him.

Leaning my forearms against the counter, I watch the exchange silently. Gia's shirt with holes for the thumbs covers a finely sculpted ass that I'd give anything to glimpse more of right now.

Rowdy scoffs, matching her step for step in his retreat. "I don't have to clean there. That's what my mom's for."

And yeah, Gia pounces. I mean really, Rowdy set himself up for it with that comment, so I don't feel bad when Gia rat-tails him in the nuts after wrestling the dishtowel from his hands. Laughter spills from my mouth, even though my thighs squeeze together in solidarity with him.

He curls into the fetal position on the hardwood floor, cupping his boys. The cotton towel is still pretty wet from drying dishes too, so I *know* he's hurting.

Gia bends down to kiss his cheek, saying, "You know I love you but that was a dickhead thing to say." She stands, looking me in the eye and making the air refilling my lungs catch. And not from fear of being rat-tailed either. No, this is a different fear entirely.

Not yet.

"What about you?"

"What about me?" I counter.

"Are you tired?"

I tip a shoulder. "I could sleep." Or not. I'd never sleep again if it meant I didn't have to leave here.

Without breaking eye contact, she says, "Tell your mom I said hi," and holds out her hand to me.

My eyebrows are just starting to pull together when Rowdy speaks from the floor, asking, "You're kicking me out?" He gets to his feet with glistening eyes.

"Well, we're going to sleep, so…" Gia lets that hang in the air while Rowdy and I glance at each other with equally lost expressions. Does she mean I'm staying?

Gia flips her hand palm side up and says, "Come on, cowboy."

I ask, "You want me to stay?" at the same time Rowdy bursts, "You want him to stay?"

Gia simply rolls her eyes, grabbing my shirt to pull me after her. "You're just as tired as I am."

Although lying next to Gia dressed in underwear and not much else will most likely not result in sleeping, I'm not about to correct her. At least not in front of Rowdy. I do have some dignity.

On the way up the stairs, I go tell Rowdy goodbye but swallow the word *whole* when I get a good look at him. If anything, I thought he'd be worried for Gia, his best friend, but the concern in his eyes isn't aimed at her at all. It's for me.

Vanilla and rosemary knock me square in the face as soon as we cross the threshold to her room and I see a candle with three lit wicks sitting on a worn oak desk next to an open laptop.

"Romantic," I tease to hide my nerves. What the hell's going on with me?

"Shut up."

She releases my shirt, then face-plants on top of a white comforter with different species of birds hand-drawn on it, making me chuckle. Above the headboard hangs a string of white lights with pictures clipped to the cord between the bright bulbs. I'm not even surprised to find photos of more birds along with candid shots with friends, her dad, and a woman whose portrait we passed in the hallway. *Vita.* It's easy to see where Gia gets most of her features from—her mom was absolutely beautiful.

One black-and-white photo shows Gia curled up in a hospital bed, her arms wrapped snugly around her mother, both of them asleep. It doesn't look like it was taken that long ago.

"Is that why you missed a year? Because you had to take care of your mom?"

She turns her head to the side, cracking open an eye. "No. I *chose* to miss school because I *chose* to take care of my mom. You have to collect every minute you have with someone, you know?"

I nod. I do. There are so many times I wish I could go back and just…collect. Enjoy. Times with Salvy that I didn't slow down and give it my all. Times when I would stare at my phone, not being fully present. Times when I would fixate on what was next instead of embracing the moment I was in.

Gia was mature enough to make that kind of choice when she was only…what? Fifteen? Sixteen? Damn. She made the right decision, but I hate that she had to make it at all. And so young.

Pictures of the moon and stars and quotes—lots of quotes—fill the rest of her walls. All of them so otherworldly, it's like she's in the wrong place, longing for somewhere far off. One quote in particular catches my eye, it reads *Just Passing Through*, and I wonder if that's true. She's always on the move for one thing or another.

I look over at her.

Not right now though. Right now, I got her, and I can collect this moment to keep for later. To keep for always.

I blow out the candle, then lie down beside her, so I'm facing her. Her closed eyelids twitch, but she doesn't stir otherwise. With my head on my bicep, I press my lips to her forehead, tucking my arm around her back and drawing her to me until her front's flush against mine.

Her sleepy voice breathes the word, "One," making a grin stretch my lips.

One. One moment to be in. One life to live in. One kiss to make Gia believe in.

Here we fucking go.

Chapter 11

GIA

The box on my passenger seat stares back at me accusingly.

"I know," I groan aloud for the fifty-eighth time today as I rethink this whole plan. Again. Roz invited me over to celebrate the Fourth of July at his place. His roommates are throwing a party, even though everyone will eventually be leaving to watch the fireworks at the town square. Everyone, but us.

After a week straight of hanging out together, you'd think he'd be sick of me, or vice versa really, but nope. The guy follows me around like a lost puppy, and stupid me, I keep giving him belly rubs. Not literally though. Ever since our "date" at the pizzeria, we haven't pushed those limits—unfortunately. Not even when I woke up to him draped across me like a poncho in a snowstorm. He takes his cuddling very seriously, that guy. I just need to figure out how to get him to snuggle without clothes now, then it'd be easier to stop with all this chummy shit because we've already established Roz and I can't be friends. Besides, I have Rowdy for that. And like a dozen other dirtbags I call friends. Once I screw Roz out of my system and wipe that final kiss off my debt, then I'll be free to move on already.

That's what I tell myself as I grab the box and hop out of my truck.

That's what I've been telling myself all along and it still hasn't stuck.

As I'm walking up, Roz dives for the volleyball, his interlocked fists bumping the ball before it can hit the ground and sending it high enough for one of his teammates to spike over to the other team. It's a far cry from the Roz I first stumbled across. Months ago, he was adrift in a sea of loneliness. Even when he was among people, he wasn't engaged, not like this. He's participating now. He's living again. He's stunning.

This right here…this is exactly why I haven't sent Roz packing yet. This is what I've been waiting to see for myself. All week Roz has been…*this*. This mesmerizing model of rebellion. Of resilience. He's played, he's laughed, joked, talked. He's gotten up and gotten out. He's taken me for more "dates" than I've ever been on and will probably ever go on in my lifetime. And he never stops feeding me. Every time I see him, he's holding food for me. I take it, but only on the condition that he has to help me eat it. He's already put some weight back on and it's only been a week. Roz is on his way to being healthy again, which is more important than being happy because happiness can always be rediscovered. Health isn't so easy to restore though. Happiness can be manufactured again and again, pulled out of thin air, slipped on as easily as a Halloween mask. But health… health can fade without so much as a single warning. Sometimes when it's gone, it really is gone. Forever.

I didn't want that for Roz. I don't want that for Roz. He's different. He treats me different than most people do. He treats me… like me.

Someone slaps the volleyball into the net, forcing a timeout to fix the lights the previous fraternity had to string the net with after a gnarly wind storm ripped out chunks of the netting. With the sun just starting to sink below the horizon, the lights are lit up, but several bulbs are burned out from being hit by idiots with shit aim. Or drunks. Probably drunks. The guys that lived here before might've been Greek by choice, but they were Irish by blood and outdrank everybody on Greek Sac.

Once upon a time, this house was my hangout every weekend. And weekdays. I was here so much, I could've pledged the frat myself. I used to get trashed out of my mind before passing out wherever my body fell for the night. Or day. That was the summer my mom got diagnosed and all I wanted was to disappear before she could. The idea of losing her nearly crippled me, but the fact that it could've possibly been prevented pissed me off and I made a lot of bad decisions with a lot of bad people, T.J. being one of them. I wanted to smother the anger that stemmed from my pain with anything I could get my hands on. But the pain I felt, the regret I had to chew on like a fatty piece of meat, after I came out of the fog I'd willingly trapped myself in, was so much worse. I'll never get that summer back and it kills me. Still. That entire time in my life makes me sick actually and this house holds a lot of memories I wish I could forget. Except Roz's room since it was the president's, and he didn't let anybody inside it. I think anyway. If I did end up in there, I don't remember it.

I was stupid then. Way stupider than I am now.

When my mom's cancer metastasized to her lungs, reality woke me the fuck up and I came to my senses in time to spend what ended up being the last year of my mother's life right by her side. I gave up everything, even school. To this day, she remains my favorite person and I don't regret a single thing I sacrificed for that time I got with her. I still find myself wishing my collection of memories with her was bigger, but then I remind myself that quality really is better than quantity.

My eyes fall down Roz's firm back as he runs a hand through his hair absentmindedly, chatting up someone beside him. He still hasn't seen me and I kinda like it—watching him, but from afar, like a fly on the wall. Or a bird in the sky.

I should leave.

Roz is on the mend. He doesn't need me anymore. *He doesn't need me at all.*

Starting to turn, I notice a platinum blonde with a pixie-cut high-five Roz and I freeze. Good. This is good. Great even.

But as she leans into him and he stares down at her like the rest of us don't exist, it doesn't feel so great. Not like I thought it would. Not like I hoped it would. I'm actually…I don't know how to describe it. It doesn't make any sense, what I'm feeling. She's wearing a floral Brazilian bikini and she's wearing it so well that if I didn't want to rip her arm from her body, I'd probably be drinking that shit in myself. Everybody else is. Especially Fletcher, who's practically drooling down the front of his hot-pink muscle shirt. To be clear, he has no muscles, but that's the only way to describe his shirt that says *Sun's Out, Buns Out* with no real sides whatsoever as it's held together with a thin strip of material at the bottom. On the opposite team as Roz, he's supposed to be serving right now, but he's so busy gawking at Pixie, he's holding up the game.

Roz's roommate, Johnny, calls out to me, blowing my cover wide open as Roz's gaze snaps to mine. *Damn.* Those eyes. Those golden eyes. When they're open, really open, they're like a portal to everything I wish I could have. *He's* everything I wish I could have.

At least I have him for a little while. For tonight. *Quality over quantity.*

"What up, Johnny?" I say when I pass, tapping Roz's roommate's outstretched knuckles with the box in my hold. It's a little sloppy, but he's double fisting a couple of spiked ciders, so he's not in a position to judge anyone. He's also the one I got that bottle of wine from the last time I was here.

I nod in greeting to a couple of others on my way cutting through the messy formation of Roz's teammates.

"G, I'm surprised you're back. Didn't think we'd be seeing you again," Fletcher says from the other side of the net and I don't miss his meaning. *I fucking know*, I want to yell for the fifty-ninth time.

Instead I say, "Don't worry, Fletch. You won't after you wake up tomorrow." And I know he catches my drift just as easily.

So does Roz because his entire demeanor changes just before I shove the box into his chest.

I lock my eyes on Pixie's so I can't see the hurt in Roz's. I've been upfront with him from day one.

"Why don't you fill that up, cowboy?" I say, my gaze still on Pixie. This…*thing* between me and Roz, it doesn't include this girl. Not yet. Come morning, that's a different story, but for now, I don't want her touching Roz. I don't want anyone touching him—tonight. Tomorrow…

Tomorrow.

Tomorrow, I'll do what I always do. Cut bait and act like nothing happened while keeping my collection of memories to myself. The one I take out when nobody's looking. It's a punishment as much as a luxury but only because punishments are meant to teach a lesson and I haven't learned mine yet. If I had, I wouldn't be here, adding more to the stack.

"Gia," Roz sighs, the pain in his voice as unmistakable as if it were written on his face.

I fight a wince. I don't *want* to hurt Roz. I just don't know what else to do.

I don't know what I'm doing, period.

"We already have—"

"Heads up!"

The ball lands next to our feet and I don't even have to look to know it was Fletcher's doing. *Jerkoff.*

Pixie smirks. *She's a jerkoff, too.*

I tilt my head to the side, telling Roz, "I'll play your spot," then place myself where he was just standing.

As Roz stalks off the spray-painted court, I finally tear my eyes from Pixie. The second he makes it over to the sidelines, he's rocking side to side on his feet. He catches me looking and I blow him a kiss, making him crack a small smile before dropping his gaze to my outfit—a gray low-cut romper with shorts. Knee-high socks and my old-school Vans complete the look. It's not as revealing as what Pixie's rocking, but it's probably the most revealing outfit I own. Scratch that, it *is* the most revealing outfit I own. I put an unbuttoned black and white long-sleeve flannel over the top, so it's just my legs that are exposed, but I'm definitely showing more skin than I usually do.

I give Pixie another glance, checking out the dimples of Venus sitting just above her ass. Shit, that's hot. Too bad she's a jerkoff.

A game and a half later, I've got a healthy buzz going thanks to somebody's genius idea to make the team that drops the ball have to take a shot. Roz disappeared for a while, but he's back now and is talking to Johnny about who knows what. They don't seem to know each other for shit, but their lips haven't stopped moving since Roz sat in the grass next to him. And I would know because that's all I can look at. Much to the frustration of the rest of my team, my attention is just not on the game anymore. I'm not sure it ever was.

Pixie had to rush inside to get an ice pack after the ball nailed her in the back of the head. It was one of those crazy instances where someone got an eyelash in their eye and they couldn't see where they were hitting the ball.

It's me. I'm someone.

Fletcher, the concerned hero, followed after her and we've just been fucking around while we wait for them to get back and the poor lit-up net is paying the price. It's down several more lights now and is flickering every few seconds.

Pixie prances down the front porch steps—I'm pretty sure someone called her Annalise, but Pixie rolls off the tongue so much better—but instead of joining the game, she cops a squat next to none other than Mr. Roswell Fancy himself.

A couple of shitty serves later, I hear a noise so nauseating I swear my gag reflex engages all on its own and I almost dry heave. Beside Mr. Fancy, Pixie has her head thrown back on a laugh while Roz just smiles pleasantly at her, clearly immune to the foul-ass sound. I don't know if she stinks, but her laugh just sounds rank.

If this is what jealousy feels like, I don't like it. It feels like somebody put me in a salad spinner and cranked that baby to full speed. I don't know which way is up, just that I might puke if it continues any longer.

"Hey, do you want me to give you a couple tips?" a guy on my team asks me.

What?

Oh. It's my serve.

I look him over. Straight black hair, jawline clear of stubble, obnoxiously present shirt.

I'm game. Jealousy only has as much control as you give it.

My teammate wastes no time positioning himself against my back, aligning his groin perfectly with my ass to give me a pretty sizeable tip—and I'm not talking about in volleyball either. Annoying mansplaining aside, he *is* cute but not enough to get my briefs wet, not when Pixie clutches on to Roz's arm again, this time in another stomach-churning laugh.

Extracting myself from the guy at my back, I stroll off the court without so much as an explanation or an apology to my team. Jealousy, the raging bitch, is in full control now because I've given up completely.

Pixie says something to Roz, but he doesn't bother acknowledging her as he tracks my every step. At the last second, I swing around the small crowd, coming up behind him before lifting his chin and flipping my hair over my head like a shield in front of my face as I bend down to kiss him full on the mouth. Despite the fact that I'm upside down, his lips are already waiting for me as they part instantly, inviting my tongue right in. One of his hands comes up to grab the back of my head, keeping me to him.

A fake cough has me pulling back, but Roz's fingers grip a handful of hair, showing me he's not done as he nibbles my lips in a tease I feel down to my toes.

"I've been waiting to do that all week."

"No more waiting, Roz. Only doing."

"That might be a problem considering that was my last kiss."

"That one was on me," I whisper, winking at him, then tilt my head to the side, asking Pixie, "Roz is stupid hot without his shirt on, right?"

Her eyes widen before ducking left. Now, how does she know what Roz looks like with his shirt on?

"When's the last time you even saw me with a shirt on?" Roz asks me, and I squeeze my eyes closed, drawing in a breath. *Shut up, Roz.*

It's true. Roz is always one or two articles of clothing away from being naked.

"That's not the point."

I stand up, Roz's fingers gliding through my strands as I go.

"What *is* the point?" His ear-to-ear grin is so annoying.

The point is Pixie knows exactly who Roz is and I don't like her touching him, talking to him, or breathing near him, but if I say that out loud…I can't say that out loud.

"You make for nice eye candy. Okay, Roz? I was simply objectifying you," I snap before mumbling, "I have to get back to my lessons."

Roz's hand latches on to my ankle and that little smile of his changes into something so sinister my insides shudder.

"Lessons, my ass."

"I didn't think you noticed." I send a glare over to the person I would've assumed kept Roz from seeing my "lessons."

"I noticed."

All I can do is smirk smugly. If Roz's jealousy is even half as strong as mine, this should be interesting. I won't admit it openly, but will he?

"And?"

"And see what happens if he touches you again, Gia."

"Ooh, what'll happen?"

"You liked me wearing my own blood?"

The downpour in my underwear is answer enough, but I cross my arms over my chest, acting unimpressed.

"This time it won't be mine."

Daaaamn, dude. Stop showing off already.

His eyes flicking between mine turn serious as his hold on my ankle tightens. He means it. He will annihilate my teammate before I even get a chance to ask him for another "tip." But as fun as that sounds, we do need to speed things along.

I drop my arms, telling him, "He's not even my type."

"You don't have a type."

"But if I did, it wouldn't be him."

"Does he know that?"

"He who?"

Our growing smiles match each other's and, just like that, I don't want to be around anyone else.

"Are we done here or what?"

"I thought you'd never ask," Roz says, getting to his feet to take my hand. It's a little too coupley for my taste, but I remind myself it'll all be over soon.

Too soon.

"Do you want to tell me what we're supposed to do with…this?"

he asks once we're around the side of the house, his gold eyes lighting up despite his obvious confusion. He likes this shit just as much as I do; he just doesn't know it yet. Or he does and feels too guilty to admit it. Grieving and enjoying life are not parallel. They overlap, they coincide, they can live in beautiful harmony if you know how to balance them correctly. It may not feel that way at first, but after a while, the agony lessens, allowing you to find a way forward, embracing both notions openly.

I take one half of the inflatable pool I bought while Roz lifts the other and, together, we carry it to the backyard. Then with his help, we drop it in the regular pool.

"Now we need blankets, pillows, snacks, and drinks."

Roz eyes the inflatable pool floating on top of the water. "What if there's a hole?"

"Then we swim." I turn for the house, muttering, "Or sink."

Chapter 12

GIA

"**W**hy didn't you just do online schooling during the year you missed instead of making it up later? I'm sure the public schools have programs like that."

"Worm," I say, and Roz drops a gummy worm into my mouth.

"You could've gotten a tutor like I did."

I scowl over at him, swallowing most of the worm whole. "You're kidding, right? Private tutors cost crazy money, Roz."

He bites his bottom lip into his mouth, so I decide against stating the obvious. Roz comes from money and I do not. But even if I did, I wouldn't have used that kind of change on myself, not while my mom was suffering. We poured everything we had into getting Mom better, and it still wasn't enough.

Roz feeds me a potato chip, then faces the inky sky again. "It's just…you don't exactly strike me as the type to want to go to a school like that."

"It meant a lot to my mom for some reason. She went there, too." To be honest, I never really understood why she wanted me to go to the all-girls academy so bad. My grandpa sent her there because after her own mother died, she no longer had a woman's influence in her life, and he didn't want that for her. A woman's touch, as they used to say. But I did have my mom. Mostly. For the first sixteen years anyway.

Maybe she was planning ahead. Preparing. It's what I'd do.

I reach for another worm from the bag on Roz's chest.

"Is she the reason you like being outside so much, too?"

"Yeah." Times like this, it's where I feel most like myself. For the last few hours, we've been lying side by side inside the inflatable pool, talking, eating, appreciating the view above us. Roz and I skipped the fireworks, but it feels like the stars are putting on their own show for us.

Every few minutes, we bump into one of the sides of the in-ground pool; otherwise, it's been a pretty smooth float. No holes so far.

"My mom loved to be outdoors. She was big on, um," I side-eye Roz, but he's still gazing up at the stars, "adventures. So we were always outside somewhere, off searching for the next one."

"And birds."

"And birds," I say, grinning, because some birds you don't have to search for at all. Some birds find you.

After a long pause, Roz changes the subject, saying, "So, you skateboard, you ride four-wheelers, what else can you do?"

"Want to find out?"

We turn our heads to each other at the same time.

"I'm not sure I'm your type." His tone is teasing, but there's a layer of genuine curiosity tucked in there, too.

"Type… Yeah, you might be right. I don't think I have one. I like everybody."

The water below us shakes from Roz's laugh.

"You really don't."

"No one I've hooked up with had any similarities, so…" *Aside from being dope-ass people that like a good time.*

"I'm not talking about hook-ups."

"What else is there?"

Roz rolls to his side to face me full-on, and I immediately try to roll away from him, hugging the inflatable pool's wall.

Laughing, Roz gives me a quick tug, making me land on my back again.

"Have you ever been in love?"

I don't blink as I meet his eyes and say, "Every single day."

His eyes harden but I explain, telling him, "Every day, I fall in love with *something.* The rush I get when I learn something new on my skateboard or four-wheeler. The excitement I feel when I teach someone else. The surprised smile from a stranger passing me on the street when I go out of my way to greet them. The smell of the ripe fruit at the summer farmer's market. The sound of a baby's laughter filling my dad's restaurant. The colors of the sky just before the sun sets."

Roz sits quietly for a moment, nodding his head like he's trying to follow along, then says, "And yet, you only showed me a sunrise?"

"Maybe I'd already fallen in love with something that day," I say without stopping to think.

"Have you ever fallen in love with a person?"

I shrug. "Yeah." He already knows about Rowdy.

"Romantically?"

"I…don't think so."

"Why?"

I turn the question over in my head, picturing what it'd look like—being in love with a person like that.

"Because I don't think you can walk away from someone you're truly in love with."

"I disagree."

My eyes dash to Roz's.

"I think if it was to save them from pain, you'd do anything for the person you love, even if it meant walking away."

"Would you?"

His gaze falls to my lips, but he just shrugs the shoulder he's not lying on.

"Have *you* ever been in love with anyone?"

Another half-shrug.

"Well, there's always tomorrow," I tell him, and with one push on his shoulder, Roz rolls on to his back, too, causing the entire pool to heave around us.

"And why not today?"

My thumb covers the moon and I close an eye, telling him, "Because it's almost midnight already."

"Were you some kind of scout or something?"

Moving my hand around, pretending to measure stuff in the distance, I nod.

"I'm just fucking around." I drop my hand, laughing. "I have no idea what time it is."

"I wonder if Annalise is still around."

Her name coming out of Roz's mouth makes me dizzy, like being in the salad spinner all over again, and I threaten to kick him overboard, like literally, with both feet.

"So that's what that kiss was all about." The twinkle in his eye is brighter than the stars over our heads. "I knew it. You were jealous."

My scoff is a little too loud, even to my own ears.

"She was nice…" he says, leaving it open-ended. *She was nice… but? But what?*

I roll my eyes, knowing he's watching my every expression. "She had a nice body, I'll give you that. Pretty face, tight ass, great rack."

"Maybe I got it wrong then. Maybe you wanted Annalise for yourself."

I shake my head so fast I give myself momentary vertigo.

"Stop saying her name. It sounds…" I say, leaving it open-ended, too. *Read between those lines, Roz.*

In one quick motion, he's on top of me, the bags of gummy worms and chips scattering out over the blankets we're on. The entire thing—the swift movement, the additional weight, the lost snacks—has me chuckling deep in my chest as I try to push him off with no luck whatsoever. There's just a lot of sloshing, kind of like being on a water bed, with a few crunches from the chips somehow making their way under my body.

"Wanna share her instead?"

We both stop moving, everything coming to a halt.

I try to keep my voice as unaffected as possible, telling him, "Nah, I'm good."

"Have you ever?"

"Had a threesome?"

He nods.

"Have you?"

"You love a question for a question, huh?" He glances at my lips, saying, "Yes, I have," before meeting my eyes again, the pupils in his much larger now. "Two guys, one girl."

"Lucky girl."

"You?"

"Once. Two girls, one guy."

"Lucky guy."

A moment of silence follows, then Roz changes his tune, saying, "I hate him," and I smirk, drawing his attention south again.

"Never mind. I don't think I could."

"Don't think you could what?"

"Share you."

Our eyes connect, and there's a raw honesty in his that he should probably be hiding a little better.

What do mine look like right now?

"Today you showed up in the sexiest thing I've ever seen—"

"Was it the tube socks?"

He groans loudly, saying, "It was the tube socks."

My laughter bounces off our vinyl enclosure.

"You showed up in your sexy-as-fuck tube socks, your one-piece thing—"

"It's a romper," I clarify, rubbing my finger on the skin between his eyebrows.

"—whatever it's called. And your tits looked amazing. And your ass looked even better. All week I've been keeping my hands to my-self, but today almost broke me. Then I had to sit there and watch some asshole put his hands on you."

"Technically, he didn't use his hands at all."

Roz drops his face to my chest, breathing out, "Jesus Christ."

"Would it help if I told you it was small?"

He waits a minute, then asks, "Was it?" his breath fanning down my cleavage, causing my nipples to stiffen.

"I don't think so." I think back. "He only had a chubby, so it's hard to tell for sure, but the way it was pressed between my ass—"

Roz's head pops up. "He's fucking dead."

I grapple with his shoulders, trying to keep him in our "boat," but it's actually pretty hard when you're also wheezing from laughing too hard, and I have to resort to wrapping my legs around his waist.

"Good gawd, Roz. I was joking." Kind of. Not really. The guy was on his way to being fully erect, and he did seem like he was packing, but my jealousy at seeing Roz with Pixie blocked it all out, straight erased him from my memory. If Roz hadn't brought the guy up, I would've forgotten all about him. Nothing about him was worth collecting.

"Your sense of humor sucks," Roz says, settling himself so his weight's on me again.

I roll my eyes, pulling his hair at the ends. "I'm hilarious. You're just a bad drunk. And mean."

Roz's own chubby thickens between my thighs, and I have to silence my moan before it can escape.

"I thought you liked it rough."

Bringing his hand up, he tugs his fingers through my hair roughly, and this moan I can't suppress at all.

"Don't start what you can't finish," I warn, my thighs tightening around his hips to bring him even closer. Roz may have a dirty mouth, but can he deliver?

"Baby, I'll have you finishing before I even start."

Gold and black eyes stare back at me in an animalistic, crazed, feral way—exactly how I feel—then his hard length lines up with my pussy, grinding mercilessly, the dampness already there soaking the material of my underwear, probably all the way through to my romper.

My eyes clamp down on a sneeze, and I instantly turn my face into the crook of my elbow. Nothing actually comes out, but it's a habit engrained in my brain from elementary school to sneeze there and now it just happens automatically.

"What the—" Roz's weight disappears as he lifts himself. "Are you okay?"

I just nod, trying to pull him down, but he remains suspended above me.

"Is it allergies?"

"Not really?"

He's peering down at me with that concern he wears like a badge of honor, and when his penetrating gaze refuses to let up, I sigh, telling him, "It happens when I'm horny, okay?" *Like, chill.*

The corners of his lips twitch.

"For real?"

"Yeah, it's so stupid." And weird and sometimes even embarrassing. "I have no idea why, but I sneeze when I'm turned on."

"You're good then?"

"Ye—"

My response dies on my tongue as Roz lowers himself, circling his hips so his dick hits my pussy like a tornado, around and around. Quickly losing myself in the rotations, I stop caring if I get consumed or not. I'm just chasing the storm, looking for a good time. *A good time for a short time.*

"Gia?"

With a hand buried against my scalp, Roz angles my chin skyward, biting my jaw, and the moan from the delicious pain is all I can manage as a response.

"Gia, I'm not ready to kiss you yet, but I'm going to lose my mind if I don't touch you soon."

"Tell me," I breathe out, needing to hear his words as much as he does. "Tell me what you want and you can have anything."

His grip in my hair tightens, and I cry out, my pussy spasming.

"Fuck, that makes me so hard, baby. I want everyone to hear you scream for me. Can you do that? Can you let me touch you and make you come apart, so the street will know who's fucking you?"

Wicked words from a sinfully deep voice make for a dangerous weapon. One I'm ready to take the brunt of. Now.

In reply, I arch my back clear off the flimsy vinyl beneath me, hooking a leg around his back and meeting Roz's swirling hips with my own. It's difficult to pull off, but Roz takes the challenge and grinds into me that much rougher, creating waves both in the water and my core.

Our breaths stutter over each other's mouths, and I consider closing the gap.

"Don't," he warns.

"Why?"

"Because I won't fucking stop. When I get my lips on you again, Gia, I won't. Fucking. Stop."

"Just my lips though, right?" He came up with some pretty good alternatives before that didn't count as kissing—according to Roz. And me too, I guess.

A light bulb above his head flares to life, and he tells me to sit up. But Roz's eyes are glossed over like a man without reason, and I need to know how we can make this possible. The inflatable pool barely fits the length of his body alone, so him trying to scoot down any farther is out of the question. Thanks to all our frenzied movement, we've already disturbed the water to the point of large waves splashing over the wall and onto our blankets.

"Sixty-nine?" I offer, saying, "I won't even kiss you. Just suck your cock like a fucking popsicle."

"Fuuuck, your mouth."

"Yeah, that's the gist of it. You fuck my mouth."

Roz curses, his dick thrusting into me so hard I whimper. Whimper. Gawd, who am I? Next I'll be mewling.

I'm not fucking mewling.

"You got a mouth on you, too," Roz grits out, his words choppy like the waves surrounding us.

"And I know how to use it."

He's still trying to prolong things. A part of me just wants him to redeem that last kiss already. Pair that with a hand job and this'll all be over in a matter of minutes.

A bigger part of me wants Roz to make good on his word to make Greek Sac hear my screams.

"But..."

"But what?"

Roz's body tenses above mine as his eyebrows sink faster than the Titanic.

Oh, shit. This might be a first.

Chapter 13

A chorus of voices echoes from the side of the house somewhere.

"Did you just…" Gia glances down between us.

"What? No. I didn't come in my pants from some dry humping. Jesus, give me *some* credit."

A glare out to the corner of the house proves whoever's over there is getting closer as flashlight beams bounce across the grass.

Fuck me. This is bad. I mean it was good. So fucking good. But now it's going to shit.

Sixty-nine with Gia? Yes, fucking please. I want to do everything with Gia. All of it. I just don't think I'll get to. She's told me as much, over and over and fucking over again. So, I need to make sure whatever I do get to do with her, I do better than I've ever done anything in my life and this whole pool-inside-a-pool situation isn't helping. Neither is the audience on its way out to us.

"We gotta go," I tell her, then quickly latch on to the cement lip when we bump into the pool's edge again. Gia finally catches on and climbs out ahead of me. After passing her all the crap we brought out, she wraps it all into a blanket that I grab once I'm back on solid ground.

She's going to run.

I know it. This is the good part and she's going to disappear, leaving me with a monster of a hard-on and a shitload of regret.

"I, uh—" she starts as soon as we're inside and, dropping the blanket sack, I spin around so fast her head jerks back.

"No. Nope. You're going up to my room and I'm going to make you come so hard, you'll swear you're still seeing stars."

I don't care how I get to do it, what I get to use, I'm making Gia come. Twice, preferably.

Gia grins. "I was going to say I need to use the bathroom."

"Oh." Okay. "You're not going to take another bath, are you?"

Her chuckle is my only answer as she closes the door behind her. So, is that a no? Or…

With a shake of my head, I clean everything up before stopping off at the cookie jar for a handful of condoms.

I take the fact that there's no water running as a good sign as I pass the bathroom on the way up to my room.

After fluffing a pillow for the third time, I give up and stare at the door, talking myself out of pouncing on Gia the second she walks in. Except, she never comes. I wait for at least forty minutes—okay, seconds—before I'm back downstairs looking for her.

Unsurprisingly, the door to the bathroom is wide open with the inside dark as night.

Fuck. She ran.

A hushed voice, not exactly a whisper, but definitely lowered for privacy, draws me over to the other stairwell—the one leading to my roommates' rooms.

The entire house is dark, so I can only make out shapes, but I'd know Gia's body anywhere and she's pushed up against what might just be Fletcher's.

Blood pounding in my ears, I start forward only to freeze when I hear Gia out of breath and threatening, *"Don't go back in there."*

"Please. Like you're any better?" This whisper is different. It's male and full of resentment. "You can't tell me you're not using Roz like you've used every other person that was stupid enough to fall at your feet."

"That's not the same and you fucking know it, Fletcher."

Called it.

But why? What the fuck are they doing?

"Might as well be." His laugh holds zero humor. "He's just as oblivious."

I take another step in their direction, happy to show my roommate just how oblivious I am, but Gia shoves away from him, pointing in his face. "Lay a finger on her and I'll run your dick through the meat grinder at Al's."

Her? Wait, hold up. Now that, I will admit, has me scratching my head.

"What's going on?" my voice booms when Gia's a few feet away, eyes downcast.

Both she and Fletcher jump, but look at each other instead of me. What the hell did I just break up?

"Who were you guys talking about?"

"Annalise—"

"Annalise is set for the night. Right, Fletcher?"

I've never been more grateful for lack of lighting than I am right now. That's who they're talking about? But, why can't Fletcher touch her?

Gia waits until my roommate nods, then skirts around me, shaking her head.

With a scowl Fletcher probably can't see, I turn on my heel, following Gia. Luckily, she takes the staircase up to my room and doesn't try to flee. I'd still chase her ass, but I'm glad I don't have to.

"Do you like my roommate?" I ask before my door's even closed all the way.

Keeping her back to me, she says, "Johnny's dope," distractedly as her hand trails over a bare spot on the wall that used to hold posters.

"Stop fucking with me, Gia."

She spins around with fire in her eyes but silence on her tongue. Those eyes move though, from me to around me. Above me, beside me, everywhere. This is the first time she's seeing my room after I removed my old life from it.

"Fletcher. Do you like Fetcher or not?"

"Fletcher's tolerable on a normal day."

"And what about today?"

"Today he can fry ice."

"What does that mean?"

"It means you've been away from New York for too long." She scoffs, no longer looking anywhere near me as she stares down at the oak flooring.

Taking her in, I realize she's shoeless. Actually, both her shoes and socks are missing. When did she take them off?

"Where are your shoes? And your socks?"

I was only half-joking about finding the knee-highs sexy. They make Gia *Gia*.

"Ask Annalise," she says a little too easily. Earlier, Gia visibly reacted when I said that girl's name aloud, but now she's using it… What? To throw in my face? Does she really find Annalise a threat? The girl whose laugh sounds like a fox's ear-piercing bark in the dead of night?

Annalise tried everything she could to get me to notice her, but with Gia on her way, there was just no hope for her. The only reason I talked to Annalise was to get back at Gia for saying that shit to Fletcher about disappearing after tonight.

But none of that explains the thing downstairs with Fletcher.

"Annalise? The girl Fletcher can't sleep with? Why is that again?"

"Because she's off-limits right now."

"Because she flirted with me earlier? Because I lied and said I'd be interested in a threesome with her?"

Her eyes fly to mine, but I'm already pinning her with my own fiery gaze. If Gia wants to go down this road, then she better fucking come prepared. Since she appeared in my life, I've felt jealousy so fucking deep, I could've sworn the devil himself replaced the marrow in my bones with the visceral emotion. And Gia's reaction to Annalise shows she feels it, too.

Her humorless laugh pierces my skin, needling its way in. That's jealousy, isn't it? She's jealous?

"Narcissism doesn't look good on you, Roz."

"Yeah, well, jealousy looks incredible on you," I argue, giving it one last try to get her to admit it.

"Fletcher was right. You really are oblivious."

"Fuck Fletcher. And fuck you, too."

Maybe I am oblivious. Maybe I've read everything fucking wrong from the very beginning. Maybe…

"Kiss me."

One command and I'm across the room in two strides, lifting Gia off her feet. Her legs swing around to cross at the ankles behind my back seconds before I slam her against the wall, my nose running the length of her jawline.

"Are you sure? Because if I kiss you now, I'm not coming up for air." I only got one kiss left; I plan on making it last. Fuck morning. Fuck tomorrow. It's just her and me, me and her.

She laughs, the sound wild—like her. "Am I gonna have to revive you?"

My laugh counters hers, and I tell her, "You already did," before sealing my lips to hers.

She takes what I give her, her nails biting into the sides of my neck as she gives it right back, too, and we kiss for I don't know how long: months, years, lifetimes. I never want this kiss to end. I want my mouth on Gia always.

Drawing her bottom lip between my teeth, I swear a purring sort of sound comes from her chest, making mine fucking swell.

With Gia pinned against the wall with my lower half, I tug her flannel down over her shoulders, pushing her tits together with the material grasped in my hands. I kiss my way down to her cleavage, murmuring, "Where's your bra?" With the exception of Salvy's funeral, I've only seen Gia wear sports bras, but now she's not wearing a bra at all. Wait, was she wearing one at the funeral?

"Where's yours?" she returns, her hands restless in my hair.

I grin against her skin before I catch the neckline of her romper with my chin and pull it down, sucking her bare nipple into my mouth. Fuck, she tastes good.

"Roz," she moans, trying to buck into me, but with me holding her to the wall, she's not going anywhere.

"Perfect," I say around her peak. Absolutely fucking perfect.

Gia removes the flannel completely, dropping it somewhere by our feet, and with my mouth busy feasting on her tits, I slide the straps of her romper down an arm at a time until her entire chest is on display.

I jerk away from the wall and walk us over to my bed, setting Gia at the edge of the mattress when I drop to my knees. She immediately tries to scoot back, but I bite one of her nipples to keep her from moving. Her yelp drips with desire.

"Don't move," I mumble out while frenching the fuck out of the reddened nipple.

I slide two of my fingers in through the opening of her shorts at her thigh, going straight for the front of her underwear.

What the fuck? Where is it?

"Do you have a tickling fetish you forgot to mention?" Gia asks when I keep fumbling around.

"Where's the hole?" I ask against her skin.

"Oh, I'm sorry. I thought you knew your way around. Do you need a map or will simple directions get you there?"

"No, the dick hole."

"Umm, Roz—"

"In your underwear." Every pair of men's underwear has one, it's how we piss without pulling our pants down. I thought I'd be able to slip right in to finger Gia, but what feels like an impenetrable wall of fabric has me struggling to get anywhere.

"These are boxer briefs for women. They don't have a hole."

"But I thought—"

"I wear both men's and women's boxer briefs." She laughs. "Today I wore women's."

I didn't even know there were boxer briefs for women. That information would've been useful before I made myself look like a fucking idiot.

I yank the crotch to both her romper and her boxer briefs to one side, breathing, "Fuck, baby," when I feel her bare pussy with the tips of my fingers.

"You're gonna need to be a bit more specific than that, cowboy. Tell me what you want and it's yours."

No fucking problem.

I kiss a trail down her stomach, biting along the way, so she can feel it through the romper. Over her hips, with a quick kiss to the inside of her thigh, I stop when I reach my destination and say, "I want your pussy, Gia." My mouth's less than a centimeter away from her pussy, so when I lick my lips, I lick hers, too. Her ass jolts off the bed and I take the opportunity to grab her airborne bottom half with my free hand, dragging her forward until she's practically hanging off the mattress to let my nose nuzzle between her folds.

I wait, just wait, listening to her breathy moans infuse my room, then with one long lick up her slit, I freeze at the top when Gia's hands tangle in my hair again, this time so much needier.

I honestly don't think I've ever been harder as I spread her legs wider, my lips teasing the ones between her hips. I kiss her pussy like I kiss her mouth, swirling my tongue at a dizzying pace, and using the tip of my tongue, I spell out my name—my full fucking name—as my own version of a branding. It's not long before her moans grow as frantic as her hands in my hair. Those same hands try to push me away, even as her heels dig into my back, not letting me actually go anywhere.

She's a fucking wreck and I've only just begun.

My name becomes a chant that's no doubt making its way down my stairwell and out the front door. "Roz." Gasp. "Roz." Gasp. "I'm close." Gasp. "Roz?" Gasp.

Not yet, I'd tell Gia if I wasn't currently tongue-fucking her because if she's coherent enough to ask, then she's not nearly close enough.

I replace my tongue with a finger between her slick pussy walls and her thighs instantly start to shake around my head.

Hers drops back as she moans my name loudly when I add another finger, telling her, "I want you to come on my face, baby."

The heat around my fingers begins constricting, so I twist the digits as I pump them in and out, then I'm sucking on her clit.

Incoherent pleas spill from her mouth as soon as I press my tongue flat against her swollen tip, letting her ride my face as hard as she needs to.

There we go. Now she's ready.

I add a roll to my tongue and a scream rips from her throat that I know most, if not all, the fraternities on the block heard.

"Stand," I say through damp lips, kissing her thigh.

"Dude…no."

"I told you until you were seeing stars, remember?"

Her laugh is hollow and wobbly. "Seeing stars? I'm swimming in them."

Around a smirk, I nip her skin, letting go just as quickly to repeat, "Stand."

Still clutching my hair, she gets to her feet, watching silently as the romper around her waist falls to the floor. And holy shit. An entire outfit just gone.

I sit back on my heels, turning my head to bite the hand that falls to my shoulder to keep from biting the rest of her milky white skin. Goddamn. She's so fucking beautiful.

"Promise you'll only wear rompers from now on."

When my eyes finally meet hers again, they're creased at the edges, and there's an icy breeze to her tone when she says, "No promises, Roz."

I nod, letting my gaze trail down her body. Perfectly rounded tits that she usually smashes under sports bras—but not today. A tight tummy she prefers to hide under a gigantic sweater—but not today. Toned thighs she typically covers with bulky jeans—but not fucking today.

My hands frame her hips, bringing her forward until my forehead rests on her waistband. I've got her pussy on my mouth, nose, fingers, and still, *still*, the smell of the real thing so close taunts me all over again until I almost bend just to take another lick.

Instead, I glide my pointer finger along the crotch part of her underwear, loving the way she fucking shivers, then crook my finger inside the black cotton, teasing her wet lips with my knuckle before dragging the briefs down her legs to join her discarded romper. I kiss from her toes up to her belly button, and when I stop, Gia's watching me through guarded eyes she didn't have a minute ago.

"Stop trying to seduce me already. I'm here. I'm ready. Let's fuck."

She wants my words as long as they're not promises. She wants to fuck as long as I don't seduce her.

"I'm not seducing you." I guide her back on to the bed, positioning her the same as before, just at the edge. "I'm memorizing you. I'm drawing this out—"

"No shit," she mutters under her breath.

"—so that I can savor every single moment." Collect them, like Gia said. "In my dreams, I've already had you in every way possible, and I'm fucking sick that I won't get to do those things to you in real life. So instead, I'm trying to make sure the next time you come to me in my sleep, I get it right. How you sound when your breath catches when I put my lips on you. How soft your skin feels under my fingertips. How hard your nipples get after I suck on them. How fucking good your nails feel digging into my scalp just before you come on my tongue." I groan at the memory, my dick fucking begging to be touched. "How your pussy tastes. How *you* taste, Gia."

Everything I say I do and every reaction she gives, I catalog the hell out of.

After giving her collarbone a tender kiss, I glance up at her, and it almost looks like her eyes are misty, but then she smirks and they're clear.

Are mine misty then?

No.

"Your turn. Tell me what you want, baby."

"A million right nows. I can't change yesterday. Tomorrow doesn't matter. I just want this moment right here, right now, with you looking at me like I hold the world in my hands. I want it a million more times," her voice wanders off, "but tonight will have to do."

"Why?" I *could* give her this a million more times. *If she'd let me.*

Gia averts her gaze, saying, "Stand."

I push to my feet, watching silently as she reaches out to undo my boardshorts. Without taking my eyes off Gia, I step out of the shorts, kicking them to the side.

She eyes my rigid cock, then my face.

"You're the star, Roz."

I shake my head, feeling my body instinctively sway from one side to the other.

Gia's hands shoot out, catching my hips to keep me from rocking. "Don't go yet, cowboy. I need you here still."

"Lose the rings," I rasp, and keeping eye contact, she does just that before bringing one hand around to fist my cock. Up and down with a half spin at the head, Gia keeps up the pattern until precum starts to build on the tip of my cock and I have to pull her hand away.

"This is what you want?" My voice is thick like molasses.

"I want…" *Come on. Come on.* "I want you to fuck me like you'll never get to again."

Chapter 14

ROZ

Gia's words float like a butterfly, but sting like a motherfucking wasp.

She said I could have anything I asked for but that's not true at all. She won't give me what I want, what I really want.

What exactly do I want?

I don't know what I want, only what I don't want, and I don't want to snowboard anymore, a decision my body wholly refuses to surrender to. Boarding used to be the only thing I did want, yet every day, I deliberately deny what my heart craves most.

Is that what Gia's doing? What happened to her that she won't even try anything other than a one-night stand?

This past week wreaked havoc on my self-control, but I know—*I fucking know*—she'll disappear the second I take things to the next level. Like the white fluff on a dandelion, she'll drift away on the faintest of breaths, leaving me to watch in helpless wonder as she goes.

I'm not like every other guy she's fucked around with. This isn't like that. She could've screwed me already, just as easily as I could've screwed her, but the fact that she hasn't yet means I can't be the only one that feels this undeniable connection we have.

Fletcher's wrong. I'm not as oblivious as all the others. I just don't want to quit Gia. I quit the most important thing in my life. *I quit my life.* I don't want to quit Gia and Gia wants what I'm giving her right here, right now, by looking at her like she holds the world in her hands. Not just because I'm losing my shit watching her stroke my cock, but because she does. She's got some kind of hold on me and I don't want her letting go anytime soon.

I twist my finger through a loose curl at her shoulder.

"Lie back."

She cocks an eyebrow. "Missionary? How basic of you."

One hand gripped to the back of her knee, I flip her to her stomach and give her ass a hard smack, making her suck in a breath.

She's probably worried about her back, but I plan on making her forget soon enough. I don't need to see her scars to remember they're there; they've already been burned into my brain. I hate not knowing how she got them, but they're one more thing that makes Gia who she is. Perfection is boring, and Gia is anything but boring, which somehow makes her perfect—imperfectly perfect.

Coming down on top of her, I run my lips over the marred skin, telling her how beautiful she is and, slowly but surely, the tension leaves her back and limbs.

With my erection rubbing against her wet slit, her moans quickly turn to pleas.

She wants this moment, but I want more, so I gotta stretch it out like I've been doing all week.

I reach under her, using my hand to spread her wetness around, then I dip two fingers inside her pussy. With her head turned to the side, I snatch up her lips in a punishing kiss.

Her ass arches up, knocking me to the side, but I push her back down with my thigh, sandwiching my hand between her body and the mattress. She grinds into my palm and my hips thrust forward, the feel of my bare cock on her bare skin a little too enticing. Fuck, I could blow just like this, and judging by Gia's jerky movements, she's already on her way to an orgasm, too.

"Who's making you come apart, baby?"

"Condom."

"A condom isn't doing this to you."

Gia's ragged voice rises an octave. "Get a fucking condom."

I slow all of my pumps, lifting my leg along with the pressure she needs.

A snarl rips from her throat, and I have to hide my smile against her shoulder. "Come for me one more time and *then* I'll fuck you."

She pushes up from the bed, swiping a condom from the pile on my nightstand before pinning me with a glare to say, "If I wanted to hump a mattress, I could've stayed home for that."

"Uh…" *What now?*

Using her teeth, she rips the package clean open, but I manage to take the condom from her grasp, holding it just out of reach.

"I'm ready, Roz."

"Sorry." I shake my head. "You're not ready until I say you are."

Watching Gia's eyes as they track my movements carefully, I roll the condom down over my shaft, pinching the air pocket at the tip.

Her hungry gaze meets mine.

"One more."

Lips pursed to the side, she reclines back on the pillows and does something I never could've seen coming…she starts fingering herself. Right here in front of me, just plays herself like a fucking fiddle while I sit open-mouthed, mesmerized.

Her eyes focus on mine, but my gaze drops lower to watch the show I don't think even I could've dreamed up.

Unbeknownst to me, my hand glides over her thigh to join the action, but Gia slaps it away with her free hand, never breaking her swirling pace on her clit with the other.

I dart my eyes up to hers.

"You're not the only one that's been suffering all week."

Fuuck.

"What do you picture?" I ask, reaching around her to grab the lube out of my nightstand.

She watches me drizzle the liquid over her hand and pussy, moaning when it gets between the two, making it easier for her to swirl.

"You," she breathes, and I pour some in my hand, too, before dropping the bottle off the side of the bed.

My tongue traces my top lip, still tasting her, and I lean back on my dry hand, taking my cock in my other.

"Every night?" I ask, stroking myself using the lube.

She nods once, her mouth falling open on a silent moan as her fingers rub small circles like she's trying to get out a stain, which is ironic, considering I'll never be able to get this memory out. *Thank fuck.*

On a gasp, her eyes slam closed and the bed vibrates with…something. The last shred of my restraint fleeing my body? Gia coming on her own fingers while she calls out for me and only me? Both? I don't know, or care. I just know I'm ready, too. So. Fucking. Ready.

In the next instant, I rip her hand away, replacing it with my straining cock. Her throbbing walls hug my cock tightly and her eyes fly open with another gasp as I sink further into her. Without letting her recover, I start moving, thrusting into her with long, measured strokes, trying to prolong her aftershocks for as long as possible. I may not know all the different kinds of underwear women have, but I do know their second orgasms are more intense than the original and can go on for longer, too.

When I dip for a kiss, she turns her face into my shoulder, making me pause for just a second, but then she bites the skin into her mouth so hard, my spine stiffens and my cock swells even more, demanding movement.

"Fuck," I breathe, my arms already growing shaky as I resume my thrusts.

Gia's nails rake down my back, leaving scratches in their wake, and I hiss through clenched teeth.

Fuck, fuck, fuck.

I'm working double time, trying to hold back my own release, but she's spinning me into a web of pleasure that's rapidly draining my strength the more she winds it. Whoever said condoms dull the sensation clearly didn't have sex with Gia. The girl is fucking everywhere. All around me she scratches, bites, praises. *Holy fuck.* She acts like my mouth is dirty, but she's about to make me come just from the whispers falling from hers.

I hike one of her legs over my back, getting a better, deeper angle. One that we both stop momentarily to appreciate. My nails bite into her thigh, holding her in place while I continue to thrust into her center. Her head falls back on a moan, so I sink my teeth into the soft flesh at her exposed throat, groaning from all the sensations.

There's a fucking flood, and I know this is my chance. I'm not sure why, but I need Gia's eyes on me. I need her to see what she's doing to me. What I'm doing to her.

Gently sliding my other hand under her to palm the back of her head, I prop her up, but as soon as our eyes connect, she instantly slams hers shut again.

"Don't go yet," I repeat her words back to her, "I need you here still."

She opens them slowly, hesitantly, staring into mine with such uncertainty, it almost breaks me wide open.

This is why she needs to see. So she can feel me like I feel her.

I keep her eyes and with one more deep thrust, rubbing against her clit with the base of my cock, Gia clenches up her body around mine, screaming out my name louder than the first time. So much louder.

My balls tighten up and all my muscles tense, then I'm fucking exploding, my own orgasm coming so hard, the elbow holding me up almost buckles as I drop my forehead to Gia's.

Jesus Christ.

Gia never looks away from me even after our breaths start to even out.

"That was—"

"Yeah," she cuts me off. "I know. Missionary sucks."

I rear back like I've been slapped with a fucking frying pan.

"Bullshit. I already told you I'd know if you were faking, and there was nothing fake about this. My face, my hand, and now my entire fucking lap is soaked. Hell, I'm practically covered in the proof you didn't fake anything."

She pushes on my shoulders, not meeting my eyes anymore, and I pull out, quickly taking care of the condom.

Her legs are over the side of the bed as she looks for her clothes, but I wrap an arm around her waist, holding her tightly but gently. "I don't want you to leave like this. Stay, please."

She glances at me over her shoulder, and this time, there's no mistaking the water filling her eyes.

"It wasn't supposed to be like this. *You* weren't supposed to be like this."

So she did feel it. She *does* feel it. She knows this is different. This has potential. *We* have potential. But she's scared.

"You've already stayed the night here before. It'll be just like that."

There's a riot inside my chest. An absolute uprising to the point that I'm pretty sure Gia can hear my heart thundering its objection. This isn't just like that. This is so much more.

"It's easier if I don't."

I bark out a watery laugh, stunned by the foreign sound. Am I crying? Excluding the day I failed to dig Salvy out from the avalanche's debris in time, I can't remember a single time I've actually cried.

What the hell?

"I don't want you driving right now. Just…sleep here. I'm just asking you to sleep in my bed for the night. Nothing else."

As the seconds tick by, I start to lose hope, so pretending like there's only one choice worth choosing, I lie back, taking Gia with me, positioning us like that first night in my room with her head on my shoulder and my feelings on my invisible sleeve.

"Don't go yet. I need you—"

"You don't though. You don't need me."

My eyebrows pull together in the dark.

"I *want* you here still. You said I needed to tell you what I want and you'd give it to me."

"Roz—"

"I want you here. I want to fall asleep with you in my arms and wake up with you still in them. No running off."

A long silent pause follows that eats away at my confidence until finally, she sighs, saying, "I'll stay for breakfast."

After a while, she melts into me, and I breathe out a shaky sigh of my own, knowing that even though I haven't won the war, I won the battle—tonight.

Chapter 15

ROZ

The next morning I'm standing at the kitchen counter, waiting for my coffee to finish brewing, when Fletcher sits up from his spot on the couch, cradling his head in his hands, and groaning.

He mumbles out a greeting when he finds me eyeballing him, but I don't bother returning the gesture. Something set Gia off last night, and as much as I'd like to believe it was blind jealousy, my roommate did seem suspicious as fuck with the way he was talking to her, and since neither one came out and told me what exactly went down, I have no choice but to assume he is.

"You get in a fight with a vacuum or something?" he asks, and I follow his gaze to the dark purple bruise on my shoulder.

"Or something."

He mutters something to himself, but Annalise, stumbling down the other set of stairs, keeps me from asking him to repeat it. Her short hair's sticking out in all different directions and her make-up-lined eyes are glassy as all hell. She widens them when she sees us staring back at her and says, "Umm, hi?"

Hi? Did she not know we'd be here? In our own house?

"Bad night?" I guess.

There's hungover and then there's this. She's the one that really looks like she got into a fight with a vacuum cleaner. No hickeys, but, her hair, it definitely took a beating.

Annalise squints up the stairs she just came from, saying, "I'm not sure. The last thing I remember is us," her eyes skitter over to

Fletcher, "kissing, then puking all over somebody's…feet? Maybe? Maybe not." Her hand goes to her forehead, pressing her palm against it like a human bandage. "I don't know. It all went black after that."

I busy myself pouring the coffee into my mug. She doesn't even know whose room she passed out in? That seems…dangerous. I mean, not in this house. Nobody living here would even think about messing with an incoherent girl. If I even thought they would…

I dart my eyes over to Fletcher again, but Gia bounds down my staircase, robbing every ounce of my attention. She's back in her romper, but has the flannel from last night buttoned all the way to the top. She's also wearing one of my beanies pulled down low over her forehead, but she's still barefoot.

"Gia," Fletcher says, "what are you still doing here?"

I eye him, then Gia.

She says, "Breakfast," like it's the only possible reason before her face splits into a grin spotting Annalise. I'm already preparing for a catfight between the two, but then Gia asks her, "How was your sleep?" before glaring at Fletcher.

This is…new.

Or is it? Her words from last night come rushing back to me. *"Lay a finger on her and I'll run your dick through the meat grinder at Al's."*

Well well. So it wasn't jealousy after all. Gia didn't want a girl, a girl she didn't even seem to like, to be taken advantage of while she was incapacitated, so she went for Fletcher's jugular to ensure she wasn't.

Gia enters the kitchen and proceeds to steal the coffee right out of my hands, taking a small drink.

Personally, I'd prefer a violent tongue down my throat as a morning greeting but…caffeine.

She hands it back, barely glancing in my direction before facing Annalise again.

"I woke up alone, so," Annalise says, her gaze plummeting, "you know?"

"I do." Gia nods. "I didn't know where to put you, but Fletcher here offered his own bed. Isn't he sweet?" There's no mistaking the undertone in her statement.

Fletcher frowns at Gia, but I frown at him. She's in the right. Fletcher *should've* offered up his room to the drunk girl. Had I known about the situation beforehand, I would've insisted Annalise take mine. I don't know where he gets off being a little bitch about it, but I'm happy to have a talk with him after everyone leaves. Gia's threat will look fucking tame by the time I'm finished.

Gia ducks into the bathroom, reemerging a second later with a bulky plastic bag in her hand.

"Oh, crap. You were the one I puked on, huh?"

"No worries." Gia waves Annalise off. "You didn't seem to know what was what, and it just kind of came out. Like legit everywhere."

Everybody groans sympathetically, and I'm really hoping someone already cleaned it up, so I don't have to. I'd rather take on that sea breeze freesia-scented water stain left behind from that bubble bath again.

"I'm so sorry," Annalise says. "Can I clean your shoes at least? Or buy you new ones?"

Gia heads for the front door, telling her, "I'll stick 'em in the wash when I get home. I do it all the time. It was good meeting you though."

A snort finally pulls Gia's gaze my way, and I realize I'm the one that made the noise. The shit with Fletcher may not have been driven by jealousy but Gia *was* jealous of Annalise before that. She nailed her in the back of the head with a volleyball for Christ's sake. I didn't buy that eyelash story then, and I don't buy it now.

"Okay…" Gia raises her eyebrows along with a hand. "Well, bye."

What? I was going to bring her breakfast in bed, but she's trying to leave already?

I grab a random muffin from a bakery box someone must've picked up before I got down here, jogging over to the entryway as I hear Annalise and Fletcher behind me talking quietly.

"I'm sorry for stealing your room."

"It's fine. I prefer the couch."

I fight a second snort.

Gia gets the door open, freezing when I ask, "Hey, what about breakfast?"

"I had coffee."

"You had one sip." I find it hard to believe that the daughter of Al, the man who makes fucking feasts for breakfast, actually thinks she can get by with a sip of coffee for a meal. And if Fletcher and Annalise weren't talking so loudly, I bet I could probably hear Gia's stomach growling right now.

I put the muffin in her hand, asking, "Wanna borrow a pair of my shoes?" She's already got at least a few of my shirts, a pair of shorts, a pair of pants, my jacket, and now my beanie. Might as well complete the wardrobe.

After glancing down at the muffin, she twists at the waist, telling me, "Nah, I don't think so."

"You draw the line at shoes, huh?"

A ghost of a smile touches her lips, and she shakes her head.

"Do you work today?"

She eyes me, stretching the word, "Yes," out.

"What time does your shift end?"

Same thing when she says, "Later."

"See you later then."

With my thumb on her lips, I lean in until mine rest against my knuckle, Gia's uneven breath audible between us as I look her in the eye.

All at once, I release her, spinning on my heel.

"Is that your idea of a goodbye kiss?"

"That wasn't a kiss at all." Not technically. We just kind of breathed each other in. "Trust me, next time I kiss you, you won't need clarification."

"I definitely won't…considering you're all out of kisses."

When I turn around to face her again, I make sure I use the same amount of arrogance, telling her, "I'll earn more."

One battle was fun and all, but the second will be even better.

I hope.

Chapter 16

ROZ

Just about every day for almost two weeks now, I've eaten at Al's. Most days, Gia ducks out before I even catch a glimpse of her, but some days, I actually lay eyes on her. Those are the days I live for. Unfortunately, her reaction when I do see her is always the same—indifference—and I could really go without that feeling. If I engage in conversation with her, she answers with one- or two-word responses and they're forced. Detached even.

I fucking hate it.

Not enough to stop coming here, obviously, but I just wish Gia would tell me why she is the way she is. Who hurt her? Physically, emotionally…sexually? I want to know.

After the night we spent together, there's no denying the chemistry between us, yet every time I run into her at Al's, she tries her damndest to do just that.

Still…I show up. I have nothing better to do. I have nothing to do, period. I thought I'd try out that bakery, but no. I'm not going there, not when I could go to Al's instead.

And I thought if I showed up earlier tonight than I usually do, I'd have a better chance at seeing Gia and…I don't know. I never really have anything planned, but that's the beauty of being around Gia, I don't need to. She leads, I follow. Or I lead and she changes course, and I end up following anyway. The second I pull in though, I start questioning if I'll get to see Gia at all. It's fucking packed. There's even a line out the door and down the side of the building.

Al's is busy every night of the week, but I've never seen it like this, and I have to park across the street. I honestly don't even know how Al handles most of the business alone normally. Of course Gia helps too, but from what I've seen there's only one other employee, a woman named Patty, who runs the register and answers the phone that's always ringing off the hook.

I make my way past the line, ignoring several accusatory glares, until I find Patty, red-faced and sweaty with a handful of menus clutched to her chest.

"What's going on?"

"Little league baseball season just ended."

"Oh…" I say, glancing around at all the tables jammed full of rambunctious preteens waiting for their food. "And Gia left already?"

"No, she's back there, too."

She is?

"Al's gotta hire someone to help you guys out. This is crazy."

Patty shakes her head, telling me, "Can't. He's still paying off—"

The phone rings, cutting Patty off, and flustered, she hands me a stack of menus, asking if I can seat the next customers in line.

Okay…

I put the family of five in a corner table, then head for the kitchen to see if there's anything else I can help with. Pushing through the swinging door, I come to a stop, shielding my eyes from a persistent ray of sunlight streaking through an open blind. A few blinks later and I feel like doing it all over again. Gia and Al are…dancing. They're dancing. Hand in hand, bright smiles on both their faces, they're dancing around the warm kitchen together to some ungodly opera-sounding song.

Gia's been so guarded with me lately, but right now, she's free, she's herself, and all I can do is stand still, holding my breath as I watch the father/daughter duo, hoping this moment lasts forever. *A million right nows.* Yeah, I'm starting to get it.

Al spots me first, gesturing for me to join them, but I look over at Gia spinning in a slow circle and point over my shoulder, yelling over the music to him, "Looks like you've got a full house tonight!"

Gia comes to a stop, her gaze snapping straight to mine. None of us move for what feels like a whole minute, then she brings up a hand in what feels like slow motion to crook a finger at... I do a quick check behind me to make sure no one else is standing there. Me? She wants...me?

My feet are already moving, putting me within inches of her, my hands opening and closing repeatedly at my sides. I ache to touch her again. *Ache.*

Through my heart banging against my ribs, up my throat, and into my ears, I somehow manage a "Hi." It's small and quiet and doesn't come close to what I really want to say to her, but it's something. Something in an endless loop of nothing.

Gia's own smile doesn't drop, but her wall does. It's almost visible, tangible. For the first time in twelve days, eight hours, and thirty-seven minutes—give or take—she actually looks happy to see me. Or at least isn't actively pretending not to be.

Every nerve ending on my body sizzles, suddenly making the kitchen feel too small. Too cramped. Too full. Until her hand takes ahold of mine and then it all disappears entirely. Her and me. Me and her.

Her.

"What are you doing?" I tease, lifting her hand as she completes another spin. "There's an angry mob out there and you're in here practicing your pirouette?"

She stops in front of me, her big brown eyes like mirrors as I stare down into them. Her finger traces down the length of my nose, starting just between my eyebrows.

"Dance with me, cowboy."

"So you're a cowboy?" her dad asks, and I glance over at him, telling him, "No, sir. I'm a snowboarder," before I realize what I'm saying.

Goddamn it.

"A snowboarder, huh?"

"Not..."

One side of Gia's mouth lifts, mesmerizing me.

"...anymore," I finish too quietly for Al to hear as he says, "Good man."

"He still carves, all right," Gia says like a praise that has my cock twitching in my pants.

"Can I, uh," I clear my dry-ass throat, "can I give you two a hand? You don't have much time before your customers start storming in here."

"There's always time to dance, Roz." Gia's body starts rocking in time with the next song, this one not quite as bad as opera but still not great. Definitely not your typical dancing music.

"You two carry on without me." The smile in Al's voice sounds like how I feel. "I got this." He returns to the stove, stirring a large pot that unleashes a mouthwatering aroma into the air. Something with rosemary.

All that's missing is the vanilla.

Grasping Gia's hips, I pull her flush with mine and inhale. When she looks up at me, I forget how to exhale.

Our bodies dance together, but her moves are unpredictable, as imperfectly perfect as she is, and after a couple more songs of me trying to keep up with Gia, Patty pokes her head into the kitchen with a guilt-inducing look, so we stop to help Al with the food.

Despite the customers being irritable and the orders I'm in charge of not being worthy of anybody's social feeds, Al takes the time to teach me how to properly seal a pepperoni roll, right in the thick of all the pandemonium, reminding me of his daughter sitting calmly in the middle of the busy skate park.

You can't control what's happening around you, which can be scary. Really fucking scary.

You can take avalanche classes, you can wear an airbag, but when the overhang your best friend is standing on suddenly drops and his own bag doesn't deploy properly, you don't have any control over that. I didn't have any fucking control over that.

I do have control now though.

I could have control, if I chose to, because like Gia said, there's always a choice. Even in a storm of turmoil, you still have choices. People like Gia and Al, they choose to be the eye, while me, I've been pretending the storm's not even there. I've been pretending a lot lately. Pretending I'm okay walking away from Gia. Pretending I don't miss snowboarding. Pretending my old life doesn't even exist. Pretending *I* don't exist.

Interrupting my thoughts, Al says, "Roz, give Gia a ride home for me, would you?"

"Okay," I reply, finding and holding his daughter's eyes.

"Gia, let Roz walk you to the door this time."

"Okay," she says, not looking away either.

I know what I want now. I want to be the fucking eye.

The entire way to Gia's house, she talks to me, and not even in exchange for me talking to her either. She fucking *talks* to me. Willingly. Openly. I end up missing the turnoff into her driveway a few too many times, and after the fourth attempt at acting like I can't see it, Gia crawls over the center console, sitting on my lap to do it herself.

"It really isn't that hard," she says, parking my Chevy.

"Not yet," I tell her, staring at the skin where her shoulder meets her neck and licking my lips. It's not that hard, but it's getting there, especially when Gia squirms on my lap and I can feel the heat of her pussy directly above my cock.

"I missed you." I don't mean for it to come out so strained, but I'm so tired of holding back. I'm so tired of not being like this with Gia more. I'm so tired of not being like this with Gia at all. I'm just so tired. I used to think pretending was easy, but really, it's fucking exhausting.

"Roz?"

"Yeah, baby?"

"I missed…"

I tear my eyes away from the newly formed goose bumps to meet hers in the rearview mirror.

"Your truck. I missed your truck." With that, she opens the

driver's door and hops down on the gravel driveway, but it takes me a little longer to get out.

She missed…my truck?

Right. Yeah. Makes sense, especially since she kisses the window easier than she kisses me. She did that again tonight—she left another kiss print on the glass. I've got news for whoever buys this truck off me when I'm done with it…I'm keeping that window. The passenger door window, with Gia's lip marks, is mine. Forever.

Trudging up the steps, Gia's phone rings, and she answers it, putting it on speaker while she fits the key to the doorknob.

"Hey, what's up?"

Rowdy's voice crackles through the speaker. "What time am I picking you up in the morning?"

Gia's hand freezes, and I nudge a splinter of paint sticking up from one of the wood planks with the toe of my shoe. As soon as I get it to stay down, another pops up next to it. The whole wraparound porch needs to be repainted. Or redone. It's in really bad shape. Inside Gia's house, it's homey and peaceful and purposely lived in, but the outside is falling apart and something's gonna have to be done soon. It's only a matter of time before the decay makes its way inside.

Rowdy laughs, asking Gia, "Did you forget?"

"The cabin. Yeah, I did. Shit."

Rowdy's voice lowers. "What's wrong?"

"Nothing. I was just gonna try to…"

Even with my eyes on my shoes, I can feel her look at me.

"Never mind."

"You're sure?"

"Yeah. It's…nothing."

There's more Gia wants to say. I know it and Rowdy knows it, because he waits before saying, "I already got work off, so if you need me to take you to—"

"No. It's all good. I'll be there."

"All right. So what time should I—"

"I'll meet you there."

"What? What about your Raptor? You're not gonna try to load it by yourself, are you?"

Not bothering with any pleasantries, Gia hangs up on Rowdy's ass. I'm pretty sure she could load it by herself.

Silence stretches between us until it hugs us both, squeezing us, but in opposite directions.

Eye of the storm.

I shake it off, straightening my shoulders and asking, "Are you going somewhere?"

"*We're* going somewhere."

I try but fail epically to hide my smile.

"Tomorrow morning, be here at eight. We're taking your truck," she says before disappearing inside her house without a backward glance.

I stand outside the closed door, waiting for her to come back out and give me a few more details, like what to bring and maybe even, I don't know, where we're going, but in true Gia fashion, she leaves me guessing.

Should I go inside and ask? I did get permission from Al to walk in unannounced.

No. *We're* going somewhere. Together. That's enough for me.

That's everything.

Chapter 17

GIA

Familiar fingers skim over the thin layer of sweat coating my inner thigh, moving inward as glowing gold eyes capture mine, holding me hostage.

"Open." His raspy voice alone makes me shiver.

"Anything," I whisper, the word falling from my lips as easily as my legs falling open to the sides.

Tight circles focusing on my throbbing clit have my hips lifting off the mattress, trying to chase that perfect pace—not too fast, not too slow, with absolutely zero letup.

"Will you come for me? Please?"

My pulse skips a beat, throwing the tempo off briefly. He doesn't usually ask. He tells. He demands.

The pressure deep inside my pussy, deep inside me, increases, bringing me back, and I repeat, "Anything," bucking against the hand between my thighs as my eyes squeeze closed even tighter.

The hand on my sticky neck glides down to my breast, pinching the hardened tip, and I stuff my face into the pillow by my head, smothering the cry ripping through my throat.

My hip thrusts grow erratic, spastic, downright violent as the swirling intensifies, and just as the orgasm begins to crest, I hear, "Do you love me?"

What?

Our eyes meet again, the raw vulnerability in his just as evident as it was when we first met. Just as endearing. Just as irresistible.

"Can you love me forever, baby?"

Tears gather at the corners of my eyes, my nod shaking them loose.

In this moment, where it's just us, and nothing else can affect who we are or what we have between us, I admit the truth I wish wasn't so complicated, confessing, "Anything," like a sinner in church would. My legs clamp around the arm braced across my trembling abdomen and my body tenses, riding along the hills of ecstasy in a motionless daze.

Opening my wet eyes, I slowly sit up, scanning the bed. My bed. My *empty* bed.

It felt real. It felt good. Not just the idea of another round with Roz, but all of it, even that part at the end, when I was able to give him anything he wanted. Anything *I* wanted.

I go to wipe my cheeks, then think better of it, tramping over to my room's attached bathroom to wash my hands instead. When I'm done, all I can do is stare at my reflection in the mirror, facing my terrible decisions that led me here—wanting. Hopelessly wanting. For the first time ever, I actually do want someone back. I want someone…longer. Longer than I've ever allowed. But this isn't a fantasy, this is the real world, where wants don't determine your future. Facts do. And the fact is, I can't keep Roz any more than he can keep me.

Gawd, giving in to that want though, if only for a second, gave me a rush like nothing else ever has. I'm still shaking.

I'm still shaking.

And he'll be here in an hour.

Fuck. This is bad.

At 7:30 sharp, Roz pulls in, staring me down like a hunter would his prey.

Grateful for the early morning breeze, I turn into the wind, letting it cool my hot cheeks as I close my eyes, wishing for strength— any and all. I'm gonna need it.

Roz did the unthinkable. He weaved his way through uncharted territory, carving lines so deep, they'll never be erased. And he did it all without a board strapped to his feet. Fucking shredder.

"Good morning," Roz greets when I meet him by his front end, tossing me a bag from my new fave bakery.

"Did you snag this off Johnny?"

"No. I picked that up myself." He pushes up the sleeves of the pullover I know he's itching to take off. "Why?"

"That's our *spot*." I give him a wink.

Instead of cracking in half from Roz's sharp glare, I just laugh, telling him, "And you say my sense of humor sucks. I eat there sometimes," *all the time*, "and I've seen him stop by before, putting in orders too big for just himself. I assumed it was for the whole house."

"I…didn't know that."

Of course he didn't. He'd have to talk to his roommates to know them. Roz has made huge progress from the glimmer of a human he was when I stumbled across him, but he still isn't one hundred percent. *What is his one hundred percent?*

"What were you like?"

"What do you mean?"

"Before."

"I was…" He exhales, swaying from side to side.

The bag crinkles in my hold. I want to go to him so badly. I want to wrap him up tight and never let go. I want, I want, I want.

"Formidable."

"In what way?"

Roz looks directly at me when he says, "Every way," and my own body sways.

I drop my gaze, pulling out the sausage and cheddar scone he got me. My frown must not stay as hidden as I was hoping because Roz chuckles before retrieving another bag from his open driver's door, handing it over and saying, "Don't worry. I've got your sweet, too."

Sure enough, there's an apple cinnamon tart waiting inside to balance out the savory scone.

"Oh, Roz, you know your way to a girl's stomach, huh?"

Roz doesn't so much as smile, pinning me with a severe look. "If that's what it takes to get where I really want."

An immeasurable amount of time passes where we remain silent, neither of us willing to expand on that statement.

Strength. I could use some right now because what a fucking line. Not even operating at full capacity, Roz is more formidable than most people firing on all cylinders.

"*Can you love me forever, baby?*" Can I? I would…if I could. If it were up to me, I totally fucking would because Roz makes it easy.

Easy to love, but not easy to walk away from.

I break the silence first, nodding and staring off to tell him, "You're not the first person to want seconds from me, you know? You should put this kind of energy toward a girl that'll actually sleep with you more than once. This," I lift the food, looking over at him, "won't get you between my thighs again."

"If all I wanted was to be between your thighs, I'd drop to my knees and bury my face in your pussy until one of us passed out."

I'm blushing, swaying, and now my underwear's soaked. This day's off to a great start.

"I want in," Roz continues, gently gripping my wrists and pulling me to him as I struggle to keep hold of both the bags and my sanity. "I want in that pretty head of yours." His eyes gloss over every inch of my face, then he drops his voice. "I want in… I want *in*, Gia."

My own voice comes out low and throaty to say, "You're a Tit."

"What does—"

"A Tufted Titmouse. They're these little gray birds that cling to outdoor walls and windows, pecking. A lot of people think they're looking for a way in, but really, they're just searching for wasp nests. You know, a snack to hold them over."

"I'm not interested in a snack. I want where nobody else has ever been."

"So…anal?"

"Oh, Gia," he mocks my previous words, "your sense of humor really does suck."

And because it's not even remotely funny, I burst out laughing.

What the fuck are we doing? What the fuck am I doing?

"Okay, cowboy." I remove myself from his hold, my skin instantly chilled from the loss. "That's enough. We need to get on the road." Before I do something dumb. Monumentally dumb.

We get my Raptor loaded into the back of Roz's truck, then I tie her up tighter than a Thanksgiving turkey while Roz gets the cab situated with the rest of our shit. I only packed a duffle bag, and it looks like Roz did as well, except he's also got several grocery bags full of food.

I shake my head, finishing with the last strap.

Why I feel the need to constantly open his eyes to what life has to offer, I don't know. Every time I see him, it's easy to picture him sitting in his room, all alone, feeling…sorry for himself? Is he feeling? That's just it. I don't know what Roz is doing. Roz doesn't even know what he's doing. He's just…here. Barely. He's not living, not fully, but I think he wants to. He's so hard up for something, anything, he's even willing to stalk me at Al's every night just to have a few minutes of not feeling so lonely.

I think the desire is there, just not the drive. There's nothing pushing Roz to live again, except me.

He needs to get outside. He needs to remember just how formidable he used to be. Some fresh air, comradery, an adrenaline rush that has nothing to do with snowboarding—Roz needs it all. He deserves even more, but this is all I'm able to offer him. All I'm able to offer anybody.

We eventually get on the road, making a quick stop at a convenience store for some coffee to go along with our pastries, but when Roz keeps checking me out, I roll my eyes at him, leaning my head against the window to see him better. He looks happy. As close to happy as I've seen him.

Keeping his left hand on the wheel—it's still got the pink and purple bracelet from Iris, and every time I see it, I get stupid happy—his right tugs on the pants I'm wearing, telling me, "I like seeing you in my clothes."

I saved all my regular riding gear for later, so I'm currently rocking the pants I first lifted from Roz's room.

His lips split into a smirk. "I'd like seeing you out of them better."

I bend a knee, planting my foot on the leather seat and cursing myself for changing my underwear before we left. What was the point? Everything about Roz makes me drip for him.

"I don't do repeats," I say more for my sake than his, but he needs to hear it, too. Probably many more times. He's…demanding, and each time he is, I'm finding it harder and harder to resist him.

"Three orgasms in one go is hard to turn down." He removes his hand, lifting it to his jaw to rub the soft scruff cockily.

"I guess," I tell him. "My own personal record is seven but that was by myself." Once I got a girl to come five times in one night by using a sucking vibe on her clit and that was pretty amazing, too. She's also the one that keyed my truck though, so maybe that wasn't such a good idea.

"Seven? What the fuck? That's possible?"

It must suck to be a man and only be able to come once before being rendered almost completely useless.

"Yeah," I say slowly. "If you've got the time and stamina." Which most men don't, so they stop after getting their woman to come once, if even at all. *Lazy.*

"Anyway, you only got two." Although the last one he got out of me was kind of split, it just kept going and going—the lube helped, but it was Roz's gold eyes piercing mine that really heightened everything—but for argument's sake, I'm sticking with two.

His head tilts my way, keeping one eye on the highway.

"Three."

"Two. One was by my own hand." I wave said hand at him. "Or don't you remember?"

"I finished that one off," he argues, making me bark out a laugh.

"You rode my coattails and now you're trying to claim the victory for yourself? Typical male bullshit."

Suddenly, my head jolts off the glass as Roz jerks the wheel over to park on the shoulder.

My eyes fly to his when we're stopped.

"I can get more."

He reaches for me, but I'm already out the door, fighting to keep myself upright as I clutch my stomach from laughing so hard. Roz is on me in the next instant, jumping over the center console, missing the passenger seat completely, and landing easily on the asphalt in front of me. *Daaamn.*

"Well, shit," I say, teasing. "Looks like the snowboarder's as good on his feet as he is on his back."

Straightening to his full height, he towers over me, and I take a step back, watching him closely.

"You haven't seen me on my back yet, baby. Or don't *you* remember?"

Roz arches his eyebrow at my follow-up sneeze.

"It's…" I wave a hand. "…your clothes. I'm not used to them."

His shirt's off and tossed behind him, into the cab of his truck… somewhere. With his muscles filling back in from the weight he's gained, Roz stands before me like a Greek god and I almost release a second sneeze.

"Better?"

"Must be your pants," I say with what I'm hoping is a straight face. He can't actually give me several orgasms right now, can he? He is leaving his engine running on the side of the highway while…

His lips lift into a smirk, but his hands drop to the button of his jeans.

He can.

He could.

Distracted, I barely manage to dodge his next grab for me, but only slightly. Dude is not only tricky but lightning fast, too.

"What? No roadside striptease?"

"Say it and it's yours."

"Stri—"

This time, I'm not so lucky as Roz darts a hand out, latching on to my Champion crewneck and twists until I'm firmly in his grasp. I immediately spin around though, giving him my back. It's easier to refuse him when I don't see those penetrating golden eyes. That's how he always gets me in my dreams.

That's how I always let him get me in my dreams.

What feels like a band of steel wraps around my waist and Roz hauls me off my feet, walking us several yards over to the tree line. Out of view from the highway, he sets me down in front of a tall birch tree, coming in close to rasp near the shell of my ear, "Let me do things to you."

"What things?"

"All of them."

I squeeze my eyes shut, forcing the words, "I can't," out.

A whoosh of air replaces Roz at my back, and I carefully turn in my spot, spinning my hat around until the bill is facing forward but slightly slanted to the side, then relax against the tree's trunk, regarding him silently because if I open my mouth, it'll all spill out. More and more I have to bite my tongue, and it's starting to feel like I'm trying to hold Niagara Falls back.

Roz closes his eyes, his fists curling at his sides. He's the visual representation of how I feel inside—coiled tight, ready to strike, ready to claim.

Slowly, he opens them, then his mouth, but I cover his lips with my fingers, telling him, "Shh. Listen."

The dirt clashes with the pine-filled breeze blowing past in an intoxicating blend of untouched earth. The wind cuts off suddenly, revealing the sound of rushing water somewhere nearby and a Blue Heron flying overhead squawks loudly like a pterodactyl ruling the sky.

Nature heals us. Nature feeds us. Nature gives us life by providing everything we require: soil, air, water, and our most powerful source of energy, the sun.

"Do you feel that?"

Aside from his rapidly expanding chest, Roz doesn't make a single move.

"You lost it?"

A slight shake of his head can't hide the agony overtaking his face. He didn't lose his connection to nature. He left it.

"You belong out here."

I drop my hand to his chest, feeling his heartbeat through his ribs while he watches me from under hooded lids.

"This is where you should be. Not locked up in a bare room, living with people you don't even care enough about to talk to."

Goose bumps start at the top of his shoulders, branching outward like a snowflake growing, and he says, "I care," so quietly I'd miss it if I wasn't paying close attention.

Rays of just warming sunlight slice through the leaves above us, bathing everything in a sea of illumination. Different shades of neon green dance over our hair and faces, and we both look up, hypnotized by the spontaneous production.

"I care a lot."

I bring my gaze back to his, finding his focus solely on me.

"I…" Am about to burst. I can't do this.

I stand from the tree, pushing him back.

"Gia, let me—"

"There will be other girls at the cabin, Roz!" I shout, scaring a dozen, if not more, birds from their perches on the boughs above us. "Lots of girls, who would probably love to let you do all kinds of things to them." I swallow the acid filling my mouth. "So, keep it in your pants a little bit longer. We'll be there soon."

"Are you serious? I just told you—"

"Then I guess we're both shitty listeners because I just. Told. You. I. Fucking. Can't."

Without waiting for him, I return to his truck, my gaze fixed on my lap. What *am* I doing?

"Where's this cabin you keep talking about?" Roz asks, slamming his door shut before shoving his shirt back over his head. "Where are we even going?"

He's pissed. He shouldn't be. He won't be. Whatever blow I just delivered to his ego will soon be soothed by someone ten times better than me.

I twist my head the other direction to hide the tears filling my eyes, telling him, "Take the next exit," as he merges back into traffic. "It's at the base of Willmont Mountain. You'll see the signs."

A tension crawls up my spine, sticking its claws into each vertebra like the rungs of a ladder.

"What's wrong?"

It's a while before Roz answers, saying, "I used to board there," between his teeth.

Exhaling loudly, I press the back of my head against the headrest multiple times. Shit.

"Yeah, so," I run my palms up and down my thighs, "I fucked up. I'm really sorry."

As if on autopilot, he tells me, "You didn't know."

"True, but I shouldn't have asked you to come along anyway." This was a bad idea all-around. The entire situation had the potential to blow up in my face—truthfully, the odds were never really in my favor—but it just detonated before we even got to our destination.

Roz side-eyes me, but I point up ahead of us, telling him, "Pull over whenever you get the chance and I'll call someone to drive me the rest of the way. I didn't think this through, like at all, so you can just drop me off around here somewhere." *Anywhere.* "And I'll cover the gas you wasted and everything."

His head starts to shake. "You're kidding, right? I'm not going to drop you off on the side of the fucking road."

I soften my voice, infusing it with a smile I don't feel at all. "Don't worry about it. There are so many other people going, I'll have another ride lined up before I even unload my quad." I could probably even ride the rest of the way there myself.

My phone's already out and I'm opening the lock screen when Roz grabs it from my grasp, wordlessly dropping it in his center cupholder.

He takes the exit I originally told him to, acting like I didn't just hit the eject button on my own seat, and I shift to face him.

"Roz, you don't have to do this."

He doesn't answer though. He doesn't say anything for the rest of the drive actually. I watch him while he watches the road, and as soon as we get closer to the cabin, I point out which turns to take until we finally arrive at the large rental home everyone went in on for the next few days. Supposedly it sleeps twenty. We invited forty, plus enough randoms to spice things up.

As Roz circles around for a place to park, I can't help but check out the competition. Technically none of us are here to race, but I still prefer my girl to be the nastiest four-wheeler in the crowd. It makes the reaction when people discover she's mine that much better. So far it looks like Rowdy's twin YFZs are the only ones even close to my league.

My smile disappears when I hear Roz basically hyperventilating next to me.

"Hey, you don't need to stick around." I jerk a thumb over my shoulder. "I'll get this unloaded real quick, so you can be on your way." I don't want to say goodbye to him, but I need to.

Story of my life.

His voice stops me as he says, "Tell me how you do it," his gaze zeroed in on the base of the giant mountain before us.

"Do what?"

He pins those lost eyes on me.

"Not feel."

"You think I don't feel?" I'm literally choking back my feelings. "I really was lucky," I say, sighing, "my mom loved me so hard, so wholly, that I can still feel it wrapped around me, even three years after her death." I peer out the window now, not really seeing. "I do miss her though. Everything about her. Every day. Sometimes I miss her so much, the pain tears up my insides, looking for a way out." My voice thins as I look at him. "But her love, it was so fucking strong, so fucking sure, it was like wearing steel armor. That armor, that love, is what keeps the pain from getting out and taking over. It's what keeps me in one piece. Because I allow it to. I choose to remember my mom and I choose to honor her by embracing her love, her life, *and* her death, not bucking it."

"How do you make it look so easy?"

"I don't know. It's not easy. It takes work, for sure, but we can't choose where we're born or when or to who. We can't choose if we're born at all. But the life we are given, it's full of choices, and I choose to live mine with no regrets. I'm going to leave this world having done everything I wanted to, just like my mom did."

Just like my mom did.

"I overstepped what I was given, so it got taken away."

"Overstepped?"

"Yeah, I think I over-lived it somehow."

"It wasn't taken away though. You *walked* away, unscathed."

"Unscathed?"

"Didn't you?" If Roz was injured in the accident, he never told me about it.

"Physically, sure." He scoffs, then he does that thing where his eyes shift left to right and back again. "I wish this was physical. Physical damage is visible. It's comprehensible. It's treatable. This shit has no form, no sound, no cure. It's fucking *killing* me."

"Do you want it to?"

"I—" His gulp echoes throughout the truck. "I did."

I knew Roz was struggling to recover from his friend's death, but I didn't know to what extent. Not really. I had my theories but not facts. His appearance, his voice, his room—the signs were all there. I just didn't know he was on the verge of…I don't even know. Suicide? Would Roz really do that? Could he? It sounds like he absolutely could've.

I look down to find myself mindlessly ripping the stitching from my sweatshirt's cuff. *Companion Parrot.* Domesticated Parrots can sometimes develop separation anxiety and will pick their own feathers when they're separated from the person they're most attached to.

"There may not be a cure," I tell Roz, yanking my sleeves down over both hands until all my fingers are hidden inside. "Grief doesn't just disappear, but relief *is* possible and it starts with a choice. A choice only you can make."

Climbing over the center console, I straddle Roz's lap, taking his unshaven jaw in my cotton-blend-covered palms.

"Please don't go yet. I need you here still."

His arms encase me, holding my body to his like a lifeline, but after a while, he whispers, "I don't think that's true."

"I do," I say just as softly before pulling back and looking him in the eye. "You've still got my Raptor."

He cracks a smile, shaking his head. "Don't forget I got the snacks, too."

"I could never forget," I mouth, my gaze locked on Roz's lips.

"Gia—"

"Choose to stay. Choose to try. Choose to live, Roz. Your friend would've wanted you to." I bring my eyes up to his. "*I* want you to."

Roz should stay. This place, this mountain, is bringing up a lot of emotions for him, but if he doesn't face them now, he might never try to again. If I have to compromise for that to happen, then so be it. There's no growth without sacrifice and Roz has already sacrificed enough.

"Okay."

"Okay?" I ask, and he nods.

As soon as we're out of his truck, there's a swarm of people gathering around to talk shop. Roz refuses to get farther than a few inches away from me, except to remove his shirt again when he decides he's done with keeping up appearances—exactly five minutes into them.

Rowdy joins us sometime later, eyeballing the shirtless man glued to my side, but I shake my head, inconspicuously telling him to drop it. He does but only because he loves me as much as I love him. At the end of the day, this is my mistake to make, even if spending time with Roz doesn't always feel like the mistake I know it is.

"G." He grins.

"Rowdy, you remember Roz," I say with the same grin.

"Hey, man, how's it going?" Roz says to Rowdy, stepping forward to take my best friend's hand.

Rowdy shakes it, telling him, "Welcome to Dysfunction Junction."

Roz forces a chuckle. "Thanks for having me."

"Need a hand unloading?"

Roz glances at me and I give him a nod before shooting a grateful look to Rowdy for not saying anything. Prolonging this charade might hurt Roz in the long run, but what if I can help him before then? What if the good outweighs the bad, only if just for a little while longer?

Lost in thought as I watch the guys work together, my fingers find my collarbone first, causally slipping over my shoulder to feel for the scab that seems to be taking forever to heal.

Rowdy's eyes pierce mine, and I drop my hand, pasting on a wide smile as I approach the back end of Roz's truck.

"Let's get this party started."

"I thought you were the party," Roz says from above, standing in his truck's bed, and I laugh, telling him, "Exactly."

A good time for a short time.

Chapter 18

ROZ

The first day in the cabin was mayhem, pure mayhem. Anyone with a half-functioning liver started taking shots around lunch, resulting in everyone being hammered well before dinnertime came around. Some people took off on foot to a nearby bar to eat while the rest of us stuck around and ordered pizza. After complaining through two slices, Gia passed out, so I enlisted Rowdy's help finding a private room I could claim as mine and Gia's. My plan was to talk to him a little more, see if I could get some information out of him, but as soon as I stood from tucking Gia in, he disappeared quicker than slush in May.

I didn't feel like going back out to socialize without Gia, or just in general, so after putting a bottle of water on the nightstand for her, I called it a night myself and climbed in next to her. Now as I blink sleep from my eyes, glancing around the rustically decorated room—sans water *and* Gia—I find myself wondering why I even bothered sticking around at all. The last time I was here was mayhem too, but in a completely different way with a completely different crowd. Some of these people snowboard in jeans. I know because they fucking bragged about it. Bragged. Like that's something to be proud of.

The door swings open, and Gia hops up onto the mattress, making the blankets I'd shoved to the foot of the bed fall to the floor with a quiet *thump*.

She's why I'm still here. One more day, one more hour, one more minute in her presence is worth it all. To get a little more time with Gia, I'd walk through fire. Yeah, even in jeans.

Her feet frame my hips as she jumps, and a smile tugs at the corner of my lips as my body bounces around. Her long, dark hair is loose around her face, moving freely with the rest of her body. A baggy white tee sits over a pair of riding pants I'd love to see her in some other time with nothing else on.

"How you feelin'?" she asks, using her hands on the ceiling to avoid hitting her head while maintaining eye contact through the repeated up and down motion.

"All right. You?"

"I feel great." Her words come out staggered as she jumps.

I run a hand up my stomach, letting my short nails scratch over the rippled abs. Gia stops suddenly, her brown eyes following along and making my smile grow.

"What's going on down there?"

I glance down at the tent in my boxer briefs.

"It's morning…and you are bouncing on top of me." What does she expect? Either of those would do it, but both…fuck yeah, I'm hard as a rock.

Taking advantage of her stunned state, I sit up quickly, yanking her hips down until she's straddling mine. She lands with a surprised laugh that I wish I could've kissed straight from her mouth.

"How'd I end up being cuddled by you?"

"You mean how'd you end up cuddling *with* me?" Gia cuddles, too. She can talk all the shit she wants, but she's a cuddler. "I put you here." We never discussed sleeping arrangements, but I didn't think we needed to. She's out of her fucking mind if she actually thinks I'd let her sleep in anyone else's bed but mine.

"I said—"

"You said I was a shitty listener." I wait for her to finish her eye roll before adding, "And I listened to that."

Groaning, she says, "There are plenty of girls here that would kill to be in your bed doing more than G-rated cuddling."

"PG, maybe even PG-13. Your hands…they roam while you sleep." It's one of the best things about sleeping with Gia, but also the worst, because then I wake up fucking starved for her only to have her run off before I even get to satisfy my appetite.

Gia completely ignores me, saying, "Promise you won't do that again tonight."

My smile slips. "I thought you don't do promises."

She doesn't answer right away, avoiding my gaze to stare at my mouth.

"I don't know what to do," she admits quietly, then raises her eyes to mine.

"I wish you did," I tell her, bringing her body in until we're pressed tightly together. "It'd make this a hell of a lot easier." As hard as I try, I don't understand why Gia, the most caring person I've ever met, seems to have the emotional maturity of a clam when it comes to relationships—specifically any involving me.

With our chests touching, I can feel her heart beating and it's going as fast as mine sounds in my ears. Having her in my arms again…I don't want to let her go.

"And what exactly is this?" she whispers.

For my answer, I lie back, taking her with me, so her mouth hovers over mine while I massage her back with one hand. My other grabs a solid handful of ass, making sure she feels what she does do to me as I tell her, "Anything."

Eyes wild, Gia rears back, gasping, "What?"

"I just meant this can be anything. We—"

"We are nothing, Roz. Not really. We just…fucked. Once."

"Nothing, huh?"

"Yeah."

This back-and-forth shit is giving me whiplash. Maybe I should start giving it back already. See how Gia fucking likes it.

I tuck my hands behind my head, studying her.

"Why are you on my dick then?"

"Is that what I'm sitting on? I thought that was—"

I thrust my hips off the bed, swapping her next words out for a moan.

"You like me."

Her laugh gets caught in her throat.

"I like you."

Another thrust.

"That's," she moans, "not my problem," her breaths slow and heavy.

Lifting my head, I grab Gia's waist, holding her suspended above me. "I'll fuck somebody else tonight, just like you want."

I slam her body back down, but she meets my thrust with one of her own as she clutches my chest, rolling her hips against mine.

It's a minute before I can get my next words out. "And while she's riding my cock, screaming my name, you'll have to listen, knowing it should've been you."

Gia doesn't even break pace to ask, "Need a condom?"

On a growl, I snatch her wrists off my chest, pulling them out to the sides so we're face to face. All movement below our waists comes to a halt as I say, "The box I brought should be good. Should be."

Something changes in Gia's face, almost like something *breaks*.

"Did you really bring a box of condoms?"

I shake my head once, loosening my hold on her.

"I brought a few." I didn't want to get my hopes up, but I also didn't want to be unprepared in case Gia did what Gia always does—catches me off guard. "Did you bring a box?"

"Yes."

I try not to let that sting. She can have condoms as much as I can, but Gia said it herself—she doesn't do repeats. So who the fuck was she planning on screwing here?

"I needed to."

"To prove something?" When she looks away, my lower jaw shifts to the side. "To me or to yourself?"

"Both." Her eyes meet mine again, full of unshed tears.

"Gia—"

"Roz, you've got some shit to figure out. You *need* to remember why you're here and what you want, what you love, without pinning it to someone else."

"What do you mean?"

"You lost your best friend in a tragic accident, but you're letting that tragedy take you, too. You already tied your happiness, your life, to someone else once before. What if you're just trying to do it again? I won't be the next person to hold you back," she says, sitting up.

"Hold me back?" I sit up with her. Where'd she even come up with that? "You've been pushing me forward since we met. Literally."

"And what happens when I stop?"

Stop pushing me?

"I…"

Relentless, she searches my eyes.

"…don't know."

"You're lying."

I am. I do know what happens when Gia's not there to push me. I fall back into a depression so deep, it feels like I'll never be able to climb out.

I did though. I fucking climbed out on my own. I didn't choose to leave my room, knowing I'd run into Gia. I just fucking chose to get out by myself. For myself. Connecting with Gia again afterward was just a coincidence. Dumb luck.

I eye Gia back.

Or was it?

For someone putting up such a fight right now, her face, hell, her entire body, is telling a completely different story. She was just grinding on my cock, and I bet if I stuck a hand in her pants, she'd be drenched.

"So are you," I tell her, and she shakes her head, freeing a few tears in the process, so I hug her to me tightly, saying, "You do like me." *Come on, baby. Admit it.*

"It doesn't matter."

"It does matter. It matters to me. I'm not tying my life to yours. Okay? I'm not." At least not yet. I could. I could see myself with Gia, but that'd be another choice, a big one, and I'm not going to make it until Gia does, too. "I just like being around you," I tell her, taking her face in my hands like she did to mine yesterday, feeling the moisture from her tears absorb into my fingertips.

If this were only about my issues, why is she crying? Gia can try to put this on me, but she's the one holding back because…I don't fucking know. She won't tell me. She's scared. She's scared of *something*, but she won't let me find out what. She clams up every time I try to.

"I don't know who or what hurt you, but fuck, Gia, I'll do everything in my power to make up for that monster's mistakes. Let me prove it to you."

"Aww, Roz. When are you gonna realize *I'm* the monster?"

"Wha—"

"Gia."

Rowdy's standing in the open doorway, still as a rock. Stupid as one too if he thinks now's a good time to interrupt. Yeah, the door was open, but we're obviously in the middle of something.

"We ridin' or what?" he asks, and Gia sighs and straightens.

Face to the ceiling, she says, "Yeah. We're in."

"Nino just got back with the coffee. Want a cup?" His eyes slide to mine and hold, neither of us breaking first. Gia said he was a Cockatoo, right? Well, repeat after me, Rowdy. *Fuck. Off.* Gia's the only thing keeping my erection hidden from his view right now.

He's lucky I didn't sleep naked last night, otherwise the awkward factor right now would be off the charts.

"You have to try this coffee," Gia says, looking down her nose at me. Her face is dry, her eyes are empty, her body lacks any previous pliancy. For all intents and purposes, Gia has moved on. The moment is officially fucking over.

"I think I'm gonna head into town actually."

"Good idea."

Rowdy's comeback lacks any real heat. He's all smoke—like a hint, not a warning. I don't take any offense; I just want to know why. What's he hinting at? Because whatever's got Gia scared, Rowdy knows about it—I can feel it—but he's keeping his bestie's secret.

"No, it's not," Gia tells her loyal friend, leveling a glare on him before turning it on me to say, "No, you're not. Now, let's go fill up on coffee that'll keep us awake until tomorrow, so everyone can fuck like rabbits tonight."

"Too late. This entire house already reeks of sex."

My hands reflexively grip Gia's hips still situated on mine, even as she twists to face Rowdy. She's with me tonight, too. I don't give a fuck. The only way that box of condoms of hers is getting opened is if she's using them with me, nobody else.

"Damn, I missed everything. Who hooked up?" she asks, and Rowdy starts listing names I couldn't care less about, so I zone out.

"You didn't tell him, did you?" he stops to ask, and Gia looks down at me, popping an eyebrow.

"You get one of the twins today."

Twins? Is she still trying to shove women in my face?

"You sure he can even handle that?"

Gia cocks her head to the side, acting like she isn't already fully aware what I'm capable of, and replies to Rowdy, saying, "I guess we'll find out."

My hands shake like leaves caught in a biting fall breeze. I should've never drunk the coffee. The name of it has the word death in it. Literally, death. Gia wasn't exaggerating when she said we'd be up for the next couple days. It's like I can feel each individual blood vessel rushing through my veins. Every part of me is fucking jacked up right now, and if I was still boarding, I'd be fit to last all day with no breaks from just one cup of the stuff. It's from a local company that claims to have made the strongest coffee in the world and I've tried enough coffee from enough places to confirm they absolutely nailed it. Jesus Christ.

Oh, and the twins I get to pick from, they're four-wheelers. Rowdy owns a pair of identical Yamaha YFZs, and according to Gia, he's letting me ride one for this little group outing.

On my way out to the parking lot where the four-wheelers are, I pass a pole with ten or so wood pieces of various lengths nailed to it. Each one has a different name of a high peak carved into it with an arrow pointing to its general vicinity. New York has three main mountain ranges but a shit ton of peaks within each of them. I'm not sure why the owners even bothered with the handmade sign honestly, but if I had to guess, I'd say it's probably a way for them to brag about the ones they've hiked. A notch-on-the-belt kind of thing.

Salvy and I did something like that, too…when we were eleven. Once I got more serious and my numbers hit double digits, I sorta lost track. Not that the places I scaled didn't mean anything anymore; it's just that after a while, I was moving too fast to fully appreciate each specific experience for what it was. I snowboarded. Period. That's just what I did, then what we did, me and Salvy, together. The two of us. Our jobs. Our careers. Our passions. Our lives.

Then in the blink of an eye, it was just mine again. My job. My career. My passion. My life.

And now…

The passion went first, followed by the dream career linked to the job I never really saw it as, then I guess the life part just kind of slipped away unannounced somewhere in the fallout afterward.

I never meant to tie my life to Salvy's. I thought that's what he wanted, too. It made everything more tolerable, more enjoyable—having a partner for what can be a very isolated lifestyle. I was always on the road, away from home—the only home I'd ever known—away from friends. But the things Gia said this morning, I'm wondering if maybe I did. We were best friends and Salvy did love snowboarding, that much I do know. As far as how much pressure I put on the two, I'm not sure.

He would've loved this though. Salvy would've eaten this shit up with a spoon in each hand. Whereas I was content having one solid friendship in my life, Salvy was always down to add new people to our circle.

If I could do it all over again, I'd ease up on both. Both the expectations from Salvy and of him. Looking back, I could've been suffocating him just as easily as the avalanche that took him out.

Hindsight, man, it's fucking brutal.

"Hey. I'm Bryce."

A scrawny guy that reminds me of a teen trying to hang out with his older brother's friends saddles up next to me, introducing himself. This has been happening since we left the room. Gia is refusing to acknowledge me now that she's off my dick, but every other person here is happy to chat me up this morning.

What's in that coffee?

I fit my hand to his, giving it a firm shake and telling him, "Roz."

He was here last night, too, but we didn't get a chance to meet. We couldn't because Gia practically tackled him to the floor when he arrived, then proceeded to sit on him for a solid hour, catching up. I hated him for that hour, but he kept his hands where I could see them, so I let it go.

His gaze touches on Gia and mine follows. She's talking with another attendee I don't care to meet, but probably will. There's about twenty or so people participating in today's bonding exercise, which is about twenty too many.

"So, you're here with Gia?"

My eyes roam her from head to toe, stopping on the ass I was just squeezing the hell out of before mumbling out, "Something like that," and grabbing the helmet Rowdy loaned me, ready to shove it over my head, and eyes, and memories. *Fuck.* Why'd it have to be this mountain?

Bryce laughs under his breath. "Damn, man. What'd you do to get on her bad side?"

Hands faltering, I look up to see what he's talking about, but Gia's still deep in discussion, oblivious to us, or just to me, I don't know. She's fucking full of mixed signals.

"Gia usually only fucks with guys she doesn't like. Makes for easier catch and release, you know?"

The little shit has the nerve to wink at me. Yes, I know what catch and release is. I've been a fisherman since I lost my fucking virginity, but I don't need this punk explaining it to me like I'm the virgin here, pining after some notorious player.

"So, she must really hate you to let you stick around," he says, making the helmet in my hold suddenly feel like putty.

"Who says we fucked around?"

Cat's got his tongue now because he's not saying anything.

"And she doesn't hate me," I say, wondering if that's actually true. That didn't feel like hate this morning. Not hate at all. A healthy dose of confusion finished off with a sprinkling of blue balls for garnish, yeah. But hate? No. "We're cool."

Are we cool though? We used to be. We tried to be. *I* tried to be.

I don't know what we are. Maybe Gia's right. Maybe I should test the waters with someone else, see if I can get over this…infatuation. Hmm, no. I don't like that description any more than I like using the word *cool* to describe what I feel for Gia. I can't even define it myself, let alone to anyone else, but it's deep. Deeper than this conversation requires.

Gia saunters over, planting a loud kiss on Bryce's nose while pulling the ugly beanie over his head a little lower.

She asks him, "How are you feeling, Bry-bear?" and his eyes find mine before dropping briefly.

"Why are you still calling me that?" he groans, exactly how I imagine an embarrassed little brother would.

"I can't help it. You'll always be my Bry-bear."

"Well, you can stop now."

Gia wraps him into a giant hug, telling him, "I'm just so happy you're here."

Jealousy wraps me up too, so snug it feels like an anaconda constricting my body for easier consumption.

"Are you up for riding with me?" I hear her whisper, and after another peek at me, he tells her, "I am but only because you're scared I'll show you up if I drive."

Gia's head is thrown back with a silent laugh. "Nobody drives my Raptor but me."

"I thought I heard a story about Rowdy driving it before."

"She told you that?"

Everything around us seems to slow down as the two fall into an odd trance, staring at one another. It's like they're somewhere else entirely, gone from the here and now and stuck in some other time, one from long ago.

Rowdy, who's been busy helping gas up all the quads, stops what he's doing to watch too, his gaze softening at the pair.

Gia shakes her head to say, "That was my old Scrambler and it was once. Rowdy had to help get me out of a hidden marsh I plowed into after sailing over a blind hill. But I may have left that part out at the time." Her eyes sparkle with past mischief, then, staring between his, she says, "She said Macaw, but I think you're a Cockatiel."

His almost nonexistent eyebrows drift closer. "Why?"

"All hiss, no bite."

Bryce laughs, gently pushing Gia off. "I bite. I can show you, if you want."

His tone leans toward the suggestive side, but in an inexperienced way. I wouldn't be surprised if he is an actual virgin.

Gia finally sets her sights on me but holds her wrist out to Bryce, saying, "Go ahead. I'm not afraid of a little blood."

"A little blood?" I step between the two, taking Gia's wrist before Bryce can. "Baby, anyone else's teeth so much as nicks you and they'll be bathing in it." My words are not quiet, my threat is not empty, and I give Gia a *push me and see what happens* look, letting her fucking know it.

Her lips lift into an amused smile, saying, "Is that a promise, cowboy?"

"No promises," I tell her before biting the side of her wrist, not enough to hurt but enough to get the heartbeat in the vein against my bottom lip to speed up. Both lips close over the skin and I suck as I let go, maintaining eye contact with Gia while I bring a hand up to plug Gia's nose before she can sneeze, 'cause I know one's building.

Bryce mutters, "I knew it," under his breath, making Gia blink first, then she's shaking me off and pulling him away.

They mount her four-wheeler while everybody else starts preparing to do the same, and I do too, breathing a little easier than I was a few moments ago. If Gia only bangs guys she dislikes, then there's not a chance in hell Gia and Bryce have ever been together because she adores the kid.

What does that say about me though? *Does she hate me?*

Her eyes meet mine a second too late, and I see a mirror image of my own lust looking back at me before she can school her features.

Definitely not hate. I just need to figure out what exactly she does feel for me. Or better yet, I need Gia to figure it out.

Familiar with snowmobiles, I only need a quick rundown from Rowdy before I'm able to get the YFZ running on my own, then we're off, all of us traveling in a loose formation—Gia and Bryce in the lead, me and my thoughts following close behind, a dozen other riders scattered about, and Rowdy bringing up the rear.

We ride like that for a couple hours, making our way around Willmont, each four-wheeler occasionally breaking from the pattern to show off in one way or another. My favorite rider to watch is Gia though. Even with a passenger, she's still fearless as fuck. She jumps insane inclines over fallen trees, then lands them with complete confidence, never questioning herself or her capabilities. Not once does Bryce seem scared, the visible smile from under his helmet saying it all.

We've already passed several trail markers, but as soon as I catch sight of one of the overhead ski lifts, I end up skipping a gear, causing the machine under me to make an unnatural noise. Gia twists her head over her shoulder so fast, I think she's going to crash, but she eases her throttle, falling back in line with me easily to ask, "You okay?"

I shrug noncommittally. Am I? I've ridden these trails before. I've boarded these trails. I've conquered these trails. It's different being here without snow though. It reveals more, all the hidden natural beauty that was covered in white. I like seeing everything through new eyes, it's like getting to experience it for the first time all over again. Not many people get that chance—a second shot. Nobody gets a third. I need to make the best of mine. I want to.

I'm going to.

I give Gia a nod, telling her I'm good and to go up ahead again. She doesn't want to hold me back, but I'm not going to hold her back either.

We pull off a while later onto a decent-sized lookout with a puddle of a lake off to the side. Boulders and tall trees surround the hidden area, leaving the view unobstructed the closer you get to the ledge.

The noisy engines cut off, allowing the vast silence of wilderness to claim it. At first nobody moves, almost as if we're all captives of Willmont's suppressing charm and the mountain's lulling us into a petrified state like the massive stones around us, then all at once, there's a flurry of activity, breaking both the quiet and the spell.

With heavy limbs, I'm dismounting when I notice something in the distance. A flash of red cuts through the trees, soaring downhill, and I squint my eyes, trying to make out what it might be. It's too far away to tell exactly, but for the briefest of seconds, it looks like somebody I used to know. Somebody with red hair. Crazy, unmanageable—not that he ever actually tried to tame it—bright red hair. An ironic sort of smile tugs at my lips, and I blink long and hard, breathing through my nose.

"A Cardinal."

Gia's voice hovers above me, waiting for the exact spot to land where I need it, and the comfort it provides, most.

She jerks her chin to where the barest of flickers of the ghost disappeared. The thousands of trees almost resemble the tops of broccoli, they're so tightly packed, but come winter, they'll look more like cauliflower, providing a better opportunity for seeing wildlife. It's amazing I was able to see the bird to begin with. Must've been the color.

"Male Cardinals are said to be messages from someone you lost."

Suddenly my limbs lose the extra weight, like they too are ready to fly away.

What message would he have for me now? That, like Gia said, I am in the right place?

"Could be for you. Maybe from your mom?"

She watches me closely for a minute before saying, "I've been wondering that myself."

She has? For how long, because we *just* saw it?

"What bird was your mom?" I ask her instead, and before I even get the full sentence out, she's already answering, "Bohemian Waxwing."

"Never heard of it."

"They're beautiful." Her eyes fill with a wonder I can practically feel. "But in an understated way. People mistake them for other birds all the time."

Hold up.

"And that's the one that's most like your mom?"

A light laugh floats past her lips. "My dad says the same thing. He thinks she was a Snowy Owl, or a Mute Swan. Something romantic. Gorgeous. Ethereal."

"But she wasn't?"

After a moment of Gia losing herself in some faraway memory, she starts again, saying, "Waxwings eat so much fruit, even the overripe fruit that's fermented."

Fermented?

"You mean they get wasted off it?"

She nods, and we share a private laugh that goes straight to my bones.

"A bird that gets drunk, huh? Did your mom like her wine or something?" I know mine does.

Gia's face loses a bit of its glow. "She didn't drink alcohol at all. She didn't need to. She was drunk off life. She always had the best time everywhere she went, no matter what the mood was." It's easy to see where Gia gets that same quality from. "She loved life so much she was drunk off it. Every fucking day. Even at the end." She drops her eyes, lost all over again.

Damn. What a sad ending for a woman with so much to live for—a devoted husband, a daughter chomping at the bit to follow in her footsteps, a successful business, a hobby bordering on obsession. And to top it all off, she genuinely loved life, the very thing others waste their precious existence resenting.

Kind of like when their best friend dies suddenly, leaving them all alone.

Fuck.

"How'd you know that one was a male?"

"Hmm?" she asks, bringing her gaze back to mine.

"The Cardinal. You said the males are messages, but how could you tell that one was a male?"

"Because he's fucking stunning. You can't look away from him when he's near. A body like no other, a face that stands out in any scenery he's in, a quavering voice used to attract his mate. You know when you come across a male Cardinal."

"Do you think that one has a mate?"

"Maybe. She'd be out of sight but still close by him. Cardinals are never far from their mates for long. They're…partners, in every aspect, really. Not all species care for each other beyond mating but Cardinals do."

I scan the trees below, asking, "What does she look like?"

"Different," is all I hear followed by Gia's footsteps, and when I look back, she's gone.

Cardinals.

Something tells me there's more to that story. A lot more.

Chapter 19

ROZ

I pop the last bit of beef jerky in my mouth as Bryce ventures over to my perch on a rock overlooking the water. It's been one visitor after the other since we stopped. They've all been nice, just weird. They're not weird. *It's* weird, the fact that so many people are going out of their way to talk to me. I've never been somewhere where everyone's interested in me, and I've done televised interviews with live audiences being instructed to be interested in what I'm saying.

Wait.

I shoot a look over to Gia. She's been steering clear after our little bird chat, but hasn't kept her eyes off me for very long. Every few minutes, she does a sweep of my area. Just like on the four-wheelers, she's tuned into what I'm doing while acting like she's not.

"Did Gia send you over?" I ask Bryce, and he shakes his head, saying, "Not me, no. But…"

Yeah. *But.*

She's not catering to me directly, but she's sure as fuck checking to see if I'm taken care of indirectly by keeping me occupied. Keeping my mind from racing, spinning out of control. *Falling into oblivion.*

We talk for a couple more minutes, then I start to dig a little deeper, asking, "So, you two never…"

"I love Gia." The hand stuffed in his pocket might as well have my heart in its grip. "But no, she's like my little sister."

"How old are you?"

"Twenty-one."

"You look—"

"Young? Yeah, I get that a lot." Bryce gets that embarrassed look again, making me feel like shit. It's not that he looks young, it's that he's really small. Sickly almost.

The day's events come back to me, slowly at first, then faster and faster. Gia was asking him how he was feeling, and while everyone else was hungover from last night, Bryce wasn't one of them. He couldn't have been because he didn't drink anything. At least not during the time that I watched him and Gia with hawk eyes.

"How *do* you know Gia?"

"Her mom, Vita, and I got chemo at the same time." He adjusts the beanie on his head, revealing hair with that newly grown-in look.

"Shit. Sorry, dude. I didn't know. Did you…"

"Beat it?" he supplies, then nods.

"That's good. Congrats."

"Last we checked anyway."

"You have to keep checking, huh? It can come back?"

"It can do whatever it wants." He shrugs. "That's the thing about cancer, it doesn't really tell you its plans ahead of time."

I blow out a breath, tugging on the collar of my hoodie.

"Luckily, we caught mine early though."

"That must've been pretty hard going through that in only your teens, right?"

If Vita died three years ago and they got treatment together, he was fucking young.

"Cancer's a real asshole." His glacial blue eyes pin me in place. "It doesn't see age."

A lump settles in my throat as I bob my head, dropping my gaze to the ground.

"It's probably a good thing Gia's so damn proactive."

"How do you mean?"

"Well…because her mom…" He eyes me carefully.

"Yeah, I heard." Gia doesn't really talk about it though, not like this. She talks about her mom and what she meant to her, but not about her death. I don't even know what kind of cancer Vita died from. "But cancer's not hereditary, is it?"

"I had Hodgkin's lymphoma, which the mutation could've been passed down to me, but neither of my parents had it, so mine probably wasn't. But, you know, Gia was practically Vita's doppelganger." He lets that linger, but I still don't really understand. Why does them looking alike matter? "Add that to the fact that Vita died of the same exact cancer her mother did and I'd be getting biopsies, too."

Biopsies?

"What's that cancer called again?" I ask, my eyes already seeking Gia out.

"Melanoma."

Skin cancer.

Biopsies.

That's what those scars are. Gia gets biopsies taken because she's worried she'll get skin cancer, just like her mom. And apparently her grandmother. But why didn't she just say that? Why couldn't she tell me? I'd…

I don't know.

"You all right, man? You're wobbling."

I look down, freezing my body in place. I hadn't even noticed. "Uh, yeah," I mumble before walking away, toward Gia, who's bent down, checking her tire pressure.

Everything starts to fall into place. The long-sleeve shirts, pants, and hats, even when it's triple digits. The time I found her in the shade when every other person would've been soaking up the sun like a sponge in the Atlantic. Her words that day. *The sun can kill you.* Everything. All of it. Even the day I first met her.

"Are you planning on dying then?"

"Not today."

"You're scared," I blurt as soon as I'm standing above her.

She squints up at me, tugging on something under the

four-wheeler's muddy body. Her head dips like she knew this was coming.

"Junior year, I had just come back after my mom died, and one day at lunch, I downed a whole carton of milk too fast and it sprayed out my nose like a broken fucking spigot. I'm telling you, nobody walked away dry that day. Anyway, this group of girls thought I was possessed, so they started filling their water bottles with water they got from the bathroom and dousing me with it in the hallways between classes. They would chant these fake prayers and everything." Sitting back on her heels to dust her hands, she says, "And I'm scared I'll never be able to get the taste out of my mouth."

What? That…took an unexpected turn.

Or two.

"You mean the water?"

After a pause, where I think she's going to take it all back, she says seriously, "It was public restroom water, Roz. You don't know what's in that shit." She even pretends to shudder.

Is she serious right now?

"What are you talking about?"

"What are *you* talking about?"

I shake the entire—hopefully fictional—story away, telling her, "I'm talking about those scars on your back, Gia. And on your wrist." She stops what she's doing, staring blankly in front of her. *That's right, baby. I caught on.* "Why do you wear clothes that cover almost every inch of your skin? Even on the hottest summer days? Why do you lurk outside funerals like you're doing research for your own?" I crouch down beside her, willing her to look at me while whispering, "Why won't you admit you have feelings for me?"

After a quick glance around to see if people are listening, she brings her eyes to mine and, fuck me, I shouldn't have done it like this. I shouldn't have cornered her because now she's pacing like a wild animal, looking for a way out, any way out. Unfortunately, the only way out is through me because I'm not letting this go. Not until she's honest with me.

"What's your deal with wanting me to like you so bad? I used to like thongs once upon a time," she shrugs, "but you don't see me parading around in one now, do you?" She stands suddenly, taking every bit of my calm with her.

I mimic her stance, crossing my arms over my chest and meeting her glare with my own. "You're scared to like me. You're scared to be with me."

"There he is. Mr. Roswell Andrews-Smith, the narcissistic asshole looking for a good fuck."

My face flinches before I can stop it.

"Take sex off the table—"

She groans dramatically. "But table sex is so good when it's done right." I try to ignore her, but she keeps going. "You have to find someone tall enough but not too tall."

"Gia."

"The table can't be too tall either though."

"Gia, stop," I try again. Softer, I say, "You're scared of dying."

"And you're scared of living." She scoffs.

"Talk to me already. You can push me all you want, but I'm not budging this time. Fucking *talk* to me."

A few minutes pass until finally she says, "You weren't the first person to notice my scars. You were just the first person to be upset by them. You're…" she groans, "it doesn't fucking matter. Every woman in my family has died of the same cancer. Do you get that?" The look she gives me silences the response on my tongue. "Yes, I avoid commitment. I'm *avoiding* commitment. But it's not for my sake. It'd be like a sinking ship inviting passengers to board and I won't do that to anybody, especially not—"

She stops abruptly, grinding the side of her jaw into her shoulder.

I take a step toward her, needing her in my arms already, but she ducks past, refusing to look at me again.

"I'll meet everybody back at the house."

"Don't do this. Don't leave," I beg, but she's not listening anymore. She's not listening at all.

The sky outside matches the storm brewing inside my chest as Bryce and I pull up to the cabin. After we made our way back down the mountain Gia abandoned us on, I let him tag along with me to the outdoor store I saw in town. He's actually pretty funny. Being in and out of hospitals, he spent a lot of time people-watching, giving him the ability to pick apart a person's personality without ever speaking a single word to them. It'd be freaky if it wasn't so goddamn entertaining.

Gia still wasn't around yet when we left, but parking now, I catch sight of her sitting sideways on her four-wheeler with her head leaned back, so her face is pointed at the angry sky.

We quickly jump out to open up the new tarp, the promise of rain sitting heavy in the air as we work to get everything I just bought covered.

Bryce stands frozen, breathing out, "She's crazy," and I don't have to see who he's talking about to know it's Gia.

"She is."

"I'll go get her."

Looking over at Gia, I instantly catch Bryce's arm, telling him, "I got her."

Out of the corner of my eye, I see him hesitate, so I jerk a nod at the cabin, saying, "Go ahead inside. I don't need you catching a cold or something." He was just telling me about being in remission and how many restrictions there are. His immune system is basically like a newborn baby's and he has to slowly work his way up.

Even once I'm alone, I don't rush over to Gia, instead choosing to watch her from a distance for a while. The rain finally falls down on to her slim frame, but still, I don't move. I can't. I'm a hostage and Gia is my captor—I'm fucking seized by her.

A crack of thunder rings out, jolting me back to the here and now. Gia doesn't so much as wince though as she fits a joint to her lips, the tenacious tendrils of smoke attempting to persevere past the drops of pounding water more affected than her. What the fuck is she doing?

I'm closing the distance with heavy, determined steps carrying me toward her a second later. The clouds above us aspire to be as pissed as I am right now.

"What do you think you're doing? It's not safe out here."

"It's not safe in here." Without opening her eyes, she points to her head, and I swear her finger grazes her chest as she drops her hand back to her lap.

The electricity hanging in the air calls to the current buzzing beneath my skin as my eyes run the length of her.

"Your clothes are getting wet."

Pulling from the neckline at my back, I take my hoodie off and move to put it on Gia, when her eyes pop open. Neither of us blinks, but the dying cherry at her mouth catches my eye, so I grab it with one hand before placing it between my lips. I get the hoodie in place on her while traces of the smoke goad me into taking a bigger hit. I do just as the last of the roach dies out.

Gia's eyes watch without a single trace of emotion before blinking back up to the sky, raindrops sticking to her now motionless lashes. There's mud up to her thighs, a twig in her hair, and her knuckles look like they're wind-chapped. She's the most beautiful thing I've ever fucking laid eyes on.

"Dance with me." The whispered plea floats between us before I can call it back.

It stirs her though, and she looks back at me, asking, "What?"

"Dance with me."

"Roz—"

Dropping the dead embers to the ground, I pull her to me using both hands, then wrap an arm around her back.

I throw her words back at her, telling her, "There's always time to dance." If she can push, so can I. She wants things a certain way? Well, so do I. And right now, I want her in my arms.

She resists at first, only giving in when it's clear I'm dancing with or without her participation, but when she does, we move in sync to the same song neither of us can hear.

After a minute, she lets out a low chuckle that vibrates through my chest, saying, "I thought you'd be a better dancer."

"Why's that?"

"The way you snowboard, you move like you're having sex. A seductive dance. An erotic show for the masses." Her eyes soften, droplets falling from her lashes onto her cheeks. "You don't dance like that at all."

"You've seen me compete?"

"For hours." She nods. "Once I started, I couldn't stop. After I met you, I had to look you up. Pro snowboarder gracing this small town with his presence…how could I not? Your skills are unmatched."

Another moment passes as our feet continue moving to the silent tune.

"I watched your friend, Salvy, too. He was good. Nowhere near as good as you though. You worked those slopes like you were teasing a well-acquainted lover in a risky game of foreplay. He looked like he was just along for the ride."

I think back to the way Salvy was always rushing to finish through runs of our prized sport. Salvy liked snowboarding, but he loved the overall lifestyle competing and winning provided us more. The constant travel, the girls, the money, the photo shoots, the *fun*. I enjoyed those aspects at different points, but as a whole, all I really wanted, what I craved more than anything, was snowboarding itself. But…

"It must've been a lover worth walking away from then since I quit."

Her red-rimmed eyes bore into mine. "Like all great love stories, you'll be back. You'll return with open arms, blind optimism, and enough passion to fuck everybody up."

I shake my head. "I've been riding alongside Salvy since we were kids. It wouldn't be the same without him."

"I saw the way you were with his mom at his funeral, you took care of her. You took care of both of them, didn't you?"

My eyes fall to Gia's mouth, watching bits of water lazily roll over her bottom lip, and I nod.

Gia clamps her eyes shut, the energy around us shifting.

"And now you're looking for someone else to take care of."

"What? No." I never said that. I never even thought that.

Her eyes open, revealing more determination than I've ever seen in them before as she says, "But, I don't need you, Roz. I don't need your help. I don't want it. I don't want *you*."

She pulls away, leaving me grasping at air.

"So, that's it then? All because you can't accept help?"

"That's where you're wrong. I've never seen a man so lost in the one place he truly belongs until I saw you out there today. I'm not the one in need of help. You are."

"Are you talking about snowboarding?"

She rolls her eyes.

"I'm fucking *done* with boarding!" I roar, spreading my arms out wide, letting the rain openly cascade down my body.

"Are you?"

"Yeah, I am. Why can't you understand that? Why are you pushing for something that's not gonna happen?"

"Why are you?" she shoots back. "You returning to the life you love, the life you were meant for, is an actual possibility. This," she gestures between us, "isn't."

"Yeah well, fuck you then. Fuck you for forcing yourself into those church doors and into my life. Fuck you for forcing yourself into my bed as easily as you forced yourself back out of it. Fuck you for forcing me out here just to tell me you regret it all. Fuck you, Gia!"

Not once does she look away, not even when I yell the last part again.

With an eyebrow raised, she says, "You want to kiss me, don't you?"

"Fuck yes." What gave it away? The outline of my hardening

cock against my jeans? The thundering from my chest that feels a hundred times louder than the clouds above our heads? Or the way my body won't stop leaning toward her like she's the north to my compass?

"Typical upper-class brat."

Air pours from my nose in quick, thick streams.

"You think everyone owes you something because you excelled at going fast down a few snowy hills? You think *I* owe you something because you were decent in bed?"

She takes a step closer to me, and I almost say fuck it all and kiss her. At least it'd shut her up. I don't want to hear this. Not from her.

"Two-thirds of the population around here can slide their ass down the side of a mountain once the snow falls, Roz. It's called having money and nothing better to do. You miss your friend? Go buy another one. It worked with Salvy, didn't it? Throw a little money at anything and you can claim it as yours. Isn't that right?"

What. The. Fuck.

Where is all this coming from? She's never judged me for the parts of my life I've shared with her, but now she's throwing everything back in my face. And with enough venom to make the most lethal snake jealous. Was she just pretending this entire time? Saving up all these misconceptions to fuck with my head when she was done fucking with my body.

"If that's true, what's your price?" I regret the words as soon as they're out of my mouth, but I'm too far in to pull out now. Might as well dig a little deeper while I'm here. I've got nowhere else to go.

Her laugh is unlike any others I've heard from her. "While you were dipping from your parents' bottomless pit of resources to kick-start a career any adrenaline junkie with a trust fund could get, I was busy creating a life I actually chose for myself. One I respect enough not to ruin by messing with miserable cowards. In fact, this is all starting to border on pathetic, and unfortunately for you, I no longer give out pity fucks."

I scoff loudly while trying to keep my body as still as possible. "Was that before or after you let T.J. eat your pussy?"

"You wanted to know what bird you are?" Her fingernail pierces my skin below my collarbone as she digs her pointer finger into my chest. "A Mockingbird. Aggressive assholes who spend their lives mimicking others instead of being themselves. You're a fucking imitation, and I'm glad to finally be rid of you."

"Is that your idea of a goodbye?" My voice is stripped raw, just like the rest of me.

"You were a good ride while you lasted, but we both know you don't last long at anything."

With my hoodie still on her, Gia turns away, leaving me here for what feels like the last time.

"You said I was a star," I call to her back. "Remember that?" It's not even what she said but how she said it—with awe. How does a person fake that?

She doesn't even stop as she looks over her shoulder with a face full of pity, saying, "Yeah, a failing star."

Fuck an avalanche, Gia herself just buried me alive. Or at least I was before she ripped my heart out of my chest.

Chapter 20

GIA

I hurry up the porch steps on legs shakier than they were after a full day of riding.

He just had to. He just had to push me to say those things and now my tongue feels like ash in my mouth.

It's okay. It'll be okay. It's for the best. It is. It has to be because the alternative…

No, this is the right thing to do.

It feels wrong, incredibly fucking wrong, but I have to believe it's better than letting Roz watch me wither away in front of his eyes, just like my mom did mine and my dad's.

The front door swings open as I'm reaching for the handle to reveal Rowdy with something that looks a lot like disappointment building in his eyes.

"I know," I tell him, but I don't. I don't know anything right now. I thought I did, then I met Roz.

Bryce passes me a bottle of gin I'm ninety-eight percent sure he wasn't drinking from, and I take it, throwing back a couple of shots in one go.

"Good gawd, that shit's nasty," I blanch, but the alcohol burns worse than the dumpster fire my mind currently is, so I toss back another gulp before wiping my mouth with my hand.

"There goes our security deposit," my boy Mikey says, his face practically pressed against the glass of the living room window. "What did you do to him, G?"

Everybody else is focused on the front yard too, but I already know what has their attention. I heard it on my way inside. Roz is ripping apart the cheesy-ass sign the homeowners obviously made using his bare hands.

"I pushed him," I say under my breath, putting my back to the window.

I pushed Roz the way I've been pushing him since we met, but I also *pushed* him. I pushed Roz away, for good.

I just hope I didn't push him too hard. There's no denying Roz is stuck. He's not doing anything because he doesn't need to. He's pancaked between what his mind is trying to convince him is normal and what actually is. Sitting around like an unfeeling zombie who doesn't let himself enjoy anything isn't Roz's normal, I know it isn't. Roz is passionate, complicated, dangerous, vibrant. But he needed one last nudge. A reason to feel again, to lose who he thinks he should be, so he can rediscover who he really is.

And I just gave it to him.

What he doesn't know is it hurt me more than it hurt him. Those things I said tasted like a straight shot of moonshine followed by a vinegar chaser and I am absolutely choking right now. *Choking.*

I swallow more gin, trying to wash it all down. Wash it all away.

"What happened, Gia?" Bryce breathes, his gaze fixed on the scene on the front lawn.

Taking a quick look out there myself, at first all I see is shards of wood flying everywhere, but then in the middle of it all, stands Roz in deep concentration, like an ice carver, except instead of making something, he's fucking destroying it.

I turn back around, choking all over again. Even in his downfall, Roz is breathtaking.

Someone cheers and several others laugh, guessing which trail name Roz will rip off next, reminding me of these raptors in Australia called Firehawks that actually feed off the panic at wildfires.

"I fed the Firehawks," I tell Bryce regretfully. Regret, the one thing I never wanted to feel. That and whatever's happening in my chest knowing Roz is in pain—pain I caused.

"Hurricane Gia strikes again, leaving *another* path of destruction in her wake," says an outlandishly tall girl named Kori that graduated a couple years ahead of me, but I don't even argue. I can't. I wish this was the same as the others.

"Everyone you touch turns into a fucking mess."

Rowdy pierces me with a disbelieving look, probably wondering when I'm going to shut Kori up already, but what can I say? Really? She's not exactly wrong. Out of line, but not wrong. I shouldn't have brought Roz, and I've left behind a fair amount of messes. None that felt like this one though.

This is a first.

I didn't tell Roz the whole story earlier today, the one about the girls chucking water at me—it wasn't all bullshit. They really did do that, but what I left out was that I didn't shy away from their melodramatic exorcism. I opened my mouth, welcoming it in because I wanted to see if it would work. If it'd magically rid whatever evil is running through my bloodstream that nature's clearly been trying to eradicate from this earth by killing off all the women in my bloodline. And although I told Roz I was worried about getting the water *in*, the truth is I'm fucking terrified I'll end up letting the rot—the very thing afflicting my entire family tree—*out*.

Theoretically that could only happen if I got knocked up, which I already decided against a long time ago. But Roz? He makes me question everything. He makes me want things I've never wanted before. He makes me go back on my own rules without hesitation. He makes me forget I even have rules…and why I made them to begin with.

"You think he's a mess?" I ask Kori over the noise, waiting until she returns her gaze to mine. "Treat him like he's not." Because my way hasn't worked so far, and I need him out of my head already.

"How?"

"Make *him* forget."

"Forget what?" She arches a flawless eyebrow, pulling a red-coated lip into her mouth.

I head for the hall leading to the back of the house, telling her, "Everything." Even me.

Especially me.

I'm in a hot tub. In my riding clothes. *Great.*

"Whose idea was this?"

"Yours," a masculine voice to my right says with a chuckle, and I fight an eye roll.

Did I black out? I don't remember wanting to come in here. I don't remember much except…

Except not wanting to go anywhere near the room Roz and I shared last night. He's in there right now. Or he was last I had my fucking wits about me. The door being closed made an impression though. A huge impression that helped the gin go down that much easier.

He's probably using the box of condoms I paid for.

Hope the ridges pay off for…what's her name again?

"Kori."

Did I say that? Or… I drag my gaze over to the guy on my left, but he's too busy fingering the hem of my shirt to notice. On my right his friend's hand teases my pant-covered knee under the water. There's a lot of stimulation. And heat. A *lot* of heat. Not like Roz's relaxing heat either. This heat's…prickly. Like itchy carpet on a summer day with ninety-two percent humidity.

"What?"

"Kori. That's who you're talking about, right? She's been in with that skier for hours."

"Snowboarder," I correct before sinking lower into the hot water, the itching spreading quickly.

Hours.

Good. Wonderful. Fuck like rabbits, just like I predicted. Just like I *wanted.*

Again, with *my* condoms.

"Don't worry, we've got condoms, too. Lots of them."

Knee guy leans in close, nuzzling the skin below my ear, and my eyes close on their own, welcoming the foreign touch. *Yes.* Now this I take full credit for. What's better than one fuckboy rebound? Two.

"Stop reading my thoughts," I mutter. "They can't be trusted." That's why I drowned them out to begin with.

"Sorry, baby."

Reality backhands some of the alcohol blur from my vision as I blink my eyes open, tilting my head away from knee guy to tell him, "Don't call me that."

"How about you lose some of this?" His friend changes the subject, tugging on my shirt. More reality comes into focus, making me wish I could just go under the water altogether. I can't lose my shirt or my scars will be on display. I can lose my other clothes though. At this point, they're just deadweight anyway, and since I already lost a 6'2", hundred-and-seventy-five-pound—

No.

I never had Roz. I coveted him, but I didn't have him.

The guy with my shirt in his grasp starts to pull it up, but luckily, someone's voice booms through the screened-in three-season room, keeping him from lifting it any higher.

I eye the material caught in his fist, willing it to be freed somehow without me being obvious about it. It's only the three of us in the hot tub, but there's people everywhere, all around us.

My other bookend doesn't stop his deep-water exploration as his hand finds its way to my inner thigh, and when one of his fingers grazes my pussy through my pants, I have to gurgle through a hiss to stifle a gag, dropping my head on the headrest, so I can't see him anymore.

With my eyes still open and on the ceiling, I catch Roz as he crosses my line of vision followed closely by Kori. I struggle to follow them as far as my odd position allows, but from what I can tell, Kori's got on a bright yellow bikini while Roz is just in plain cargo shorts.

It's their expressions however that have me lifting my head to get a better look. They're both wearing a pair of matching frowns like an old married couple sitting in a restaurant full of people with absolutely nothing to say to each other. I see it all the time.

I don't exactly know what I was expecting from Roz and Kori, but frowns weren't it.

Afterglow fuzzies.

Tender caresses.

Self-righteous smiles.

Not...whatever this shit is.

"Nice."

You can *taste* the disapproval in Roz's tone as he scowls at us, and I have to suppress another gag using the back of my fingers against my mouth.

I track him leading Kori over to the opposite side of the hot tub. He's dirtier than I thought he'd be. Don't get me wrong, his mouth is straight filth normally, but this is like actual dirt. Flakes of it coat his palms and forearms that he tries to hide when he notices me looking. *What's that about?*

"Back at you," I fling at him like an accusation. "You owe me fifteen dollars and sixty-nine cents, by the way."

Roz eyes Kori and I scoff, shaking the thought of him actually using them with her from my head. Thankfully, it sinks to the bottom of the boiling water when two pairs of lips start in on my neck.

Roz's golden eyes find mine again, and before I can stifle it, a moan escapes, drifting over the steamy surface, straight to his scowl, making it deepen.

It feels good in the worst way possible. Right eyes, wrong lips. Right guy, wrong girl.

If only I wasn't wrong for Roz. If only...

"What'd they do to earn that?" Roz sneers, piercing the tension with a knife and twisting.

"They..." They... They... They did nothing to earn this. Nothing to earn me, my body, my time. Not like Roz did. He earned more kisses than I let him have. He earned more time than I gave him. He earned more from me than I thought possible.

But I took it all away before cancer could.

The heat rises and rises and rises, surrounding me, invading me, until it's too much and my throat fills with acid the second another finger joins the first one in an attempt to stab awkwardly at the outside of my crotch.

I push the two fuckboys away, avoiding Roz's heavy stare.

Rowdy pokes his head out the slider, asking, "G? You good?" He knows I don't ask for permission for anything I do, but he still likes to make sure I'm coherent enough to make those choices for myself. I just wish he would've thought to check in with me *before* I decided to get into a hot tub fully clothed because that's a choice I should've never made.

I give him a nod that feels like a shake. What is good? Because this doesn't feel good. Nothing about these guys feels good. Not their lips, not their hands, not even their attention. Roz's attention didn't just affect me, it changed me, and now nothing else compares.

"She's being fucking mauled and you're okay with it?" Roz spits at Rowdy, his expression not matching his words. There's anger, for sure, but there's also a lot of pain. Pain I'm still putting there.

This isn't to *hurt* Roz. It's to hurt him *less*. Him watching me die wouldn't just hurt, it'd debilitate him. Look how he handled one death. He couldn't handle another. He shouldn't.

He won't. Simple.

"She's a big girl, Roz."

Roz switches his glare from Rowdy to me and, raising my own eyebrows, I mouth the word "big" for him in case he missed it the first time even though I don't feel big right now. I feel tiny, insignificant, but I've gotten really fucking good at faking a bigger presence around men thanks to them constantly trying to challenge me, like Mitch did.

"She knows what she's doing." Rowdy pins me with a hard look, then mumbles, "Most of the time," while turning away.

Maybe I'm not as good as I thought.

Shirt guy chimes in, saying, "You're welcome to join us. If you and Kori are up for round two."

"Or three or four," says his friend.

Even though I shouldn't, I wait with bated breath, listening for Roz's answer. Kori doesn't give anything away as she drops her gaze shyly and Roz... Roz just hesitates, his thumbs rubbing roughly over his grimy knuckles all the while his jaw tics like the seconds hand on a clock.

Well?

Kori interrupts the stretched moment, suggesting, "What about a game of two truths and a lie?"

A game? How fucking camp counselor of her. No wonder Roz is out here looking for a fight instead of banging Kori's brains out.

Unless he already did.

Did he or didn't he?

I reach for the half-empty bottle of gin sitting on a tall table off to the side. Unfortunately, it's out of my grasp in the next instant as Roz pulls it away and tosses the entire bottle out the propped-open screen door.

Rude.

"Rich people are so wasteful," I tsk.

Not nearly concerned as I am about the spilled gin, knee guy asks, "What are the rules?"

Kori smiles up at Roz and I have to fight to keep myself above the water. I told Kori to do this. I don't have any right to be upset. But…

But I hate her. Roz, too. Mostly Roz, for falling for the cheap shot he should've seen coming a mile away. A stupidly hot girl dangled in front of his face seconds after I stomped out his little crush? Come the fuck on. He can't really be that naïve.

Of course, even if she went for him on her own, I would've had to do the same thing I'm doing now—nothing.

I'd have to watch her steal my ice cowboy right out from under me.

My ice cowboy.

"I'll start," Roz says, that deep voice of his setting off underwater shockwaves.

As soon as Kori started talking, I tuned her out, so I have no idea what the rules are but, apparently, we're all playing, including Roz.

"My first job was at the mall serving lemonade, I have eight gold medals, and the last thing I said to my best friend before he died was 'you go first.'" Roz's gaze drops to his lap.

"Damn, that was deep. How are we supposed to guess after that?"

I lick the inside of my cheek. *Lemonade? Really?*

"The mall's a lie." I know the medals are true, I practically memorized his record. The one about Salvy sounds like something that might've happened, even though I hope it didn't. It'd explain why Roz feels so gawd-damn guilty all the time.

Roz brings his head up slowly, saying, "She's right."

The vibe changes suddenly, becoming much more charged, and I glance around, asking, "What does that mean? Is it my turn?"

"Not yet. He gets to choose who you kiss first."

My pulse picks up speed as I sit up, making waves that go over the edge of the hot tub walls. Why did I open my mouth?

I open it again to try and backpedal, but am cut off by Roz saying a name I didn't expect but totally should've.

"Kori."

Touché, Roswell. Touché.

Kori looks like she just chugged the lemonade Roz never served as she quirks her perfect eyebrow at me, a hundred questions written on her face.

It's a little late for that, Kori. She should've questioned me hours ago, when I first gave her the assignment she's currently failing. Roz hasn't forgotten anything, not even me. Especially not me.

Forced to stand since Kori's a giant and not fully submerged yet, I grab a handful of hair at the back of her head to bring her face within inches of mine. I hold the position, waiting for her permission, since I know she doesn't like me, but then she clenches my waist, pulling me to her so hard, we almost head-butt each other, and I have to knock her chin with mine just to create a little more space. She closes it in an instant though, darting her tongue straight into my mouth with both the enthusiasm and expertise of a Saint Bernard puppy.

Two loud groans sound off behind me with absolute silence from Roz next to us. Silence so cold and thick it burns like dry ice.

All at once, I release Kori's hair and lips, returning to my seat in a daze.

The girl is fired up, that much is obvious. Like *bad*. If they really are on round two, three, or four, you'd think Kori would be a little more…chill. But she's not. I'm lucky she didn't rub against me like a bear trying to scratch a day-old itch on a tree. Day old…or *hours* old. What were they doing in that room?

Am I out $15.69 or not?

"Your turn," somebody says, and with my eyes on the surface's bubbles, I say, "I've never ridden a horse, I took apart my first quad by myself to sell the parts, and for the last three years, I've woken up early every morning to listen to my dad cry when he thinks no one can hear him." *Excluding the mornings I spent with Roz, that is.*

This is why I suck at real games. I follow no one's rules but my own, and even those I'm having a hard time with lately.

"I can be your first horse ride," one of the fuckboys offers, but before I can take him up on it, Roz's jagged voice slices through the double entendre with, "Your first quad is currently a loaner at the racetrack you teach at."

"Is he right?"

A shoulder bumps me and I nod absently.

"Okay, pick a name. And remember, you can choose yourself." Another bump to my shoulder, this one from my other side.

I feel like I'm on a roller coaster down on Coney Island during summer break. It's too hot, too humid, too bumpy, and there's trash everywhere I look. I want off but…

Contrary to what I told Roz earlier, the ride isn't over. Not yet.

"Kori."

Roz's tongue runs across his top teeth, then with every single muscle below his neck taut as a bow, he moves for her. Kori's got a dopey smile plastered to her face, but I can't even blame her. Roz kisses better than he used to snowboard.

Eight gold medals. *Eight.*

The second his lips touch hers, I commit the image to memory, collecting it for the moments when I'm weak because I know they'll come. They're already here now.

It's over as quick as it started though, then Roz is speaking in the next breath, saying, "I once landed an 1800-degree quad cork, I knocked my front four teeth out on a bunny hill, I haven't washed my truck in two months."

Unable to stop myself, I unclench my teeth from around my thumb ring to murmur, "Bunny hill."

"No shit? Only like four people have ever landed that jump," shirt guy, or maybe knee guy, says. I lost track. I lost track when I gave up pretending anything about them was collectible—right about the same time Roz showed back up.

Never away for long.

Roz's eyes on mine, I watch as they abandon their normal color of gold and light to umber and murky in a flash and, almost like he's handing out punishment, he announces, "Kori," completely ignoring everyone else.

"Damn, Kori. You're having all the fun tonight."

Except, she isn't. She didn't fuck Roz and he sure as hell didn't fuck her. There was zero familiarity in their kiss. Zero chemistry. Zero emotions.

Watching Roz the entire time, I make my way over to Kori again, kneeling on the bench her feet are on to pull her into the water by the backs of her knees, so she's straddling my lap. With my hands cupping her jaw, I pull her to me, licking her soft lips once before opening them to slip inside.

Roz's appearance gives nothing away to the naked eye, but I know better. I know *him* better. His fists tightening shows he's struggling to keep it together right now. While every other guy at his house party was happy to fetishize two women together, Roz didn't offer so much as a single fuck when my friend and I were dancing, just like he doesn't actually give a fuck that Kori and I are kissing. He does care that *I'm* kissing Kori though, and because he can't kiss me himself, he's using her as both a conduit and a punishment.

Massaging Kori's overactive tongue with mine, I'm able to tame it into submission until our mouths are kneading each other's rather than the all-out wrestling match from before. She's sweet like cherry soda and makes my lips fizzy.

Or maybe that's the bubbles bursting all around us.

Never once breaking eye contact with Roz, I keep up the pace until Kori starts rolling her hips atop my thighs. I'll kiss her, but I'm not about to give the girl her first orgasm of the night. I'll leave that to…someone else.

Staying where I am, I break the kiss to say, "I prefer graveyards over hospitals, I've never had sex with the same person twice, my prom date had three balls."

Rowdy protests from somewhere outside the hot tub, saying, "I don't have three balls," a second before Roz says, "Prom."

I don't even hide my grin when I say, "Kori."

Still standing half out of the water, Roz leans down before taking Kori's mouth in a kiss that has a lot more emotion than the first one. My premature smile falls clean off when he does the exact thing I just did—continues kissing Kori while watching me.

Shit. Talk about the perfect combination of pain and pleasure.

My own hips start to buck under Kori's, and I have to fight to keep my eyes open and on Roz's. If I just pretend…

Roz's teeth clamp down on her bottom lip, drawing it out from the rest of her mouth, causing me to moan out loud, but when Kori's fingers dig into my upper arms, tempting me like a siren coaxing a sailor to their demise, my control starts to splinter off in different directions.

Dilated eyes locked on mine, Roz groans, too, gathering all my resolve back into one direction—his—and I thread my hands through Kori's hair, pushing her further into him, pretending it's my lips he's devouring, not hers. Round after round, Roz goes in for more, never backing down, never looking away until I'm breathing so heavy, I don't even notice another hand joining the mix, grabbing the back of my neck to turn my head.

A second hand—I'm not even sure whose—guides my cheek the rest of the way until my face is over my shoulder.

Out of the corner of my eye, I see Roz tear his mouth from Kori's, but then my lips are brushing someone else's.

"Get the fuck off her."

The lips on mine disappear as Roz shoves both guys backward, making them fall into the water with two huge splashes.

"Why?" I press, and he blinks at me like he's speaking in Morse code. I don't read Morse code though. It's outdated and I'm drunk. Or…I was. I was drunk on *something*, but now I'm just drunk on *someone*.

"What the fuck, man? Now you're bogarting both girls?"

"Not both. Just one. Her."

One of the boys reaches for me again as he tries to find his footing, but Roz knocks his hand off, telling him, "Don't fucking touch her."

"Don't tell my fuckboys what to do," I tell Roz, sliding Kori off my lap to stand in the middle of the hot tub.

"Fuckboys?" one of them says, offended, while Roz parrots, "Yours?" before shaking his head once, twice, then steps off the wraparound seat down into the center, too, putting us at eye level with each other to say, "Fine. Let them touch you again, Gia, and I'll turn this water red."

"Why?" I repeat, looking into his eyes.

"I didn't go yet." He shrugs, his voice stale and not at all convincing.

"Well, that much is obvious."

We both stare the other down while the other people in the hot tub…I'm not sure what they're doing. Are they even here still? All I can see, hear, and feel is Roz. All I *want* to see, hear, and feel is Roz.

Wanting is the kindling for needing though, and I've tried to train myself not to need anybody. Needing people when you're at your lowest means possibly draining them and I won't risk that.

I can't.

"So?" I goad, rolling my finger in a circle for him to get on with it.

"I use a hypothetical as a crutch, I mess with people's heads for my own amusement, I make it seem like I'm fearless but really, I'm the fucking coward."

I knew Roz had a backbone, I've just been waiting for him to use it against me so I can get some closure already.

Let the closing ceremony commence.

"I waste every opportunity I've been given because I know I'll never run out of them, I'm clingy to make up for the attention I didn't get growing up, I wish I was a coward but I'm just tragic."

Leaning into my face, Roz grits, "Fuck. You," and in a knee-jerk reaction, I say, "Ki—"

"I thought this was supposed to be a game," one of the fuckboys complains, saving me from saying something I shouldn't.

I shake my head, saying, "It was never a game," instead.

"Really?" Roz sneers. "Because it sure as fuck feels like I got played."

"You knew what you were getting into from the jump."

Roz throws his hands up, sending water droplets into the air. "How could I know *anything* when you lied every step of the way?"

"I didn't lie. I just didn't share every little detail of my life with you. There's a difference."

"Is there? Is that what you tell yourself at night after you're done finger-fucking yourself thinking about me?"

"And I'm the liar? Weren't you the one that said you didn't kiss and tell? Loose lips sink ships, Roz."

"Good thing I'm not a sailor then, baby." He pushes into me, his chest heaving. "'Cause I'm a fucking snowboarder."

He doesn't even flinch when he says it either. *Finally.* He finally remembers, and like everything in life, it's both beautiful and heartbreaking.

I lift my jaw in a single nod, then look around at the eyes on us, admitting, "I'm done," quietly.

I am done. I've done everything I said I would and now I can finally walk away from Roz, knowing he's back on the right path.

At least the only person I had to screw this time was myself.

Chapter 21

ROZ

Where the hell does Gia think she's going after pulling all…*that*? I'm already out of the hot tub, charging after her because no, no fucking way is she done.

Honestly, I don't even know what all that was. I feel like I'm still playing catch-up. Like how long was that whole threesome shit even going on for? I tried to hurry, but damn, I wasn't gone for that long. Was I?

Oh well. It doesn't matter. I'm here now, and those fuckfaces—because they're *not* fuckboys, at least not Gia's fuckboys—are lucky they're walking away with all their limbs the way they were pawing at Gia. I thought I made myself clear this whole time, but our blow-up must've tipped off everybody in a fifty-mile radius, making them think Gia was fair game.

She's not. Not as long as I'm around. Yeah, I went fucking ham for a while, but I didn't actually go anywhere. Not far anyway.

After I'd gotten most of my anger out, I tried getting my head in order again by revisiting my plan from earlier, the one I had Bryce help me with. I had no idea what I'd be coming back to when I was finished, but now that I do, there's no way I'm giving up.

Gia can be scared. I get it. Damn, do I get it. But she doesn't get to act like an asshole under the pretense of martyrdom. It doesn't work like that. *I* don't work like that.

Being near Gia is like being kissed by the warmest rays of golden sunshine, but the shadow cast from her absence is like being spat on by the harshest of downpours, and even though I've spent my life adjusting to cooler temperatures, I'll never get used to that kind of cold.

And I don't care what she says, I'm not a Mockingbird. I don't give a fuck. I looked those things up, and yeah, no. Not me. Not now. Not fucking ever. The only time I've ever been aggressive in my life is when it comes to Gia and the need to protect her, to have her, to keep her. As for the rest...I'm done pretending.

The door to what was our shared room bounces off the wall as I fling it open and come to a full stop, staring down Gia's back.

Oh yeah, this is happening. She pissed me off, but I've never been more sure of anything.

We're both standing in our own puddles, but the lamp on the small bedside table casts an orange glow over the room that I pause for a second to absorb.

Gia looks over at me, asking, "Where's my bag?" breaking the moment.

"Come with me and I'll show you."

"No, I told you I'm done. I'm *done*, Roz. If Kori took—"

"Kori?"

When I was moving our stuff out to my truck earlier, Kori came in asking if she could crash for a bit. Apparently, the room she was in originally was being used for some sort of board game—yes, real board games—competition, so she needed somewhere quiet to hang. Since I knew Gia and I wouldn't be sleeping in here tonight, I left her to it, so I could get the rest of my shit done. Kori didn't have a chance to touch anything, but how'd Gia know she was in here to begin with?

"Yes, Kori. The girl whose mouth you just had your tongue inside."

"Same mouth yours was in," I say, crossing the room and throwing her over my shoulder with a spongy smack to the ass.

"Are you fucking kidding me?" she grumbles, not sounding angry so much as tired.

She hits my back the entire way through the house, but there's also a tremor no amount of half-strength blows can hide, telling me she's intrigued.

"I'm gonna puke," she groans, going limp, and I give her ass another slap, telling her, "Good. I need you sober for this next part."

Rowdy blocks the front door with a frown firmly in place and asks, "What's going on, Roz?"

"Nothing, man. Why don't you go ahead and get the fuck out of my way, so we can keep it that way?"

Gia squirms in my hold, forcing me to tighten my grip on her hips. I'm not gonna fight Rowdy. He's her best friend. I just need him out of my way. This night's already on the brink of failure, and I refuse to fail anymore.

Turns out, I'm not very good at it. I'm much better at excelling.

"I can't do that."

Oh, this is where he draws the line? But that whole scene in the hot tub, where Gia was getting felt up while her eyes were close to rolling in the back of her head, was okay? Right.

"You got my—"

"That's right, I got her." I get in his face, everything around us going quiet. "*I* got her." And I'd like to see him try taking her from me. I'd like to see anybody try, and that includes Gia, too.

Gia sighs, calling Rowdy off.

"That's what I thought," I tell him on my way out the door and past the newly reconfigured yard sign. It's nowhere near perfect, but I tried my best to piece it back together again.

I set Gia down by the passenger door of my Chevy, careful to keep her facing toward the front end.

"You done now?" she asks, and I try not to laugh, telling her, "Not even close."

Her knee lifts so fast it's a blur, but I manage to shoot my hands out in time to keep her from connecting with my balls.

Jesus Christ, that was close.

"Don't ever pull that shit again."

I press into her, peering down my nose to tell her, "Don't *you* ever pull that shit again." My voice rises as I continue, "I had to sit there and watch your *fuckboys*," plural because, fuck me, "grope you while you lapped it up! You're lucky a couple smacks on the ass is all you got."

"How much longer until you get it?" She's full-on yelling, too. "What else do I have to say to get you to go away?"

I take a step back. "You can start with the truth."

"We tried that, you went fucking psycho."

"Yeah, I broke some stuff, but you tried to fuck me out of your system."

"You could've done the same," she mutters.

"What was that?"

"Nothing." She waves a hand. "Who says you left that kind of impression? And what makes you think I haven't already fucked someone else?"

I growl, pushing back into her. "I've had it with you and—"

"Good! Fucking great!" Her hands flail at her sides before she uses them to shove at my chest. "I've been waiting for this moment. It's really not that deep for some of us. It's sad that you're incapable of understanding that, but I promise, Roz, the only person you're hurting is you."

Lies. I was about to say I've had it with her and her lies. Even now, nothing in Gia's expression matches what she's saying.

"Are we making promises now?" I murmur, but instead of answering, she tries to shoot past me.

I block her with an arm on the side mirror and lower my voice to rasp, "Don't. Don't go yet. I need you here still."

She jerks her head to the side, jaw locked.

"Come on, Gia. Go on an adventure with me."

That word does the trick, and she slowly lifts her gaze to mine. She waits a minute, then gets into the passenger seat without another word. *I knew she was intrigued.*

Around the other side, I fist a fresh pair of shorts and, using the open back door as a barrier from the house, I drop the wet ones along with my boxer briefs in one fell swoop. Gia's breath catches from the front seat and I swallow a scoff. *Why you looking, baby?*

I step out of the wet pile, making sure I keep my eyes on Gia's. She holds my stare the entire time…until she doesn't.

She looks all right, drinking me in like a castaway after a drought and damn if my cock doesn't love the thought of that scenario.

"Still think I'm pathetic?" I give her a little wink when she makes her way back to my face. There's a sheen to it that she can't even begin to hide.

"Still want to kiss me?" she counters.

"Always."

"Then yes."

My smile widens if only just to piss her off. She rolls her eyes, facing forward again, and I yank on the dry pair before closing the door and climbing into the driver's seat.

"Where are we going?"

Taking a page from Gia's guidebook, I don't answer her. I don't give any hint at all. I just drive, ignoring her next to me—well, trying to—as we make our way up the mountain. Technically, vehicles aren't allowed up this far, so I had my work cut out for me when I came back out here myself a couple hours ago. Following the trails our four-wheelers had previously made was a bitch thanks to the rainstorm that came through, but my four-wheel drive helped. Moving enough debris by hand for my truck to fit on those trails was a whole other challenge.

I reverse until my back tires hit the rocks I already put in position.

"I thought you were about to *Thelma and Louise* us."

Uh, who are they?

At my silence, she shakes her head, asking, "Weren't we just here?"

I retrieve her bag from the back seat, dropping it in her lap. "Yep. Now put something warm on."

Even though there's still a reassuring warmth in the air now, it'll get cold later. The mountains have it all in the summer—hot days *and* cold nights.

"Why do you have my stuff? And whose clothes were in our room?"

Our room. She knows. She fucking knows and still, she fights me.

"Kori's probably."

"Probably? Wouldn't you know?"

I shrug. "No, not really." It's no longer my concern now that I got Gia out of there.

"You spent *hours* with that girl in there and you don't know if those were her clothes?"

Hours? "I didn't spend hours with Kori. You were there the entire time I was with her. In the hot tub." Unless… "Is that what you meant about owing you fifteen ninety-nine?"

"Fifteen *sixty*-nine."

"Whatever. You thought I used your condoms? With Kori?"

She's got a dry shirt draped over her now, with the previous wet one slipping through the armpit and she stops to ask, "You didn't?"

"No." I half-laugh. Clearly that idea never even registered. Kori is…not Gia. Even though I put on a good show with that kiss, that's all it was—a show. My lips might've been kissing Kori's, but my mind was fucking Gia's.

She groans, lifting her ass off the seat to pull her stiff pants down her thighs. "See? You're wasteful. I put her right there for—"

"Wait. What do you mean you *put* Kori there?"

When she refuses to meet my eye, I say, "So I'd fuck you out of my system, too? Is that it?" That *is* it though. That's exactly it.

She continues avoiding me, messing with the pants bunched around her ankles. The moonlight filters in through the truck's windows, casting a spotlight on Gia's exposed skin, making it look luminescent. Wet strands of hair stick to her face and neck and shoulders, and as her body twitches with each yank of her sopping clothing, she could pass as a misplaced mermaid.

"Don't come out until you're dressed," I warn, leaving her inside so I can…breathe. Or something.

I undo the straps I used to secure everything earlier, then remove the tarp, setting it all up—the snacks I packed along with the sleeping bags, blankets, and pillows I bought with Bryce from the outdoor store.

After placing two coconut waters off to the side, I take a huge breath, then another, holding it for a count of ten before releasing it fully.

The other times I was up here today weren't right. They just… weren't. One was with too many people, the other was with too many distractions. Or one in particular anyway.

Now, my mind can home in on what this place really represents— change. I thought quitting snowboarding was an end. A departure from what had always been. But really, it's a beginning. The start of something else entirely. Something I never would've found had it not been for sacrificing damn near everything first.

I've felt a pull so strong, so undeniable, since the moment I saw Gia, almost as if she's been the finish line all along.

"You're a Flame Bowerbird now?"

"What's that?"

Wrapped up in a giant hoodie that matches her joggers, Gia hesitates by the tailgate, surveying the stocked bed before smirking at the combination of perfectly balanced snacks. She looks tiny, fragile even, but has a personality the size of an entire defensive line. How she manages to pull off both feats, without so much as trying, I don't know.

"It's a bird in New Guinea that builds these fancy bowers, basically a nest or a bed, that are supposed to impress a mate, but really, it's just to fuck in."

"That's not what this is." I didn't do that.

I didn't *mean* to do that.

"Uh-huh." She picks up the black device closest to her, instinctively fitting it to her eyes, and asks, "What are these?"

"Night vision binoculars."

She breathes out, "Whoa," as she looks around, then pulls them away just as quickly, asking, "Why do you have them?"

"I just bought them today, I swear." Fuck, I look like a douche.

Her glare doesn't let up an inch.

"I got them for us, for you, so you can watch for any birds that might be out here. I don't know, like an Owl maybe?" Or something like that. I thought nocturnal birds were a thing, but with the way she's looking at me, I'm not so sure.

"You did this…for me?" She uses the binoculars to gesture at my truck. "All so I could bird-watch in the middle of the night?"

"I mean, yeah." Pretty much.

"After everything I said to you?"

I nod, eyebrows furrowing.

"And after everything I did?"

I bite my cheek.

"After you saw me with those two hot guys—"

"Fuck that," I say, unable to hold it in. "Those guys were fucking scavengers. What birds are scavengers?"

"Crows."

"Worse than Crows."

"Turkey Vultures."

"Turkey Vultures, that's what they're called?"

She nods, and with a shaky smile forming, she asks, "So, even after the Turkey Vultures, you still wanted to do this for me?"

"Yes."

Her lips split wide open into one of her best smiles I think I've seen so far.

"You're something else, cowboy."

Cowboy. What a stupid fucking nickname. I still have no idea what it means, but the moment I hear it leave her lips all the fight, all the fire eager to spread, just disappears, leaving my body completely as that calm Gia creates settles back into place.

"I aim to please."

She snorts. "Not Kori."

"Not Kori," I repeat, hopping up onto my open tailgate.

"Why didn't you go for her?"

I hold my hand out, telling her, "I came here with you, I'm leaving with you."

"I would've left with you even if you fucked her."

My eyes hold hers for a beat.

"Yeah? I thought you were glad to be rid of me."

She flinches, putting her hand in mine, and with a small voice says, "I could never."

Never what? Be rid of me? Or be happy about it?

Using both hands, I help pull her up until she's standing next to me. Neither of us moves at first as we take in the view, then I step behind her, telling her to close her eyes.

"No."

"Why not? You don't trust me?"

"Up here? After the day we had? No." She laughs.

"I won't hurt you. I *promise*."

"Roz—"

"Just close your eyes."

I can tell the moment she does because her shoulders rise an inch, like she's preparing her body in case I do push her.

Fitting my hands to hers, I lift all four out to our sides, like wings.

"Open your eyes," I whisper, "we're flying."

Thankfully the storm is long gone, the sticky veil of humidity along with it, leaving behind a fairly mild night with only a puff of occasional wind.

Up here, above it all, we've got the perfect bird's-eye view. There's not a ton of light, save for the moon and the twinkling stars in the sky overhead, but it's enough to see the highlighted treetops spread out below us. Just under them is a hidden playground full of critters providing the night's soundtrack even though we can't see them.

Gia's back expands against my chest, and when she talks, her voice quivers.

"Do you know what a failing star is, Roz?"

I shake my head, my arms going slack momentarily. Is she really gonna try this shit again? Here? Now?

"It's not what it sounds like. Not in a bad way anyway. It's a star that's too big, so it becomes a dwarf planet."

Okay. That sounds a lot better than she made it seem originally. But we both said some fucked-up things to each other.

"Some failed stars explode in a supernova, leaving behind a black hole."

That part doesn't sound good though. What's she doing?

"Black holes have so much gravity, that nothing can get out, not even light."

"Is that what you think of me?"

"No. That's what I think of me."

Now my chest expands into her back, and I strengthen my arms, holding Gia's up again.

"You're the one responsible for bringing the light back into my life. You."

"But you're the one that let me," she whispers, and now that I have a better perspective on everything that's happened, I see that she's right. It was a choice and I chose to let the light shine through my life again.

Our fingers slide along each other's, making every nerve ending on my body stand at attention.

"You're so much bigger than a star, or a dwarf planet. You're the sun, enhancing everyone's beauty with your own. The sun's so confident, so powerful—without even trying—that even on the darkest of nights, its light can still be felt, reflecting off the moon. When I look out there," I nod at the scenery before us, "all I see is the light, not the dark. All I see is you, Gia."

She says, "Right now that's all you see," bringing our arms down to curl around her middle.

I hug her tighter. "That's all I've seen for four months now, and it's not changing. Even if I fall back into the dark, I'll still see you. I'll still *choose* to see you."

A beat of silence passes between us, but I'm not sure if that's a good thing or not.

"Do you know what I see?"

I shake my head.

"Unfocus your eyes."

I don't want to. I don't want her to tell me anything that'll ruin the picture I've engrained in my mind, but I listen anyway, letting my eyesight drift lazily without focusing on any one thing in particular.

"What am I looking for?"

"Just wait."

It takes a bit of effort, but after a while, everything around us changes. Where there was only a stationary setting before, now is a lively production of lights. Tiny flickering lights. Everywhere.

"What the—?" I look down, finding Gia gazing up at me instead of the landscape before us. "Are those fireflies?"

She nods slowly, glancing down at the forest's version of a pyrotechnic display.

"Not everyone realizes they're there. They're tricky like that." I can hear her smile. "They put on these magnetizing performances at night, but as soon as their natural glow's no longer visible, they're forgotten about, almost completely."

"So…bugs? You see bugs when you look out there?"

"You. I see you out there. I saw you when you couldn't, when you refused to. I see you when you think nobody else ever will. I see you for everything you were then and everything you are now. I see you when I'm trying not to. I've seen you from that first day and I haven't stopped, not even once, because to me, you do still glow, whether you're drowning in shadows or you're basking in the spotlight. But I'm fucking terrified that when my time comes to explode into nothingness, I'll swallow it up like a black hole."

"Maybe mine already blinked out."

"It didn't."

"It feels like it did."

"As soon as you stop trying to suffocate it, you'll feel it again. You took away snowboarding as punishment to your friend for leaving you, but hurting yourself in the process *is* the punishment. Your first love was boarding, but Salvy's wasn't. You're self-sabotaging for no reason other than to self-sabotage."

"I could say the same thing about you. You're avoiding a relationship with me for self-preservation."

"It's not for my protection." She spins in my arms, staring up at me. "It's for yours."

"I'm sorry your mom and grandma got sick," I tell her honestly. "I'm sorry you think it's going to happen to you, and I'm sorry you think I'm too weak to stick around even if it does but, baby, I'm not quitting you."

Her brown eyes fill with tears.

"You do realize cancer is fatal, right?"

"Some is. But some is treatable. And you don't have cancer, do you?"

"No." Barely above a whisper, she says, "But I will."

We sit in silence as my eyes search hers, wanting to see that spark I love so much. The one I hope is still there. Every other time I've tried this, I've failed. Gia doesn't break. She doesn't fold. She stands tall, waiting for an equal, but never really expecting one. The only way to get Gia's walls down is to knock down some of my own first.

"I told Salvy to go first because I wasn't ready. The cornice he was standing on, the same one I would've followed him down on, broke. It just fell away, without warning, and it swept my best friend up in a wave of snow so deep it buried him alive. I had all the supplies to dig him out at my disposal, but it didn't matter because I was too late getting to him. All because I wasn't fucking ready. I let him go without me, and he died because of it."

"You didn't have any control over that, just like you don't have any control over this."

"Maybe, but I'm not letting you go ahead without me. I'm not making that mistake again. I'm ready now."

"I can't ask that of you. I won't."

Needing to touch her, to feel her, to show her, I cradle Gia's face in my hands, promising, "You don't have to," because I've made my choice, and it's her. It'll always be her.

Chapter 22

ROZ

"**W**hatever you're about to do, wherever you're about to take this, remember someone else was just there, attempting exactly what you are," she says, her breath teasing my lips.

After all that, she still thinks she can scare me off?

"You forget I know when you're faking," I tell her, blowing on her lips and making her moan before I drag my hands down her neck and then her chest to capture her tits in my palms. "And when you're not." I squeeze, feeling her ribs swell beneath my fingertips. The nipples in my hold pebble through both her shirt and hoodie, and I have to stifle a groan to say, "The Turkey Vultures didn't get this far."

"How do you know?"

"Because you have a tell."

I grip the back of her neck, putting our lips within millimeters of each other's, then drop one hand to her waistband, slipping inside her boxer briefs.

Her scoff is forced and I feel her words more than hear them as she says, "You weren't around long enough to know if I sneezed."

My tongue slips out to wet my bottom lip, and Gia does the same, touching hers to mine. I almost give in and kiss her. Almost.

Fuck. I want to taste her again so badly.

She sucks in a breath as my fingers make contact with the top of her slit, and I pause, meeting her eyes.

"Do you wish it was them touching you?"

She jerks a nod that I don't believe for a second.

Fuck that.

I shove my hand the rest of the way in, feeling her drenched already.

"Who's got you wet right now?"

"Them," she grits, closing her eyes tightly.

"Do you like it?" I make sure my lips touch hers with each word. "Do you want more?"

She nods again, her eyes still shut.

The moment my fingers spread her pussy lips, the lines between her eyebrows crease, but as soon as I push inside with my middle finger, they smooth back out.

Gia wants me as much as I want her, but she feels guilty for wanting me. If I were dying, I'd probably feel the same way. But Gia's not dying. Not today. So today, I'll prove to her why her guilt is pointless...because I'm already hers.

Even though her eyes are closed, the skin on her eyelids continues to move like she's watching an action flick.

"What are you seeing? Tell me."

I sink another finger between her folds, and we both moan, our noses crashing into each other's as air pours through our mouths. Mine, hers, I don't know whose is what anymore, and I don't care. She already has all of me.

"The hot tub," she whispers.

"Who's in there?" I ask, pumping in and out of her warm pussy.

"Kori."

My hand freezes. *What?*

Gia's lower half begins moving, rotating onto my motionless hand as she rides my fingers.

I crook them both inside her, adding a roll of my own.

"What's Kori doing?"

"Watching."

Okay...

"Watching who? Who's she watching?"

My hand matches her pace, thrust for thrust, as my cock stands upright in my shorts, ready to be released.

"Me."

Jesus Christ.

Faster and faster, we work Gia's pussy together. My own hips mimicking the movement, crushing my hand between us but helping my fingers go even deeper.

"And what are you doing, baby?"

Her eyes finally open, and looking straight into mine, she says, "Fucking you."

Fuck. Yes.

Suddenly her eyes squeeze together again, and just when I think she's about to come around my fingers, she twists her head to the side, a sneeze tearing out of her.

I slow my hand, letting her recover, then the second she faces me, I seal my lips over hers, eating up every last drop of uncertainty she could possibly have. I earned that sneeze and I earned this kiss.

"Mmm, Roz," she moans into my mouth, making my heart pound.

"Hold on," I murmur, removing my hand.

She whimpers until I pull both her pants and underwear down, dropping to my knees at her feet.

"So, was Kori watching you fuck me…or my face?"

The spark in her eyes rivals the moonlight shining down on us as she hooks a leg over my shoulder and closes the gap between my face and her pussy.

"Fuck Kori."

She looks so good jealous.

"Fuck Kori," I echo before diving in to do what I've been dying to do—taste her.

I lick up, I lick down, I swirl my tongue like I'm chasing the streams of melted ice cream running down a cone, and it's only a matter of seconds before Gia's hips are bucking wildly against my face. Without stopping, I glance up to see her losing it.

Above Gia's flushed face, the stars come into focus, reminding me of not only Gia herself and how otherworldly she is, but also about the fireflies she pointed out.

I see Gia, but she also sees me—the real me, not just what the public saw—which is something I haven't felt since I lost my best friend, someone that knew everything about me and loved me anyway. And that's what Gia confessed. That she understands not only who I was but also who I am.

Wait, does Gia love me though?

She lost someone she loved more than anything and wouldn't wish the same fate on her worst enemy, let alone someone she…I mean, maybe. Maybe she loves me and that's why she's tried so hard to scare me off.

"Roz."

Hearing my name fall from her lips brings me back, and I pick up the tempo, fucking her with my tongue.

I slip a hand up behind her, using the cum still on my fingers to lube up and down her crack in time with her hips rolling.

"Oh my gawd," Gia gasps on a tremor, her rhythm stuttering between shakes.

She never slept with the same person twice, but that's because she hadn't met me yet.

Like I told Rowdy, I got Gia now.

One last rotation over my tongue followed by a possessive growl sends Gia over the edge, and in this moment, she *is* the sun. Hot, dangerous, and so beautiful it hurts.

Her leg gives out, so I guide her down my body, shedding her hoodie and shirt in the process. Thankfully she didn't bother with a bra or else that'd be coming off, too.

"The cowboy wants a cowgirl," she says lazily, smirking down at me with her arms crossed over my shoulders.

"Reverse," I tell her with matching slaps to her ass cheeks that press her on to my cock. "Turn around, baby."

"You got a condom on you?"

I reach over, grabbing one out from under the sleeping bag we're on, and hold it up for her inspection.

"Flame Bower," she tsks, shaking her head.

Helping her to turn around, I get my shorts down one-handed, kicking them the rest of the way off.

Okay, yeah, maybe it was a little cocky stuffing condoms back here. This part, though, the part where I show Gia what she means to me, that's just confidence. Confidence in the way I feel, in the way *we* feel—together.

I roll the condom down over my already leaking cock, keeping my gaze on Gia's as she looks back at me once she's firmly situated on my lap with her knees tucked between my thighs.

Before she can lower any farther, I catch her with an arm, pulling her in close to my chest to inhale deeply.

"Close your eyes."

"Are you gonna make me fly again?"

"Hopefully." *No pressure.*

I lean back just a bit and lift Gia to line her pussy up with my cock, watching inch by inch disappear into her opening as she eases her way down my shaft.

"Fuck," we say in unison once I'm fully buried. With her legs pressed together instead of on the outside of my thighs, it's a deep, *tight* fit, and I swear to God, I could come right now. Holy shit.

Keeping that same position, it's all I can do to watch through heavy lids as Gia takes over, rising up with her hands braced on my upper thighs, then sliding back down in a maddeningly slow pace. Her spine is ramrod straight with her hair piled on top of her head in a bun and it's all a little too…nice. Gia's not nice. She's a fucking masterpiece. A messy, chaotic, rare piece of art that makes you *feel.*

I untie her bun and grab hold of the loose strands, arching her neck back so her face is to the sky. She hisses at the pain, but quickens her pace like I knew she would, moaning my name like a chant. The combination of pain and pleasure is what gets her. A girl in search of constant balance, Gia can't have one without the other, and I'm happy to give her both. Always.

My other hand goes around to her front to rub her clit.

"Are your eyes still closed?"

"Yes," she pants.

I suck the side of her neck into my mouth, swirling my tongue between my teeth, nicking her delicate skin.

"Oh gawd!" Gia's scream echoes out around us, and I groan, thrusting up from below each time she takes the plunge down my cock. I want to hit her deepest walls. I want every part of her to have my stamp.

Mine.

Mine.

Mine.

I let go of her hair to grip where her shoulder meets her neck and notice a small raised bump by my thumb. I move my thumb over an inch, avoiding it, then use the added leverage to go even deeper.

Clutching the back of my neck with her own hand, Gia brings me in for a kiss as she twists her head to the side. It's sloppy and wet and imperfectly perfect. She can't get enough of me, and I'll never get enough of her.

"Baby," I say, my breath rushing out in spurts, "you're gonna come with me."

She nods her head clumsily, and I'd laugh if I wasn't currently using every fucking muscle in my body to hold off this orgasm. Honestly, I'm surprised I've lasted this long, but I need it all to line up or it could backfire. This might very well be my only shot and I can't fuck it up.

"Open your eyes," I whisper against the shell of her ear. "See that?" The shimmering sky above and the twinkling land below, it all blends together in a sea of us. Just us. "This is ours. It'll *always* be ours and *nothing* can ever take it away from us."

Her hand on my neck tightens and she warns, "Roz…"

"Today and every day after, I'm here with you, Gia, and I'm not going anywhere. I love you," tumbles from my lips as I thrust upward one last time, spilling everything I have, everything I am, into her.

Gia continues to milk my cock with shuddering contractions from her own release, screaming, "Fucking Roz!" The sound slicing through the waning night air and bouncing off the pool of spring water in the distance to impale my ribs. It burrows into my chest, nestling against my strongest muscle—my heart. It's never given up on me, even when my head wanted to. Even when *I* wanted to.

"Did you just say—"

"Yeah. I did. I love you."

"You can't."

"And yet, I do."

She moves to sit beside me, reaching for her clothes first while I take care of the condom, wiping myself up with one of the blankets.

"Roz," she starts when her pants are back in place, but I cut her off, telling her, "I'm not asking you to say it back. I just need you to know where I stand. We can go around and around, again and again, just like we did today, but it won't change how I feel about you. Nothing will."

Gia's actions tell me everything I need to know anyway. She can deny it, but I *know* she loves me, too, even if it's in her own way. I'll take her love, any form of it, over her anger or even worse—indifference. That shit's gotta stop. Love me or hate me, but never act like I don't matter. I'm here and I'm hers, whether she's willing to accept it or not.

All she does is exhale loudly, then turn her gaze out toward the trees below and, not used to going topless like me, she shivers next to me, so I wrap the blanket around our backs, keeping my arm draped across her shoulders.

"Oh, uh, I think you got a bug bite or something," I tell her, remembering the bump I saw.

She stiffens, asking, "What'd it look like?"

"It's like a sore with some crust on it, I don't know. It wasn't a mole though." I don't think.

"On my shoulder?" I nod. "That's not a bite. It's a scab."

"Do you think you should get it checked out?" I flinch when I say it, the thought of her possibly getting another scar from a biopsy making my stomach turn. Why do they leave such bad scars? I've gotten incisions before and never came away with scars like Gia's.

She pops a shoulder, shifting the whole blanket. "Only if it doesn't heal."

"Let me know if it doesn't and I'll take you myself."

The following silence amplifies nature's backdrop as we sit quietly with our own thoughts for a while.

Out of nowhere, a flapping noise has me looking up to see a flurry of rapidly beating wings above our heads.

"There's your birds," I tell Gia, blindly reaching for the binoculars.

She tilts her head to the side, like she's listening at first, then squints one eye skyward, saying, "Those are bats."

"What the fuck?" Everything in my body tenses while hers begins to shake with laughter. "Are you serious?"

"Yes. Bats…that are…catching lunch, I'm guessing. Or breakfast maybe."

"Right above our fucking heads?" I'm already hunching over, trying to make sure mine is off the menu, but Gia just remains upright, completely unfazed. I pull her down too, which makes her laugh even harder.

"Hey, we're in their territory. They're doing some serious hunting, and we're the ones in the way."

"We can't stay out here," I say, tugging the blanket up to cover our heads.

"They don't want us. We should be okay if we leave them alone."

I shoot her a scowl. "What if one falls on us? And it has rabies?"

"What happened to that adventurous spirit you used to get me up here?"

"Gone. It's gone. Shriveled up like my dick from the cold."

She barks out another laugh.

"We're leaving. Now," I tell her, and before she can say anything else, I scoop her and the blanket up, hopping off the lowered tailgate, grateful my lazy ass didn't get around to taking my shoes off yet.

I drop her in the back seat, shoving all our shit to the floor to make room. "Move to the front and I'll get the rest of the stuff," I tell her, stealing the blanket off her to use as a shield. Her laughter shadows me as soon as I take off with it over my head like a makeshift umbrella.

Real sexy here. Real fucking sexy.

After getting my shorts back on, everything is moved from the bed to the back seat—with a good shake to check for any unwanted stowaways—and then I flip my truck around, putting the overlook on display through the front windshield instead.

Gia and I both grab shirts from my bag sitting on the center console. Her bag is still on the floor in front of her, but she went out of her way to grab mine from the back. She loves me. She so loves me.

Well, she loves my clothes at the very least and that I can live with.

We crack the windows and recline our seats, then I motion out the windshield, asking, "Do you think they're eating fireflies?" That'd be a pretty foreboding nightcap.

"No. Their lights warn bats off." She looks over at me, explaining, "They're toxic to most predators."

There's a loud nasally cry followed by what sounds like a truck roaring past, then it stops, the rushing of air disappearing altogether like it never even happened.

"What was that?"

Gia's already got the night vision binoculars fitted over her eyes, leaning forward on her seat.

"That's a Nighthawk. And they actually do eat fireflies. I've never seen one before."

"I'm honored I get to help you check it off the bird bucket list."

"There is no bucket list. Not a physical one anyway."

"What? Do you just remember them all?"

She nods, absorbed in whatever's flying across the sky.

"Really?" I don't even think I can remember every country I've been to.

"Mmhmm."

"Even without the pictures saved on your phone?"

She lowers the binoculars to her lap, her gaze on the glass in front of us. "I only did that for my mom. I'd come home and show her my findings from the day and she'd listen to me tell her all about which bird had done what. After she died, I didn't really feel like stopping, so I didn't. They're all there." She gestures to her bag. "That's all that's on there. I don't bother with pictures of anything else." She shrugs, swinging her gaze to mine. "I save mental snapshots for that."

I want to ask if I've made any of those but don't. Instead, I ask, "But you remember every bird anyway?" She nods gently, watching me. "Why keep the pictures then?"

"Maybe I'll be able to show her again one day and tell her all about each of them. What they did that made them so interesting. Why they caught my eye. How they kept it." The cords in her neck flex on a swallow. "She'll want to know everything."

There's something in her tone, the way she's looking at me, scrutinizing me almost, that has me curious.

I wait until she looks back out the windshield before bringing my phone up to take a picture of her.

"Why'd you do that?" she asks without moving her eyes.

"I'm collecting, too."

I see her lips tug to one corner as she shakes her head, and as soon as she turns my way, I snap another picture.

She grins at me, so I take a third.

"Do you have any Mockingbirds on your phone?"

Her smile floats away like a sailboat caught in a breeze.

"No. No Mockingbirds."

"Wouldn't want any aggressive assholes on your phone, huh?"

"Definitely not," she says, lying back in her seat, turned on her side, so she's facing me still. "Look, I'm sorry for that and all the other shit I said. It was—" She pulls the sleeves of my shirt down over her wrists, tucking her hands completely inside and fidgeting with the opening. "I was ugly to you. Beyond ugly. I'm sorry."

"Me too. I'm sorry for what I said, too. It was just…wrong." Any way you look at it, I was wrong. I was pissed and jealous and worried, but I was wrong.

"I've just never dealt with this…with these feelings. It's a lot. I don't know what to do with them. Or you really. I don't know what to do, period. This is new to me."

What's new? Having feelings for someone? Loving someone? I'd give anything to know but can't push her too much or she'll clam up or run.

Or both even. I wouldn't put it past her.

"Then let's just see what happens. You're good at not following a plan, right?" I've never really seen her with one anyway. "So, we can keep doing what we're doing and see where it leads us."

"Mmmm," she replies vaguely, snuggling further down into her seat.

Is that a *yes*? A *no*? A *we'll talk about it when I'm not half asleep*?

Also, and I'm not just exaggerating, but how the fuck is she even tired? I'm pretty sure if I were to cut my arm open right now, that coffee from this morning would come pouring out, still piping hot and caffeinated as all hell.

I'm not ready for this to end. This is the first time where I don't feel like she's holding back. Well, mostly. She actually confided in me for once and I don't want to let that go just yet.

But how can I keep her up?

Chapter 23

GIA

Warm. So warm. The warmest I've ever felt is when I'm around Roz, I swear. We're not even touching and the bone-deep warmth is still here, enveloping me into a cocoon of comfort.

"What's your favorite bird?" I hear Roz ask quietly as I struggle to stay awake. He's given a lot tonight. He's also wanting a lot, even though I can't return a fraction of what he deserves. It doesn't matter that I want to, that I want to give him everything he's asking for, it's not fair. It's not fair to him, even if he thinks it is.

Orange and red hues dance in front of my closed eyelids, the warmth closing in on me.

"Gia? Baby, what's your favorite bird?"

His fingers graze my face, and I lean into his heat, greedy for more.

"Mmm, Cardinal."

And that's what I mean about Roz being tricky. He gets me to admit things I wouldn't normally admit. First, that whole firefly confession, now this.

"The red bird?"

"That's just the male."

"Right. And the females look…different?"

I smirk, nodding. "Attractive in her own right but not stunningly so like her male counterpart, she's able to camouflage with the best of them. Most people overlook the female, blinded by their own assumptions and leading them to mistake the Cardinal for a dozen other birds, which is exactly the point. She's essentially hidden in plain sight. The male is meant to draw attention but the female… she gets to blend in."

The cab is quiet for a while, but just when I'm about to pass out, I hear Roz say, "She's the one whose mate's always close by…" trailing off before a loud commotion next to my face startles me enough to crack my eyes open again. He tilts the center console up, opening more space across the bench between our seats, then scoots closer, stretching out his lean body alongside mine. With the seat still reclined, he props my head on his shoulder, snuggling tightly against me.

"Never far away for long," I whisper, looking into golden eyes rich with love.

Too scared to say more, too fucked in the head to try, I snatch Roz's lips in utter selfishness and watch helplessly as he steals the rest of my undeserving heart.

Both Roz and I are moving a little slower than usual after spending the night in one uncomfortable position after another, and there's a stitching imprint along the entire left side of my body from Roz's leather seat.

He stands a few feet away, talking with Mikey, and despite his hair sticking up in every direction and bags under his eyes, he still manages to look utterly fuckable. I, on the other hand, look as approachable as a Wild Turkey as I scrape the stubborn mud splotches off the seat of my four-wheeler with my bare nails.

Bryce walks up, asking if he's still riding with me today, but before I can answer, Roz breaks away, saying, "What about Rowdy's extra?"

"With you again?" Bryce asks, surprising me. I didn't know he rode with Roz. I would've expected one of the more experienced riders to pitch in after I left him yesterday without a ride back to the house.

"I was thinking you could try by yourself." Roz shrugs a little too nonchalantly. What's he getting at?

"Who will you be with?"

Roz shoots his gaze my way.

Oh.

No.

Bryce attempts to smother a laugh while Roz leans in, but I dodge his lips just before they make contact with mine. I thought we were gonna keep with the whole fucking undercover thing, not…the couple thing. Does he want us in matching pullovers, too? His and hers travel mugs?

"Uh…"

"I don't have anyone to ride with," Kori says, gracing us with her overly tall self as she shuffles over like an Emperor Penguin. "I could ride with you, Roz."

I narrow my eyes at her, and she rushes to add, "If that's okay?"

Roz straightens to his full height, crossing his arms over his chest and pinning me with a hard stare. "Yeah, Gia. Is that okay?"

No. It's not okay. But I don't know what else to do here. What does Roz want me to do? Claim him publicly? What does that achieve? In the long run, it only complicates things.

Even dead ends can look appealing for a little while. Until you realize they're just that—dead ends. They lead nowhere.

"Bryce." I drag my eyes away from Roz's to hand Bryce the same spare helmet he used yesterday, telling him to get on the back of my Raptor because we're riding together.

The rest is out of my hands. Whoever rides with who…I'll just have to deal. Or close my eyes and pretend I'm back to last night when things felt so much simpler. So much better. Because no matter how hard I try, I don't regret what happened with Roz in that truck. He needed that. I needed that. We needed that.

It's everything else I don't know how to navigate. It's this. I. Don't. Know. What. To. Do.

"Not this shit again," Roz gripes, letting his arms fall as he begins rocking side to side, and Bryce drops his gaze to the ground, not as amused anymore as he climbs on to my four-wheeler.

"You got a helmet?" he asks Kori, shoving past without sparing me a second glance.

"Are you okay?" Bryce asks as soon as Roz and Kori are out of earshot.

"Golden Eagle," is all I say.

"Is that bad?"

"The worst."

The Golden Eagle pierces its victim's heart with its talons, killing them instantly, and that's the only way to describe what it feels like watching Roz leave with Kori, except for me, there is no relief from an instant demise. No, I'm stuck sitting here, suffering while the puncture continues to openly hemorrhage. And at my own doing no less. My fucking talon. My fucking pain. My fucking bad.

"I thought maybe it was some kind of fucked-up revenge or something, bringing him here with you, but… Look, you're a bird-watcher, right? You watch everybody the same way you watch birds, Gia. With interest, but only for a short time and from a safe distance away."

"What's your point, Bry-bear?"

"My point is you look at him differently." He points at Roz, but I don't dare glance in that direction.

"How do I look at him?"

"The same way he looks at you, like you found the one person you want to watch for the rest of your life."

I flatten my eyes at him, and he puts his hands up, saying, "Take it up with karma, okay? I'm just telling you what I see."

"Karma, huh?" I say, turning my keychain over in my hands, fingering the feather on it.

"What about this one?" I hold up a gray feather with white at the tip to my mom.

We've been hiking around this place after she surprised me with a picnic dinner of chili dogs and cheese fries from a nearby drive-in restaurant. I love Dad's food, but sometimes it's nice to eat other things from other places, especially when we don't have to make it ourselves.

She said the small waterfall we ate by earlier would make a great spot for sunrises, but the sun's just starting to set now, coating the clouds overhead with purples and oranges just past the tall trees all around us, and I think it's perfect.

It'll be dark soon, but that won't stop Mom. She'd stay out here all night if she could and if I didn't have school in the morning, she would. She's so fun. Dad is too, but in his own way. Like when he tosses pizza dough high in the air, then tries to catch it before it can land on his head. Sometimes he lets it just to make us laugh. But Mom, she doesn't have to try to be fun, she just is. She's so naturally herself and doesn't get embarrassed by it.

She inspects the feather closely, a smile lighting up her soft face as she says, "Ah, a Dove. How fitting. Do you know what this stands for?"

I shake my head, my hair falling in front of my eyes. It's so wavy, even more so with the damp summer air. Last week a kid said I should cut it all off since I look like a boy anyway, but I don't want to. I like my hair.

"Dove feathers signify harmony."

My mom looks at me expectantly, but I don't know what that means, so I just shrug.

"Balance."

I shrug again and, laughing, she tells me, "It'll make sense one day. I promise."

I love when she does that—promises. Everything seems possible when she does, like she'll always be here to make sure it is.

"They also represent beauty."

Her eyes meet mine and I smile. Everyone says I look just like my mom, but she's the prettiest, so I don't know if I believe it. I don't care so much about being the prettiest, but my mom is also the happiest person I know, and I think that's better. Maybe I can be that instead, because I want to be exactly like her.

"And love," she says, but I pull a face.

The girls at my school talk about the boys nonstop, like that's the only thing worth caring about. Most of the boys aren't even nice, but because they're "cute," we're all supposed to go crazy for them. I don't get it.

"What?" She laughs. "Love is a renewable resource, it's created and you can never run out of it."

She tucks the feather behind my ear with a curl, telling me to keep it. That maybe I'll need it someday.

"How is love created?" I ask, brushing the feather with my fingertips.

"With a choice. You can create love for anything you choose."

"Anything?"

"Anything, even birds."

I love birds. Maybe not as much as my mom does, but I love watching them, too.

"You can also love anyone."

"Anyone?" I ask, to make sure, and she smiles, saying, "Anyone. You can love anyone, Gia, as long as they earn it."

I think about that as we start walking again.

"You can even create love for friends." She looks over her shoulder, winking. "Like Rowdy."

That makes me feel better because I do love Rowdy. We just started hanging out at each other's houses, even though he's not one of the boys the girls call cute, but I don't care. I don't see him as cute or not cute. I see him as the shy, new kid that never gets chosen for dodgeball in PE because he's too busy pretending he's racing one of his four-wheelers around the gym. Sometimes I pretend with him, so he doesn't feel so alone. It's actually pretty fun and makes me love him even more. I don't want to hold his hand or kiss him, but I love him a lot.

When we stop to watch a Downy Woodpecker hop its way up the front of a rotting tree, my mom whispers, "The love parents create for their children is a pretty special one, too," before pressing a kiss to my hair, staying a little longer for some reason. Maybe a leaf fell in it.

"What about the love you and Dad have?" I ask after the black and white bird with a little red spot on his head flies off.

She's quiet while she listens to a series of chirps, then says, "That one can be a little trickier sometimes because you don't always have a choice in who you love, only what you do with that love when it's created."

"Does that kind take a lot of work to create?"

"To create? No…but everything that's worth having takes a lot of work, and it's your choice if you put in the effort or not."

This is getting kind of confusing.

"But that love, along with all the others, they only happen when you conquer the most important love of all first—the love you create for yourself. None of those matter if you don't have that one down pat."

I frown. "How do you do that?"

"With another choice."

There's so many choices. How do we know if we're choosing right?

"What makes you happy, Gia?"

I picture all our outings together, bird-watching, finding fun stuff to do. I picture the four-wheelers at Rowdy's house. He lets me ride one when I go over there, and I always like how dirt sprays out behind me when I go fast. I picture the movie I saw last summer during the drive-in's throwback night, too. It was about the skateboarders in California that made the sport popular. There were girls that skated too and they were so confident, the way they kept up with the boys.

"Those things you're thinking about right now, choose to do them. Even if they're big, scary things. Even if nobody else likes them, do them. Every single one of them. Would we have as much fun looking for birds if they all looked the same with the same voices and mannerisms?"

I shake my head, my hand coming up to grab the feather so it doesn't fall out.

"No, we wouldn't. It'd be boring, and eventually we'd stop looking for the beauty in the world because there wouldn't be any worth appreciating. Diversity makes the world beautiful, but it can only exist if you find what makes you happy, what makes you different, and run with it. Never back down from what makes you happy and never apologize for being yourself. You're the only person that gets to live in your skin and in your head and in your heart, so make sure it's somewhere you want to be all the time. That's how you love yourself."

"You know all that from a feather?" I ask, and she laughs again.

"The choices we make determine which path we take in life, but birds have a different vantage point than us, so they can show us things we might not be able to see on our own. Free will dictates what ultimately happens, but birds give us signs along the way, including warnings. We must always keep an eye out though, because some are even messages from our loved ones that can't be with us anymore."

"Like Nonna?"

I never got to meet my grandma, but my mom talks about her a lot.

"Uh-huh." She nods, walking again, and I hurry to catch up.

"Will you give me messages, too?" I don't want to think about her dying, but she says that's how it's supposed to be, that parents aren't supposed to live longer than their kids.

We stop at the same time as she looks over at me, saying, "I promise."

No, not karma. Vita.

My mom. She sent Roz. I suspected it was her for a while but didn't want to accept it because that would mean…what does it mean?

A reminder to let myself embrace the light in my own life? Because when it comes to the way Roz makes me feel, I've been chasing that happiness away like a Northern Shrike would another bird, denying myself the opportunity to have it, or him, long-term.

Do I have Roz though? I didn't think I did.

There's only one way to find out.

"Treat her well," I tell Bryce, tossing him the keyring to my Raptor.

"What?" he asks, but I'm already on the move.

"Sorry 'bout the mix-up, Kori, but you're gonna have to find somebody else to ride with."

"Why?" Her gaze rakes over me, then Roz.

"Because Roz is with me now."

Putting his feet in front of mine, Roz asks, "Oh, am I?"

"Unless I got it wrong…" I trail off purposely. This is why I don't do this shit. It's awkward. I shouldn't have even—

"Baby, I've been taken since you crashed my best friend's funeral."

A disgusted scoff to the side goes unchecked. Hey, we're unconventional. Didn't she pick up on that last night?

"You have me today, tomorrow, and every day after that. You take up way too much space in my mind for me to be anything but yours, so the better question is, are *you* taken?"

His eyes latch on to mine.

"I don't do labels."

"Cut the shit, Gia. After last night, everyone on this mountain knows you're mine."

"Only this mountain? Guess you'll have to try harder next time."

He buries his hands into the hair by my ears, pulling me in until his lips are an undeniable temptation. "As soon as you tell me what I already know."

"You're like a dog with a bone, you know that?"

"What? No bird reference?"

I roll my eyes. "You're a Common Swift—"

"I'm a Cardinal."

My heart skips a beat as I try not to react.

Fiercely loyal. Gorgeous beyond words. A creature made for the spotlight, everyone notices the male Cardinal.

I did.

That streak of red he wore at the funeral caught my eye and refused to let go. *He* refused to let go.

Roz is so protective of me from everyone and everything, has been since he put his jacket on me that cold March day. Just like a Cardinal, he'd hurt himself before he ever hurt me.

And the food. He's never not trying to feed me.

"What makes you say that?" I ask carefully.

"Because you are."

Reaching down, he lifts me by the backs of my thighs, and I automatically wrap my legs around his waist, hooking my feet behind his back before he walks us toward the house, forgetting all about the four-wheelers and the audience next to them.

Chapter 24

GIA

By the time we get my Raptor unloaded and Roz walks me to my front door, it's close to midnight. We spent the morning in bed—a real one—then met up with everybody after a relaxed lunch of grapes and spray cheese and crackers on the deck. *So fancy.*

The rest of the afternoon was full of riding, swimming, and general fucking off. I even let Roz take a turn on my Raptor, too, which wasn't as bad as I thought it'd be watching someone else ride my four-wheeler. There's something about putting your trust in someone worthy that makes the small stuff seem inconsequential.

He insisted on taking me out for a real dinner, so we stopped off at a little diner on our way home. We even sat on the same side of the booth and everything. All that was missing was a bowl of mile-long spaghetti.

It was all very normal. But strange. I feel like I'm in an alternate universe, and I'm just watching myself right now.

"Come stay with me."

Roz peppers kisses along my neck, the light above my front door casting shadows over half of his face.

"Damn boy, don't you want some time alone?" I laugh.

"I've been alone for months…it's overrated."

"Okay…go chill with one of those roommates of yours."

"I wanna chill with you." The sharp ridges of his teeth scrape my skin, making me curse. "Only you."

"I need to sleep and shower and stuff." Emphasis on the stuff part.

"All things you can do at my place."

"Roz."

Sly fingers venture up my shirt, grazing the bottom of my boobs.

"Roz."

His lips spread against my collarbone before he finally looks up, his eyes dilated and crazed. "Sorry. Were you saying something?"

I can only shake my head. Does he even realize where we are?

"Seriously though, thanks for the last couple days."

"It was a shitshow, Roz."

"A fucking wreck," he agrees, nodding.

"But it was…"

"Amazing."

"I was gonna say fun."

"You would've done our time together a disservice if you did."

I roll my eyes, shoving him back a few steps. "Don't be dramatic. We had fun."

He catches my wrist in his grip, pulling me to him again. "I had you. The rest was forgettable."

"You're so cheesy."

"I can't help it." He pops his shoulder. "My girl fed me cheese straight from the bottle."

"Your girl?"

"My girl."

"This is such a bad idea," I say, rethinking this whole thing—again.

"It doesn't feel like that to me."

"Yeah, well, lust and love can do that. They imitate the other like one giant cosmic prank on humanity."

"I loved you before I ever even lusted after you."

I raise an eyebrow.

"All right, maybe that's a stretch, but I think they're distinctively different. The two get confused because while each one can stand on its own, they both give the same impression that you're either incredibly happy or decidedly miserable. Lust is temporary. A figment. But love…love is all-consuming. It seeps into your every pore, saturating your entire being for the rest of your life."

"For someone that's never had a girlfriend, you sure talk a good game."

"Never before now."

It's not posed as a question, but the uncertainty in his eyes tells me it is. He's waiting for me to make this official. What he doesn't realize is, it already is.

What'd he just call it? Being saturated in love? I'm saturated by my feelings for Roz.

"Okay, cowboy, we'll give it a go."

He gathers me into his arms, gazing into my eyes.

"So, was I right? Are we Cardinals?"

"We're Cardinals." *As if there was ever any doubt.* "But Cardinals mate for life. For *life*," I repeat, leaving the rest unsaid. I don't know how long I have left here—none of us do—but I don't want to waste any more time fighting this. Roz makes me happy. So incredibly fucking happy.

"Then it'll be a life worth living," he says before his lips lower to mine, making me the kind of promise I actually do accept.

We say our goodbyes, then I watch until his taillights disappear on to the road. Turning for the door, I notice a lump on the porch, just below the sitting room window, and stop. My dad built the wrap-around porch specifically for him and my mom to grow old together, while sitting outside in their matching rocking chairs, but he doesn't keep up with it anymore, so it's starting to wear. It's not unusual for it to be dirty, but we're talking leaves and pollen, not…a bird?

Closer, I bend down to inspect it. *American Goldfinch.* Its small yellow and black body already stiff and cold. On the window, there's even a faint outline of its spread wings.

My throat constricts.

Birds give us signs, including warnings.

A bird running into a window only means one thing—death.

Chapter 25

ROZ

"**Y**ou got anything going on tonight?"

There's a steady thrum on the other end, like a vibration.

"Besides sleeping?"

I quickly check my rearview mirror before merging into the right lane and answering, "Yes," to Gia.

Her laugh crackles through the speakers, making me grin. We've spent the past two months together practically inseparable, and I don't think I can hold my parents off any longer for a family dinner. I thought taking Gia sounded like a good idea. Not only because I hate being away from her, but I also want my mom and dad to finally meet her. I've never brought a girl home, but Gia's not just any girl. She's my girlfriend.

Girlfriend. I used to fear the term. Like it meant something so serious, so final. Now it feels almost like a mockery. Gia's more than a word, a title. She's just more.

"Shit!"

The vibration cuts off followed by a couple of heavy thuds.

"What happened? What's wrong?"

"Nothing." She mutters something under her breath that I miss.

"What are you doing anyway?"

I wanted to meet her for lunch at Al's, since she's supposed to work today, but I'm running a bit behind after the meeting with my financial advisor.

"I'll call you back."

"Don't worry about it. I'm almost to the pizzeria now."

"Why?" Her voice comes out clipped, which is…unusual.

"Umm, to see you." Do I need another reason? "Is that a problem?"

Some rustling from Gia's end fills my cab, then she grounds out, "Shit," again, making my eyebrows dip. "Hey, I gotta go, okay?"

The line goes dead a second later, leaving me in a state of total what the fuckery. Seriously. What was that?

I contemplate beelining it to Al's anyway but ultimately decide against it. Maybe this is one of those times where she needs a breather. Lately we've been spending almost every waking moment together in one way or another, whether it's at my place or hers or off on some spontaneous excursion.

Maybe she's on her period.

When *does* she get that? Actually, now that I think about it, she hasn't had a period since we got back from Willmont, and by my estimation, she should've. At least once.

Although she is on the pill, so maybe not? I'm not sure because she's never told me. The only thing Gia has been clear about is that even though she's on birth control, she still wants me wearing a condom every time we have sex.

That'd explain why she was snippy on the phone. And why she might not want to see me.

But why couldn't she just say that? I wouldn't care. I'd still want to hang out, even if we couldn't have sex or whatever. Can women have sex on their periods? It seems like it'd be messy but still doable. I mean, if she wanted to. Which isn't a requirement for us to hang out.

No wonder she's dodging me. I'm a fucking idiot who doesn't even know when his girlfriend's cycle is…or what cycles even are exactly.

A grocery store comes into view, and I pull in, finding a spot away from other cars to do a quick internet search. It's still warm out, being the end of September, but there's a breeze with a bite to it, announcing that fall has arrived, and I don't want any doors slamming into the side of my Chevy.

After learning more about periods than I ever planned on

knowing, I head inside to load up on all things Aunt Flow might require for her stay.

A double-pack of pain reliever, heating pad, four kinds of chocolate, and a pint of ice cream later, I emerge through the automatic doors. I stopped by the tampon section, but yeah, no. That shit is way above my skillset. There were different sizes, scents, and materials. Does she use organic? Applicators? And why, if applicators are an option, are there ones without them? Do women carry around their own applicators then?

What the fuck *is* an applicator?

I almost asked someone for help but chickened out. Unless Gia herself gives me a detailed list of exactly what to get, I'm never going near that part of the store again if I can help it. Too many choices, too many possibilities to get it wrong.

I also grabbed two face masks for us to try along with foot massage cream I could use on Gia. I figured I'd distract her with some spa stuff. And despite my findings saying to avoid salty foods, I got some popcorn to balance out all the sweet. Who really cares about a little bloating when your uterus is literally shedding itself? If a woman wants salt on her period, she should eat salt. All the fucking salt.

Back in my truck, I catch sight of a brown-haired skater I'd know anywhere, except she's not skating; she's strolling down the sidewalk with her skateboard up behind her head, an arm on each side. One of her back wheels is missing, which explains why she's walking but not where she's walking to.

I thought she had to work all day. She told me she had to work all day. *Didn't she?* Either way, she's not working now.

So…what is she doing?

I hit redial on my dashboard screen, then start my engine, shifting into Reverse. I can take her wherever she needs to go.

Gia pulls her phone out, but with one look at it, returns it to her back pocket, the call going to voicemail.

Stomping on the brake, I shift back into Park.

What the fuck was that? It can't be period related. *Right?* She's not even giving me a chance here. I bought mint chocolate chip ice cream for fuck's sake.

My finger hovering above the redial button, I watch as she cuts across a yard to a pale blue house with a wheelchair ramp and pushes through the front door without so much as knocking. Who the hell lives there? More importantly, why is Gia blowing me off to visit them?

It's not a guy…is it?

Fuck that.

My tires squeal across the asphalt as I pull onto the street and over to the parking lot beside the house Gia disappeared into.

Scoping out the place, my eyes snag on the lined parking spaces. What kind of house has a parking lot instead of a driveway?

Another car parks in the spot next to mine and a couple gets out—an elderly couple—then they pass a weathered sign as they inch their way up the ramp. *White's Dermatology.*

Some of the properties along the main street of this particular hamlet can double as residential houses as well as offices or retail spaces. It took me a while to get used to the concept after moving back, but since I have yet to go in one, I kind of forgot about it.

This is why she blew me off? To go to the dermatologist? I already offered to take her myself. I could've sat with her in the actual exam room. Hell, there's not an inch of skin on Gia's body I haven't been over myself—many, many times—maybe I could've given the doctor some pointers. I'd love to meet the hack who's incapable of performing a single biopsy without leaving an ugly-ass scar behind in the process.

There hasn't been anything that's stood out to me except for that scab thing that never did heal properly. *It didn't heal properly.* And Gia said she'd get it checked out if it didn't heal, but we've been so busy with each other, she's just now getting to it.

Damn.

Did I keep her from going to an important appointment? I never meant for that to happen. I don't want to be that kind of boyfriend. The kind that sucks up every moment of his girlfriend's time, stopping her from having any life outside of the relationship. It's just that…I like her. A lot. Of course, I love her, but more than that, I actually like being around her. She brings out the best in me. She makes me feel alive when I was beginning to wonder if I even was anymore.

And how do I repay her? By monopolizing all her time, then holding a stakeout in her dermatologist's parking lot, spying on her.

Before she can come out and catch me, I get back onto the road toward my house. I need to care more about her instead of just myself and how I feel.

I hate that I can't be the first person she sees after a stressful situation, and I really don't like the idea of her walking from the appointment, but I need to let her have this time by herself. I need to respect her wishes.

Gia gave me a gift by trusting me, and I don't want to fuck it up by only thinking about myself.

If she wants to come over later, then I'll be here waiting with open arms…and period provisions that may or not be necessary.

Chapter 26

ROZ

Inside our favorite bakery, I give my order of two loaves of cinnamon bread and six butter danishes to-go to the girl working the counter. "And a French vanilla espresso for here," I add on before telling Gia to get whatever she wants. It's become our Sunday morning tradition to pick up breakfast for the house together, so after not hearing from her for the past two days, I drove over to her house and picked her up like I usually would. She hasn't said anything about her appointment with the dermatologist and I'm still debating if I should bring it up or not. I'll look like a paranoid asshole if I tell her how I know about the appointment, but it's killing me that she won't just tell me herself.

Gia orders a strawberry shortcake scone and a bacon sandwich, then asks Kylin about her plans for the upcoming week while I pay. She always does this. She chats up people everywhere we go, genuinely interested in hearing about them, and Kylin's no exception. She's as quiet as a mouse, and by the looks of the way she's struggling to keep her gigantic sweatshirt on correctly, she might be as small as one, too, but Gia never misses an opportunity to talk with her.

With my drink in hand, I keep the other one on Gia's lower back, guiding her over to a table by the window. The bakery's this crazy triangular shape perched on a misaligned four-way intersection. There's not a lot of traffic usually, so it's a nice place to sit and relax for a while. A few college students take up the other tables with their laptops out and one guy in particular keeps stealing glances at

Kylin. I've seen him before at a couple parties, but not at my house. I think he's a frat bro, maybe even a president.

As Gia sits down, I stand behind her, trying to see if I can make out a bandage or anything else that might be sticking out of the top of her neckline, but it's useless since Gia's enveloped in one of my flannel jackets and her wavy hair blocks out the rest of her neck, so I just take my seat across the table from her instead.

She slides my espresso over to her side before I even get a single sip in, then we sit in silence, waiting for the food. It's not comfortable but it's not uncomfortable either.

It's uncomfortable.

I'm yanking up the sleeves to my long-sleeve shirt, wondering why it's unacceptable to go shirtless in here if it's going to be so goddamn hot, when I notice Gia smirking at me knowingly. An errant ray of morning sunlight strokes across her face like a painter's brush, highlighting her lips, and I stop fucking with my shirt, going completely still to stare back at her.

Damn.

A million more of this moment wouldn't even be enough. I never want this to end, and I'll do whatever it takes to ensure it doesn't.

I prop my phone up, stealing a photo of her.

"What are you going to do with that?"

"Add it to my collection."

Gia tilts her head, her gaze on me, not so much narrowing as intensifying.

Feeling even hotter, I shrug. "I'll probably hang it on my wall." It's still bare and could use a little art.

"If you think that's a good idea," she says, getting up to grab her order.

Now my gaze is narrowing.

"I do…" I say to her back. At least I did.

No, I do. It's a great idea.

Unless Gia has a reason to think it's not…

She returns, and I open my mouth to talk about Friday, but the bell above the door jingles and there's something about the way this one sounds, the way it feels—like change—that pulls me from our little bubble.

My mom and dad come waltzing through the bakery's front door, casting their gazes across the small eat-in area. As soon as they spot me, their postures elongate, causing their noses to lift.

"Canadian Geese," Gia mutters, unaware they're my parents.

So, it's not just me seeing it. Do I do that, too? Lift my nose like that? God, I hope not.

I stand to greet them both, hugging my mom and giving my dad a firm handshake behind her back.

Pulling out of the hug, I gesture to Gia, but my mom says, "Oh, our apologies. We didn't mean to interrupt. You weren't home when we stopped by, but Fletcher told us where we could find you."

"Mom. Dad. This is Gia, my girlfriend."

If Kylin dropped a muffin right now, you could hear it. Gia's hands tighten on her bacon sandwich, the wrapper crinkling loudly, and my dad clears his throat, shifting on his feet.

"Oh, right. I think Roswell mentioned something about a girl-friend," my mom says dismissively, and I frown. That's not how I'd put it.

"Hello, dear. I'm Lynnette, and this is my husband, Warren." She extends her hand to Gia but Gia's wide eyes swing from my mom's to mine, and leaning out of view of my parents, I give her a subtle headshake. *I didn't set this up.*

There are certain lengths I'll go to. Stalking my girlfriend outside her doctor's office, yes. Ambushing her with a surprise visit from my parents in a public setting, no. I wouldn't do that to anybody.

Gia sets her food down to take my mom's hand. "Nice to meet you both. Roz talks about you all the time."

Now everybody's lying? I don't really like talking about my par-ents. Not with Gia. Mainly because they pale in comparison to hers.

She shakes my dad's hand too, his stare falling to the many rings lining Gia's fingers. He's been quiet so far. Too quiet.

"Roswell, I have to be honest. I didn't think you had it in you to settle down, son."

There's the Warren Andrews-Smith I know. The one that doesn't pull any punches.

"What can I say? I was waiting for the right person," I tell him before Gia can try to gut me in front of my parents by correcting him. While we may not be "settled down" exactly, I am serious about Gia. She has to know that by now. I even gave her the top two drawers of my dresser. They're technically still filled with my clothes, but they're my clothes that she wears when she's over. And when she leaves. Basically, she's always wearing my clothes these days, but the way I figure it, with the amount of time I spend consumed by thoughts of her, it's only fair she be wrapped up in reminders of me.

"Um, want to join us?" Gia's wide eyes flit around the small group. "Kyle over there makes a killer scone. They're super moist." Immediate regret registers on Gia's face and I bite down on my lips.

After my parents turn for the counter, I release my laugh, saying, "Moist, huh?"

"Shut. Up. I can't be held responsible for what comes out of my mouth around parental figures."

We drag over a couple chairs, adding them to our table.

"That's not true. Most of Al's customers are probably parents."

"They're not the parents of the—"

"Man you've fallen in love with?" I wink at her. "I get it. It's tough. But last week I ate you out with your dad on the other side of your bedroom door."

"He didn't even know."

"Yeah, because you kept up a conversation with him the entire time."

"He wanted to know what kind of toothbrush I prefer."

"But did you have to go into detail about what you like about it? Right then?"

"Mouthcare's important." She pops a shoulder like that explains it.

"Anyway, the point is, that's not really my specialty either, but I did it for you."

"Uh-huh. And you didn't get anything out of it?"

I drop my eyes to her lips, smirking. "I didn't say that."

"Exactly. This is totally different, Roz."

"If you want, we can go into the bathroom real quick so you can return the favor." My eyebrows bounce as hers sink.

"Nice try. I'm sure Mr. and Mrs. Fancy would love that."

"Just be yourself and they'll love *you*. If that fails, just say moist again."

Her ring-covered fist connects with my bicep a second before my parents appear on the other side of the table, and I cover the grunt with a laugh while sitting down. I tuck Gia into my side, placing my hand on the knee closest to me. Gia sits with her legs spread so damn wide the other knee's in the next town over. Hamlet. Next hamlet over.

There's some small talk at first, letting everybody get settled, then the personal questions start up.

"So, Gia, is that short for something?"

"Gianna, but I don't go by that."

"That's a beautiful name."

"Thanks. It was my grandmother's."

"Was?"

"She passed away."

"I'm sorry to hear that. On your mother's side? Or your father's?"

"Uh, my mom's. It happened when she was only nine years old."

I knew Vita was younger when her own mom died, but I didn't know she was *that* young.

"Your mother must still miss her immensely if she named you after her."

"She did, yes."

"Did? My goodness. Don't tell me your mother has passed as well?"

"Mom," I say in warning.

Gia glances at me briefly, telling my mom, "We lost her three years ago."

"My sincerest apologizes, Gianna."

My mom prefers to lengthen everyone's names, making them, and her, sound more sophisticated. I never minded before, but hearing her do it to Gia makes the hairs on the back of my neck rise, especially because Gia just said she didn't go by that name.

"Roswell's been dealing with a loss himself. We all have. Salvatore was a part of our family." My mom dabs at the corners of her eyes, careful not to smudge her makeup in the process.

"Yeah, Roz has told me a lot about him. I'm sorry I couldn't meet him."

"Yes, a shame indeed. Similar to your grandmother, correct? You never met her either?"

"Unfortunately, no."

"And how did she die?"

Jesus Christ.

"Mom," I growl, earning a pair of blank looks from the other side of the table.

This is not the way I saw this going.

"It's a little curious, Roswell. Wouldn't you say?" My mom's eyebrows go as high as her Botox allows. "Two women in the same family not making it to their…fiftieth birthdays?"

Nobody makes a single sound.

"Fortieth?"

The leg farthest from me starts swishing back and forth as Gia bobs her head slowly, neither confirming nor denying anything.

"Mom? Drop it."

Gia's head turns my way, then she says, "Cancer. It was cancer."

A gasp leaves my mother's lips while my father covers a cough with a napkin.

"Both? Or just—"

"Both." Gia looks at my mom again. "Same kind. Skin cancer."

Honestly I'm not even sure how to take this. It took me forever to find out what she just told my mom in minutes, and it wasn't even Gia's doing, it was Bryce's.

"And we celebrated my mom's thirty-eight birthday like it was her fortieth. We knew it was her last one, so my friends and I got a bunch of people together to drive by the house. She couldn't get out of bed, so we brought the party to her. It was a parade of motorcycles, dirt bikes, quads, everything, in one long line. It lasted for hours."

My father speaks up finally, asking, "Your mother, she enjoyed that?"

"She loved it." Gia's lips split into a reminiscent smile, hopefully unaware of the looks being exchanged between my parents.

"Is that what you enjoy, Gianna? You drive those types of off-road vehicles?"

"*Gia,*" I emphasize her preferred name, "rides four-wheelers and skateboards."

"If it's got four wheels, I'm down to try," she adds with a laugh, reminding me one of her skateboards is currently missing a wheel.

I should've said something. I shouldn't have waited.

Damn it.

"Those both require a lot of time outdoors, correct? In the sun?"

Gia studies an old Nova passing by and swallows before saying, "Being aware and being terrified are two different things. I'm aware of how dangerous the sun is, but I'm not going to live my life being terrified of it." She turns her head back toward my parents. "Even though I'm outside almost every day, I still do my best to protect myself against its rays. A soldier showing up to battle unarmed isn't brave, they're just stupid."

"Well, if that doesn't sound like a snowboarder's motto, then I don't know what does," my dad says, steering us back to the topic they love to beat over my head. "How about you, Gia? Do you snowboard, too?"

Her eyes flick to mine. "Nothing like Roz here."

An image comes to mind—that same one from before—and without looking away, I tell Gia, "I bet you'd tear up some fresh pow though." And maybe in another life, one where I'm back to boarding, I'd actually get to see it firsthand because, as it stands now, it's just a pipedream.

My feet start rocking under the table.

"You should take her up to the cabin once the snow sets in. You two lovebirds—"

"We're Cardinals," I correct my mom, and Gia snickers, dropping her gaze. I don't know if lovebirds are real birds, but they don't sound half as cool as Cardinals.

My mom blinks at me, her face frozen, but I don't backtrack an inch. I'm proud to be a Cardinal, and I don't care who knows it.

"Well, you both are welcome there anytime. Just let us know beforehand and we'll have everything stocked and ready for you. You can make a weekend out of it. Go snowmobiling, snowboarding—"

Heat spreads up my arms, right to my neck. "I'm not saying this again, so let these words sink in…I *quit* snowboarding. That part of my life is *over.*"

She looks to my dad, and he shakes his head.

"Roswell, you're one of the lucky ones. You could have a long, illustrious future doing something you genuinely enjoy. Not everyone can say the same. Gianna knows that better than anyone."

I see Gia flinch out of the corner of my eye.

"Your girlfriend doesn't let fear hold her back, so why do you?" my dad asks.

Standing suddenly, Gia says, "Excuse me, I need to use the bathroom. Or restroom. Washroom? Whatever," before disappearing into the small gender-neutral bathroom.

I stare at the closed door for a minute, making myself cool the fuck down before facing my parents and telling them, "I used to think I was one of the lucky ones, too, because of the way I grew up, the lifestyle we had. Then I let it all go. I gave everything we had, everything *I* had, up. I just…gave it up."

"Roswell—"

"And now, I have something in my life that I could never give up. That's what makes me lucky." There will always be more snowboarding, just like there will always be more money, more material items. There may not always be time with the woman I love though, and I consider myself the luckiest that I get to spend any of it, even the briefest of moments, with her. "I'm not letting fear hold me back. I'm just choosing to put my energy somewhere else." I may have had a lot of opportunities handed to me because of my parents' wealth, but

I'm not sure I ever really had choices in my life's path. It was always gonna go one way. It took an avalanche to throw me off course, then a brown-eyed, brown-haired, boxer brief-wearing ball of light to teach me about the choices I do have and how to make them for myself.

"I'm sure she's lovely, but those genes…they're not promising."

This weekend I had a lot of time to think—you know, since my girlfriend never returned my phone call—and I kept coming back to the birth control thing. Any kids I've seen Gia around, she's amazing with, but she told me after that first four-wheeling class that those girls were the closest she would ever get to having kids. If Gia had some kind of medical condition that kept her from getting pregnant, she wouldn't require both birth control and condoms. Technically, she wouldn't need either. So that means she's purposely choosing not to have kids, and if I've learned anything about Gia, it'd be so that she can't pass on a disease that has the potential to be hereditary.

"Jesus, Mom. I'm not with Gia to breed."

Not every fear is unwarranted, but there are almost always alternate routes around it. And if Gia and I do settle down, and she decides she wants kids after all, I'll take whichever path she chooses, whether it be fostering, adoption, surrogacy, or anything else I may not be aware of yet. Our story doesn't have to work only one way. It just has to work.

"I'm with her because there's literally nowhere else I'd rather be." Not Switzerland, not Canada, not Alaska, not France, Austria, or Japan. I've been to them all plus dozens more and none of them, not one, compares to being next to Gia.

"Roz, son. We're glad you're doing better. You need to be healthy mentally as well as physically if you're going to have a chance at qualifying. If you started training now—"

"I think it's time you guys get going," I say, pushing out of my chair. "Don't expect me for dinner anytime soon."

They look up at me, then each other, slowly getting to their feet as well.

"See yourselves out." I point to the door leading outside, heading for the bathroom myself.

I wait until they leave to prop my hands against the doorjamb to the bathroom, telling Gia, "You can come out now. I scared them off."

From the other side, I hear, "Did you swallow them?"

"What? Swallow them?"

Gia pulls the door open, saying, "Yeah. Barn Swallows, Tree Swallows. They can be pretty ruthless scaring off predators."

Did I *Swallow* them… Nope. Still not a good use of words, especially not in reference to my parents. Or anyone's parents.

"I don't know about that, but I did get rid of the *parental figures*," I mock her previous term, and she rolls her eyes, tossing a paper towel in the garbage.

I stop her in the doorway, telling her seriously, "I'm sorry about my parents. They were—"

"Right. Your parents were right."

What's this now?

She pushes past me, saying, "They're total Brown-Headed Cowbirds, but they're right about snowboarding."

"What are those?"

"Brood parasites. Shit parents."

I shake my head, following her back to our table to throw away our trash with more force than necessary.

I do still miss snowboarding and I have to fight certain urges. Not like I used to, but it's definitely still a part of me. When I first moved back to New York, it was worse. Ignoring the constant need. Fighting my body's natural setting.

Now it's more manageable.

Soon, it might even be nonexistent.

But why is that such a big deal to everyone?

"Don't think before answering. If you could do anything for the rest of your life, what would it be?"

Easy. "Be with you."

Gia stares at me silently, then pushes through the door, holding it open for me while I grab the to-go part of our order from Kylin. I've been calling her Kylin because her name tag clearly says Kylin, but Gia calls her Kyle for some reason.

Jesus Christ. *Am I my mother?*

I instantly duck my head down, making sure my nose isn't high in the air.

"Don't you want more out of life than just a girlfriend?" Gia asks over her shoulder.

"Don't think before answering," I tell her, and she freezes at my Chevy's passenger door. "If *you* could do anything for the rest of your life, what would it be?"

"This," floats out of her mouth in a whisper.

I wrap an arm around her, nuzzling her neck. "If your life is enough, why can't mine be, too? It's the one I chose." And will continue choosing.

"What if you chose wrong?"

I spin her around, so I can look into her eyes when I tell her, "I didn't."

Why do I get the feeling she's pulling away?

She stretches up to kiss me, but it's not the reassurance I thought it'd be. It's slow and soft, things Gia isn't usually.

"I love you," I say when her lips stop moving to breathe me in.

Getting the door for her, I don't miss the way she avoids my eye as she climbs inside or the fact that after two months, she still hasn't said "I love you" back. I know she does and I thought we were finally moving toward a place where she'd feel comfortable enough to express herself, but something's still keeping Gia from saying the words.

Your girlfriend doesn't let fear hold her back…

I'm not so sure about that, and judging by the way Gia reacted to my dad's comment, I don't think she is either.

Chapter 27

ROZ

Voicemail.

Again.

How fucking convenient.

Gia's been pulling this shit all week. The only time she even answers her phone is to give me some bullshit reason about why she's so busy.

"I'm on my way out."

Funny how I'm never invited along anymore.

"My phone died."

Coincidentally, neither of the two new portable power banks I bought and dropped off at her house have prevented that from happening.

"The shop is slammed."

That one's my favorite, considering I've helped out at Al's enough times now that I should have my own apron.

And here I am, once again, listening to the generic-ass voicemail recording, wondering why the fuck my girlfriend wants nothing to do with me all of a sudden.

I knew she was pulling away. I knew it. But was it something I did to cause her to pull away? I'd fix it if I could. And if I couldn't, I'd try anyway.

But, as usual, Gia takes things into her own hands, leaving me in the dark, alone and grasping at straws.

Fuck.

What if it's not fixable though? Did something happen at the dermatologist? Would she tell me even if it did?

No, she wouldn't. She'd do exactly what she's doing now—clam up on all the bad, so only the good shows, except in this case, Gia's not showing me anything. She's fucking running.

Snatching up my keys and wallet, I pound down my staircase, my heartbeat matching my heavy steps. I didn't earn eight gold medals for nothing. I'm light on my feet, barge every jump I ever encounter, and I'd never even considered bailing midway through a run, no matter how bad my chances look.

Gia can try to dodge me, but I'm a motherfucking snowboarder. I'll catch her.

It's keeping her that's gonna be the hard part.

Hopping down from my truck, I hesitate with a hand on my door.

What the *fuck?*

Gia and Rowdy are loading the back of her vintage truck with her Raptor. Technically, Rowdy's loading it while Gia keeps trying to help, but he waves her off, shaking his head each time she reaches out.

My muscles tense to the point of numbness, and I approach the two, staring Rowdy down when he makes the mistake of locking eyes with me.

He knows. He knows what's going on, and he's been keeping it from me, too. Rowdy and I aren't what I would call friends, but we talk. We talk enough that he could've reached out at any time to tell me what's going on with my own girlfriend.

She is still my girlfriend, isn't she?

"Baby?" I look at Gia. "What's wrong?" I don't even beat around the bush. Something is wrong, and I need to know what. Now.

Gia spins on her heel, retreating to the garage at the back of the property.

Here's where my skills come in clutch.

I catch up to her in three strides, blocking her path. She tries to dart around me, but I move with her, planting my feet and grabbing her shoulders.

"What's wrong?"

She lifts her shoulders, knocking my hands away.

"Nothing. We're going riding, Roz. I didn't know I needed your permission."

"You don't." She knows I don't care if she goes riding. I care that she's hiding something from me though. "Why are you acting like this?" I ask, looking between her eyes.

"Like what?"

"Like you're scared." Gia's fearless most of the time, so when she's scared, she gets angry because she's not used to the feeling. It's foreign, and she doesn't like it.

What has her scared?

There's a flicker. The tiniest trace of emotion crosses her face before she's moving again, skirting around me and throwing over her shoulder, "I can't with this. You're so clingy."

Rowdy stands in the bed of Gia's truck, towering over the scene. His hands toy with the straps as he watches on, but that emotion she just let through, it's written across Rowdy's face now, too.

My chest grows even tighter.

"What's wrong?" I yell out to him. Somebody better start talking, and since she's refusing, I'll get her sidekick to. I don't care what I have to do.

"Rowdy, don't!" I hear behind me, followed by the absence of crunching rocks under Gia's feet.

"Tell me," I say quieter, knowing damn well I don't need to raise my voice, but he doesn't. He doesn't and Gia doesn't either.

I had a best friend once and he would've sold me out long before now.

If I didn't love Gia so much, I'd hate Rowdy. He gets the uncensored version of Gia; he gets to be there for her in ways she won't let anybody, not even me, and he keeps his mouth shut tight while doing it. He's the kind of friend that'd help bury a body.

Hell, he's doing it right now.

"I know about the dermatologist," I say, turning to face Gia. "I know you were there last week."

Tings from birds pecking at seeds from Vita's birdfeeders fill the silence.

"New Year's Eve is our craziest time." Gia's voice comes out smooth, too smooth, and she keeps her gaze trained on my feet, hiding the real emotion. "One New Year's, it was fucking insane, and I got sidetracked somehow when I was reaching in to grab a pan out of the oven without a glove on. I didn't even realize my mistake until I heard the pan clatter to the floor across the room." She swallows, dragging her eyes up to mine. "My brain sensed the danger before my body even felt the pain and acted fast enough to save me from permanent damage."

With her palms turned out to me, I quickly scan both.

"There's no scars."

"Mistakes don't need visible reminders for the lesson to stick."

"Gia." I take a step in her direction. "I won't hurt you. I *promise*. Fuck, I *swear*. I *love* you."

"You're not the pan, Roz!"

Colorful leaves swirl at her feet like a tornado building, and when she looks at me, her eyes fucking raging, she shifts from being the eye to the eyewall—the most dangerous part.

"You're the one that's too distracted to realize what you're getting into, so I'm stepping in to save you before you can get hurt any worse."

"You don't have to save me from anything." I reach for her, missing those same hands as she backs up. With each word, my voice rises, burning my throat from the inside out. "I didn't go into this blind."

I knew there was a chance my time with Gia would be limited, but it didn't stop me from falling for her. I don't think anything could've.

"Just tell him, G." Rowdy sounds closer, like he too is struggling with whatever she's not saying.

"I got it," she says, and one second I'm staring directly into the most beautiful face I've ever seen, the next I'm looking up at it from the ground as my knees buckle beneath me. Pebbles pierce the skin on my shins while I fight to catch my breath.

"The scab?" It comes out as light as the wind dancing between us, as broken as the dried leaves under my knees.

Gia nods and Rowdy, inching closer, says, "She just got the results back for it yesterday."

"Is it melanoma?" I ask anyone that'll answer. Melanoma is the deadliest form of skin cancer. It can still be treatable, but it depends. It depends on a lot, like when it's discovered.

We should've had it checked sooner. I shouldn't have taken up so much of her time. Gia's right, I am clingy.

"Squamous cell carcinoma."

I remember seeing that one come up when I researched skin cancer. It can be deadly as well, but it's treatable, if you catch it in time.

"What stage?"

"I have to see an oncologist for that."

"Where?"

Gia looks away.

"Where?" I demand. The good thing about where we live is we're three hours away from several big cities with all sorts of top-of-the-line specialists. Where other people have to fly in from all over the world to get that kind of care, we only have a short drive.

"Somewhere local," Rowdy mutters.

Another quack running his practice out of a multifamily house? Why would she do that?

Because not everyone is born with their noses in the air.

Fuck me.

Al probably doesn't even have health insurance, and how else would Gia be able to cover the medical expenses she's about to rack up?

Unless she's not planning to at all.

"I tried to tell you this would happen," Gia says, staggering forward several steps, tears streaming down her face. "You didn't wanna listen."

"Are you saying you wouldn't do it again? Because I would. I'd fall for you again and again and again." I drag her to me, pressing my forehead to her middle and close my eyes tightly.

Ultimately, there's no way to really know what someone's fate will be. Vita couldn't have known that she'd die of cancer just like her mom. And just because Vita did, doesn't mean Gia will. She can fight this. We can fight this. Just like in Switzerland, I have the resources, but now I actually have the time, too. I have the fucking time…as long as time's still on my side.

Using a finger, Gia lifts my chin, forcing me to look into her eyes.

"I'm saying I'm not doing it this time." *No.* "I'm ending this now. I'm not taking you down with me." *No, no, no.*

She pushes, and I sit back on my heels, mashing my lips together. "We're through, Roz."

This can't be it.

She walks past me, stopping when she hears me whisper, "How many more times are you gonna kick my legs out from under me?"

"Until you stop getting back up." She drops her voice. "Stay down. *Please.*"

A car door opens and closes, then an engine flares to life. I expect a second one to follow, but when it doesn't, I glance behind me, finding Rowdy hesitating.

At first, neither of us speaks, so I slowly get to my feet, turning around to ask him, "Were you more worried about me? Or her?" Because he's never wanted us to be together. I could see it in his eyes, even from the beginning.

"Her. It's always about her."

Yeah, I know the feeling.

"Back in the day, I was that awkward new kid that changed schools in the middle of fifth grade. Everybody had grown up with everybody since kindergarten, so I didn't fit in anywhere. But Gia was…"

"Gia."

"Gia was Gia." He nods. "Even then. She was fearless, she was different, she was happy. But she went through it with Vita's death. It was brutal on everybody, but especially Gia, because she was right there with her mom, every step of the way. She spent a year by Vita's side, watching her die. Her fucking mom, man."

Rowdy blurs in front of me, and when my vision clears, his eyes are just as bad—red and brimming with tears.

"At the end, when there was nothing left for her and Al to do but sit and watch the center of their universe slip away, I could see it, I could see the way Gia was shutting connections off, left and right, to everyone except me and Al. We're the exception, but just barely. Just fucking barely, because Gia would never willingly put anyone else through what she went through. Then, something happened. You happened. You're the only person I've ever seen her keep around and the fact that she's fighting so hard to cut ties with you means she loves you as much as her own family."

She loves me.

Gia honks her horn and he runs a hand over his fauxhawk, telling me, "I'm sorry, but Gia needs me."

She does need Rowdy. And she needs Al.

But she needs me, too. I hold one of those ties she told me would keep her here. Otherwise, if she was just tied to Earth, she could float away like a balloon.

She's crazy, absolutely nuts, if she really thinks I'll stay down, this time or any other.

Sometimes you gotta out-crazy the crazy.

"What are you gonna do?" Rowdy asks, half-turned.

"What I always do after a wipeout. Get my ass back up and go twice as hard."

"You better be ready, man. This shit won't be easy."

I'm ready.

"Do me a favor and drop her by my house when you're finished."

"She's not gonna go for it. You heard her. Her mind's made up."

I let a smile pull the corner of my lips. "So is mine."

Chapter 28

GIA

"Rowdy, what the hell? What are we doing here?" I ask, slinking down in my seat so I won't be seen.

From the driver's seat, he just exhales, but in an ominous way that I don't like the sound of.

Seriously?

I'm so tired I can barely lift my arms, but I do anyway, telling my best friend to speed up before Roz or any of his roommates can come out and see my truck lingering outside their house. He knows what it was like for me to break up with Roz. He's been the one catching the pieces that keep shedding off me in jagged shards ever since we left Roz standing in my driveway.

At one point, the tears clouding my vision got so bad, I had to pull over and let Rowdy drive the rest of the way until we reached the telephone lines we ride along every fall. Then when I was riding, it didn't matter if I could see or not. I know what's out there; I have it memorized like a mental vision board of inspiration. The poles are kept clear of vegetation the entire way down the lines, for miles and miles and miles, with lush borders on both sides of deciduous trees currently in the middle of the color change New York is so damn good at. After the trees shed as many of their leaves as possible comes the big freeze, killing off anything stubborn enough to still be attached.

Even with my nose being stuffed up, I tried to breathe in the earthiness of plants hunkering down in preparation for winter to remind myself why I'm doing this—closing in on myself, making my reach smaller, so when the cold does take over, and the harsh, icy tendrils of cancer grip my heart, there's no one else there to feel the blast.

I've been doing it for months, for years, long before Roz showed up and took hold of my most fallible organ like he alone would take on the abominable end, *my* abominable end.

Rowdy and Dad are a gimme. A rule I'd never try breaking. It doesn't mean I have to put them through the worst of it though. Unfortunately, I won't be able to shield them completely, but whatever the oncologist says, I can water down. Internalize it. Let them think it's not as bad as they believe. *As bad as I believe.* I'm not sure how exactly, but I have to try. My dad will be wrecked, but if I can keep Al's from going under, then he'll be wrecked with a steady income and a solid purpose to keep going.

With football season back in full swing, Al's is busier than ever, but the bills will eventually pile up. The *debt* will pile up. It'll bury Al's first, then me.

Me.

Buried.

Gawd. No matter how much preparation you go through, it doesn't help. It doesn't fucking help. I feel like I've been getting ready to die ever since my mom did, and I'm still not ready. I feel like those plants out there, desperately gasping their last breaths before winter shows up, unleashing its suffocating snow in a vicious test of perseverance. I want air. I want to breathe. I want to live.

I stuff my hands in the front pocket of my hoodie to hide the shaking.

At least Rowdy would come out all right. Wrecked but all right. He's got his boys, his hobbies, his whole life to help him bounce back.

It's Roz though… Roz has nothing. Nothing to win, nothing to lose. He'd go for broke trying to save me, and bankrupt he'd be…of everything. He'd lose himself entirely. He would. I know he would.

"Roz told me he had some of your stuff he wanted you to pick up," Rowdy says, slowing to a stop. "I thought it'd be easier if we just grabbed it now so you're not alone."

I side-eye him. Most of the stuff I use at Roz's *is* Roz's.

He shrugs, saying, "Who knows? It's probably just rings and shit," before parking and getting out.

Roz's Chevy sits idle in the driveway.

I crack my door, calling to Rowdy, "I'll wait here while you get it all, okay?"

It's easier when I don't have to see those golden magnets Roz thinks pass as eyes.

"He left everything out back. Said you'd know where to look. I don't know what that means. Grow a pair and come on."

A pair of what? Those overly sensitive lumps filled with ra-men-noodle-looking tubes? The ones men act like us women should covet while simultaneously bowing down to? Nah. I've got several pairs of things on my body that make me twice as strong as those crybabies with overly sensitive sacs.

With an eye roll, I jump out, following him to the back. Why would Roz put my jewelry out here?

One ear trained for any noise from the house, I do a quick scan around the backyard, then say, "I'm not seeing anything. Let's go."

"Oh, shit." Rowdy perches down at the pool's edge, rubbing a hand over his thick strip of hair.

"What?"

"Is that…?"

Oh my gawd, what's in there?

I stalk closer, imagining all the glittering metal I'm about to see at the bottom of the pool. I didn't expect Roz to stoop this low. I knew he'd take it hard, but being petty enough to toss my shit in the pool? I gotta say, it's not so fancy.

As soon as I approach, Rowdy shoots to his feet, latching on to my arms and angling my back toward the pool. Giving me an apologetic look, he says, "Sorry," before I feel the water slap my back, robbing my breath right from my lungs.

By the time I get my feet under me again, my dude is long gone, and I can vaguely make out my V8 pulling away over the sound of my teeth chattering.

I'm so buying him a pocket pussy for Christmas and letting him open it in front of his grandma. *If I'm still here.*

I shed the heavy layers on my way to the back door, not giving a shit who might see my bra and underwear. The pants alone are like walking in sheets of ice, the hoodie like an oversoaked sponge, continuously leaking streams of freezing water.

In front of the sliding glass door, there's a folded colorful beach towel next to a long foam dart gun with a note taped to it. Shoving everything aside, I fist the towel with numb fingers, rubbing it over my shivering body.

The note catches my eye again, probably because it's Roz's handwriting.

Behind a locked door sits a hot bath.

Winner gets the key.

Come find me.

I dare you.

This is the shit I'm talking about. He knows adventures are my weakness, Roz himself being the biggest one. How am I supposed to turn this down?

Tricky. He's tricky.

I'm doing it for the bath, I tell myself as I fling my head forward, wrapping the towel around my hair, then secure it into a tight twist before standing again. I slip my boots and socks off and head inside—with the gun in my hold, a finger on the trigger, and a smile on my lips. *Game on, Roz.*

The dark living room meets me as I enter, silently sliding the door closed behind me. I immediately duck behind the kitchen counter, poking my head over the top and sweeping the darkened area, only to come up empty. The adrenaline buzzing over my arms chases away the cold as I take stock of my ammo. The cartridge holds six, but Roz only gave me four. Shit. That's not nearly enough.

A foam bullet whizzes past my head, hitting the wall before landing at my feet.

Five.

I add it to my arsenal, carefully remaining perched beneath the countertop. Going off of the angle the bullet came from, I aim my gun in that direction, then take off across the kitchen, the towel on my head falling at my feet as I go.

Two more bullets suction to the fridge at my back and I laugh from the string of curses that follows.

I make it to the front door, pressing myself flat against it while listening, my gun in front of me, searching for any movement.

When no one appears, I push off the metal, creeping forward. Coming up on the stairwell leading to Roz's room, I stop, straining my ears since I can't see a thing, then fire off a couple bullets of my own into the blacked-out space.

Nothing.

I pass it, continuing my sweep of the house. Every room is checked, and every room is cleared, even the bedrooms upstairs, and by the time I make it back downstairs, I'm starting to think I imagined the entire thing. The only thing keeping me from believing I did is the door to the bathroom being locked like the note said.

With my gun hanging at my side, I notice a glow that wasn't there before, so I lift it again, moving my feet in the direction of Roz's stairwell.

I could've sworn it was empty before.

Coming into view first, the handrail has a string of white lights wrapped around its wood, giving off a healthy amount of light, but the strings of lights hanging overhead illuminate the entire stairwell. Pictures, dozens of them, decorate the walls, stairs, and…door. Which is closed with Roz sitting calmly in front of it with his gun at his feet and his heart bleeding out on to his face.

I fire off my last shot. The other two were used on Fletcher's room for stealing my underwear that first night I stayed here. I'm still not over it.

Roz drops his gaze to his chest, saying, "You shot me."

"You dared me." I pop a shoulder even though he can't see it.

When he lifts his head, his smile doesn't reach his eyes. Pain, pain, pain—that's all I cause.

"Where's the key?"

"Don't you want to know what all this is?"

"No." I keep my gaze trained just below his, so we're not making actual eye contact.

"It's my own collection, of all the moments worth remembering."

My eyes rise to his.

"It's my life, the parts I *want* to remember."

I shift my gaze to the right of Roz, then up and over to the other side of the stairwell, touching on every single one. The pictures are… of us. Not his snowboarding days, not his childhood. They're all recent pictures he took over the last couple months. Some are just of me, but most are of our time together. There's even birds and a couple dishes from Al's I know he's responsible for by the obscene amount of garnish on each one.

This wasn't supposed to go on this long, but I'm not sorry it did. If that makes me selfish, then oh well. I'm selfish. I wanted Roz all to myself, just for a little while, before the reality I feel like I've been outrunning my whole life caught up to me. I *want* Roz all to myself. Still. Even with disease invading my body, my thoughts, and my own bleeding heart, I still want him. He's the one adventure I wish didn't have to end.

But I don't just love Roz, I fear him, too. I fear he's going to take my life's projected path and shape it into his own with his skilled hands.

I fear he already has.

Roz stands suddenly, asking, "Have you heard of a sympathetic trigger?"

"A what?"

He drops down a couple stairs.

"A sympathetic trigger. It's when one avalanche sets off another."

A few more steps down.

"Don't tell me. I'm the second disaster?" Kori said it best, I'm a hurricane that leaves messes everywhere I go.

He lands on the last step, coming face to face with me and looks directly into my eyes.

"The second one happened when I met you because I fell for you faster than any of my record-breaking times that won me medals. All-consuming, blanketing everything in sight, I never stood a chance." His hand comes up to cup my cheek. "I didn't leave my heart on the slopes, Gia. It's been with me this whole time, leading me to you."

My nose stings and a hiccup burns my throat.

"You said if you loved someone enough, you could walk away from them, so please…walk away. I'm begging you."

"I didn't know what I was talking about when I said that. You were the one that had it right. If you love someone enough, you *can't* walk away. I can't walk away, baby."

"Key," I say while I still can, holding out my free hand. "I earned it."

Roz hesitates, his eyes searching mine, but he places it in my palm, saying, "It was a cheap shot, but a deal's a deal."

"Cheap shot was having Rowdy do your dirty work. This was payback." I yank the dart off his bare chest, pushing past while sucking in mouthfuls of air to hold off the tears.

"You're lucky I love you," he says to my back, and only when I'm out of earshot do I respond, whispering, "I know."

The warm water mutes all sound to the outside world and accepts my tears, claiming them as its own. It even imitates the fluid in my body, tricking me into believing I'm somehow safe.

Lies.

I don't need any more lies. I'm already full of them. Lies for the right reasons still taste like lies, but they're easier to swallow when they're for the ones you love.

A shadow falls over the bits of my face still exposed and I look up to find Roz standing above me.

He jerks his head to the side, then climbs in as I sit up. Still wearing his shorts, he positions himself behind me, pulling my back against his front. His arms wrap around my middle, and he holds tight, allowing me to fall apart at the half-assed seams I've been work-ing like hell to fasten before anyone could notice. His sobs mix with mine, and soon, we can't get close enough. We're both grasping for help, begging for someone to feel what we're feeling.

The thing is though, I do. I know what he's feeling because I've felt it. I lived it. I lost the person I loved most and I would've rather died myself than have my mom push me away like I'm doing to Roz.

How can I not though? How can I continue letting him love me, knowing it will only end in heartbreak?

Do I even have a say? In any of this? It's starting to feel like I don't.

Maybe I never did. Maybe it really was some natural force, big-ger than either of us, that caused our paths to collide, then intersect again and again until they merged into one.

"I need you to make me a promise, Gia. Promise that no matter what we find out, you'll fight. I *need* you to fight."

"I've been fighting," I say, wiping my cheeks. "Fighting to live a life I'm proud of, one that I love and cherish. For me. Not for any-body else."

And that can't change. I refuse to stay afloat because someone tells me to, even if I love that someone with every breath I take.

"Am I not enough?" His voice breaks, not just in his throat, but me as well. His voice breaks me. How could Roz ever think he's not enough?

Because I made him think that. Over and over again.

"Is that why you're willing to walk away?"

I spin in his arms, slipping each of my legs over his hips, then run my finger between his eyebrows, smoothing the angry skin.

"You're so much more than enough. But I won't live a life for someone else. That's not fair to either of us. I've lived the life I want. Meeting you was just the cherry on top. I've enjoyed every moment with you. Your eyes. Your mouth. Your laugh. Your scowl." I laugh when his forehead wrinkles. "I will die knowing that heaven does exist because I've been staring at it for months now."

"You're killing me here, Gia. Give me something."

Tears stream down over my fingers roaming his face.

"I'd give you my heart, cowboy, but you've already wrangled it away from me."

I'd always planned to fall in love with as many things as possible. Things I could walk away from when the time came. Falling in love with Roz was never part of that plan. But now that I have, I'm finding it difficult to walk away. Before, when I'd try, I would bring out my inner monster and let her bat Roz around, hoping he'd do it himself. He hasn't yet. He refuses to walk away, no matter what I throw at him.

I'm not just tired physically right now, I'm tired mentally, emotionally. I'm tired of pushing Roz away. And I don't want that to be his last memory of me either. I want him to be free and happy, not battered and broken.

"I just thought you'd be a good one." I told him that when we first met. "An adventure. I thought you'd be a good adventure, but I was wrong. You weren't just a good one, Roz. Loving you has been my greatest adventure."

His golden eyes darken. I've never said it back to him before. I've never said it to him, period. *Love.* I held off on saying it because I thought it'd make things easier. I was stupid. When it's real, nothing is easy.

"I love you," I tell him finally, and his lips capture mine in a rush, like we don't have time.

We don't.

"But I can't make that promise," I say against his mouth, tasting the salt. "I'm not scared of dying. I'm scared of taking you with me."

Roz leans his head back against the wall, regarding me as he says, "I knew you'd say that, so I already worked everything out with Al to have your shifts covered…" He shrugs. "Indefinitely."

"By who?" I straighten my spine, eyeing him right back.

"You don't need to worry about that."

"Excuse me?"

"The only thing you need to worry about is choosing."

"Choosing?"

"Choose to stay. Choose to try. Choose to live, Gia. I'll take care of the rest."

"It doesn't just work like that, Roz. This isn't a therapeutic retreat in the woods. Cancer's formidable, too. More than you ever were."

"We don't even know how bad yours is yet and you've already got one foot in the grave, making decisions that don't need to be made right now. Baby, we're not there. If you choose to fight, I'll fucking fight enough for both of us, I swear to you."

"And if I choose and it still doesn't work?"

"If it doesn't work, if cancer wins," he lifts his head again, swallowing, "then just make sure you stay nearby, okay? Because I don't want to be anywhere but by your side, down here or in the sky."

He's such a Cardinal.

I pull his face to mine, kissing him deeply, roughly, thoroughly, before my sneeze eventually breaks us apart.

Roz's chest rumbles with a laugh, but he doesn't try to take things further. That's not what this is about. I'm just…stunned. Roz is always stunning, but this is different. He's feeling again. He has a purpose again. *He's alive again.* So beautifully alive.

"We have an appointment in two days with the best oncologist in all of New York."

We have an appointment.

"Where?"

"In the city. I'll drive us down tomorrow, and we can stay the night."

"Roz."

"*Everything* will be paid in full, including travel expenses and any possible treatments available."

My head shakes even as tears fall from my chin.

"I've had money my whole life, and it didn't make me half as happy as you do. I'd use every dollar I have to spend even one more day with you, Gia."

"I know." But I refuse to do that to anyone, especially Roz.

"So then let me."

"I can't," I sob.

He uses my own words, telling me, "There's always a choice."

A thousand choices fill my head, not just the ones I'm faced with now, but also the ones I've made and the ones I never even got to make, like falling for Roz. Why'd it have to be him?

Because he earned my love. Because his love's worth having. Because *he's* worth having.

"You've been pushing me since the day we met," Roz says, "always making me do things when I didn't think I could. It's my turn to push you. You don't have to live for me. You just have to choose."

I drop my forehead to his, and he pleads, "Don't go yet, baby. I need you here still."

My vision grows blurry watching his do the same, our eyelashes thick with tears.

"I'll do anything. Anything."

"Anything?" I manage to ask, and with his own hoarse voice, he promises, "Anything."

Chapter 29

ROZ

White surrounds me as far as the eye can see, welcoming me back, welcoming me *home*.

And even though it's a long overdue homecoming, everything's exactly the same as I remember it—the smell, the chill that doesn't affect me in the slightest, the rush I get from just being out here.

Except me. I'm not even close to the same as I was the last time I did this. After everything that's happened in the last few years, how could I be?

I take a deep breath, dropping my head between my shoulders to mentally collect the image above me. Neon green with streaks of blue twist across the sky in a chaotic rhythm that reminds me of Gia in the best way possible, and I can't help but smile. *Of course I see her.* They're light—polar light but still light.

I pull my phone out of my pocket, snapping a picture before my battery can shut down. I never used to take my own pictures of the places I'd visit. Like everything else in my life, I took them for granted.

Not anymore. Now I cherish it all, even the same aurora I've seen dozens of times before, because you never know when your last time seeing something will be.

Is she seeing this?

Passing the small holes in the snow that hold continuous flames, thanks to the resort keeping whatever they fill them with that's flammable lit, I step into the glass igloo, mindful of the cold Finnish air trying to slink its way inside as I shut the door quickly.

"It's not a bluebird, but it'll do. Ready to go, Mrs. Andrews-Smith?"

"That's Mrs. Fancy to you," Gia says from the bed, before pulling back the thick quilt and getting to her feet.

She was seeing it, just from in here. I told her to stay inside and keep warm while I went to check on conditions.

"How could I forget?" I tease, running a quick check over her thin frame, but with her wearing a one-piece set of long johns, there's only so much skin I can make out. *Thankfully.* We are in a glass igloo after all and, with the northern lights putting on an erotic-as-all-hell show, you can bet we're not the only ones awake right now.

It's okay though, I did a more thorough check earlier…multiple times.

"Oh, like you forgot your promise to me two years ago." She arches an eyebrow while pulling her snow pants on.

"I didn't forget."

"Mmhmm."

"We were a little busy," I say, making her laugh.

Thankfully, Gia did choose. She chose to fight, but on the condition that I snowboard again. Not professionally, but she wanted me to have something to strive for if…if she wasn't around to push me herself.

After that first appointment with the oncologist, Gia started receiving simultaneous radiation and chemo treatments almost immediately. We were in and out of the hospital for the whole first year, and we've been taking things slow, getting back out in the world now that she's in remission. Her body's still healing from everything it was put through, but she's currently cancer-free according to her last several appointments.

"You could've gone without me."

I frown. "No. I couldn't." There's literally nothing that could've pulled me from Gia these past two years. "Besides, we've discussed this, I was waiting until you could join me."

She stands, fastening her pants, and I walk over to hand her one of my sweaters.

"That wasn't part of the deal," she says once her head's free of the neckline.

"Well, I'm a shitty listener like that." I wrap an arm around her back, closing the gap between us. "You know I wanted you beside me."

"I'm beside you now," she tells me, draping her arms over my shoulders.

"You're beside me always."

"For better or worse."

I finish the vows we just took, promising, "In sickness and in health."

Fuck, I love my wife. We've only been married for a week, but we were bonded way before that, having already gone through the thick of it together. There's not a doubt in my mind that Gia's my soulmate and I wanted to make it official, so this past summer, after clawing her way back from the pits of emotional and physical fatigue hell, when Gia finally started feeling like herself again—her new self because she'll never be the same either—I asked her to marry me. Unfortunately, she turned me down, straight rejected my ass. But then New Year's Eve came along, and as we were counting down in our new home, down the road from her dad's, she looked into my eyes, and I knew—we were about to have another adventure. A life-long adventure.

New Year's Day we got married, starting the year off right, with as many friends and family as we could scrounge up. Rowdy was there to be Gia's man of honor while I chose to leave the best man role open, in honor of Salvy. My old roommates showed up surprisingly, even the underwear thief, Fletcher, and we all watched teary-eyed as Al struggled to hand his daughter over to me. He and Rowdy were involved in Gia's journey the entire time, just not in-person once we had to rent an apartment in the city for a while when traveling back and forth to receive treatment became too much on Gia. I kept them both up-to-date on her condition though and the three of us grew closer because of it. They're the only two people that love Gia as much as I do, so we were all in the trenches together, fighting the same battle to keep Gia alive.

We also invited my parents to our impromptu wedding, but they weren't in town, off on some vacation or another. They never did come around about our relationship…until they heard where we were honeymooning. Gia calls them Woodpeckers, peck, peck, pecking for any little morsel regarding my old life, and I bet they're absolutely feasting on the fact that I'm getting ready to snowboard again. It's too bad they won't get to see it. If they ever get around to pulling their noses out of the air, then maybe. *Maybe.*

"Dress warm." I give my wife my own peck, smacking both her heavily padded ass cheeks. "Extra warm." Her team of doctors barely gave us the green light to come here. Gia being in remission, her body's still more susceptible to infection right now, so we've gotta be careful in everything we do. We're even going night boarding to avoid crowds.

"Are you even wearing a coat? A *real* coat?"

"My body doesn't need as much gear."

She slides her arms through her own coat, muttering something about her husband being singlehandedly responsible for global warming, the words "my husband" coming out of her mouth making my cock start to swell. I swear that shit better not ever wear off. I love hearing her call me that.

"Or we could stay in and I could warm you up myself," I generously offer before catching the beanie my wife throws at my face.

"Don't even think about it. You seducing me will not get you out of snowboarding."

"Baby, I haven't even started seducing you yet," I tell her, putting the beanie on the top of my head so the majority of it sticks up. We're only thirteen hours into our honeymoon and I've already seduced her every which way, but it's good for her to wonder what my next move is. Gia's always keeping me on my toes, so I gotta return the favor every now and then.

Plus, I saw that her long johns have one of those ass flaps and I plan on taking full advantage of the easy access as soon as possible.

"I'll be outside, getting everything ready," I say before I change my mind and actually seduce her. "Now hurry up, Mrs. Fancy." I swirl my finger in an exaggerated circular motion, causing us both to laugh. Yeah, I can't pull it off as well as her.

Back outside, I take in the length of my board, studying the clean lines and vivid colors of the brilliant, almost glowing, poppies swaying in a light breeze as tiny snowflakes dust their orange-red petals. They were Gia's parents' flowers, and now they serve as a reminder that it doesn't matter what goes right in life, only what feels right. Perched on a branch in the middle of the field of poppies is a male Cardinal. Head held high, he's ready to take on anything.

Gia's board is an exact replica of mine, except instead of a red male Cardinal, hers has the tan female. Side by side, her bird's looking forward, toward the future, but mine's looking at her, his future.

During Gia's many appointments, I commissioned an artist to custom design them for us as a way to represent me watching Gia's back, even when she's not looking, even when she can't see me. Because even when she couldn't open her eyes from sheer exhaustion, I was there, making sure she was taken care of, never once considering being anywhere other than by her side.

Tears I didn't think I still had fill my eyes.

It's been a long road to get here. For both of us.

Gia meets me outside our private igloo and immediately stops to gaze up at the impressive sky, breathing, "Whoa."

"Beautiful," I agree, and she looks directly at me, saying, "Stunning."

I go over all the safety gear with Gia, making sure she's all set, then we start off toward the chairlift just past the copse of colossal evergreens coated with heavy snow that separate the lodging section of the resort from the trails.

After what feels like another two years on the lift, we finally crest the top of the mountain and clear the ramp. It's something I've done before hundreds of other times, if not more, but now feels like the first time all over again, and I get a fucking high from it as I look down at what awaits us below.

You getting this? I send up to Salvy because I know he's watching. I still miss my best friend, but I no longer use that grief to punish myself. I'll snowboard today, and maybe after this, and it probably won't be the same as before, but expecting anything in life to remain the same was unrealistic. We're always moving, changing, growing. I was rejecting that concept though, instead choosing to stay stationary. Life is a gift; one we should live intentionally. My wife taught me that, but so did Salvy, and I want to honor him by choosing to live, all day, every fucking day, as long as I can.

Several other night boarders line up on both sides of us as I bend down to activate the LED lights built into our boards. The sensors spring to life, and Gia bends backward, setting off a sequence of colorful lights along the rim of her board. I do the same with mine while she straps her other foot in, then get my own bindings adjusted before checking hers.

"How you feelin'?" Next to me, Gia stands tall, illuminated by the floodlights surrounding us as she watches me closely.

She just battled and beat cancer, and she's worried about how I'm doing?

"I'm good," I tell her honestly. It may not be the honeymoon most people envision, but it's ours and it's perfect. Imperfectly perfect.

"We'll see about that." Hands to my chest, Gia pushes, making me fall flat on my ass, then angling her body toward me, she smirks down at me and says, "Try to keep up, cowboy," before proceeding to shred the absolute fuck out of the slope we're on, leaving sprays of pow in her wake. She said she could board, but she never told me she could rip. Fuck. Me.

Pushing to standing again, I alternate between watching her ass and the LEDs rapidly lighting up in reaction to her every move before I realize we're back to where we started—me chasing after her without a second thought.

I shake out my arms, filling my lungs, and after the first hop, I lose almost all conscious thought as my body takes over, guiding me back into familiar movements as natural to me as walking or breathing.

Damn. I missed this.

I don't regret walking away from snowboarding—I wouldn't have met Gia otherwise—but damn, did I miss it. My brain, my body, my heart, my fucking soul missed it, and now that I'm back, I feel peace, a peace I'd been denying myself out of near-crippling guilt. It wasn't my fault Salvy died though, only how I handled it afterward, and for that I take full responsibility. I'll never go back to that place again because now I know, there's always a choice. I can choose wrong, or I can choose right, but the choice *is* mine to make.

Easily catching up to Gia, I match her move for move until about halfway down, she pulls off to the side next to a wooden split-rail fence.

"What's up?" I ask, yanking off my helmet to instantly check her over. "Is everything okay?"

She lifts her goggles to the top of her helmet, meeting my eyes to say, "I thought I saw a Pine Grosbeak."

My ribs stop aching and I take a full breath.

Pointing out over the trees, she says, "But don't you think this would be a good place to have your ashes spread?"

Not this again.

I lift my chin, exhaling through my mouth. The warm fog rises, getting lost in the light show above us.

"You planning on dying?" I slide my eyes over to her, but she's already looking my way, wearing the same smile she first caught me with.

She grabs my hand, squeezing tightly through the fat cushioning of our gloves, and shouts, "Not today!" into the air for the world to hear.

Fuck yes. *Here we go.*

Check out my website amarieauthor.com for playlists,
inspiration boards, and up-to-date news.

Also by
A. MARIE

Creekwood Series

Detour

Changing Lanes

Blind Spot

Roundabout

Standalones

Let The Light Shine Through

The Comedown

Acknowledgments

First, thank you, Mare. It was never my intention for life to imitate art writing this book, but once we found out it did, I'm so grateful you chose to fight. Our family definitely needs you here still. Should you ever forget that, don't worry, I'll be here to remind you all over again.

Next, a massive thank you to you, the reader, for picking this book up. This story was so special to me for so many reasons and I'm so appreciative you took a chance reading it.

An even bigger thank you goes to my family for their endless support. You're all amazing and I love you with my whole heart, forever and always.

Huge thanks to my beta on this one. Shanna, you do so much for me and I appreciate every single bit of it.

Thanks to the team that helped me get this book ready for the public—Murphy, Becky, Judy, and Stacey. It's gorgeous, inside and out, thanks to all your help.